ROGUE

D. E. BARTLEY

VINCI BOOKS

Vinci Books

vinci-books.com

Published by Vinci Books Ltd in 2026

1

The publisher and the author have made every effort to obtain permissions for any third party material used in this book and to comply with copyright law. Any queries in this respect should be brought to the attention of the publisher and any omissions will be corrected in future editions.

A CIP catalogue record for this book is available from the British Library.

Paperback ISBN: 9781036711962

The EU GPSR authorised representative is Logos Europe, 9 rue Nicolas Poussion, 17000 La Rochelle, France contact@logoseurope.eu

By D.E. Bartley

*To my husband Nick and our three boys, who have supported and encouraged me, whilst I try
and make sense of my ramblings. Thank you for all the cups of coffee, glasses of gin, and space during my many meltdowns. I love you.*

Prologue

Two years ago

Gradually, I start sensing things around me as I regain consciousness, knowing better than to open my eyes, I remain still. I need to ensure I'm alone first.

I lie here on the mattress, which stinks, and listen. I can hear the crickets as well as the familiar sound of the wind blowing through the trees outside. An owl hoot tells me it must be night-time, then nothing. I strain my ears to check; the tell-tale sign of his breathing is absent. I let out a sigh of relief; he's gone for now.

Slowly, I start to open my eyes, but only one opens fully. From the painful throb, I know the other is swollen shut.

The room's dark, the only light coming from the moon outside and the light around the doorframe. Was it light when he came in? The last thing I remember before the blow was the look of anger on his face. I'd refused him; I had fought him, attempted to stop him, and begged him to leave me to rest for one day. So he'd beaten me, knocking me unconscious. From the pain radiating from between my legs, he had taken what he desired, not needing me to be coherent as he never had before; why would he start now?

Why had I fought him? I've promised to be a well-behaved, loving mate and to work with him, to let him impregnate me with his pups. He's going to build a pack, him at the head of it, me obediently by his side. Him, the undefeatable Alpha and me, the magical Luna, who can use their magic to ensure he's the strongest he can be and protect his pack from any threat. All I have to do is be good, listen and obey him, and, most importantly, behave how a Luna is expected to behave.

"You're not his Luna. He is not your Alpha or your mte. Your true mate is out there. You're worth more than this. Your true mate will show you what it means to be loved."

Shut up, just shut up!

There she goes again, that voice in my head, my wolf, telling me to fight, to be strong, to do the opposite of what he wants. But where has that gotten me? I'm lying on a stinking, filthy mattress, which is covered in every bodily fluid you can think of, most of it my own. Locked in this tiny little rundown room with nothing but this mattress, a bucket to piss in, and a covered window.

"Be strong. You're giving up. Fight."

For what? Fighting has brought me nothing but pain and sorrow. As long as I behave, my family and coven are safe. That's all that matters. The longer I do as I'm told, the chances of me seeing them again will increase. That's what he keeps telling me.

"If you keep listening to him, you will end up dead! Just like the last girl who he tried to make his Luna! You know this; you heard it yourself."

Just shut up.

2

The way she goes on, you would think I want this, I don't.

I want to go home, I want my family, I want to feel my uncle's arms around me as he hugs me. I want to taste my auntie's cookies, fresh out of the oven and so hot that the melted chocolate burns your tongue. I want to feel the sun warming my face and the grass in between my toes, to smell the rain, and to feel the breeze on my skin. I want it all, but most of all, I want to be free, free from the pain, free from this room, free from *him*.

"Then FIGHT!"

Suddenly, the sound of footsteps pierces the silence. I close my eyes and try to lie perfectly still, hoping he will think I am still unconscious. I hear the lock on the door click just before it opens. The door closes, and his footsteps get closer.

"Time to wake up, sweetheart," he whispers as his fingers brush over the bruising on the side of my face. I instantly flinch from the touch and know I have no choice but to open my eyes now. The first thing I see is his dark grey eyes looking at me, then that smile. How can he smile when he can see what he has done to me?

"Because he likes it, he's a sadist. He likes the pain he inflicts on you."

"Do you realise what tonight is, sweetheart? It's a full moon." Oh no, not already. I'm hurting enough; not tonight, please. "I was going to let you out with me to run. You've been so good, so well-behaved. But then you ruined it, so now you'll have to stay here again." The softness leaves his face, that look which screams a warning of the pain that's on the way, replacing it. I quickly sit up; I can feel the tears burning in my eyes.

"I'm sorry, I really am. I don't know what came over

me. Please forgive me, Alpha, please don't hurt me again." I feel a sob escape my lips. He runs a finger over my cheek, collecting a stray tear, before lifting it to his lips to taste it.

"Do you think I like hurting you? I wouldn't have to if you did as you're told. How can I trust you to come out with me if you won't even sleep with your mate without fighting them?"

"I'll do better, I promise." I watch as that grin spreads across his face, his eyes darkening. I shuffle back away from him until my back's pressed against the wall, and I know I can't go any further.

"Oh, I know you will because if you don't, I'll start killing members of that precious coven of yours, one by one, starting with the leader, your uncle." I jump forward to beg him to leave him alone, but he hits me with a back-hander across the face, sending me back against the wall with such force I hear my skull crack as everything goes dark.

Chapter One

DAISY

Present Day

Just when I thought my sneaking-in days were numbered, here I am doing it like a pro. Ethan Hunt ain't got shit on a girl trying to avoid looking like she's doing the walk of shame.

I slowly slide my key into the lock of my apartment door. Cautiously twisting until I feel the mechanism slide with the slightest of clicks. Taking a deep breath, I ease the door open, praying to every God and Goddess I can think of so that it doesn't squeak, waking my sleeping friends inside.

Ensuring there's enough room, I squeeze through. Slowly carefully, I release the key before removing it from the lock. Once inside, I slide the door back into place with just as much caution while holding the handle. It gives the tiniest of clicks, causing me to freeze, listening to the silence for any sign of my friends stirring, but thankfully, I hear nothing. Releasing the breath I'd held, I turn towards my room.

Considering that was the first time I've snuck into this dorm at stupid o'clock in the morning, I think I'll take this as a success. Tired and aching after the night's activities, I creep to my room before repeating the mission of unlocking the door without waking anyone. I've just opened the door when there is movement from another room. I throw my bag through the gap onto my bedroom floor, knowing it is too late to hide; they'll hear my door as it closes.

"Daisy, is that you?" A voice comes from down the hall. I turn to see one of my dorm mates walking into the hallway, quickly letting out a sigh of relief; it's only Tony.

"Yeah, it's me. Sorry, did I wake you?"

He yawns, ruffling his black curly mop of hair before stretching as he walks towards me, wearing nothing but his boxers. I hold my bedroom door open for him so we can talk in private.

"No, I was already awake. Did everything go okay last night?" he asks. I scrunch my nose in distaste.

"As well as it could have, I guess." I can see the sympathy written all over his face. "What are you doing up so early?" I ask, trying to quickly change the subject.

"I thought I'd get a coffee and chill in front of the TV for a bit before everybody else gets up." Tony looks at me with his warm brown eyes, smiling gently. "Plus, I wanted to check if you got back okay. I was a little worried about you." I'm about to scold him for worrying when he reaches towards me and pulls a leaf out of my hair. "It's a good thing I saw this before one of the girls." He laughs, waving the leaf in my face. I swat it away, which just makes him laugh more. "Wouldn't want them thinking you were out for an early roll in the bushes with some strange local, would we?" he adds, wiggling his eyebrows at me playfully.

"You're such a child," I mutter whilst turning away, smiling, heading to my small bathroom.

"I'm going for a shower. I'll be back in fifteen. I expect there to be coffee in the pot and toast on a plate." I stick my head out of the door and point at him. "And put some damn clothes on, for the love of the goddess; we don't need to see those chicken legs this early in the morning."

I hear Tony chuckling to himself as I head back to the shower, and he walks towards my door. Although to be fair, his legs are far from weak-looking, his body isn't a bad sight either.

"Oh please, you just hate seeing what you can't have, witchy bitch."

"Really? Why would I want what everybody else has already had, demon boy?" I call back; I can hear him laughing as he closes my door.

Have you ever met someone and wondered where they've been your whole life? That's what it was like when I first met Tony, not in a romantic way, not at all. Instead, we just became instant best friends. I'd been worried I'd be on my own here, but meeting Tony has been a blessing. I can honestly say having him as a friend will make this journey a lot easier.

I let out a deep sigh as I step back into my room and take it in—home sweet home.

Two weeks ago, I moved into the student dormitories at a university in North Wales. I'm twenty-two and living away from what little family I have left for the first time. When I was six, my mother died suddenly. My father, whilst visiting family in Ireland a year later, was caught up in an IRA bombing. His body was never found. Luckily, I was taken in by my Auntie Mary and Uncle Nigel, who brought me up. They've loved and cared for me like I was their own child. I couldn't be more grateful for them; they have been my rock over the years, and I love them dearly.

Turning to my chest of drawers, I look at the picture of my auntie and uncle I have next to one of my parents and me, just before everything changed. I wonder what my auntie and uncle are doing now. I am sure my auntie would be baking some goodies for my uncle's breakfast whilst he reads the paper in his favourite chair in the kitchen. I miss them so much.

I quickly grab my phone and send a text, letting them know I survived last night and I will call them later to tell them about my first day of classes. Then, I grab my wash bag before heading back into my tiny shower room.

Once there, I start stripping as the shower warms up. Catching my reflection in the large mirror over my sink, I stop in my tracks. Thank the Goddess it had been Tony who caught me sneaking in, and I'd been covered up. It would have been harder to convince the girls I hadn't been up to something if they'd seen all the mud up to my right arm and across my shoulder. I turn and look at my back. Yep, there would have been no excuse for this amount of mud on my body. I guess I could've told them the truth. I can just hear how that conversation would have gone. "The thing is girls, I was curled up under a bush in the middle of nowhere where I spent six hours as a wolf."

That's right, surprise! I'm a werewolf.

Last night was a full moon, so I'd snuck into a local woodland, curled up and hid from the world to ride out my forced shift. Guess you can see now why I can't tell people the truth about where I've been. Of course, Tony is aware, but that's only because he's also supernatural, a fire demon, to be precise. Hence, he understands a little about what I go through. He is part of our world; the girls who also live here are not, so we keep what we are from them. Thankfully, we have each other.

I hate being a werewolf; even the word makes me feel sick. Changing into a wolf once a month is still new to me, as I wasn't born a wolf.

Two years ago, I was changed against my will. Not long after, I had to learn to deal with what'd happened to me alone. Because I'm not part of a pack, I am known as a rogue. This means I had nobody to teach me or help me learn how to be a wolf or control her. Getting the courage to approach a pack for help has always been difficult for me. What if they treated me the same way as the asshole who did this to me? Would they treat me differently, as I have heard they don't trust witches?

That's right; I hit the supernatural jackpot: two supernatural abilities for the price of one, a magical werewolf hybrid; yay for me! Yes, witches and sorcerers are real, too. I was born a witch. Every member of my family is of magical blood. They are also all in the same coven. My coven has never left my side through it all, but I have never been able to go back to any meetings. The main reason is that they are usually on a full moon. Yeah, I'm a little preoccupied those nights. Secondly, I'm ashamed of what I've become; I don't feel I deserve their loyalty or support. Thirdly, my magic has never been the same since I was turned. It's much weaker, and we have no idea why. I miss how it was before; I was stronger with it; it was part of me; it was my birth rite.

I quickly snap out of my thoughts before jumping into the shower to wash away all the evidence and memories of how I spent my night. Plus, I really need my morning coffee.

Once showered and dressed in my favourite jeans and hoodie, I head into the kitchen, where Tony is now sitting fully dressed, nursing a cup of coffee and a bowl of cereal.

"There's coffee in the pot," he announces as I walk in. I thank him before heading to it; goddess, I need coffee.

"You look knackered. Didn't you sleep after you shifted?" Tony asks as I sit opposite him at the table, shaking my head.

"Nope, never do. My hearing becomes too sensitive, so even the silence is noisy," I reply as I take a big sip of my coffee, relaxing in my seat, savouring the sweet-bitter brown nectar. I rely heavily on my morning caffeine to help me function. Plus, I really want to avoid all questions regarding last night. Tony seems to realise and thankfully changes the subject.

"Are you ready for the first day of classes?"

I nod, unable to answer verbally as I have a piece of toast hanging out of my mouth and am busy tying my chest-length dark blonde hair into a messy bun on the top of my head. Tony just smiles at me before carrying on. "Yeah, me too. Feeling nervous as hell, though."

"I'm sure it will be fine." I take another sip of my coffee and then smile at my friend. "Just think, in about five years, when we are high-rising lawyers, taking the supernatural world by storm, today will feel like a lifetime ago. We will look back wondering why we were so nervous."

Tony glances up at me from his cereal bowl.

"Don't think I will let you forget about our plan to become business partners," he winks playfully.

"Oh, don't worry, I won't. I can't wait to have you as my coffee bitch," I laugh.

"We'll see. Pretty sure it will be your bitchy arse bringing me my coffee, not the other way around."

Tony and I sit and talk until an hour before class. Then, he heads out to meet a couple of the guys we met yesterday. I decide to head off early myself, as I will pick up a few of the cafeteria's muffins before class. They are so good they always sell out quickly. I missed out yesterday, and I don't plan on making the same mistake twice.

Chapter Two

DAISY

I pop into the cafeteria for the muffins and a bacon sandwich to eat now. The four slices of toast I ate with Tony earlier didn't fill the bottomless pit that is my stomach.

Tony is always laughing at me as I eat continuously. The high metabolism is a significant perk of being a shifter; we quickly burn off the excess calories. As a result, it's nearly impossible to gain weight, which makes this twenty-two-year-old extremely happy. I loved my food before I became a wolf, but being able to eat as much of it as I want now without the fear of going up ten dress sizes is fantastic. However, I'd give up the unlimited food if it meant I'd no longer be a wolf in a heartbeat.

When I get to the cafeteria, I'm shocked at how busy it is. I've never seen it so packed at nine-thirty before. I guess people are all up early, ready for the first day of classes, as Tony and I were. It takes a while for me to get to the front of the queue, but luckily, there are still plenty of muffins left, so I grab one of each. Hey, I'm not kidding when I say they are amazing, no judging, okay!

For the middle of September, it's still surprisingly warm. The grounds are all filled with bright flowers and leafy trees. The witch in me longs to spend some time in nature. I check my watch, realising I have a bit of time before I need to start heading to class, so I find a bench to sit and read for a bit.

As I'm rummaging through my bag, searching for my book, my wolf perks up. *"Wolf"*. The scent hits me as I'm about to question her.

Shit, there is another wolf. I turn to face the direction it is coming from. Two men are walking towards me, deep in conversation.

"Wolf," my wolf repeats; surely it can't be one of them. I subtly sniff the air again; shit, it is.

My heart starts racing as I take in the two men; I realise that the shorter of the two is Martin, the head of the Law Department. I met him briefly a couple of days ago. I know I hadn't picked up on a wolf scent then, so it can't be him. I look over to the other guy; my stomach drops. Holy shit, he is hot. Not just desirable, but clamp your legs tight to try and stop the aching in your lower stomach hot, I want; no, I *need* him, now!

I look at this definition of pure sex walking towards me; he must be at least six foot eight as he's towering over Martin's short five-and-a-half-foot frame. He has dark brown hair, which is slightly longer on the top, just long enough for me to entwine my fingers into it to pull his gorgeous, kissable lips to mine.

What the hell? Get a grip, Daisy! I can't tear my eyes away from him as much as I try. It's like I can't see anything but him.

Just as he walks past me, the breeze shifts and his head snaps around. He looks straight at me. He stops in his tracks and stares. As soon as our eyes meet, I feel a warmth rush through me. The pull to be near him, to touch him, is overwhelming.

Shit!

I watch as he opens his mouth to say something, but I panic. I jump to my feet, grab my bag, and walk away from him as fast as I can, cursing myself.

"He's a good wolf!" my wolf tells me. You don't know that; he was probably going to shout at me for staring. *"Doubtful, he may have wanted to chat."* I quickly tell my wolf to shut up. Oh god, he had probably picked up on my scent, too; he will know I'm turned on. Shit!

I never even considered that I'd bump into another wolf here. I knew it would happen at some point in my life, but am I ready to be around one now? I've avoided them for the last two years. Hopefully, I won't be seeing him very often. A girl can hope, right?

I shake my head, trying to think straight, before attempting to work out where I'm going. I glance over my shoulder; he's still there behind me. He has carried on his conversation with Martin but has his eyes trained on me. I notice bathrooms down the far end of the corridor. I rush towards them, almost slamming the door into the wall behind it as I barge in to get away from him.

I rush over to the nearest cubicle, shutting the door behind me. I slam the toilet seat down to sit on it. Placing my head in my hands, I bite my bottom lip to stop myself from screaming in frustration. As soon as I close my eyes, I see him there, staring at me. It sends a shiver down my spine, causing my wolf to stand on edge; this is not what I need right now.

He was gorgeous. All werewolves tend to be muscular, or so I have been told, but I never dreamt one would be that

… I try to think of a word that defines him, but words fail me; there is nothing that could do justice for that man.

My stomach flutters as I think about how it felt when our eyes met for those brief seconds. I got the strangest feeling of deja vu, which is ridiculous as there is no way I've ever met that man before. Unless he has done a complete Neville Longbottom, I wouldn't forget someone like that. You know, going from the loveable chubby kid to hottie in a couple of years, making him unrecognisable then, no, I haven't met him before.

"You going to hide in here all day?" my wolf asks. I check my watch, and see I have ten minutes before class starts, and I still need to get to the other side of campus. Shit, I really need to get it together. I give my head one last shake in an attempt to clear it before leaving my little panic room, praying he's long gone by now so I can get to class.

Thankfully, it doesn't take as long as I feared; I make it with five minutes to spare. The room is unlocked; there are a few people already inside. I spot an empty table for two in the centre of the room; I head straight for it. I promised to save a seat for a girl I met yesterday.

The lecturer isn't here yet. I pull out my notepad and pen before looking around again, this time at the room itself. Like most places on campus, the place seems plain and boring, with the bare minimum in each room.

"You still saving a place for me?"

I look up to see Beth standing next to me, smiling.

"Depends. Did you bring the coffee?" I ask, smiling. Beth smirks as she places two to-go cups on the table.

"I did, but did you remember the *amazing muffins* you wouldn't shut up about?"

I smirk as I pull two out of my bag, placing them on the table next to the coffee.

"I think we are all set." We both pick up our cups and tap them together, smiling before chuckling.

I look over at Beth as she sips her coffee whilst playing with her long, red, wavy hair; I get envious every time I look at it.

"How are you feeling today?" I ask; she had been home-sick yesterday. Having moved from Central Manchester.

"Alright, I guess. I still can't get over how quiet it is around here. How about you?"

I open my mouth to say I am okay when I hear a loud group of people behind us. I turn around just in time to see three guys stumble through the door, laughing loudly. Of course, Tony is in the middle of them.

"Hey! Biatch! What happened to saving me a seat?" he calls, heading over to me. I pout my lips whilst frowning.

"I'm sorry, do I know you? I think you must have me confused with someone who would respond to being spoken to in such a way. I'm a lady; as such, I expect to be spoken to as one good sir." I reply, putting on my poshest voice. Beth is trying desperately not to laugh next to me, whereas Tony just roars with laughter.

"Please, I live with you. I know there is nothing ladylike about you." He winks at me as he walks three tables back from us. I just laugh, turning to face the other way, but as I do, I make sure to flip him the bird over my head.

"Boyfriend?"

I turn to the sound of Beth's voice, unable to stop the laugh that escapes me, shaking my head.

"Hell, no. Dorm mate, a.k.a, the royal pain in my arse." I reply.

"I heard that bitch," Tony calls across the room; Beth laughs as I turn in my seat to face him.

"Then stop listening. I'm talking about you, not to you."

I turn back to Beth, who's still laughing, when I notice a man walking to the front of the room, heading straight for the teacher's desk. As he does, his scent hits me; I instantly feel my cheeks burn as my heart stops. Oh crap, it's the wolf. I can't believe he's here. I quickly nod in his direction to Beth.

"Is that the lecturer?" I ask her quietly; she looks over and nods as a huge grin spreads across her face. Oh, double crap. Only I would have a wolf for a lecturer.

"Hot, isn't he?" she winks. I roll my eyes, trying desperately not to give away the fact that I'm falling apart at the seams just from looking at him. I quickly grab my phone to look busy for a second so that I can compose myself.

What if he recognises me from earlier? He's probably already picked up on my scent; if I can smell him, he can smell me. Ohgods, his scent is so unique, like a fresh woodland area, the perfect mixture of pine, wood, musk, and a smidge of fresh rain. That scent does things to me I never thought possible. I want to rush into his arms, forcing him to hold me. Thankfully, I feel my phone vibrate in my hands; it's a text.

Tony: Is he a wolf???

Daisy: Yes! What do I do?

I feel myself starting to panic; what the hell is wrong with me?

I quickly look back at Tony, who just shrugs his shoulders at me. I mouth 'thanks' at him, and he gives me that 'sorry' look. Why do I keep him around?

I hear the wolf clearing his throat at the front of the class; slowly, I turn to face him. As soon as I look up at him, my heart races, my breath gets stuck in my throat. He is even better looking up close. I know it's a romantic cliché, but he really does take my breath away. I look at Beth only to realise it's not only me he has this effect on. She is staring with her mouth hanging open. I nudge her, and she snaps out of the trance. She looks at me, eyes wide open.

"Wow."

I nod my head, smiling at the look on her face.

"Morning all. I'm Michael Adams, and I'm one of the law lecturers who'll be teaching you for most of the units you'll cover this year. I'm also new here, so if you have any questions that I can't answer, I'll do my best to find them out for you." While standing, he looks at each person individually. When he gets to me, I'm sure his blue eyes darken for a second, but when he blinks, they've returned to the deep blue they were before. I quickly put my head down, breaking eye contact. I can feel my cheeks flushing.

Get a grip, Daisy, for crying out loud.

"This morning, I'd like to hear a bit about yourselves, who you are, where you're from, and what made you choose to study law." He picks up a bean bag. I hear a few giggles and moans from people around me.

"I see some of you can guess what this is for. But I will explain for those of you who don't know. Whoever has this bean bag tells us about themselves. Then, when you're finished, you simply throw it to someone else," he explains, smiling. Oh, dear goddess, his smile is mesmerising.

"Right, how about I get us started, as it's only fair," Michael announces. He stands at the front of the room, tossing the bean bag from hand to hand, casually leaning back against the desk with his legs crossed in front of him. He is the image of a god. I try to study his face but can't help glancing down at his chest. He is wearing a white fitted shirt, and by fitted, I mean that shirt really is an excellent fit. The fabric stretches against his muscular pecs, and the buttons seem to be straining ever so slightly to stay in place.

"As I have said, my name is Michael Adams. This is my fourth week working at this university. Before, I was working in a different facility. However, I was asked to help here for a while. I'm not going to say how old I am, as I'm sure I'm a lot older than all of you in this room, so I'll leave that to your imagination. But put me in my forties, and I will fail you." He smiles, causing everyone to chuckle. I take a quick glance around and notice all the girls are leaning forward, listening to Michael's every word. I purposely sit back so I don't look as deranged as the rest of them.

"Yeah, real smooth, like he can't smell your arousal," my wolf laughs.

Of course, he can't, can he?

I clamp my legs tight, just to be on the safe side. I swear I hear my wolf chuckle, bitch.

"Right, so I've started us off; who should be next?" He looks in my direction, smiles, and, of course, points at me. "You," he says as he throws me the bean bag. I catch it quickly and look up at him.

"Thanks," I sigh sarcastically, smiling. Michael just winks at me, causing my stomach to flip. Pull yourself together for crying out loud, Daisy! I scold myself. "I'm Daisy Andrews; I'm twenty-two years old. I've just moved here from Cornwall." I find myself smiling. "Before anyone can ask, no, I don't surf. I can bodyboard, but only for fun. Yes, the jam goes on before cream on a cream tea, and yes, I drink cider. I think that's all the typical Cornish questions covered."

Michael laughs at the front of the class; a few others do as well.

"I chose law because I want to be able to become a lawyer to represent the victims. I want to ensure they get the voice they deserve and are not ignored, as unfortunately so many are." I risk a glance at Michael to see him looking at me like he understands. I give him a one-sided smile before quickly throwing the bean bag backwards over my head, knowing Tony will easily catch it. Instead, I hear him cursing me and everyone else laughing as he drops it, including Michael, as I relax into my seat, smiling.

I listen to everyone's introductions until the last person throws the bag back to Michael. He then starts throwing it to each person, asking them questions. I sit and pray he will not ask anything about my family.

I hear him say my name as I see the bean bag flying towards my face; thank gods for my wolf instincts. I manage to catch it before it breaks my nose. By the look on his smug face, the prick did that on purpose, knowing I would catch it. Dick.

"What do you miss the most about Cornwall?" he asks, still looking smug. I lift one eyebrow and give him that "really" look. I swear he is trying not to laugh. But, instead, I feel my face soften.

"That's easy; the sea," I reply, throwing the bean bag back to him, possibly a little harder than I should have, but I know he will catch it. Just a shame it will not hit the bastard.

"Why?" he asks as he catches it without taking his eyes off me. "There has to be a reason why the sea is so important to you?" he carries on. I find myself shrugging.

"I don't really know. I guess it's because no matter what happens in your life, the sea is always there waiting for you.

Like our moods, constantly changing, some days it's mad, some days it's calm, but no matter what, it's still there to welcome you, to make you feel like you are home." Wow, where did that come from? I look up at Michael, and we look into each other's eyes for a second. I can only describe the feeling when our eyes meet, as if electricity courses through my whole body. It disappeared as quickly as it started. I'm left with an unbelievable desire to reach out to him. I look away quickly, clutching my hands together over my aching stomach.

"Good answer," he replies, clearing his throat. Wait, did he feel that too? Of course, he didn't, but what was that?

My mind wanders for the rest of the class. I have no idea what he asks the others. I'm too distracted, thinking about those eyes and how I felt when I looked into them and desperately trying to ignore the need to be near him.

It has been two hours since we started class. It's been surprisingly fun listening to other people's stories. Still, I'm glad I haven't been asked to say anything about my life before coming here.

Finally, Michael declares that that is enough for today, explaining that lessons will start properly tomorrow. He dismisses us, and the room erupts with the sound of scraping chairs and people talking.

"Fancy another coffee?" I turn to the sound of Beth's voice. She has a massive smile on her face.

"One thing you need to know about me is I *never* say no to coffee," I answer, returning the smile as I pick up my bag. Just as we are leaving our table, Michael walks past us. He smiles in our direction before walking out of the room.

"He's hot!" Beth exclaims as she watches him smiling.

"Oh, he is hot, alright," a voice comes from behind us. I look around to see a short girl with blonde hair. I remember her name's Sam. She looks at us with a massive smile on her face.

"I think every girl in the uni already knows who he is. They're all trying their hardest to get him to notice them. Not that he seems to."

"Maybe he's gay," another voice chimes in. This one is Rosie; she is as tall as me, slender build with exceptionally long brown hair which hangs poker-straight down to her hips.

"God, I hope he's not gay. But, then again, all the good-looking men I meet seem to be." Beth answers; she looks disappointed. I think about it for a second.

"I don't think he is; then again, I have been wrong in the past."

The others laugh.

"Well, maybe there's hope for one of us yet after all," Sam replies. We all laugh again as we leave the room.

Rosie and Sam decide to join us in the Student Union. After we've gotten our drinks and snacks, we head over to a table where Tony is sitting with Kellan and Mathew, the guys he had been seated with in class. As soon as he sees me, he jumps up and drags me to one side.

"Are you okay?" he asks the second we are out of earshot of the others. I nod in response. "Are you sure? Having a wolf as our lecturer was a hell of a shock."

"Yep, it was the last thing I expected, but I think it'll be okay." I can't explain it, but I trust Michael.

"Well, if he makes you feel uncomfortable at any point, just say the word, and I'll cremate the bastard, wolf or not," Tony says, looking all defensive. I can't help but laugh.

"I see having a fire demon as a best friend is going to come in handy." I wiggle my eyebrows at him as I turn back to the rest of our friends. I feel Tony step beside me.

"Hey, say the word, and he'll disappear, literally." He plants a kiss on my cheek before we join everyone else. I can't help but smile as I know he really would do anything for me and to help me feel safe. The feeling is mutual; we have each other's backs.

We quickly catch up on the discussions which are happening around the group. First, we are all talking about the course and what we know about it so far. Then, the conversation moves on to the lecturers. Next, the girls try to decide if Michael is seeing anyone, as they know he is not married or doesn't wear a ring at least. Apparently, it was the first thing Sam had checked for. Finally, we settle on him being around thirty; he looks far too young to be a lecturer.

As lunchtime approaches, we all head off to the cafeteria to get some food. I can see this being a great class; we are all getting along so well, and everyone is up for a laugh. I can see already that this year is going to be fun.

Chapter Three

MICHAEL

As soon as I end the lesson, I grab my bag and head straight for my office.

It's as if there's a wolf in my class, not just any wolf, but a smart-mouthed one that gets my pulse racing in a way it hasn't for years. Dear goddess, the way her lips move when she speaks or how her cheeks flush when I catch her looking at me. Gods, this is going to take some significant self-control to handle this situation.

When my previous post asked me to transfer to a different university for a couple of years, I initially refused. But then my Alpha told me I would have to make the transfer as the university needed a new supernatural advocate. My old role was part-time, which was perfect as I'm busy with the Pack Protectors I lead. But now I'm back working full time, and to say I'm unhappy is an understatement.

I unlock my office door and step in. Throwing my briefcase onto the spare chair, I dig through it for my personal mobile. Just as I find it, it starts to vibrate.

"Hey," I answer without even checking the screen.

"Well, hi to you too. What's crawled up your arse, Bro?" I hear my brother Jonathan answer as I walk around to my office chair.

"I'm fine. What's up?" I ask as I sit down.

"Nothing much, just calling to see how my little brother is."

"Jon, you're only three months older than me," I point out, leaning back into my chair. My parents adopted Jon when his mum, our mum's best friend, died in a car crash when he was three; his dad was long gone before he was born.

"Still older, though, Mikey," he chuckles down the line.

"And don't you just love reminding me of it," I reply, looking up at the ceiling while shaking my head to myself. But then, I suddenly remembered why I was looking for my phone. "Oh, Jon, you'll never guess what!"

"What?" I can hear the curiosity in his voice.

"My first-year class has a wolf and a fire demon." I've been teaching for a few years and have never had a supernatural in my own class, let alone two.

"Shut up! Seriously? I take it the demon is male. What about the wolf? Male or female?" I should have known that was going to be his first question.

"I'm not telling you, you sex pest."

"Oh, so it's female. When can I meet her?"

"You can't," I say instantly. I can hear Jon dramatically huffing and puffing on the line. There is no way I would let him anywhere near Daisy.

"You're no fun! What if she could be my new best friend, and you are purposely keeping her from me?" Maybe that's why I am keeping them apart; I can see them becoming best friends very quickly, and I don't want to share her.

"Yeah, you keep telling yourself that," my wolf laughs. I ignore him.

"Jon, she has more than a couple of brain cells, so she will probably find you as annoying as the rest of us."

"Oh, har har Mikey, I will have you know I'm loved by all who meet me."

I just smile whilst raising my eyebrows.

"All?" I ask. Jon breathes in through his teeth.

"Well, almost all. I think Desmond and Alaric may be a little pissed at me right now." When aren't the Alpha and his Beta pissed with my brother?

"Do I even want to know what you have done now?" I ask.

"It wasn't my fault."

If I had a pound for every time I heard that sentence come out of my brother's mouth, I would be a very rich wolf.

"It never is. What'd you do?"

"I may have accidentally knocked Alaric into the river last night during the pack run."

I can't help myself as I burst out laughing.

"Sounds like something you would do. I want to hear all about it, but I need to call the Alpha about this wolf. What are you up to tomorrow night?"

"Nothing much, why what are you thinking?"

We quickly arrange to meet at Mum's tomorrow for dinner and then go for a run with the rest of the team.

I hang up, feeling a little calmer after speaking to my brother. He may be annoying, but he has always been my best friend.

I quickly check my emails for anything from the supernaturals on campus, just in case there was a late one from Daisy. But there's nothing.

It shocks many to learn that every educational facility has a supernatural advocate. This ensures that all supernaturals, or sups, are monitored and supported whilst away from family, packs, groups, and covens. Students are usually still learning how to handle their powers when they start university. Advocates can help them find whatever support they need, whether it's locating a local coven, pack or just someone to talk to who understands how hard it can be to hide our powers around humans. All supernaturals know to contact the Supernatural Council to inform them where their kids will be attending. The council then advises us advocates who will be attending and of any needs they may have.

That's why finding a wolf in my classroom was such a shock. I have already received the list of sups coming into the uni this year, as well as the ones already attending; there was not a single wolf on the list for my classes. I knew a demon would be attending my class and a witch, who hasn't seemed to have arrived yet. Their name was not on the class register anyway, an N. Evans.

There's a handful of other supernaturals throughout the university, including demons, wolves, witches, sorcerers, and a couple of necromancers. The wolves I know personally as they are part of the pack. We never tend to travel far from home. It's an easy gig, to be fair. The necromancers give me the creeps, though. I hate the idea of one of them losing control and raising the dead from the graveyard down the road. I involuntarily shudder at the thought.

I glance down at the phone in my hand; I need to get this call over and done with. So I dial the number for the Alpha's office and wait for him to answer.

"Hello?" his deep voice answers on the third ring. My wolf instantly stands to attention, as he always does around our Alpha.

"Morning, Alpha, it's Michael." It's pack etiquette to address the Alpha by his title, the same as his Luna and Beta. However, I tend to get away with calling them all by name a little more often than most.

"Morning Michael, I wasn't expecting to hear from you until this evening. Is everything okay?"

I decide to get straight to the point.

"Yes and no. Did you know there was going to be a wolf in my class?"

"Are you sure?" I can tell by his tone that he is not completely surprised.

"I think I, of all people, know a wolf when I smell one, Desmond." I hear the Alpha let out a deep breath on the other end of the line.

"I did receive an email regarding somebody who had shown an interest in moving to this area, but I never received a confirmation, so I didn't follow it up."

"Is that why you were so insistent that I take this post? Because you knew there was a chance she would be coming?" Why do I feel played?

"No, Michael, I ordered you to take that post because the only position was for a law lecturer. They already wanted you, so it was a guaranteed appointment. With Paul the sorcerer retiring, we needed somebody there."

I lean back in my chair, biting my tongue so I don't push the issue further.

"So?" he sighs down the line; I can hear the frustration in his voice. "Are you going to tell me anything about them? Or do I just have to guess?"

I sigh, knowing that's his way of saying he will not be questioned further.

"Her name is Daisy Andrews; she is twenty-two years old and has just moved from Cornwall. That's all I know at the moment; I only met her today in my first class." I take a deep breath to calm myself. "Do you want me to make contact with the packs down there to see who she belongs to?" I ask, hoping he will say yes so I can find out a little more about her, for professional reasons, obviously.

"No. I will contact the council's secretary first and see why I was not informed she was coming here. Do you think she is going to be an issue?"

"No," I reply without hesitation. Nothing about Daisy screams threat; in fact, it's quite the opposite.

"You sound very confident there, Michael."

"I am." Does he doubt me? I really am not in the mood for this today.

"Okay, I will leave you to contact her and let her know of your post as you do all new sups. If you have any problems, then you are to contact me as soon as possible."

"I'm fully aware of my role here, Alpha." I find myself sighing, frustrated that he seems to feel the need to tell me how to do my job.

"Michael, I know how well you are trained; I trained you myself, after all. I'm also aware of how well you work with students. Do we have an issue here that I'm not aware of?"

I consider telling him that yes, we do, that I can't continue teaching Daisy as there is more to it than her being my student and a wolf. I know that if I tell him what, I suspect he could have me pulled from the uni in a matter of weeks rather than years. But what would happen then if I was wrong about her ability? What if Daisy does require help at some point? Do I want to leave her here without a wolf to contact for assistance? Would I have an excuse to see her again if my instinctive feelings towards her were right? I need to think about all this before telling the Alpha the truth.

"No issue, Alpha. I guess I'm just more tired than I thought after last night." The sigh I hear tells me he doesn't completely believe me.

"Okay, Michael, if you say so. Keep me posted with any developments, and I'll let you know when I hear more about where the possible rogue came from."

"Her name is Daisy." I'm not sure why it irritates me that he just referred to her as "the possible rogue", but it does.

"You're right; I'm sorry. I'll try and find out more information about Daisy and get back to you. I'll contact you when I have something new. Goodbye, Michael." He hangs up before I get a chance to say goodbye. I flip my middle finger at my phone before dropping it onto my desk; I haven't done that in years. I laugh as I remember seeing Daisy doing it to one of the guys behind her earlier. She's rubbing off on me already.

I turn on my laptop, which I use for contacting the sups in the uni. Only to realise I don't have Daisy's email address or any other way of messaging her. For fuck's sake. Nothing is going to be easy with this, is it?!

I slam my laptop shut before grabbing my bag; I need some fresh air. My head has been fried since I first saw Daisy on that bench. I decide to head out for a coffee before my next class in an hour.

Chapter Four

DAISY

The tempo of my feet pounding the pavement increases as my breathing quickens. I try to push myself harder, desperate to burn off some of my excess energy. I keep pushing myself in the hope of some sort of release, but there's none.

I curse out loud with frustration as I come to an abrupt stop. I'm in the middle of nowhere, with no one else around. I lean against a tree, trying to catch my breath. Unbelievably, my legs are still aching to run, my body twitching as if on a caffeine high. I can hear my wolf begging for more. I look at my sports watch. I've run fourteen miles, yet I feel like I could run another fourteen. What do I have to do to find a release?

Yesterday, I ran ten miles and spent two hours in the gym; it was pointless, as I felt no different when I woke up this morning.

The problem with going to the gym when others are there is that I can't lift the weights I need to feel like I've worked out. I can lift so much more than most women; people look at me differently and start asking questions. It draws too much attention. It's the last thing I need when all I want is to fit in. Therefore, I run in the early hours of the morning so that way there is no chance of someone spotting a woman running at Olympic speeds just for fun.

I really hate being what I am; why can't I go back to being just a witch? Life was so much simpler then.

Just as I catch my breath, my wolf jumps to attention.

"Wolf," she calls out. I quickly sniff the air and look around, but the scent has gone. I send out a sensing spell, but there's no one there. Maybe I sense something just on the outskirts of the spell. But my magic isn't as strong as it should be, so it will only reach a few meters. I still have that feeling of being watched, but again, when I look around, I can see no one. My wolf is getting antsy, so I decide it's time to leave and head back home.

Slowly, I step away from the tree and head back in the direction I came, trying to keep to an average running pace. It means I can keep my senses about me and listen out for who was around before. The fact that I only smelt the scent for a millisecond could mean it was from a wolf passing through another day. It's not rained for a few days, so it's possible. There are obviously other wolves around here, such as Michael. What are the chances that it's him? It did smell a little like him, but it was so quick I couldn't be sure.

Why do I care if it is him anyway? He's a wolf; after all, wolves cause nothing but trouble to females; it's best to stay away from them.

"But he's different," my wolf adds. I ignore her as usual and concentrate on running back to the dorm.

Twelve miles later, I get back to my building, and sweat is pouring from me. Thankfully, my legs feel a little less restless. I really need to find out why I feel this way after each full moon; surely, it can't be normal. I never felt like this in the beginning.

Before, a short run in the morning would be all I needed. But now I have to run for longer and further each month; it's getting ridiculous; there has to be a point when things start to level out.

"*Speak to Michael,*" my wolf suggests for the hundredth time.

No, I refuse to admit weakness to a male wolf. That's what got me in this mess in the first place.

"*Stubborn fool.*" My wolf responds. No, it's called self-preservation; there's a difference. My wolf must be sulking as she has no snarky comment for once.

I walk into my building and climb the stairs to the third floor, where my dorm is situated. After running a full marathon, I shouldn't be able to climb the stairs this easily. I'm hoping it is due to my advanced wolf healing rather than the fact that I'll need to run again later.

I enter my floor and head straight for my front door. There are three other apartments on this level. Each has its own kitchen and lounge area and four bedrooms. I can hear chatter and laughter from all the dorms I pass, so I know others are awake. At least I don't have to sneak in this time.

I enter my dorm and am met with silence. I check my watch as I close the door. It's eight o'clock; surely somebody else is up. I shrug my shoulders and head to my bedroom door. As soon as I walk in, I aim straight for my bed and collapse onto it.

Thank the gods, my class isn't until ten. I've plenty of

time to shower and eat my body weight in food. Hopefully, it will wake me up a bit as I'm exhausted. A bucket full of coffee may also help me to stay awake in Michael's class, not that looking at him doesn't. I curse at myself for thinking of him again. I grab my phone and connect it to my speakers. It's time to blast some music and get in the shower in the hope of distracting myself from thoughts of Michael.

By the time I finish in the shower, I'm singing along to Ed Sheeran and have forgotten all about a particular wolf … What? I have!

Once I'm dressed, I head out, rushing down the stairs before running out of the front door. The cool, fresh air hits my face, and I breathe in the scent of fresh food in the air. I'm starving. Just as I turn in the direction of the canteen, I hear someone call my name; I turn to see Tony jogging up to me.

"Hey Dais, where you heading off to so early?" I check my watch and see it's only a quarter to nine. I place my hands on my hips as I glare at him.

"Shouldn't I be asking you where you've been all night?"

Tony just laughs.

"I got a job last night in The Crows. It's a supernatural bar; you should check it out. The owners, Carl and Richard, are wolves, too. We had a few too many drinks after my interview, and they let me crash there."

I can't hide my shock; I never knew there were such things as supernatural bars. There seems to be a lot of sups around here. Does that mean there is a pack nearby? Is that why my uncle wanted me to come here? So many thoughts start flying around in my head; if Michael is a wolf and the owners of the bars are wolves too, then surely there's at least one pack. My ears start to ring as my heart rate increases, and my breathing becomes rapid as my chest tightens. I can feel a panic attack starting.

"Woah, Daisy, calm down. I'm sorry, I shouldn't have said anything." I feel Tony take my hand, giving it a reassuring squeeze. He places a hand on my cheek and manoeuvres my face so I look into his eyes.

"Breathe, you're okay; I'm right here."

I stare into his brown eyes as his hand warms slightly against my cheek. I know he's using his powers to give me something to focus on rather than the building panic. I take a few deep breaths with him until I feel myself relax. Then, I close my eyes and take one last breath before stepping away from him.

"Thanks, Tony. Sorry, I need to get used to there being other wolves around."

Tony squeezes my hand, which he is still holding.

"Hey, no need to apologise; you are handling it all amazingly. I forget you are new to the whole wolf thing; I guess there aren't many where you live."

I shake my head.

"One small pack, I think; that's why we moved there."

Tony pulls me into a tight hug.

"Well, sorry to say it, Dais, but there are a lot more around here, so you will have to learn to deal with it. But I'm here, okay; we can take it one step at a time, starting with that supposedly hot lecturer of ours. Who's just turned up and looked at us very strangely."

I jump out of his arms and turn to see Michael walking away from us.

"So, I take it you are on the ever-growing list of admirers," Tony winks as he moves out of the way of my fist.

"Oh, sod off. Now go get a shower before class; you

smell like you slept in a brewery." I laugh as I turn away from him. I hear him shouting for me to grab him a coffee and some food as I head off to the cafeteria; I wave a thumbs up as I keep walking.

Chapter Five

I can't believe it has been three months since I left my life in Cornwall, making the move to Wales. They're not joking when they say time flies when you are having fun. Because, oh dear goddess, have I been having fun.

Besides my monthly shifts, I've enjoyed uni life so much more than I ever thought possible. I've got a great group of friends, especially Tony and Beth. The three of us have developed a special kind of friendship; we may be known to cause havoc wherever we go, especially in the bar where Tony works.

As for my dreaded monthly changes, they're not getting any easier. In the days after, the effects on my body are still getting harder to control. I have to run harder and further each month. Tony has also been lending me his weights to help me train in my room so I don't have to go to the gym in the early morning hours to avoid everyone else. I still go every other day, but it is mainly to do proper stretching and use the punch bags.

Tony has been fantastic in supporting me as I learn to juggle my wolf's needs and uni life. Although I wish he would stop telling me to speak to Michael or the guys he works for. He is convinced Michael can help me or give me some advice on why I feel as restless as I do all the time. But I just can't bring myself to ask him for help. I know Tony is worried about me, but he knows I will ask for help if, or when it becomes too much, not before.

As for classes, they've been great; I'm getting top marks in everything. As a class in general, we all get along so well. The lecturers are great, they are down to earth, and we can joke around in class, but goddess help us if we push our luck in Michael's, as Kellan has learnt the hard way several times. I don't know what he has done to piss Michael off, but he is forever getting on the wrong side of him. I'm sure Kellan does it on purpose and gets a kick out of how far he can push it. I must admit I don't think I would want to get on Michael's wrong side. I'm sure he holds back when in class, but the way he looks at Kellan at times makes me wonder if he could actually kill him, dispose of his body, and get away with it if he really wanted to.

As for Michael, well, where do I begin? I would love to say I'm over that little crush I developed during my first few classes with him, and I no longer think or dream of him constantly, but I would, of course, be lying. Nope, it seems like this crush is here to stay for the long run; yay for me!

Am I able to hide my crush on him? Gods, I hope so, but there are times I'm sure he knows that I'm staring at him or that my mind has taken a simple comment he has made and turned it into an R-rated movie that would make a porn star blush. I've decided it's his own damn fault, though. I mean, the man is a god.

I wish it was just in the classroom I had to see him, but we always seem to pick the exact same times to go to the gym. Watching him working out in a pair of sweatpants and a vest top. That man is built to pure perfection; his body could have been made by the goddess herself. The way his sweat runs down his back, his muscles flexing as he pulls himself up on the pull-up bar with ease. I quickly stop my mind from going any further as I'll lose track of where I am or run into a lamppost. I really need to stop daydreaming while out running.

I turn down the usual dirt road that I run down every morning, and for the briefest of seconds, I pick up on that scent, the one which I've smelt daily since my first week of classes. I sniff the air, hoping to find it again, but it's gone. It never comes for more than a second. However, the feeling that I'm being watched will continue for a while. If I'm honest, it's the reason I run down this road every day. Them being near makes me feel safer than I have in so long; I relax more into the run. My whole mind and body become at ease; nothing else matters but the feeling of calm that washes over me. I close my eyes and breathe in deep, allowing myself to feel it all. It's such a fantastic feeling; I can't help but savour it. I'll miss it when I return to Cornwall for the holidays, even if I only go for a week. A week without this morning routine and seeing Michael feels like a lifetime.

The sun is quickly rising. I know the guys will be getting up soon, so I need to get back; otherwise, my phone will be ringing with Kellan wondering where I am.

Kellan has been sleeping on our sofa most nights as he is the only one in his dorm who has not left to go home for Christmas. It's been fun having him around most of the time. But sometimes, he is a nightmare. He hates the idea of me running in the morning. I know he is just worried that something will happen to me, but that really isn't an issue; I'm perfectly capable of looking after myself. If only he knew how strong I really am, he would understand then. But it isn't like I can show him that I could lift and throw him out of my way easily. Although it would be fun to do; I have been tempted to do it a few times when he is really frustrated.

As fun as Kellan can be, he has made it obvious he would like us to be more than just friends, but I'm just not interested. I have tried to make it as obvious as possible for him to understand. I really don't want to hurt his feelings as he has been a good friend. But I can't wait for him to go back to his own dorm. Sometimes, he makes me feel really uncomfortable, to the point that I have even gone to work with Tony to avoid being left alone in the apartment with him. I want to feel at ease in my own place again.

I head back to my dorm, taking the shortest route to make sure I get there quickly. It doesn't take long before I look up and see that I'm back. I've been running on autopilot the whole time. As I approach the building, I start to slow down. I'm just coming to a stop at the main door when it opens, and Kellan walks out.

"Hey, where have you been?" he greets me with a smile. I have to stop myself from rolling my eyes at him in frustration. How does he always know when I'm not in my room?

"Climbing a mountain, where does it look like I've been?" I reply sarcastically, leaning on my knees, trying to catch my breath. Kellan just laughs.

"Yeah, I guess it's pretty obvious. I was just worried as you've been out for over two hours." This is the exact behaviour I've been thinking about. The guy seems to know every step I take.

"Kellan, I run in the morning, you know this. So there is no need to worry about me. I'm out so early that the druggies are all still in bed; nobody is around to jump me."

"Daisy, I only worry because I care. What if one day someone *does* jump you?"

"They would have to catch me first; trust me when I say I'm fast, so stop worrying, please," I say as I unlock the front door. Kellan holds the door open for me, and I walk through.

"Okay, I'm sorry I can't help it. I just don't think it's right that you run on your own in the morning. Maybe I should start coming with you. It could be fun, just the two of us. What do you think?"

"*No, absolutely not,*" my wolf growls, and I agree. There is no way Kellan could run as far or as fast as we need to, to even work up a sweat. He jogs to the stairwell door and holds it open for me. It is like he doesn't think I can do anything for myself.

"Sorry, but no. Running is something I do on my own; it's how I sort my head out and take time for myself to start the day. It's nothing personal; I just don't like to run with others. Anyway, what do you mean '*it's not right that you run on your own in the morning*'? Is it because I'm female, and you think I should be escorted everywhere?" I ask as I walk past him.

"Well, that's not exactly what I meant, but-" I spin around and stare at him, gobsmacked.

"Do not finish that sentence; otherwise, I may not be held responsible for my actions. I never had you pegged as a male chauvinist pig." I look at him as we head up the stairs.

As we get to my floor, he holds the door open again, and I can feel my temper rising further.

"Why will you not let me run with you? It could be fun," he says, completely ignoring everything I just said. As we get to the front door of my apartment, he unlocks it with Tony's keys, like it's his own freaking place.

"Kellan, I just like to run on my own. I run fast and far, around ten miles or further, which I like to do alone. I don't think you'd be able to keep up with me. If I was ever worried, I would just sprint out of there. I'm not some poor, defenceless female who needs a man to do everything for them. I can look after myself," I say louder than I mean to as I storm past him straight into my room, slamming the door behind me.

As soon as the door closes, I start feeling guilty.

Daisy, you bitch.

I know Kellan doesn't understand how capable I am of looking after myself. I'm stronger and faster than him. But, for crying out loud, what could he do against a threat that I couldn't? I think I may have been a little harsh on him, though. Maybe I should apologise. I turn back around to find Kellan to apologise. But before I even step out of my door, I hear voices coming from the kitchen.

"Dude, I did warn you about Daisy and her running. It is the only time she allows herself to completely relax. I told you she would never let you run with her," Tony says.

"I know; I just can't help but worry about her being out there on her own in the dark; what if something happens to her?" My stomach tightens with the guilt. "Tony, if any harm came to her, I don't know what I would do," Kellan continues. Well, don't I feel like the world's biggest bitch right now? Why does he have to be so lovely when I am in bitch mode?

"Kellan, I get that; trust me, I do. But believe me when I say Daisy can protect herself better than you and me combined. If you've ever held sparring pads for her as she punches them or seen how fast she can actually run, you wouldn't doubt her." I can't help but smile. I don't hide my strength and speed from Tony; he has seen what I'm actually capable of.

"Really?" I hear Kellan ask, followed by Tony chuckling.

"Fuck aye! That girl's a machine. I actually feel sorry for anybody who tries to get the jump on her. She is perfectly safe and will take it as an insult if you suggest otherwise."

"Okay, I guess I've some apologising to do," Kellan replies. I feel even worse for snapping at him now.

I take a deep breath before walking into the kitchen. Kellan spots me and jumps up from the table.

"Look about earlier; I'm so sorry if I annoyed you-" I hold up my hand to stop him mid-sentence. He shuts up instantly, looking worried, making me feel even guiltier. He didn't deserve that before.

"Look, Kell, I'm sorry for being a bitch. I just like my own space; I get snappy when people get in it. I know your heart is in the right place, but please don't push me about this; I really won't budge." I take a deep breath before smiling at him. "I am going to head into town in a bit to grab one last present before heading home tomorrow for Christmas. Would you like to join me?" I quickly glance at Tony, "That goes for you too."

Tony raises one eyebrow at me; he knows I'm really begging him not to leave me alone with Kellan.

"Yeah, that sounds great," Tony replies, rolling his eyes when Kellan isn't looking.

"I have to call into work to grab my wages so we can all

have a drink on me whilst we're there," Kellan says excitedly. He now works in The Crows with Tony. At least a drink may make this afternoon a little easier. "I'm going to go have a shower and get changed, then will come back for you about eleven." He kisses me on the cheek as he walks past, then wrinkles up his nose. "Do me a favour and have a shower as well. You smell," he laughs, smiling at me, ducking quickly as I swing to playfully punch his arm.

"Some of us have worked up a sweat this morning, you cheeky bastard."

Kellan just laughs, walking backwards as he leaves.

"You might stink, but you're still gorgeous," he says as he blows me a kiss, opening the front door. I turn to pull a face at Tony.

"I would normally complain about being the third wheel. However, this time, I think I may be needed," Tony sighs as he stands.

"How does he always make me feel guilty for him being the problem, and then somehow we end up spending more time together? It's unreal." I moan, rubbing my face. Tony walks up to me and kisses my cheek as he leaves. I watch as he also wrinkles up his nose.

"Kellan might be a bit of a dick, but he is right about one thing, you do stink. Please go and have a shower before we head out," he adds, waving his hand under his nose playfully. I make a show of sniffing under my arms. I know I smell a little, but seriously. I still pretend to be offended, placing my hand over my heart.

"Tell it as it is, why don't you," I reply. I try to keep a straight face, but I can't.

As I head back to my room, I wonder what Michael is doing and if he is enjoying his Christmas holidays. As always, I wonder if he has a girlfriend, fiancée, or wife. That one always puts me in a bad mood, so I quickly shake that thought off. Instead, I start imagining what it would be like to kiss those lips whilst running my fingers through his hair. Tugging on it slightly to give me access to the thick muscular neck, his hands roam down to my hips before moving across and cupping me between my legs. Fuck, the fantasies I have of that man. This is why my showerhead is constantly on the massage setting if you get my drift.

Chapter Six

MICHAEL

Gods, I hate shopping. Why does Christmas require us to spend so much money? You send cards to people you only ever speak to once a year and avoid for the rest of it. Plus, don't even get me started on the food prices. Shifters eat a massive amount of food every day, so Christmas is no different. It just costs twice as much.

Tonight is the night of the team Christmas party; I really don't feel up to it. Since classes ended, my head has been all over the place; I know it's because I'm missing a particular wolf.

It feels wrong being away from Daisy as much as I am. My wolf is constantly nagging me to go to work on the off chance we will spot her and know she is safe. Because apparently, one check a day isn't enough. I know she'll be heading back to Cornwall in the next few days, and I've no idea what I'm going to do then to keep my wolf calm.

I walk out of the packed shop and take a deep breath, hoping some fresh air will clear my aching head; instead, I breathe in that one scent that drives my wolf, heart, and

46

body wild. I search the busy high street, looking through all the last-minute shoppers until I find her.

They're walking away from me. My heart flutters at the sight of Daisy but quickly freezes when I notice that she isn't alone. Kellan Cole is there, walking next to her. I watch as he puts an arm around her shoulders, pulling her closer to him so he can whisper in her ear. Kellan kisses the top of her head, and I start to hear the blood pounding in my ears.

"*Get him off her now!*" My wolf howls. I want to storm over and tear her from him, to steal her away and keep her to myself. But I can't. Instead, all I can do is turn away from them and head in the opposite direction to go home alone.

What is she doing with him? Why is she letting him hold her?

"*Well, you're not holding her, are you? If you don't make a move, how is she to know you care about her, dickhead?*" God, my wolf, is a prick and right all at the same time. I need to run; I need to get as far away from here as possible.

Rushing to my car, I drive as fast as I dare, not wanting to be done for speeding. I don't stop shaking the whole way. More than once, I consider turning around and finding her, but I keep telling myself that I just need to get home, and all will be okay, all will be alright.

"*Yeah, right, dickhead. Keep lying to yourself.*"

I pull up outside of my house and jump out of the car, not bothering to lock it behind me or take my bags out of the trunk. Instead, I just head straight around to the back of the house and into the woods. Every part of me is screaming to go back and tell Daisy how I feel, to take her as far away as possible, to make love to her and make her mine. But I know I can't, and it's killing me. I quickly strip before allowing my wolf to take over. Hoping a run will help calm me. It's always worked in the past, but that was before she walked into my life.

———————

Why am I here? I'm sitting in a loud club surrounded by drunk idiots I don't know, and the ones I do know are all starting to piss me off. As much as I don't want to be here, I can't miss the team Christmas night out, not when I am the team leader. My pack brothers would never allow me to miss it anyway. They would want to know what was happening, and I'm not ready for that conversation yet.

I'm sitting in a booth in a club with the four other team members, drinking expensive bourbon and pretending to enjoy myself. When in reality, all I can think about is Kellan touching and holding Daisy. Are they in bed together? Is she kissing him with those soft lips? Are his hands getting to feel and touch her amazing body? Is the cupping her firm bre....

"Mikey, what the hell!" Jonathan's voice breaks me out of my thoughts at the same time; pain radiates through my hand. I look down to see I've shattered the glass I was holding, sending the drink spraying everywhere, all over myself and Jon, who's next to me.

"Shit," I exclaim as I drop the broken pieces onto the table and start pulling bits out of my hand.

"What the fuck just happened?" Jon asks as he reaches over for a napkin. I wish I could explain to him, but the thought of admitting everything out loud terrifies me, so instead, I just shake my head as I take the napkins from him, wrapping them around my hand. I nod towards the back wall where the toilets are before moving around the booth to head into them.

Walking into the disgusting toilets, I head straight for the sink, instantly running the tap. As soon as I open my hand, I can see that there's still quite a bit of glass in the wounds; it's bleeding badly as well. Luckily, I know that the wounds will start healing quickly, and all traces of the cuts will be gone within a few days. Thank the Gods for wolf-speed healing. I look down and concentrate on the blood-stained water that's pouring down the sink. I don't even hear my brother walk over to me until I spot him standing in the mirror to my side.

"Fuck, that looks bad. What the hell were you thinking about to make you squeeze the glass that hard?" Jon asks, taking my hand to examine it. I shrug as he pulls another shard of glass out of my palm.

"I can't remember." I lie.

"*Tell him the truth. You were imagining all the things Kellan is doing to OUR Daisy, all the things you should be doing to her right now.*" I hear my wolf say. I growl out loud before I can stop myself. Jon looks up at me inquisitively. I quickly pretend it's because of the glass he's pulled from my hand.

"What's going on with you? We've been looking forward to tonight for weeks. You were up for getting blind drunk when we all met up."

I just shrug again.

"Guess my mood changed; it happens." I pull my hand out of his grasp and rinse it again under the water. The bleeding is already starting to slow down.

As I pull another piece of glass out of my hand, I can see my brother shaking his head in the reflection of the mirror.

"I think it's time you started looking for a distraction; you are too lost in your own mind these days," Jon says next to me. "Why don't you think about dating Mikey? Have you ever been on a date in the last six years?"

I look at him and give him a look, warning him I'm not in the mood. But Jon, being Jon, hasn't finished yet.

"It's been six years since she left you for her mate, Mikey. She couldn't help it; there was nothing that you could have done to prevent it. The ten years you were together was just borrowed time; you know that. Carly isn't coming back."

"Jon, this has nothing to do with Carly. Just leave it."

He backs off with his hands in the air.

"Fine. Shutting up and leaving you to it. Like I always do. Maybe I just want to see you happy for a change."

"I am happy," I snap. My anger is rising, and my brother might as well be painting a target on himself.

"Bullshit, bro, you haven't been happy for a long time. Do you think it's easy for Mum and me to see you so quiet and reserved all the time? We don't know what to do to drag you out of it. The only person who would have known is Michelle. She's the one you need the most right now, and she isn't here!" he yells at me. Hearing her name is like a slap to the face. Judging by Jon's face, he knows he has gone too far, too. "Mikey, I wasn't thinking. I'm so sorry."

"You had to bring her up today of all days, didn't you? Because the anniversary of our sister's murder is not hard enough, you decide I need reminding that she's not fucking here. Fuck you, Jonathan." I turn on the spot before pushing my way out of the crowded toilet, heading straight to the exit. I jump into the first taxi I see and give them my address.

I sit and take a few deep breaths to try and calm down. I can't believe Jon would bring Michelle up tonight of all nights. I have been trying to ignore the date all day. But it's a date that is burnt into my memory.

Four years ago tonight, Jon and I'd been sitting in a bar, getting drunk and playing pool with Marcus, Will and Carl. That night, everything in our lives changed forever. I still remember it like it was yesterday. I was sitting leaning against the bar laughing with Jon when the landlord shouted to say there was a call for me.

"Hello?" I couldn't hear anything. I repeated myself, sticking a finger in my other ear to see if it would help. Finally, I could hear what sounded like someone sniffing on the other end.

"Mikey, is Michelle with you?" The voice was so panicked it took me a second to work out who it was.

"Mum? Is that you? What's wrong?"

She sounded terrible.

"Michael, is Michelle with you?" she asks again. I notice that this time, she sounds agitated.

"No, of course not. Michelle said she was going to meet up with a friend. Mum, what's happened? Are you hurt?" All I could hear was Mum sobbing.

"Michelle hasn't been seen since this afternoon. She never made it to her friend." The tightening in my stomach, which has been bugging me all day, suddenly gets worse, and I realise it may be linked to my sister. As fear grips me, I try and hide it from my mum.

"You know Michelle, she has probably got distracted by another friend and forgotten who she was meant to be meeting. I am sure she will be home in no time."

"Michael, something isn't right. When Jayne called her

mobile, she heard a strange noise but she didn't hear Michelle, and then there was a weird cry. Jayne thought maybe Michelle was in wolf form and didn't think anything of it until I asked her if she had seen her."

That didn't sound right. I turn to Jon and ask him to call Michelle. He doesn't ask any questions, as I know he will be able to hear everything. He puts his phone to his ear and then almost instantly shakes his head. I can catch the call going straight to the answerphone. Shit.

"Okay, Mum, when and where was she last seen? Jon and I will get a couple of guys to come with us, and we will look for her."

Mum tells me quickly she was last seen by the pack running ground. I knew she had been planning on going for a run before meeting with her friends later that day. I told Mum to call the bar with any news, as it is right by the grounds, and we would search for our sister.

As I hung up the phone, I turned to see Jonathan already asking others in the bar to help us search. Luckily, it's a wolf bar, so I asked the guy behind the bar to call the Alpha. In less than five minutes, two wolves walked into the pub. They quickly shifted into the Alpha and his Beta. It turned out Jayne had told the Alpha that Michelle was missing. Desmond informs us that he had sent his lover, Jayne, round to sit with Mum so she could try to keep her relaxed and calm.

We quickly filled him in on the areas we would search and shifted into our wolves before heading off to look for Michelle. Thankfully, there were now twenty of us. We were hoping she would be found quickly.

Jon and I separated into our different search teams and headed in opposite directions. Both were too scared to acknowledge that there was a chance we would not find our sister. I ran at full speed to an area where Michelle and I usually hid when we needed time to clear our heads. Only we knew about it; even Jon and Mum had no idea it existed. I was so sure I would find her there. But when I arrived, the place was empty. Her scent was barely there. She hasn't been in days. I quickly turned around and headed to the next destination.

I had only been searching my area for fifteen minutes when I heard a howl coming from the woods. I instantly turned and ran to where the sound was coming from. Within seconds, Jonathan was by my side and we ran together, praying that Michelle had been found safe and well.

The whole way, my stomach was flipping and crashing as if there were a ton of rocks inside it. Even though I kept communicating with Jon through the mind link that everything would be fine, I could feel that something was seriously wrong in my gut.

As soon as I saw the Alpha, I shifted into human form, rushing up to him.

"What's happened? Have you found her?" I asked; I knew Jon had also changed and was standing next to me. Suddenly, I realised how Desmond was looking at me, and my stomach dropped. "Desmond, you need to tell me what you found," I start to look around him. That's when I noticed a bag by his feet. I knew straight away it was Michelle's. She had persuaded me to buy it for her six months before. She never went anywhere without it. I reached down to grab it, but Desmond stopped me.

"Michael, Jon," he whispers, looking between the two of us. I heard Jon gasp next to me and turned to him. He had his hand across his mouth and was shaking his head.

"No," he whispered. At that moment, it was like a train

hit me. I couldn't breathe, I couldn't move, my whole body became unresponsive, and I couldn't stop myself as my knees buckled and I fell to the ground. Desmond and Jon both grabbed me at the same time. As I fell, I caught a glimpse of a group of guys below a short ledge looking up at me. Behind them, I see a single hand sticking out from underneath a blanket or a sheet.

I heard a sound at that moment, and I didn't know if it was a human or a wolf. It was a sound I never thought I would hear and never want to hear again. I turned and saw my mum standing behind me. Jon had let go of me and rushed to her. He had her in his arms and helped to lower her to the ground. Within seconds, I was also there. Holding our mum as she screamed and sobbed, her whole body shaking uncontrollably.

After what felt like hours, I now know it was only minutes, I looked over at Desmond, who had stood beside us the whole time. I could see he was trying to be the Alpha he needed to be right then, but his heart was breaking with ours. I found out later that the whole pack was close by within minutes. I don't remember seeing any of them. I had tunnel vision. All that mattered at that moment was my mum and brother in my arms. As well as my twin sister, lying on the cold, damp forest floor, dead.

I do remember looking at Desmond and asking what had happened. I will never forget the look in his eyes as he said the words, "We think she was murdered."

I lost it then. I screamed at him to let me find out who had done this to my sister. I begged him to let me see her. When he said no, I pushed past him and fought him until he realised I would not stop until I knew.

He held me up as he walked me down to where my sister had been found. There was a blanket over her body. I remember praying that when they pulled it back, I would see that it wasn't my sister but someone completely different. I was praying that there had been a mistake. But the second the blanket was pulled back, I knew. There she was, my Michelle.

It's a sight I will never forget. It has been etched into my mind and will haunt me until my last breath. There was my beautiful sister lying on her back, looking straight up at the tree above her. She had bruising all over her face, and I could see she also had bruising on her wrists and marks on her neck. You could see where someone had strangled her with their bare hands. I knelt next to her and brushed some hair off her face.

Whoever had killed her had stripped her down to her underwear. At least she looked like she hadn't been raped.

"Michael, the police will be here in a minute. I need to move you back." Desmond explained next to me. I nodded. I knew this was beyond our pack's abilities. We had no choice but to report this to the human police. Before they arrived, though, I leaned forward and inhaled the air around my sister. The overpowering stench of death was already overriding her natural scent, but that wasn't what I was looking for. I was trying to pick up the smell of the person who had done this to her. It was there, but it wasn't somebody I knew; I could tell it was another wolf, though. I felt Desmond place his hands on my shoulders and assist me back onto my feet; he then led me back to my brother and mother. Both had been standing a little further away.

"Who was it?" Mum asked me as soon as I was close to her. I just shook my head.

"A rogue?" Jon asks. I can see the idea of a rogue being on pack land and harming one of our own was as unbelievable to him as it was to me. I heard Desmond answer next to me.

"It must be as that scent does not belong to any of my wolves." He turned to me and tipped his head towards one of our guys approaching on the phone. I knew instantly he would be calling the police, and that we needed to get out of there fast.

I looked at my brother and mum and knew their faces reflected my own. Anger and pain were etched on each of them. I knew that I needed to be strong for them at that moment and all the difficult ones that I was sure to follow. I turned to Desmond.

"Can you take control of this? I want to get them home and away from it all."

Desmond nodded at me and told us he would be with us when the police had finished with everything. I turned and looked at my sister's body one last time, lying on the cold forest floor, battered and bruised. At that moment, I promised her that I would avenge her. I would find the person who did that to her, and I would make them pay for taking her away from us. My best friend, my sister, my twin.

———

I'm brought back to the present by the driver pulling up outside my house. I pay him before heading inside. I'm just pouring myself a large whisky when Jon walks through the front door. I knew he would follow me; I already had an empty glass waiting for him. As Jon enters the kitchen, I pour him a drink and push it forward as I down mine. He picks it up quickly, knocking it back so I can refill our glasses. There's no need for either of us to apologise; the other doesn't need to hear it to know how they feel.

It's me who breaks the silence.

"You are right."

Jon looks up at me.

"I wasn't right. I shouldn't have said what I did."

I hold up one hand to stop him from going further. I have to get this out.

"No, you were right. I've not been happy, not for a long time. I'm content, but I'm not happy. I don't feel I deserve to be. Michelle had everything going for her when she died. A large part of me died with her. I miss her so much. The pain has never gone. I've just got used to living with it."

He just nods. I know Jon understands. She was his sister, too.

I down another shot and pour us both another glass.

"You know Michelle would hate for you to be unhappy. I'm so sorry I pushed the whole dating thing. Especially tonight of all nights, but I just get so frustrated with you. I love you, bro; you know that. I want you to be happy. But you need to start somewhere."

I nod to show that I understand, and I honestly do. But I just can't tell Jon what I'm really thinking. That the woman I'm sure would I'd be happy with is possibly in bed with another man as we speak. I knock back another drink quickly before I start thinking about them together again.

"Maybe you're right. Maybe finding someone would be good for me, but I can't see me finding someone I can start a relationship with, in a bar." I watch as Jon opens his mouth to say something, but I hold my hand up to stop him again. Jon is more than happy to have short, meaningless relationships and one-night stands. But I'm not like that. I never have been.

I hold up the glass to take another sip but realise it's empty. I've drunk enough for tonight. I look at Jon and watch as he sways slightly. He notices, and we both start chuckling.

"Okay, you may have a point," he says, putting down his glass and holding on to the breakfast bar. I take a deep breath and try to gather my thoughts. The only thing I can think about at this moment is Michelle.

With my head spinning, I know it is time to call it a night. Looking at my brother, he needs to call it a night, too. I reach over and pick the bottle up to put it away before heading towards the stairs, turning the lights off as I go. I don't have to check to see that Jon is following me. As we get to the landing, we wish each other a good night before heading to our rooms. As soon as I'm inside mine, I collapse onto the bed. Not bothering to strip.

What the hell was I thinking drinking so much? I don't usually drink like that. As I start to dream, I see Michelle looking at me smiling; she turns and faces Daisy, who looks back at her smiling.

"I like her," Michelle whispers. "Stop being a dick and make your move, Mikey." Before I can do or say anything, I fall into a deep sleep where everything stops existing, everything but their smiles.

Chapter Seven

DAISY

I'm so glad I'm almost back at the dormitory. Driving all the way back from Cornwall without so much as a toilet break was a terrible idea. I swear my arse went dead a hundred miles back.

I've decided to return a day early in the hope of avoiding all the traffic with people travelling home after New Year's Day with family. It worked out well, as I managed to make the journey in six hours, which is fantastic timing. Not so much for my arse, though.

I had a lovely time down in Cornwall. It was so good to catch up with my auntie and uncle. They wanted to know all about uni and if I had a boyfriend. They asked lots of questions about Kellan, as he kept messaging me all week. I ended up turning my phone off or leaving it in my room just for a break from him. Like I said to Auntie Mary, he's just a friend. He may want us to be more, but I really don't. He is funny, handsome, and an old-fashioned gentleman. I'm sure he would make some woman very happy, but not me. He isn't Michael. It wouldn't be fair on Kellan to start something when I feel so strongly for someone else.

The time away from Michael hasn't changed my feelings towards him; if anything, they have become stronger. He's the last thing I think about as I fall asleep; I dream all night about him and then think about him as soon as I wake up.

It is like I'm constantly looking out for him, waiting for him to make his move.

"He will. If he doesn't, then maybe you should." My wolf is convinced Michael feels the same way as I do. I wish I shared her confidence.

Finally, I pull into the car park and head straight for my usual parking space outside my dorm. The second I switch the engine off, I hear a beeping behind me. I turn to see someone angrily waving at me. What the hell is his problem? I get out of the car and hold my hands up. He lowers the window and starts shouting.

"That's my spot."

I place my hands on my car and start looking around.

"Don't see your name, so I think not," I reply, slamming the door closed as I turn away from him.

"I always park there, so move." This guy is pissing me off now.

"Dude, I've been parking here since September. I've never once seen your piece of shit here, so move along and find somewhere else. I'm not going anywhere." I turn my back to him and hear a car door open. Oh, for fuck's sake, here we go. I turn around, watching as the guy starts getting out of his car. I brace myself for an argument or worse.

"Right bitch..." Did he just call me a bitch? I storm towards him when I see somebody get there before me.

"Apologise to the lady, now!"

Shit, it's Michael standing over the guy with a face of thunder. The guy looks tiny in comparison to Michael's large, well-built structure. The guy obviously realises that there is no way he can win this and turns to get back into the car. However, Michael isn't going to leave it. "I said apologise," he growls. The guy turns and faces me. I can smell the fear and humiliation coming from him and can't help but smirk at him.

"Sorry," he snaps, looking pissed off. He looks at Michael, who nods. The guy jumps in his car and drives off as quickly as possible. Michael turns to look at me. For a second, he seems worried, as if expecting to find me upset. Instead, I just start laughing. Michael relaxes and laughs, too.

"Thanks; I thought I had a fight on my hands then, and I'm not in the mood to dispose of a body right now," I say, leaning against my car. I watch Michael look back in the direction the guy has just sped off in.

"I would have helped," he laughs as he looks back at me. "What the hell was his problem anyway?" Michael asks, walking over to me as I shrug.

"Apparently, I've parked in his space."

Michael frowns at me.

"But you've always parked here?"

"I know!" I say dramatically. Causing Michael to laugh at me.

"Did you have a good Christmas?" he asks, taking another step towards me. Gods, I wish I could just pull that body against me and hold him. Instead, I settle for looking into his deep blue eyes.

"It was good, thank you. Yourself?" I ask. He leans casually against my car, placing an elbow on the roof and leaning his fist against his temple. He is standing so close, smiling that one-sided grin that makes me weak at the knees. Does he know what he is doing to me?

"Yes," my wolf sighs. Shit, is she just as turned on right now?

"It was alright, thanks. When did you get back?" His voice bringing me back from the dirty thoughts filling my once-innocent mind.

"Just. I've been stuck in that car for six hours non-stop. I'm ready to get my crap upstairs and crash," I say, almost kicking myself as I'm not ready to say goodbye to him yet. Gods, I've missed that face and that scent.

"You got much to carry up?" he asks.

"Quite a bit," I reply.

"Ask him for help," my wolf suggests. I watch as Michael smiles and tips his head towards my trunk.

"Come on then, I'll give you a hand." I can feel the smile spread across my face.

"Thanks, that would be amazing." I walk past him so I can open the trunk. As I do, my arm brushes across his and my body automatically reacts. It's like every hair stands on end; my heart stops and then restarts, causing my head to spin. I start losing my balance, but luckily Michael grabs hold of me.

"I've got you," he whispers softly as I look up at him. He has his arm around my waist, his hand on my side, holding me tightly against him. I gaze into his eyes and feel myself melting into his hold.

"See, it's natural," my wolf whispers. As if bringing me back to reality, I quickly stand up straight and take a step back out of his arms.

"Sorry, I guess I'm more tired than I thought."

Michael looks to the side of me, then quickly back. Was that disappointment I saw in his eyes?

"You have nothing to apologise for. Let's get your stuff upstairs, and then you can eat and rest," he replies, smiling. But, this time, the smile seems forced somehow.

"Yeah, sounds good," I say, clearing my throat. My mouth suddenly feels like I've been chewing on sand. I open my trunk; Michael looks in and whistles behind me.

"Somebody did well this Christmas."

I can't help but laugh. The trunk is filled with bags from my auntie.

"Nah, most of this is my auntie making sure I've plenty to eat. Must be enough to feed an army for a month in those bags."

"So, a hungry wolf for a week then," Michael replies, winking at me as he grabs the larger bags. I can't help chuckling.

"Now, you know a full week is pushing it."

I notice he has all but two of the bags. The ones left are also the smallest. "You okay with all of those?" I ask, which earns me a sideways glance.

"You're asking *me* if I'm okay with these bags. You know full well I won't even break a sweat, and before you ask, no, you can't take any of them. You need your hands free to open the doors." I nod, realising that he's right. I close my trunk and lock the car.

"Okay, point taken. Come on, macho man," I wink at him.

"That's *Mister* Macho Man to you," he says, giving me that one-sided grin again. I can't help but giggle. Why do we have to get along so well? It would be so much easier to get over this crush if we hated each other.

"Have you ever been in any of these buildings before?" I ask as I hold open the front door. He shakes his head.

"Nope. Smells better than when I lived in dorms,

though. All I could smell then was weed, rotten food and hormones."

I nod whilst wrinkling up my nose, causing Michael to laugh at me.

"It can get like that here, too, especially at certain times of the month when my senses are heightened. I've had to hold my breath and run to my room on a few occasions," I say, smiling. I hear him groan playfully.

"Do you like living here?" he asks as I hold the staircase door open for him. I smile and nod as we walk up the stairs.

"I've been lucky with my roommates. As you know, I get along with Tony really well. We're even going to house share when our year is up here."

"That's good. You and Tony do seem close. Did you know each other before September?" he enquires, smiling as I hold the door to my floor open. My front door is only a few steps from the stairwell. I shake my head in response.

"No, we met a week before classes started. We just instantly clicked. I always wanted an annoying little brother, so I guess he fills the void." We walk up to my front door and stop.

"This is me," I say as I unlock the door. Michael places the bags just inside the door and shakes his hands whilst wiggling his fingers.

"Bags too heavy for you, after all, *Mister* Macho Man?" I smirk, putting emphasis on Mister. Michael just rolls his eyes at me.

"No, just cut off the circulation to my fingers. I didn't even break a sweat as I said I wouldn't." He's correct; he hasn't. He *does* smell amazing, as always.

"Do you want to come in for a coffee?" My mouth blurts out before I can even think. I feel my eyes widen. "Oh my god! I do actually mean coffee and not ... well, you know." Michael just laughs at me. Gods, I'm so embarrassed.

"Trust me, I know you mean drinkable coffee; it's you, after all. Everyone knows about your addiction to the 'brown nectar' as you call it. But, as much as I would love to say yes, I'm sure there is some sort of policy about lecturers in students' dorms." He looks at me, and I see something in his eyes.

"*Regret,*" my wolf whispers. No, I don't think it's that, or is it?

"Yeah, you're probably right. Thank you for your help, though. Not only with the bags but with that moron earlier."

Michael's eyes look fierce at the mention of him.

"You don't need to thank me. I'm always happy to help you. If you have any more problems with him, make sure you let me know."

I smile to break the tension that's building at the mention of the dickhead.

"I can't see him trying that again. Not after macho man intervened." I pat his chest without even thinking. Michael instantly puts his hand on top of mine, holding it there. I can feel his heart beating against my fingers. I look up, and our eyes lock as time stands still.

"Daisy, I -" Michael starts, but I quickly pull my hand away, shaking my head, my face burning with embarrassment.

"I'm so sorry. I don't know why I did that. Thank you for your help, and I'm sorry to be rude, but I need to pee after driving for so long. I'll see you later." I quickly walk through my front door and shut it before leaning against it, releasing a deep sigh.

"He feels the same way," my wolf whispers softly. Shut up; no, he doesn't. Michael was about to point out he is my lecturer. I can't believe I acted like that!

I feel the door move as somebody leans against it.

"He is still there." My wolf whines. I turn and place my hand against the cold door, longing to go back out there, wondering what would happen if I just opened the door and walked straight into his arms. I place my hand on the lock, ready to open it, but freeze. I can't. I can't bring myself to open it. I can't risk the heartbreak or the pain. Growling at myself, I turn and walk away from the door and straight to my room. I want to kick myself. Why did I tell him I needed to pee? Daisy Andrews, you're such a dumbass!!

Michael

I step forward to stop her from leaving as the door closes in my face. I take that last step and place my hand on the door, followed by my forehead. Oh, Daisy, please open back up, I think, unable to say the words out loud, I need to see her again.

I can hear her just on the other side of the door; I want to knock and get her to open it. I know she feels this between us; I saw it in her eyes, in the way it felt when she touched me. But she is refusing to accept it. Is it because she is unsure of what it is or because she wants to reject me? I jump away from the door as I hear her growl inside. I hear another door close in her dorm. I'm guessing it's Daisy going into her bedroom. I missed out on a chance to talk to her again.

I head towards the stairs, feeling deflated. What can I do to make this right? What can I do to show her that we could work? Don't think I haven't thought about leaving my post here because I have.

"Can't you tell she is scared and confused? You need to be forward and tell her what you want," My wolf growls as I walk on autopilot down the stairs.

I walk out of the building and come to an abrupt stop. What the fuck am I doing? My wolf is right. Why am I walking away again? Daisy seems confused. What if she doesn't understand this between our wolves and us? What if she feels as lost as I do? One of us needs to make the first move; why not me? I turn to head back into the building. I need to speak to her now. But the door is locked behind me. I look at the intercom on the wall next to the apartment. What number was her door? I can't remember. I was so distracted by Daisy that I didn't even register how many floors we had gone up.

I pull out my phone, planning on calling her when someone bumps into me. I turn to find myself staring straight at Kellan.

"For fuck's sake, talk about bad timing," my wolf moans. I agree.

"Hey, what are you doing outside the student dorms?" he asks, frowning. 'None of your fucking business,' I want to reply, but I bite my tongue instead. I had forgotten all about him, balls. It's not like I can have this conversation with him around. I feel my hands curl into tight fists at the sight of him. The image of him holding Daisy pops back into my mind, and it takes all my willpower not to punch him in his pretty-boy face.

"I saw Daisy struggling with her bags, so I gave her a

hand, that's all," I reply, trying to keep my hatred for the kid out of my voice. Instead, I watch as Kellan grins.

"Oh, great, she's back. I'll head up to see her now. I've missed my girl." I feel like I've been punched in the stomach by those two words.

"Your girl?" I ask. Kellan smirks, nodding as he walks past.

"Yep, I seem to have finally won her around and made her realise we are perfect for each other. See you next week," he calls as he lets the door close between us.

I can't seem to move; my feet are planted to the spot.

"*Not his girl,*" my wolf growls. "*Our girl,*" I tell him to shut up and let me think. "*No, you need to act and act now. We will lose her, you fucking idiot, and then where will we be?*" If she doesn't want us, what can I do? I reply as I head towards my car. "*You need to stop being a limp dick and go back into that building and get our girl!*" my wolf growls.

"Shut up!" I growl back out loud. I realise how close I am to making a complete fool of myself. I quickly jump into my car and drive out of the car park. Addressing my wolf whilst I go.

"You think I don't realise what a mistake I'm making? Do you think I don't feel the pain you feel when we're not with her? Do you really think I don't want to walk into that building, tear that little prick apart and claim her as my own? Well, I do! I want to do all those things. I want to feel her in my arms, pressed against me as my mouth devours every soft inch of her, savouring every sweet ounce of her. I want to feel her wrap her legs around me and scream my name as I make her cum with my fingers, my tongue, and my cock." I take a deep breath. Every part of me feels like it is on fire with the need to do all those things and more.

"But I'll not do anything she doesn't want me to. I'll not

force her hand in this. If she chooses him over us, then that is how it is going to be, even if it is killing me, us." I hear my wolf growl loudly.

"How can she choose him over us when she doesn't even know that we're an option? Stop running from this, from her! Stop worrying that she will reject us and let her know we are here," my wolf howls at me before retreating and leaving me to think about everything as I drive home.

Shit, he's right, isn't he?

Chapter Eight

DAISY

I walk into the classroom and take my usual seat next to Beth. Instantly dropping my head onto the table, moaning. I'm really not in the mood to be here.

"You okay, Dais?"

I just shake my head against the cool surface.

"I want to go back to bed and sleep for a month," I reply, sighing. Knowing that'd never happen because, one, it's a full moon next week, and two, my body will not let me sleep at all. I've not slept for more than an hour a night for the last week. I'm exhausted and quickly hitting breaking point. I don't feel like anything has gone right since I got back from Cornwall two weeks ago.

Ever since I returned, all I feel like I've done is fight to keep control of my wolf. Every part of my body aches; my head hurts continuously, and my skin itches. As for my heart, it feels like it's breaking every time I think of bloody Michael. Ever since that moment, we had outside my dorm, it has been harder to ignore my need to be near him, which is just causing extra friction between my wolf and me.

"Be careful, Beth, she's in a foul mood," I hear Tony shout across the room.

"Fuck you too, dickhead," I call back. Not even bothering to lift my head, I feel Beth nudge me.

"Michael's here," she says next to me, but I just moan in response. I'm not in the mood for him and his ability to not feel like crap all the time.

I sit up and look to the front of the class; he looks at me and frowns. Great, he knows I feel like shit. I just look away and slump further into my seat, eager for this class to finish already. I want to go home and crash out onto my bed in peace.

Why can't I be a typical student and just pull a sicky every now and again? What the hell am I doing here other than forcing myself to hold back the growing need to burst into tears and smash up everything in sight?

By the time we're halfway through class, I've snapped at Beth, Michael, Tony, and Ben when he asked me where Kellan was. How the fuck should I know? The last time I saw him, I shouted at him to give me some space as he is forever at ours, hassling me and trying to get me to go out with him on a date. But unfortunately, the guy is not taking no for an answer. Michael has just announced a break, and Beth instantly turns on me.

"Right, don't even think about leaving this room. What the hell is going on with you? You're in a foul mood, snapping at everyone who dares speak to you. Talk to me, Daisy, please. This isn't like you. What's going on?"

I look at my friend, and I see how worried she is. I long to talk to her about everything, but I can't. I see Tony approaching our table. I'm surprised he will risk coming near me after I snapped at him this morning and again in class.

"Beth, can you give us a minute? I need to talk to Daisy in private," he asks, placing a hand on her shoulder. Beth looks between the two of us. She seems a little annoyed for a split second but then nods before standing up. She leans over, taking my hand.

"Please talk to Tony. If you need a female voice, you know I'm always here for you. But please just speak to one of us." She gives my hand a squeeze before leaving the room, closing the door behind her.

"Right, now it's just us. What the hell is going on with you?"

I look up at Tony and see Michael has now joined us. Tony is next to me, whilst Michael is at the front of my desk, leaning on it with his hands.

"Please talk to us, Daisy," Michael says quietly. "I can feel your wolf's magic from across the room."

"I don't know what's wrong with me," I reply, rubbing my arms as the aching starts again.

"*Speak to Michael,*" my wolf begs. I'm beginning to think she's right. Maybe I need to bite the bullet, pull up my big girl panties and ask Michael for help. I take a deep breath as my eyes fill up with tears. "*Just speak to him, please.*" I look up at Michael and can tell he sees the pain in my eyes as his whole face and body softens.

"I think I need help with my wolf," I whisper, my eyes instantly dropping to the table as a single tear falls.

"Tony, can you stand outside and stop anyone from entering until I say? Make any excuse you need to just keep them out." I can feel Tony moving next to me. He places a hand on my shoulder as he pulls me into a hug.

"I'm proud of you. You have been struggling alone for too long. *Please* let Michael help you. I love you, Dais," he whispers into my hair. He kisses the top of my head before leaving. I listen as Tony walks away from us and hear the door close behind him. Enclosing me in this small room alone with Michael, my heart starts racing. I keep my eyes on the table, unable to look at him, scared I will burst into tears.

The thought of looking into his eyes as I admit I need help terrifies me. I don't want to see pity or annoyance in them. The idea of Michael being annoyed with me makes me want to stand up and leave. He doesn't give me the choice of hiding, though. He sits in the chair next to me. Gripping the leg of my chair, he turns it, ensuring that I'm now facing him. He takes my hand under the table and holds it gently.

"Speak to me, Daisy. Not just as a tutor, not as a wolf, but as a ma ... friend whose heart is breaking as I can see you're hurting, but I don't know how to make it better. Please, darling, let me help you."

I look up at him. I can see he means it.

"I don't know where to start," I admit. Michael starts rubbing the back of my hand with his thumb. With each small circle he draws, I relax that tiny bit more.

"Then tell me what you are feeling," he prompts.

"Like shit," I reply. Looking up at Michael, I feel the tears right there on the brink of escaping. I rub them away with my other hand. But he pulls it down so he can look into them.

"Don't hide your pain from me; don't hide anything, not from me. I can't help you if you do. Describe how you are feeling, and don't leave anything out. Then, I'll be able to work out what's going on."

I take a deep breath and finally start letting everything out.

"I feel like my whole body is aching continuously. The only way to ease it is to move and run, but no matter how much I do, the restlessness never leaves. All of my senses are on full alert continuously, and my mind won't shut off. I can't remember the last time I slept properly or even felt semi-okay. I feel like I'm going to lose control that she is going to take over," I blurt it all out. I wish I could say I feel better for saying it out loud, but I don't. I look at Michael; he seems concerned.

"Daisy, when was the last time you ran?" he asks. "And I don't mean on two legs," he adds quickly. I look at him. What the hell can I say that doesn't make me sound like a wimp? But he seems to realise I'm holding back from answering. "What do you do when you shift?" He asks. I look away, scared that he will think I'm weak if he finds out; I just hide. I hear a deep sigh radiate from him as his hand squeezes mine.

"Darling, am I right in thinking you were bitten? Where is the person who bit you? Do you need me to contact them for you?"

My head flies up, my eyes finding his. I can feel the panic building in my chest at the thought of *him* finding me. I can feel my chest getting tighter. It becomes harder to breathe as the anxiety takes hold. Michael instantly realises what is happening. He starts rubbing my back with the hand which isn't holding mine. My heart races as my body starts shaking.

"Breathe, Daisy, I won't contact them, I promise. I'm so sorry I upset you." He starts talking me through some breathing exercises, helping me to calm down to regain control.

"Don't ask me about him, please. He doesn't know where I am; that's all that matters. He did this to me, and then ..." I can't bring myself to say anymore. I don't want Michael to see me as a victim. I can't bear the thought of him looking at me like that or thinking any less of me. I feel his grip tighten reassuringly on my hand, his other still rubbing my back.

"He changed you without your consent, didn't he?"

I nod, unable to respond verbally. "Daisy, if I had known you needed help, I would've helped you. You could've spoken to me. I'm so sorry I failed you."

I look at him, shocked.

"You never failed me." I want to tell him that this is all on me, that my wolf has been telling me to speak to him, but I've ignored her like I always do.

"Obviously, we can't talk openly here. So please meet me tonight, and we will discuss this further and run. I'll send you the address for a forest I use."

I glance up at him, panic building again.

"But it's not a full moon until next week. I've never forced a shift before. I've only ever shifted with the moon." I see the shock in his eyes again and realise there's so much I don't know about being a wolf. I need his help more than I realised.

"I told you he would help." My wolf whispers, reassuring me.

"Darling, we need to shift more than once a month. Please trust me to show you, teach you, and protect you." I can feel his thumb drawing circles on the back of my hand again. I don't even have to think before responding; it comes naturally.

"Okay." I see him relax a little and smile. Michael picks up my pen and rips a page from my notepad, asking me to give him my number. I feel my heart flutter as he folds the paper I hand back and he folds it before pushing it into his pocket.

"I'll send you a text from my personal phone with an address and a time to meet me. If you have any problems, just message me. From now on, use that number to contact me day or night, but keep it between us, okay? I'll help you. I give you my word." I slowly nod to show that I believe him. "Thank you for trusting me."

"I don't know why, but it feels natural to trust you."

He smiles gently at me.

"You have no idea how great it is to hear you say that. I won't let you down again, Daisy, never." He gives my hand one last squeeze before letting it go. I watch as he stands up and heads back to his desk, nodding once at the door. Within seconds, it opens, and people pile back in. Beth sits back down in her chair.

"Feel better?" she asks. I look at her and nod.

"A bit." She pulls me into a hug, and I hug her back. She is a good friend, and I don't deserve her. I see Tony heading to his table; he looks over at me and winks. "Thank you", I mouth to him. He smiles and blows me a kiss before sitting down. I'm so lucky to have these fantastic people in my life.

Chapter Nine

MICHAEL

It's now nearly nine o'clock at night, and I'm on my way to meet Daisy. I'd messaged her the details straight after class. I'd been worried she would have second thoughts, but she responded in minutes to say she'd be there. My heart's racing with the idea of spending time with her outside of the classroom.

I'm extremely concerned about how little she knows about being a wolf. I know some rogues turn humans and abuse them, telling them all sorts of lies to keep them under their control. As much as I hope Daisy's not one of those victims, I think she may have been, judging by her reaction earlier.

I really could kick myself for not realising sooner what was going on. So much for being there to support her. I've let her down, but I intend to make it up to her, starting tonight.

I pull into the area I said to meet with ten minutes to spare. I wanted to make sure I was here when Daisy arrived, so she didn't have time to panic. I don't have to wait long, though. Within minutes, I look up the road and see two small lights slowly getting closer. I know it will be Daisy, as no one else ever comes here, which is why it is perfect for tonight.

It feels like it takes forever for her to get to me. Finally, when she does, I lean on the roof of my car, looking over it towards hers. Ensuring that I give her space, knowing she will be scared and nervous about tonight. I watch her open her door and slowly get out. She looks terrified; it takes all my willpower not to rush around the car and take her in my arms to put her at ease.

"*Take it slow,*" my wolf reminds me for the hundredth time today.

"Hey," I say, smiling at her. She looks at me and smiles back.

"Hey." I can hear the nerves in her voice, and it pains me. She's so anxious and scared. It makes me want to find the prick who did this to her and end them.

"Did you find the place, okay?"

She nods, looking around.

We've parked in a small parking bay, and the only thing around us is trees. This forest goes on for miles, and it's a great place to run as humans never come near here at night.

"Your scent is the same as this forest," she states, looking at me. A smile spreads across my face as the comment makes me happier than it should.

"Is it? Yours is like a spring meadow, full of fresh flowers." Daisy seems to relax a little and blushes as I get a warm feeling in my stomach. I want to see that look on her face more. I don't think I've ever seen something so endearing.

"*Focus!*" my wolf growls again. I give my head a slight

wobble to righten my thoughts. I glance over and can tell her thoughts have also run away with her. I step away from my car and slowly walk over to Daisy. Gently, I place my hand on the top of her arm.

"Tell me what's going on in that head of yours?"

She lets out a deep breath and looks out at the forest. She seems so overwhelmed and scared.

"I'm just stuck in my own head, I think. I'm worried about tonight."

Placing a hand on her cheek, I gently turn her head so she is looking at me. I look into her eyes and smile softly, knowing she will see with her advanced wolf sight.

"You're going to do fine. You'll feel so much better after you've spent some time with your wolf and let her take charge for a little bit. Please trust me to look after you and help you along the way. You never know; you may even have some fun."

"Does it always hurt so much?" she asks. I shake my head slowly.

"No, the more you shift, the less it'll hurt. I haven't felt pain in years as I change at least three times a week."

"Really?" I can see the hope in her eyes, making me smile as I nod, hoping to reassure her further.

"Really, I could never lie to you." I quickly look down to see what she has on, a hoodie and some yoga pants. "Do you have a change of clothes with you?" I ask. She looks at me, nodding. "Good, let's get our stuff and get going." We both grab our bags and start heading off into the woods.

We walk in silence for a few minutes before Daisy starts to speak again.

"Were you bitten too?"

I shake my head.

"No, I come from a long line of wolves on both sides.

So, if you have any questions, please just ask them, as I'm sure I'll be able to answer." We walk in silence again for a few minutes before she speaks again.

"Are you part of a pack?" I nod as she looks at me, "The person who did this to me said that a female's job was purely to provide the pack with pups. Is that true?"

I stop in my tracks, turning to look at her, expecting to see some sort of sign that she's joking, but her face is poker straight. What the fuck? I can't believe what I'm hearing. I look around and see a tree stump. I know what I need to do before we go any further.

"Daisy, can we sit and talk for a minute? I've got a feeling you have been fed a lot of bullshit. I want to try to put your mind at ease." I signal towards the stump, and Daisy walks over to it and sits down. I squat in front of her, taking her hands in mine. This is what I'd feared, her being taught to fear packs and all that they represent. No wonder she never asked for help sooner.

"I don't know what you've been told, but packs aren't a thing you should fear. We are a family, whether through blood or the pack bond. As family should be, we're all very protective of each other, many of us knowing each other from birth. We believe that males and females are equal; they're given the same respect and opportunities. That's why it's laughable to believe that anyone could force our females to be used as some kind of birthing mule. It just wouldn't happen. I have many female friends who have no plans on having kids, and they certainly would never be forced to." I look at Daisy and see that she is looking at me with tears in her eyes. I lift her hands to my lips and kiss her knuckles, trying to offer her some form of comfort.

"*If* you ever feel like you want to join my pack, or any other pack for that matter, I will personally take you to meet with the Alpha. Then you can see for yourself what pack life is really like. You would love our pack, especially the women. They are forever putting us men, in our place. I know I'm asking a lot for you to believe me, but please trust me enough to protect you and to know I would never put you in harm's way."

"I do trust you, a lot. There are *very* few people I trust more."

Again, I lift her hands to my mouth and kiss them, wishing they were her lips. My wolf growls a warning, and I internally roll my eyes.

"Thank you. I promise I will never abuse that trust. Now, how about we go for that run?"

She lets out a deep breath and nods before I pull her up with me as I stand. Our bodies are so close it takes all my willpower not to pull her closer to me. Instead, I step away, not before placing a soft kiss on the top of her head.

"Let's go," I say, winking as we turn back in the direction we had been heading before.

This time, the air feels a little less forced and more relaxed, and I realise I'm still holding one of Daisy's hands. I tighten my fingers very briefly to see what she does. When she tightens hers back, I know she doesn't want to let go. I am more than okay with that.

We walk for a while until I'm comfortable that we are far enough away from civilisation and turn to Daisy.

"Okay, here's what we are going to do. First, I'm going to help you shift, and then I'll shift myself once you have recovered so I can communicate with you in human form." I can see she's worried. "Trust me, it's a lot easier than you think," I reassure her, but she just rolls her eyes at me.

"That's easy for you to say," she replies sarcastically. I

just smile in response. I take my bag and pull out an old t-shirt I had brought with me. I hold it out for Daisy.

"I'm sure you don't want to shred those clothes, so I thought you might want to borrow this to shift in. I was going to bin it anyway." But she shakes her head.

"It's okay. I'm happy to strip down to my underwear; I hate this set anyway."

I nod as I put the t-shirt back in my bag, not trusting myself to speak without giving away how turned on I am now. I internally turn to my wolf. Okay, Mister, answer for everything. Any tips on how I stop myself from coming on to her right now?

"Uhm ... umm... yeah, you are on your own with that one. Good luck." My wolf sounds flustered, which just heightens my arousal. Fuck, time to think of anything other than the pending sight of Daisy almost naked. The last thing she needs right now is to see me with a raging hard-on.

"Sorry. Is that is going to bother you?" I hear Daisy stutter. Shit, she's taken my silence to mean I'm bothered by the thought of her nearly naked.

"Gods, no! No, it's great. I mean, fine. I mean, as long as you are comfortable." I realise I'm making a complete fool of myself, but when I look at Daisy to apologise, she smirks at me. Does she know what she is doing to me right now? I quickly clear my throat and take a deep breath in the hope of calming my racing heart.

"What I mean is, whatever makes you comfortable." I try not to stare as Daisy takes off her clothes, leaving on nothing but a light blue cotton bra and hot pants. But, when she turns around to face me, I swear my jaw drops open. I always knew Daisy was beautiful inside and out, but standing here in the middle of a forest, with nothing but the moonlight and her underwear, she's radiant.

"Breath-taking," I whisper before I can stop myself. She starts rubbing her left shoulder.

"*You are making her uncomfortable, idiot.*" Fuck, my wolf is right. I apologise under my breath as I quickly clear my throat, holding out her bag so she can put her clothes into it. I put it in a tree so it is out of the way. I then do the same with my clothes, leaving nothing but my boxers on. When I turn to look at Daisy, I'm sure I catch her staring at me. Our eyes meet, and I'm suddenly very aware of how close we are standing and how little we have on.

Her scent fills my nose, and it's impossible to miss the slight hint of arousal. It takes every ounce of control not to take her in my arms. We need to get this show on the road. Otherwise, I can't promise I won't do or say something wildly inappropriate. or my body will give away how much I want her.

"You ready?" I ask. "It's a lot simpler than you think. All you need to do is relax, find your wolf, and let her come to the surface. She will do the rest. It will be swift as long as you stay calm and relaxed." I watch as Daisy nods to show that she understands. She stands in front of me and takes a few deep breaths, trying to relax. She then closes her eyes, attempting to focus. But I can see instantly it won't work; she's still too tense and not loosening up. Less than a minute later, she lets out a breath and opens her eyes.

"I'm useless. I knew I couldn't do it." I roll my eyes at her dramatically, which earns me a raised eyebrow. I smile, trying not to laugh.

"That was no time at all. Let's try again, but this time, I want you to do as I say." I move a step or two closer. "Now, close your eyes." She does, "Good. Now, I want you to truly relax. I want you to let your body become loose and allow all your muscles to relax. Whilst you do that, I want you to breathe in through your nose and out through your mouth."

She opens one eye and looks at me, smirking.

"Do you want me to sit in the lotus position as well?" I close my eyes, shaking my head, unable to stop myself from smiling.

"I'm going to fold you into the lotus position in a minute," I murmur. I open my eyes as Daisy sticks her tongue out at me. A loud laugh burst from my lips. Daisy's face breaks into a massive grin as she starts laughing too. By the time we both manage to achieve some sort of composure, Daisy is looking a lot more relaxed.

"Right, let's try this again. Close your eyes, and your mouth, and breathe. Gradually letting yourself relax." I watch as she rolls her shoulders a few times and then does as she's told. Slowly I can see her body loosen as she concentrates on her breathing. Finally, when I can see she is almost entirely relaxed, I get her to move on to the next step.

"Now, I want you to look inside yourself until you find your wolf; let me know when she's there." It only takes a few seconds before Daisy whispers she has her. "Can you feel her trying to come to the surface?" Daisy nods, "Now, all you need to do is let her. She will do all the hard work. Just let her take over." I can feel her shift starting, but then she starts to fight it. Her mind is telling her it will hurt and that she needs to stop it, but at the same time, she is trying to let it happen. "Breathe, darling, I'm right here. You are doing great; just let the change happen." I can feel her starting to relax, but she tenses up again as her bones begin to shift. This is why the change causes her so much pain; she doesn't let her body do what it needs to.

I can't stand the sight of her in pain, seeing her body

spasming, trying to shift and not shift at the same time. I know I need to do something to help her. So, I do the only thing I can think of. I pull her into my arms, holding her tightly against me, whispering encouragement into her ear whilst stroking her hair. Instantly, it starts to work, and she starts to relax. Slowly, I lower both of us to the floor until she is curled up in my arms.

"Just let it happen, baby. I'm here; I've got you. I promise I'm not going anywhere," I whisper. Suddenly, she relaxes completely; the change happens so quickly I barely have time to move out of the way. In less than a few seconds, I'm looking at the most beautiful wolf I've ever seen, with the brightest green eyes.

Chapter Ten

DAISY

I did it! I *actually* shifted without the moon, and it wasn't as painful as I thought it would be. I continue to lie on the forest floor, catching my breath, but my breathing is still a little rapid from the shift. I look over and see Michael kneeling on the ground next to me. His face lit up with a massive smile. I can't help myself; his smile is contagious. I jump to my feet, well paws, and start bouncing around him, yapping with excitement. His laughter fills the air around us. Before I even think about what I'm doing, I rub my head into his shoulder and inhale his scent. I feel him lean into my touch as he runs his fingers through my fur gently, sending waves of pleasure through me.

"You are the most beautiful wolf I've ever seen," he whispers into my ear. I savour this moment of closeness before moving away from him. I start to nudge him, nipping at his fingers playfully. Finally, he seems to understand as he starts laughing again and I knock him onto his ass.

"Okay, alright, two seconds." I watch as he stands up, taking in his amazing muscular body in the moonlight.

"Want to see how quickly you will be able to shift after a bit of practice?" he asks, grinning; I nod. "Don't blink," he adds as he winks at me. I roll my eyes, which feels weird in wolf form, and watch as one second, Michael is standing in front of me in nothing other than his snug boxers. He leans down to put his hands on the ground, but as they land, they are replaced by paws, and a brown wolf is now standing where Michael was less than a second before. His boxers are now shredded on the floor around him. I instantly jump away, shocked by how quickly he shifted; how is that even possible? I look at him again and take in the gorgeous wolf in front of me. I swear his blue eyes are even brighter in this form. They remind me of the sea on a clear day.

I walk up to him slowly and push my nose into his shoulder, rubbing against his neck again, checking it's him. I hear a low moan escape him as he does the same to me. I can't explain it, but being with him in wolf form pushes away all the confusion I had about my feelings for him over the last three months. Now, I know that there is a reason I feel this way. Michael is important to me. He is part of me. There is no other way to describe it other than he feels like home.

I feel Michael step away. When I turn to look at him, he nods towards the trees, signalling for me to follow him as he starts walking away. I lift a paw to follow but freeze. Michael stops, turns around and looks at me. I realise he wants to run, but I can't get my body to move. It's frozen to the spot. I look away from him and scan the area. What if someone sees us? What if I can't do this? Michael walks towards me. He leans down and places his forehead against mine.

"*Are you okay?*" I hear him perfectly, but in my mind. I look at him, shocked.

"*How can I hear you so clearly?*"

Michael looks at me just as surprised.

"We are mind linked, I'm not sure how, as it's usually just pack members that can hear each other. But I can feel the link there as clearly as I can feel my packs."

"But I'm a rogue, I could never hear ... his voice?" I can feel myself starting to panic, but Michael is there in a heartbeat, leaning against me, letting me use him to ground myself just like he did in the classroom earlier and when I was shifting. He always seems to know exactly what I need and when I need it.

"Maybe your wolf is letting you know you are safe with my pack and me, that we would never hurt you like he did," Michael replies in a soft tone.

"He is right; you are finally safe," my wolf whispers. I start to feel myself relax again. Maybe Michael is right; perhaps it's time to start trusting my wolf. She has never caused me any harm; she isn't to blame for what was done to me, to us.

"Thank you," I whisper to him.

"You don't have anything to thank me for," Michael replies. Again, he rubs his head against mine as I relax into him. Suddenly, he knocks me on the shoulder, and I stumble slightly. I look at him, shocked.

"What the hell?" I swear he laughs, then gives me a cheeky wolf grin.

"Catch me if you can," he says as he darts away from me. I watch his tail fly into the woods.

"Don't just stand there; get the bastard," my wolf orders. I laugh at her as I push myself towards the direction Michael has just rushed off in.

I've never felt so alive, so free. I thought I would land face-first in the mud as soon as I attempted to run, but my paws know what to do. They land softly on the ground, the wind blowing through my fur, making my whole body feel alive. I never realised what it was like, what I was missing by hiding in my little den during the full moons these last two years.

We've been running and playing for what feels like hours. We explored the forest and played in the stream. I even pushed Michael into a deep pond, and he then dragged me in with him. Michael has made the whole experience fun and enjoyable. The entire night felt so natural. Being with Michael feels natural.

Sometime later, we find ourselves back in the clearing where we shifted. Just as we get there, I feel Michael nip at my hind leg. I turn around and pounce on him. We playfully wrestle like we have most of the night until he pins me down, our eyes lock, and I can't see or hear anything else. All that exists at that moment is Michael. I lift my head, placing it on his shoulder again, breathing in his scent and just enjoying him being so close.

A low growl radiates from his chest. I know there is no threat in it; it's one of pure pleasure. Then, just as he lowers his nose to my shoulder, I feel his whole body tense, his head shoots up, his ears pointing to attention as if listening. I find myself freezing underneath him. I can hear something approaching; I try to smell what it is, but the wind is blowing in the wrong direction. Shit.

Michael jumps up, standing in front of me as I get to my feet. He starts moving backwards, so I've no choice but to move with him. I am backed up against a tree. Michael's ears are now pinned back to his head, his lips pulled over his teeth, as he snarls at something approaching. He's protecting me, using his body as a shield. I look around him to see what the danger is as another wolf walks into the clearing. This one is as big as Michael but with a light brown coat, Michael stops growling and relaxes instantly, but he doesn't move from in front of me. The other wolf tilts his head and then tries to look around Michael, but Michael moves to block his view.

"*Not now, Jonathan,*" I hear Michael say in a low tone.

"*Who's your friend?*" the other wolf, Jonathan, asks.

"*I said not now. I'll speak to you later.*" Michael obviously has some kind of authority over this wolf as he replies that he will wait for his call before running off in the direction we have just come from. Michael stays in front of me a little longer before turning to check I'm alright.

"*I'm fine,*" I reassure him.

"*I'm sorry. I didn't expect him to be here tonight. He wasn't a threat; I just couldn't pick up on his scent to start with.*"

"*It's fine, honestly. No harm done.*"

"*Hang on, I'm going to shift back,*" Michael says. I turn my back to him, and within seconds, I sense that he's shifted. I hear him messing with the bags and getting dressed.

"Okay, you can turn around now," he calls.

Michael is standing a few feet away, dressed in just his grey sweatpants from the gym, whilst holding a blanket.

"Lie down, and I'll put this over you. That way, I can help you change if I need to, but I won't see you naked." I find myself rolling my eyes at him, but he just laughs. I lie down on the ground and feel the blanket fall over my body.

"Do you know what to do?"

I nod and close my eyes. When I open them again, I'm back to being human. Michael's squatting in front of me, smiling. "Well, that was quicker than I thought it would be. Your bag is here. I won't be far, I promise. Shout if you need me," he says as he walks into the trees. I can't help but admire his muscular back before moving down to his firm tight, well, you know. I quickly change into my yoga pants and hoodie.

"You decent?" Michael calls after a minute or two.

"Yeah," I reply as I quickly gather my hair and chuck it up into a messy bun. As soon as Michael walks out of the trees, I run up to him excitedly. I jump up, wrapping my arms around his neck; he catches me with ease and holds me tight, laughing.

"I did it! I actually changed without the moon!" I squeal happily.

"I never had any doubt. You were amazing!" Michael says as he lowers me back down to the ground. I step back, smiling as he smiles back at me. I miss being in his arms as soon as he releases me.

Tonight, I haven't just enjoyed being a wolf for the first time. I have loved every second I've been with Michael, not reminding myself he is my lecturer continuously. He flirted with me as much as I flirted with him.

"So, how was your first run?" he enquires, grinning at me.

"That was amazing! I felt so free." I swear I'm bouncing on the soles of my feet with excitement. Michael stands in front of me, his arms crossed against his chest, chuckling.

"I told you you'd love it, didn't I? You shifted back so quickly as well. You really are a beautiful wolf." I can't help but smile. It was the first time anyone other than my auntie or uncle had seen me as a wolf. Plus, to know that he thought I was beautiful in that form makes my heart sing. God, I'm getting cheesy in my old age.

"I take it you knew the other wolf well?" I ask. He looks at me and nods.

"Unfortunately, yes." I notice he's grinning, looking in the direction the wolf has just left.

"Is he part of your pack?"

Michael turns back to face me and nods.

"He's my brother. I never told him we would be here. I'm so sorry if he scared you."

I place my hand on his bicep.

"Honestly, I'm fine. I didn't feel as threatened as I thought I would. Maybe it helped to have a macho man here to protect me." I wink as Michael starts laughing.

"That's Mister Macho Man, remember."

I roll my eyes at him, shaking my head.

"Oh, how could I forget." I take a second to admire Michael laughing. I look up at him, feeling my heart swell, "Seriously though, thank you. Not just for the support tonight but for protecting me when you thought I was in danger."

"I'll always protect you," Michael whispers, looking at me. I feel the butterflies flapping in my stomach. I look at his lips and wonder what it would be like to kiss them. Would he let me? I consider leaning forward to see what would happen, but I bottle it, too scared of facing rejection.

"I need to get back to my dorm before someone realises I'm still out."

Michael nods and grabs both of our bags. He holds out his hand, and I place mine in it, smiling.

"Come on then, let's get back to the cars," he says as he smiles back at me before leading the way.

As we walk back, I find that I'm a little unsteady on my feet. It's like coming down from an adrenalin rush. One minute, I'm fine; the next, I'm struggling to lift my legs so that I can walk. Michael seems to notice and offers me his arm rather than just his hand. I take it willingly and lean against him slightly, needing the extra support, as well as wanting to be near him.

"You're exhausted; at least you should sleep tonight. Do you think you will be okay to drive?"

I want to say yes, but I'm not sure. The last week, on top of tonight, has caught up with me. The more I think about it, the more I realise that I'm not safe to drive. Michael seems to notice quickly. He let go of my hand before wrapping his arm around my waist, giving me that extra support I desperately need right now.

"I'll drive you home. There is no way I'm letting you drive like this."

I shake my head.

"It's okay. I'll nap in the car for a bit, then head back," I mumble, apparently too tired to speak properly. I feel Michael's chest vibrate as he growls.

"Do you really think I would leave you to sleep in a car in the middle of nowhere? I'm driving you back. That's final." I can tell by his tone that there's no arguing with him.

"But how will you get home?" My eyelids are getting heavier, and I stumble slightly. Before I register what's happening, Michael scoops me up into his arms and pulls me against his chest. I can't resist; I put my arms around his neck and snuggle into his hold.

"Sleep, baby, I've got you," he whispers against my hair; I only just about mumble an "okay" as I fall asleep, listening to the sound of his heartbeat.

Chapter Eleven

DAISY

I roll onto my back in bed as I stretch out. Gods, I've not slept that well in so long. I turn to get my water bottle from my bedside cabinet when I spot my alarm clock. Shit! It's eleven o'clock! I jump out of bed and grab my phone. I have a bunch of missed calls from Beth and Tony, messages from most of the class, plus one from Michael checking I'm okay.

"Fuck!"

The class started an hour ago. Rushing into my en suite, I make short work of getting washed and dressed.

I'm hopping out of my bedroom door, trying to put my shoes on when I stop. "Balls, my bag!" I rush back in and grab it, as well as a packet of chewing gum off my side. I'll have to brush my teeth later. I rush out our front door and down the stairs, jumping the last five.

Racing through the grounds towards class, I curse myself continuously. I can't believe I overslept; I know I set my alarm! I must have turned it off and gone back to sleep; I just don't remember doing it.

I swear the whole class turns to look at me as I fly into the room. Every single person is smirking at me.

"Oh, so you're not dead?" Tony calls as I walk past his table.

"You could have knocked and woken me up, tosser."

I hear everyone laugh; Tony just smiles at me.

"I did, more than once, but there was no way you were going to hear me over all that snoring."

I spin around and stare at him; my jaw nearly hits the floor.

"I don't snore, you bastard!" I'm so embarrassed. I flip him the bird as I walk over to my chair next to Beth, trying to ignore all the giggling around me.

"Sorry, I slept in," I say to Michael when I finally get the guts to face him. He's laughing with the rest of them. Bastard, it's his fault I'm so tired.

"I gathered. Late night, was it?" I hear Michael ask from the front of the class; I look at him through my eyelashes, and I swear he winks at me. Oh, I'm up for playing if he is.

"Yeah, I had to help an old man when I was out for a late-night run. Unfortunately, it meant I was out longer than I should have been. But you know, care in the community is essential," I say, raising an eyebrow at him. I swear to the gods, he chokes on thin air as the rest of the class looks confused. I look at Beth, who is on the verge of bursting with sarcastic comments, so I just show her my middle finger while muttering for her to shut it.

"Rude!" she mutters, trying to look offended, but the smile says it all.

"Come and see me after the lesson, and I'll fill you in on what you have missed," Michael adds before continuing with the rest of the class. I quickly nod and start pulling my notebook and pen out of my bag.

"You look like you are in a better mood," Beth whispers next to me. I look at her and smile.

"I feel a lot better about things," I whisper back.

"Well, whatever has put that smile on your face, I hope it continues to do so." She whispers back before carrying on with her work. I can't resist looking up at Michael, who is standing by his desk doing something on his laptop. I feel my phone vibrate.

Michael: You do look better. Glad you managed to get a decent sleep. X

I quickly type out a reply.

Daisy: I feel a lot better and happier. Thanks for getting me back last night. Mr Macho Man saves the day again. x

I hear Michael chuckle under his breath from his desk as my phone vibrates again.

Michael: Mr Macho Man is always happy to help his favourite wolf. Xx

I can't help but smile as I start looking at the questions on the board and attempt to catch up with what's going on.

At the end of class, I tell Beth and Tony I'll meet them in the café, then wait behind to see Michael. When the last person leaves, they close the door behind them.

"I'm so sorry I was late; I've not slept like that in ages," I say before he has the chance to say anything. He walks around to the front of his desk and leans against it. Folding his arms across his chest and his legs in front of him. God, he's so sexy when he stands like that. It makes my pulse race every single time.

"It's amazing how tired someone can be after a good run. How are you feeling today?" Michael asks, leaning his head to one side, looking a little concerned. When he folds his arms, the fabric of his shirt is stretched around his broad shoulders and thick biceps. The fact that he rolls the sleeves up on his shirt just adds to the wow factor.

"Better than I have in a long time. My legs ache, but I'm not surprised after leaving a big oaf for dust all night." I'm shocked when Michael throws back his head and roars laughing.

"Oh, I remember that 'big oaf' having to slow down for you a few times."

I casually wave off his comment.

"Please, I was holding back so he didn't sulk like a giant baby."

Michael roars, laughing again, shaking his head. I don't know if it is just me, but I feel like our relationship has changed. Like we are openly flirting with each other now.

"Anyway, let me give you this work, and we can both be on our way."

I nod and move next to him as he turns to face the desk. He goes over the part of the lesson I missed and gives me a couple of handouts. Our hands are right next to each other as we lean on the desk. Occasionally, he reaches out with his little finger and rubs it against mine. As if testing if I will move away from him. I don't; instead, I do the same to him.

After about ten minutes, I'm all caught up and relieved I hadn't missed anything important.

"Thanks for that, Michael, and thanks for last night. Means a lot that someone would help me." I look down at the floor, embarrassed.

"Hey, look at me," Michael says softly. I look up at him, and our eyes meet. Gods, I could stare into those blue eyes all day. "Daisy, I wasn't kidding when I said anything you need; I'm here. All you have to do is call or message, and I'll be there. I would love it if you ran with me again during the full moon next week."

I can feel the smile creeping up my face and the heat in my cheeks.

"I would love that." Then, just as I'm about to add more, my phone starts ringing. I look down at it and realise it's Beth. "I better go. I have held you up enough, plus Beth and Tony are getting impatient. I haven't even had my morning coffee yet, so I can feel my mood shifting," I chuckle. Michael smiles next to me.

"By all means, don't let me stand between you and your morning coffee. Go!" he laughs. I thank him again before grabbing my stuff and leaving, sneaking a quick sniff of the air so I can take in his scent. I always feel like it is easier to be away from him if I can remember it.

As I get to the door, I quickly turn to face him. He is leaning against the desk again, watching me. Let's see how flirty we are going to be.

"Message me any time about the run. I like hearing from you," I smile at him. Michael's own grin spreads across his face.

"Same goes for you. Message me at any time, day or night," he replies, not taking his eyes off me. I can feel my cheeks, as well as other parts, heat under his gaze.

"You will get sick of me," I admit as my pulse races. Michael slowly shakes his head at me, making my heart race.

"I don't think that's possible."

Yep, fifty shades of flirty it is.

Chapter Twelve

MICHAEL

It's Saturday night, and for the first time in years, I'm out in town.

Jon had arrived at mine just after lunch and declared we were going out. There's a band playing in The Crows, which he really wants to see. I agreed straight away as it is always a good night when a band played in the pub, especially if Carl had picked it. Usually, I only go there on a quiet day when I know that only the owners will be there. But things have changed recently. I've changed, and I no longer want to hide away from everyone. There is also the incentive that Daisy said she was going into town tonight, so I'm secretly hoping to bump into her.

The booze is flowing as we go from one pub to another. I'm in an excellent mood for the first time in a long while. This is precisely what I've needed—a lad's night out with my brother.

When we finally get to The Crows, he tells me to get the drinks as he heads off to find us a seat. I make my way to the bar and get our friend's attention.

"Alright, Mikey. Jon said you might pop in," Richard calls as we shake hands over the bar.

"Hey Rich, don't tell me you've given Carl a night off?"

Richard barks out a deep laugh.

"Not a chance. He's helping the band set up. What can I get you?"

"Just the usual, please."

"We always have a bottle kept especially for you two in the cellar. Let me pop down and get it; I'll be right back."

I tell him to take his time as he hurries off. I start looking around to see if I can spot where Jon has decided to sit when someone else catches my eye.

There she is on the dance floor, her arms up in the air as her hips move in perfect time to the music. Her long blonde hair cascades down her back in loose waves, her black jeans enhancing her perfectly shaped backside. I can't take my eyes off her. As always, Daisy has me frozen to the spot as I watch her and become mesmerised.

She turns suddenly, catching me staring. Her eyes light up as a smile spreads across her beautiful face. She holds up a hand and waves, and I quickly wave back, unable to stop myself from smiling. I watch as she holds up a finger to Beth before leaving her on the dance floor and heading over to me on her own.

"Hey, what are you doing here?" Daisy asks as she stands close to me.

"I'm here to see the band with my brother." I notice she's wearing a large badge and nod at it. "Is today your birthday?"

Daisy rolls her eyes, nodding. I reach down and take her hand without breaking eye contact; I bring it up to my lips and gently kiss her knuckles, watching as her cheeks burn bright red and her smile becomes even more prominent.

"Happy birthday, darling," I whisper as I slowly lower her hand back down, not letting it go.

"Thank you," she whispers back. I can't tear my eyes away from hers. We just stand there staring at each other, holding hands where no one can see them, lost in the moment.

"Two glasses, Mikey?"

I turn quickly to face Richard as he bursts the bubble Daisy and I have created. I nod as he looks between Daisy and me, smiling. Shit, he's realised. Daisy lets go of my hand, which immediately feels empty without hers.

"Please, Rich, plus whatever the birthday girl is having. None of your watered-down house shit, though."

Richard just flips me the bird as he walks away, muttering that he gets no respect whilst we laugh at him.

"Free drink and not even the cheap shit. Adams, you are spoiling me."

"Class it as a birthday treat. Next time, it's tap water for you, Andrews." We both start playfully arguing and chatting as we always do. There are never any awkward silences when we are together. We are in mid-conversation when Richard returns with Daisy's drink and two glasses for me.

"Thank you for the drink, Michael. I'm sure I'll see you in a bit," she winks as she turns away from me, heading back towards Beth, who is still on the dance floor, drinking her drink. I'm sure there is a bit more swagger in her step than when she came over before.

"Close your mouth, Mikey, you're catching flies," Richard whispers as he leans over the bar, grinning at me.

"Not a word, Richard, not even to Carl or Jon," I warn without taking my eyes off Daisy. I hear Richard chuckle; as I turn to pick up the two glasses, I spot Richard pretending to zip up his lips.

"Mum's the word, but Mikey-" I turn and look at him properly. The grin is gone, but he is still smiling softly. "You haven't smiled like that in years. Don't waste time waiting." Before I get a chance to reply, Richard heads off to the other side of the bar, asking others what they would like to drink. I carry on watching as Daisy starts dancing again, but this time, she looks over at me and smirks as if she's flirting with me from across the room.

"You checking out my girl?"

I quickly turn around and see Kellan standing behind the bar. At first, he looks annoyed, but then he smiles, and I promptly smile back. Fuck off calling her your girl. He hardly ever turns up to class anymore. When he does, he sits silently watching Daisy. We are already in discussions on whether he will be continuing next term.

"Just being sociable," I reply quickly. Kellan nods, looking past me towards Daisy. There is no missing the fact that he likes her and obviously wants to be with her. However, she has never once mentioned him. I consider asking him outright if they are in a relationship, but I don't think I will get an honest answer.

"*She belongs by our side, not his,*" my wolf chimes in.

"Well, enjoy your night working. It must suck when all your friends are getting drunk and enjoying themselves." I quickly pat him on the shoulder before making my way away from a rather pissed-off-looking Kellan. I can't help but smirk, knowing that he is pissed off because of me.

I find Jon sitting at a table with a perfect view of the dance floor. I hand him his drink and take a seat, ensuring I can see where Daisy is still dancing with Beth and a few others.

"You spotted them as well then?" Jon says, next to me. I

just nod, taking a sip of my drink. "I might go and introduce myself."

I turn and face him, growling.

"Don't you dare." Jon looks over at me, shocked. "They are my students, and I'm not dealing with the fallout afterwards," I quickly add. Jon looks at me and pouts, and I start laughing as he just looks ridiculous.

As the evening progresses, the alcohol flows, and the flirting across the room continues between Daisy and me. Richard leaves Kellan and two other staff members to deal with the bar whilst Carl and him join us. It has been a long time since the four of us just hung out.

We are all laughing at Jonathan's failed attempt to chat up a good-looking woman when Carl signals for someone to come over. I look up as Daisy and Tony head in our direction.

"Whatever you think I did, I didn't," Daisy protests as soon as she's close enough for us to hear. Carl shakes his head at her, smirking.

"You haven't *yet*, which is why I called you over," he says, raising one eyebrow at her as she rolls her eyes at him. "Now, it's busy; I think it's time to remind you of the rules," he declares as she crosses her arms over her chest. Looking bored.

"Daisy has her own set of rules?" I ask.

"Gods, yes!" Tony, Carl, and Richard all answer in unison as Daisy continues to sulk.

"I don't understand why I have to have these special rules; nobody else does!" She turns and looks at me, pouting. "Michael, tell them I'm an angel."

I lean back into my chair, crossing my arms.

"I could, but I was brought up not to lie," I answer with a smirk. Daisy looks at me with her mouth hanging open in shock. "I think I need to know what these rules are first before I decide if I will make an exception for you," I add with a wink. Daisy sticks her tongue out at me before turning back to Carl.

"What's rule number one?" Carl asks. Daisy rolls her eyes before answering.

"No hassling the staff to serve me first."

I clamp my lips between my teeth to stop myself from laughing.

"Rule number two?" Richard asks. Daisy's face lights up as she points at Richard.

"HA! It doesn't apply as it's a band, not a DJ."

I look at Carl, raising an eyebrow. He holds up a finger, signalling for me to wait with the questions.

"The band does covers and requests, so it applies," he points out. Daisy huffs as she answers, looking defeated.

"Fine, no demanding they play my requests."

It's getting harder not to laugh out loud now.

"As it's busy, what's rule number three?" Carl says, grinning at her. Daisy looks shocked and then outraged before throwing her hands up in the air dramatically.

"Oh, come on! It's not THAT busy." Carl looks at her, raising both eyebrows this time. "Fine. No taking my shoes off." She flops down on the seat next to me as Carl continues to look at her. I start coughing, trying to hide the laughing fit that's threatening, earning me the side eye from Daisy. Richard leans forward, looking very serious.

"Now, the most important one, rule number four." Daisy looks at him and gives him the most prominent puppy dog eyes I have ever seen. I thought Jon was the master of that look, but hers is a whole new level.

"If she ever does that to us, we are screwed," my wolf whispers. I can feel it in my gut that he's right. This woman

would have us well and truly wrapped around her little finger.

"What if I am *really* careful?" she bargains, but Carl shakes his head. I glance at Richard, who is grinning from ear to ear.

"Oh, I know *you* will be careful; it's the people who will see you and think they can do it too. We can't afford to be sued because someone broke their neck. So, what's the rule, Daisy?"

She looks at Jon and me as if for help. I hold my hands up.

"I can't help you. I'm just here for the entertainment. Plus, I'm intrigued to know what you have been doing that could cause others to break bones," I add. Daisy lets out a large sigh and stands up from the chair. Throwing me a dirty look as she does.

"Rule four is 'tables are for glasses, not asses, or dancing.'" That's it, I'm done. I howl, laughing at the same time as everyone else. Daisy looks around at us, shocked. "I don't see what's so funny. You are ruining all my fun!" Tony leans over her shoulder from behind her so his cheek is against hers, smirking.

"It's okay. I'm working Friday; we can have a lock-in. The rules don't apply then."

Daisy looks at us all smugly before pointing at Carl and Richard.

"Just remember that. There will be no stopping me then." She then turns to me, pointing. I stop laughing but can't get rid of the smile on my face. She is so fucking adorable when she's annoyed. "And you are no help! Don't think I will forget this, Adams." I watch as she reaches down and picks up my glass of bourbon. I'm left speechless as she knocks it back without so much as a shudder, grabs Tony's hand and waltzes back to the dance floor.

"Now, *that's* my kind of girl." I hear Jon say next to me.

"*That is **our girl**,*" my wolf says excitedly. I nod in response to both of them, unable to reply or tear my eyes away from Daisy. She starts dancing with Tony but glances over her shoulder at me. She winks before turning back to Tony. The sight of her hips swaying, fuck. There are no words for how uncomfortable I will be all night as I feel my trousers getting tighter.

The night is slowly winding down, the band has finished, and people have started to head home.

It has been a fantastic night. Good music, great company, and a lot of flirting with a certain rogue. Just what I needed.

Daisy, Tony, and Beth joined us a few times for a drink. Whenever Daisy was with us, she would sit close to me. A few times, I felt her touch my hand under the table—others, I would just take her hand in mine. Sometimes, we forgot there were others there and just talked between the two of us until someone would ask us a question. We were like two naughty teenagers trying to hide our feelings from our friends. It was kind of fun, okay, it was really fun. I've loved every minute of it. I had planned on cornering her before she left to see if she would meet me tomorrow evening for a run, planning on talking to her about this between us, but her group just disappeared without so much as a goodbye. Beth was pretty drunk, so I guess she needed to get home.

Jon and I are pretty wasted ourselves. I've been feeling a little weird for the past half an hour. I'm sure it is just the alcohol as well as the lack of food. So, I decided to get some fresh air. Carl and Richard have already invited us to stay the night. I know I need to attempt to sober up a bit before making a complete fool of myself. I also plan on messaging Daisy to check she got home okay.

As I walk out of the door, I hear someone call my name. I turn to see Beth and Kellan standing further along the street. I instantly look around excitedly for Daisy, hoping I will get the chance to speak to her after all.

"We don't need anyone's help, and certainly not his," Kellan hisses at her. I can see something is wrong by looking at Beth, so I head over.

"What's the matter, Beth?" I ask, ignoring Kellan. Now I am closer, I can see that she looks agitated.

"Daisy's been missing for about forty minutes. We thought she had just gone home, but Tony has just got there, and she's not in the apartment. Doesn't look like she's been there at all."

"Any chance she is just getting food?" I ask. Beth shakes her head and holds up a bag.

"I was getting it; I'm really worried about her." She's not the only one. Something is wrong here. I can't explain it; I just know.

"Was she drunk? She didn't seem that bad last time I saw her."

Beth nods her head.

"It was strange; one minute, she was fine, a little tipsy, but I was in a worse state than her. Next thing, she could hardly walk or talk. It came on so fast."

I realise I need to find her fast.

"Give me one minute. I'll be back, to help you look for her." I turn to head back into the pub to get Jon. I can hear

Kellan moaning about me getting involved, but I couldn't care less about what he wants.

"I need your help," I call as soon as I am in sight of Jonathan. He looks at me and frowns as I lean on the table in front of him.

"What's up? You look pale."

I feel physically sick. I don't like knowing that Daisy may need help and could be in any sort of danger.

"Daisy has gone missing; we need to help find her." As expected, Jon looks a little weary.

"You're sure she hasn't just gone to get some food or gone to one of the clubs?"

I shake my head.

"No, they've checked at her place as well. She's not there." Jon nods and grabs our jackets; he passes me mine as we leave, telling Richard and Carl what's happened. Carl instantly informs us he will help us look. Richard's going to stay put in case she comes back.

We walk outside and find Beth and Kellan, where I left them. They inform us that there is still no sign of her anywhere.

Beth tells us where they've checked, and we quickly decide where else to look, agreeing to split up to cover more areas. We'll meet up in fifteen minutes. I asked her to send me a picture of Daisy to show around. I then quickly sent it on to Jonathan and Carl. As soon as Beth and Kellan have got out of earshot, I tell Jon and Carl to keep everyone away from me. If I can't find her as a human, I'll go as a wolf—years as a Pack Protector has taught me how to be discreet even on a busy Friday night.

I stand by the door for a minute to see if I can pick up on her scent. It's tricky, though, as hundreds have passed through here tonight; the smell of stale alcohol makes it even harder. Luckily, I spot a couple of guys hanging around, so I approach them. I show them Daisy's picture, claiming she is my sister. They tell me she left after having an argument with *"some guy that works behind the bar."* Well, Kellan kept that quiet. They point me in the direction she went in. I thank them and head off after her.

As soon as I'm out of sight of the pub, I sniff the air, praying for her scent to be strong enough. I need to kneel so I'm closer to the ground and pretend to tie my shoelace until I finally pick up her scent. It's so faint, but it's there. I head off in that direction, stopping at every alleyway or road to check which way she was going.

As I get further from town, her scent gets stronger as fewer people have been this way, so it isn't as disguised, but it's different. I hadn't noticed before, but now I can separate it from other scents, I've picked up on the chemical smell mixed into it. Has she been drugged? Gods, I hope not. I pick up the pace. A drugged werewolf is never a good combination.

I need to find her now!!

Chapter Thirteen

MICHAEL

I follow the scent down a street when suddenly I lose it.

Shit.

Panic starts to build in my chest. Why would her scent just stop? Every scenario runs through my head: did she get into a taxi? Did someone grab her? Where the hell are you, Daisy? I retrace my steps, praying I took a wrong turn somewhere. A few meters back, I realised there was a tiny alleyway I had somehow missed. I pick up her scent as it's stronger down here.

I rush down, and there she is on the floor, leaning against a wall. I drop down beside her, terrified of what I'll find. She's freezing.

I quickly shrug off my jacket and place it around her shoulders as she violently shivers. This isn't good; it takes a lot for a wolf to get this cold.

"Daisy? It's Michael, can you hear me? Are you hurt, darling?"

She turns her head to look at me.

"Michael?" her voice lower than a whisper. If it weren't for my wolf hearing, I would have missed it.

Now I am in front of her; I can smell the drugs. I have a feeling they aren't something she would have taken voluntarily.

"It's me, baby. Are you hurt? Has anyone hurt you?"

She shakes her head, and I let out a sigh of relief. I can't smell anyone else on her except her friends and Kellan. If he has hurt her, I'll kill him.

"Do you think you can stand, darling?" I ask; she sluggishly nods her head. I reach down, trying to help her get up to her feet, but I know instantly she can't stand unaided. I catch her as she stumbles before lifting her into my arms.

"You left," she mumbles, looking up at me through heavy eyelids. I shake my head at her frowning.

"I was in the pub, darling. I wanted to see you before you left." I feel her shudder deeply.

"I don't feel right. Something's wrong," she whispers

"I know, baby, but I'm here. I've got you. I'm going to get you somewhere safe and warm, okay?" She nods; her head is a little more flaccid than it should have been. I pull her close to me. I'm holding her into my chest, making sure the jacket stays around her as she rests her head against my shoulder.

"Daisy, I have to ask; did you take anything?"

She shakes her head. My jaw instantly clenches as I'm furious with whoever did this to her.

"You found me," she mumbles, tightening her hold on my neck. I look down at her and press a kiss on the top of her head. Even with the added chemical smell, her scent helps to calm the anxiety racing through me.

"I'll always find you, baby. Always," I promise as I hold

her tighter, taking a moment to savour her there in my arms.

"I know," she replies, going limp. Her arms slip from around my shoulders. Fuck.

"Daisy! I need you to stay awake for me, baby. Do you think you can do that?" I feel her hands fist into my shirt.

"I'm so tired. I just want to sleep, but I'm scared." I can see it written all over her face. She knows something is very wrong.

"I know, baby, but I've got you now. I promise nothing, and no one will hurt you." She mumbles a thank you before falling quiet again.

I rush to the pub but find Carl, Beth, and Jon on my way. I let out a sigh of relief as they will know what to do for the best.

"Is she okay? Is she hurt?" Beth asks quickly. I can see she is out of her mind with worry.

"She's blind drunk. Jon, what do you think? Home or Hospital? She doesn't seem injured, just very drunk. She was kind of responsive when I first found her." As he starts to look her over, I whisper low enough so only someone with advanced hearing will hear.

"What do you smell?" I watch as he takes a deep breath, his eyes widening as the smell hits him, confirming my suspicions. Fuck.

I look up at Carl, who looks furious. He can smell it, too.

"Daisy, can you hear me? Are you alright?" Jon asks quietly; she replies with a mumbled "Yes" and tightens her hold on my shirt again. Jon is the drug expert on my team; his scent is greater than that of nearly every wolf I know, so he has spent years learning the scent of each drug and other substances.

"She needs to be somewhere safe, but I don't think she needs a hospital at the moment. I can't see or feel any bumps on the head. She should be fine as long as she warms up and responds when spoken to."

"Bring her to the bar. She can have the spare room. She knows and trusts us. We can keep an eye on her, plus we are closer to the hospital if she needs to go," Carl offers. He pulls out his phone as it starts ringing. "Tony? Yeah, we have her. Where are you? Meet us at the bar. We are going to keep her there tonight ... alright, see you in a couple."

I look over at Beth, who looks lost.

"Are you okay with this, Beth? I promise she'll be safe there. I would never put her in danger."

Beth looks at me and nods.

"Tony is going to be here in a minute; he can stay with her." Carl pulls her into a one-arm hug, and Beth nods.

"It's not that I don't trust you. I just feel like I let her down." We all start protesting that she hasn't, and we finally get through to her as we approach the bar. Tony and Richard are standing outside the door, waiting for us. Tony turns around and looks at Daisy in my arms.

"Are you sure she's going to be okay?"

I nod at him, glancing down at her, sleeping peacefully in my arms. I ask Jon to call Beth a taxi and to stay with her until it comes. Tony and I follow Carl up to their private apartment above the bar and into the spare room.

I place her gently on the bed in the recovery position, pushing the duvet behind her to stop her from rolling onto her back just in case she's sick. There's a little bin in the room; I place it by her head, just in case. I'm checking to make sure she has everything she needs when Carl walks in with a glass of water and puts it on the bedside cabinet. He then pulls a blanket from the drawer under the bed and hands it to me. I nod my thanks before placing it over her. I wish there were more I could do to help her.

She quietly mumbles my name in her sleep as I gently brush some hair off her face. I watch her for a few minutes, terrified that if I look away, she will stop breathing. Eventually, I feel she is settled and safe enough to leave. I turn on the bedside lamp as I retreat from the room. I turn the main light off before propping the door open a little.

Richard, Jon, and a very angry-looking Kellan burst through the front door as I leave the bedroom. I place a finger over my lips, signalling for everyone to move away, not wanting any shouting to wake her up. We all head into the lounge, and I close the door.

"What the hell, man? Thanks for letting me know you had found her!" Kellan shouts. I spin around and glare at him; the sight of him infuriates me. How dare he raise his voice at me right now. I take a step forward, rolling my shoulders back; Kellan has no choice but to look up at me.

"I found her down an alleyway on a freezing cold night. Do you really think I was going to keep her outside any longer than I needed to? Do you have any idea what state she is in? She is unconscious. It's fucking lucky that I found her when I did. Because if somebody else had, there is no way she could have defended herself. She could've been attacked, raped, or killed. So yes, I brought *'your girl'* here to make sure she is safe." I catch sight of Tony, who is standing behind Kellan, looking furious.

"His girl? Daisy isn't his girl! Is that what he's been telling everyone? What the fuck? He's obsessed with her. It's gotten to the point we have stopped him from coming to the apartment, as he makes Daisy feel uncomfortable in her own home." Tony takes a step towards Kellan. "Beth said you were reluctant to ask for help finding Daisy tonight. Is that because you had something to do with the state she's in?"

"How can I be blamed for how drunk she is? I was working the bar all night," Kellan yells back. Tony takes a step forward; I open my mouth to intervene, but Jon touches my arm.

"Let's see where the demon kid is going with this," he whispers in my ear.

"Yes, you were working the bar. It wouldn't surprise me if you made her drinks stronger than she requested."

"I wouldn't do that to her. I would never put her in danger," Kellan protests, but Tony just smirks at him.

"Wouldn't you? Even if it meant you could play the knight in shining armour afterwards?"

"Do you really think I'm that sick? After everything she has been through, do you really think I would do that to her?" Kellan demands.

"Yes! Absolutely!" Tony bellows in return. Now they are nose to nose; the rest of us are waiting for the fight to start as we know it will.

"Did you slip drugs into Daisy's drink?" Carl asks over Tony's shoulder. Tony spins around and looks at him, confused.

"What?" It's impossible to miss the look of shock on his face as Carl nods slowly. I can feel the air in the room getting warmer as Tony realises someone has drugged his best friend. Shit, he is going to lose control.

"Daisy's drink was spiked with drugs, not alcohol," Carl explains, not taking his eyes off Kellan. I watch, amazed, as Tony spins around, his eyes burning as red as flames as he punches Kellan in the face. Before Tony can get to him to hit him again, Carl and Richard grab him.

"You are dead, Kellan; do you fucking hear me? If you

so much as look at Daisy again, I will make sure her face is the last thing you ever see. As I will tear your fucking heart out." I hear Carl whispering that he needs to calm down before Kellan sees his eyes as he and Richard drag him out of the room.

Jon and I have hold of Kellan, who is fighting to get to Tony. I have no worries about Tony getting hurt; if anything, I think he could kill Kellan. I'm more worried about Kellan seeing what Tony is. If he realises that Tony's not human, how long until he notices little things about the rest of us and puts two and two together? How long until he realises what Daisy is? I can't have her in any more danger than she is already. Keeping Kellan safe will protect Daisy, which is the only reason he is still breathing right now.

"I'm going to fucking kill you, Tony," Kellan yells. Jon gets hold of Kellan and starts dragging him towards the front door.

"The only thing you are doing is going home."

I place my hand on Jon's shoulder and shake my head so that he will wait a moment. I take hold of Kellan's shirt and throw him against the wall, pinning him so his feet are only just touching the floor.

"If you did have anything to do with Daisy being drugged, I strongly suggest that you don't return to classes. If I find out you put her in danger in the hope of achieving something for your own selfish needs or any other reason, I will end you. No fucker will ever find your body, and no one will suspect me. Is that understood?" I lean back as Kellan stares at me; I can see he is trying to act all big, but deep down, he's terrified.

"Go to hell. You can't threaten me," he hisses through his teeth. I just smirk, showing him a bit of teeth. I let him get a glimpse of the leader of the Protectors, Michael, the one that every rogue knows to fear. I watch as his face straightens and his whole-body language changes.

"Kellan, that's not a threat. It's a promise. Now get the fuck out of here and *never* approach or even look in Daisy's direction again." Jon doesn't give Kellan time to respond as he drags him out of the room, away from me and, most importantly, away from Daisy.

I stand there on my own for a minute, taking the time to control my anger and stop myself from going after Kellan and killing him. The only thing stopping me is that I don't want to leave Daisy for even a minute. I take a deep breath to calm myself before going to check on her.

As soon as I enter the room, I can see a little colour has returned to her face. That's a good sign; at least she is warming up. The relief is short-lived, though, as she starts to moan, and I only just make it in time with the bin in hand as she starts throwing up.

I hold the bin by her mouth and her hair from her face as she is sick. The more she throws up, the more I wonder if she should be checked out. Jon pops in and reassures me it is a good thing; her body is rejecting the drugs. He offers to stay, but I ask him to check on Tony for me. I know how close he and Daisy are, so I know he will be struggling with her being put in this state. His importance to her makes me surprisingly protective of him.

When Daisy has finally stopped being sick, I use a flannel I find in the bathroom to clean her mouth.

"Thank you," she murmurs without opening her eyes. I brush my knuckles over her face, and she relaxes into my touch. "This doesn't smell like home."

"It's not, baby. You are above The Crows. Carl, Richard, and Tony will look after you tonight; they are all here. But if you need me for anything, you tell them to call me. I will get here as fast as I can. I'm not going far."

Her eyes fly open. For a second, I think she is having another reaction to the drugs, but then she grabs hold of my shirt.

"No, please don't go. Please don't leave me," she begs. I instantly place my palm against her cheek, rubbing my thumb against her soft skin. Then, leaning over to place my lips against her temple, I whisper,"If you want me here, then I'm not going anywhere."

"Promise?" she murmurs as she starts to relax. I nod before kissing her on the forehead.

"I promise, baby. Go to sleep. I'm right here."

She nods as she drifts instantly back to sleep. I watch her for a couple of minutes with the bin ready before I feel it's safe to leave her alone again. Then, as I stand from the floor at the side of the bed, I notice Carl and Tony standing at the door.

"How long have you known?" Tony asks. I instantly try to act dumb, but from the look on their faces, they know. I look down at Daisy and sigh, unable to stop the smile that creeps onto my lips.

"From the moment I first laid eyes on her."

Tony looks at me, smiling gently.

"She doesn't understand what it is, does she?"

I shrug my shoulders at the same time as shaking my head. I really don't know what she knows right now. Tony tips his head back towards the lounge, and we all leave so as not to wake her. Leaving the door open behind us.

We head back into the lounge, where Richard and Jon are sitting with a drink in hand. Carl walks over to the coffee table to pour three more before handing one to Tony and me. I take mine and thank him before walking over to the window. I look out towards the now quiet town and try to work out how the night took such a drastic turn.

We had all been having so much fun. Daisy was happy and safe, but it all changed in a heartbeat, and I didn't even notice until it was nearly too late. I let her down again.

"We let her down. It's not all your fault," my wolf adds.

"She feels it too, you know; I have seen the way she looks at you. The way she responds to the sheer mention of you. She just doesn't know what it all means." I hear Tony say from where he is standing. I close my eyes, leaning my head against the cold glass.

"What are you on about?" Jon asks. No one answers. They are waiting for me to be the one to tell him. I almost smile realising that he is probably the last to know, which he may kill me for. The others have all picked up on how Daisy and I have acted around each other tonight. "Mikey?"

"Daisy is my mate."

I hear Jon gasp behind me. I pull myself away from the window to turn and face the room.

Tony is standing by the door smiling, Jon is pale, with a look of complete shock on his face, and Richard is leaning into Carl. The latter is sat on the arm of the chair beside him, Carl's arm around his mate's shoulders, neither of them looking shocked as I suspected.

"Well, that explains why you just threatened to kill that Kellan prick and why you were so obsessed with the girl this evening."

I look at Jon and smile sheepishly. I should have known he would notice my behaviour this evening was different around Daisy. "But as if you never told me! I knew something was different about you recently, but I never dreamt it was this. I thought it was just a crush or something. This is huge!" he shouts, jumping from the sofa, launching himself at me, and pulling me into a bear hug. I quickly shush him, telling him to keep the noise down, but he just pulls away from me, smiling, and then punches me on the arm.

"What the hell, Jonny?" I ask, rubbing my now bruised bicep.

"That's for not telling me and letting the demon kid know before me."

"Hey, I'm right here. It's not my fault your wolf brain is too thick to work it out yourself," Tony protests. Jon just turns and flips him the bird, which Tony replicates with his own one-finger salute. Jon laughs before turning back to me.

"Hey, it's got nothing to do with the wolf brain. I worked it out the moment I saw the way Mikey couldn't take his eyes off her this evening," Richard says, winking at me.

"Bitches please; everyone could see they have it bad for each other. That's not just a booty-call look. That's a mate look!" Carl laughs as he looks up and smiles.

Jon looks around the room, amazed; he then turns back to me, grinning.

"Mum is going to have pups; you know this, right?"

I roll my eyes, walking away from him to sit on the sofa.

"What's been going on, Mikey? Why do you look so worried? Is it because she's your student?" Richard asks. I look up at him, shaking my head; I can honestly say that is one thing that doesn't bother me about everything.

"I have my notice ready to hand in," I admit for the first time out loud. A couple of people whistle, and I just shrug. "If Daisy wants to accept our bond, then I will quit so we don't have to hide. If she wants to reject me, then I will leave, as there is no way I can see her every day and not be with her."

"You really think she will reject you?" Jon asks as he sits beside me; again, I shrug my shoulders. I hear Tony chuckle from his spot by the door. I look over to find him grinning.

"There is no way that girl is going to reject you. Firstly, have you seen you? No girl is going to turn down a lifetime of looking at that." He holds his hand out in my direction and waves it up and down.

"He has a point. If I was single, I certainly wouldn't say no." Richard says from his seat; Carl slaps his chest.

"Hey! I am sat right here, you know!" he points out as Richard laughs and he kisses his mate's head.

"Yes, you are, and I wouldn't change you for the world," he quickly adds, kissing his mate again.

"Better," Carl mumbles as he leans back into Richard. I can't help but smile, watching them interact together.

"Anyway, secondly," Tony says, laughing, "The way you two were tonight, you weren't fooling anyone. We all knew you were holding hands under that table. Even if we didn't know about the hand-holding, there was no way we could miss the way you were both flirting with each other. As well as staring into each other's eyes, like no one else at that table mattered. So just talk to her and let her know what you are to each other; I know you both will feel better for it." I watch as his face becomes solemn as he continues.

"But be warned, I will not think twice about cremating you if you hurt her in any way. I will make sure your body is never found. That girl is the most important person in the world to me; she is my best friend and my big sister from another mister, all in one gorgeous package. You hurt her; you sign your own death warrant as I will do anything for her."

I look up at Tony, who looks at me. I don't doubt him in the slightest. I know how much he cares for Daisy.

"If I ever hurt her, you have my permission to kill me. I don't think I could live with the thought of causing that woman an ounce of pain," I reply. I look at Jon, who is still grinning; I feel a smile spread on my face. Could this finally be happening?

I open my mouth to ask Tony what my next move should be. When I hear a groan followed by a thud coming from the bedroom, I jump to my feet and push past everyone.

I rush into the bedroom and find Daisy lying on the floor, curled up in the fetal position, groaning. Her hair is soaked in sweat, her skin boiling to the touch.

"Call Edward!" I shout to no one in particular. Tony is next to me as I lift her head and place it on my lap. Shushing her to try and calm her, I hear a gasp as she mutters my name before moaning in pain again. I try to lift her off the floor to put her back on the bed, but she screams out in pain, so I have no choice but to put her back down.

I start stroking her head in the hope of soothing her. I don't think I have ever felt as helpless as I do right now. I remember back to her first shift in front of me. It's just like that, but this is so much worse. I can hear Carl on the phone to Edward, the pack healer. I listen to him telling Edward that she's my mate. I turn to look at Carl as he holds the phone out for me to take. I ask him to put it on the loudspeaker and hear Edward's voice instantly.

"Michael, have you marked her yet?"

"No, what do I do? It's like her wolf is trying to force a shift, but the drugs have confused it." I feel Daisy tense again as a new wave passes through her. I feel her back arch as the shift starts to progress, then stop again, "Fuck Edward, tell me what to do. She's losing control," I shout as the panic sets in.

"Shift Michael, your wolf should be able to calm hers." I lift her head from my lap to move away from her; she starts moaning and crying out as soon as I'm out of her reach. I freeze, not wanting to leave her for a moment but knowing I need to shift.

"MICHAEL NOW!" Tony shouts as Daisy screams. I don't even attempt to strip. I step back and shift. The second I'm a wolf, I move back to her and curl up around her as Tony moves out of the way. As soon as I'm lying down next to her, she relaxes; she turns so she can curl into me, threading her fingers into my fur. Her heart rate begins to lower, back to an almost average pace. I can feel her wolf there, relaxing now that mine is close.

As her heart rate decreases back to its normal rate, her body temperature lowers, too. In less than a minute, she is completely calm and fast asleep. I move slightly as she lifts her head so she can use one of my front legs as a pillow. I love how she is instantly relaxed by having me near; there are no words for how amazing that feels. I just wish it hadn't taken some prick drugging her to experience it.

I can hear Carl giving Edward an update on the situation, but I am not paying attention. All that matters is that Daisy is calm and curled up to me. I relax and wrap my body around her further. I hear my name on her lips as she falls back into a deep sleep. I close my eyes as my nose rests on her head. Allowing myself to just enjoy the feel of her touch and being so close to her.

Chapter Fourteen

DAISY

As soon as I start waking up, I know something is seriously wrong. I open my eyes and look around the strange room I'm in. My heart starts racing. It almost stops completely when I sense somebody behind me. I jump off the bed and grab hold of the first thing that I see: a bedside lamp. I spin around and face the bed. There, kneeling on it is Tony, holding his hands up in defence.

"Daisy, it's only me. You're okay. I promise." I'm not okay; I am far from okay.

"Where the fuck am I?" I yell; I can hear noises outside the room. Tony hears them, too, and shouts out.

"We're okay. Give us a minute, guys." No one replies, but I hear the footsteps retreating. "We are above The Crows. Richard and Carl let us crash here last night. That was them then. You know they would never hurt you. What do you remember?"

"Nothing! I don't remember anything! What the fuck happened, Tony?" I watch as he slowly moves towards me.

"Don't. Don't come near me." He stops abruptly and nods once.

"Whatever you need, Daisy, I'm right here. I'm not going anywhere."

Not going anywhere.

Why do I remember somebody saying that to me? I feel my head jump up as I remember.

"Where's Michael? He was here. He promised me he wouldn't leave."

Tony nods. I can feel my whole body shaking. Whether it's from panic, fear, or anxiety, I just know I want it to stop.

"He didn't want to leave. He tried everything to stay. But he had promised to take his mum to his auntie's. Michael wanted to be here when you woke up. He only left an hour ago. I can call him back if you want?" Tony pulls his phone out of his pocket before holding it up for me. I want to take it and call Michael. I need him here; I need to know what happened. I don't feel safe or like I have any control of the situation. Michael will help me regain control. He'll protect me; I know he will. I can't concentrate on anything other than the need to have Michael here.

"It's okay. Michael said that you're to call him if you need him; he doesn't mind. He'll want to know you are awake anyway." Tony's face softens, "He really didn't want to leave you, Daisy, but it was a family situation he couldn't ignore."

I look at the phone in Tony's hand again. As much as I want to call Michael back here, I won't. He is helping his mum; she is more important than me having a meltdown. I shake my head as I slide down the wall that's behind me. Once on the floor, I place the lamp next to me. I pull my knees up to my chest and wrap my arms around them.

I sit silently for a few seconds, trying desperately to

understand what is happening. Tony slowly makes his way over to me; I don't look up, but I know he is taking his time to make sure I don't freak out on him again.

"I'm okay," I say quietly. I feel Tony slide down next to me. He places an arm around my shoulders and pulls me to him. I rest my head on his shoulder.

"Are you sure?" I feel a curt laugh burst from me before I can stop it. I look up at him.

"No, not in the slightest. What the hell happened? How the hell did I wake up here with no recollection of what happened? Was I drugged?" I watch as Tony nods his head.

"Tell me what you remember, and I will try to fill in the gaps." I sit there silently, trying to think.

"I really don't recall much. I remember the band finishing; I ordered a drink at last rounds; I wasn't drunk enough for that last drink to have pushed me over the edge. I danced with some random people as Beth had gone to get food. But then I started feeling lightheaded. I thought I was just hot from dancing all night, so I went outside for some fresh air. I knew then that something was very wrong; Kellan was there, so I asked him to get Michael for me. He said Michael had just left with some woman and that he had heard them trying to decide whether to head to the nearest hotel or her place."

The pain in my chest tightens as I remember thinking Michael had played me. I can feel tears falling down my cheek as my heart starts to break again. Tony near enough explodes next to me.

"He said what?! The son of a fucking bitch lied to you! Michael never left the bar! He was still there when he found out you were missing. Trust me, Daisy, there was no other woman. Kellan is fucking jealous, that's all. The prick is sick in the head." I don't even question Tony, as some part of me knew Kellan was lying to me. I don't remember anything after that. The drugs must have been in that last drink.

Tony explains that Beth had gone looking for me after returning with the food, but I'd gone; Tony had rushed home to check if I was there.

Apparently, I was missing for an hour, and it was Michael who found me down a dirty alleyway. I place my face in my hands, hiding from the embarrassment.

"I can't believe he saw me like that. He must think I was a right idiot letting myself get drugged." Tony reaches up and flicks me on the top of the ear. "Ouch, what was that for?"

He looks at me, annoyed; I feel myself leaning back from him; Tony never gets annoyed at me.

"For thinking that Michael would think you were an idiot for having your drink spiked! Do you have any idea how frightened that man was when we couldn't find you? He was furious when he realised someone had drugged you. He wouldn't let anyone else near you; he looked after you all night."

I feel my eyes filling with tears again.

"He really looked after me?"

Tony looks at me wide-eyed, nodding.

"That might actually be the understatement of the century." Tony tightens his hold on me. "Dais, he carried you through town, bringing you here. He then took care of you as your body rejected the drugs. Your wolf went into a panic and started to shift, but it couldn't complete it and became confused. So, he shifted himself, shredding his clothes to save time. He then lay down on the floor with you all night in wolf form just to ensure your wolf was at ease and stayed dormant. He didn't leave your side, not once, in case you started to shift again. I'm not lying when I say he didn't want to leave you today. The poor man was torn between you and his mum. I near enough had to force him out the door, knowing that you would understand."

I'm speechless. I can't believe he did all that. Little snippets of last night come back to me. Michael was holding my hair whilst I was sick, and there was a feeling of fur in between my fingers, surrounding me and making me feel warm and protected. The gentle touch of a wolf's nose on my cheek, wrapping itself around me. The tears start falling freely again.

"Why would he look after me like that?" Tony just lifts one eyebrow whilst tipping his head.

"Probably the same reason you two were flirting and holding hands under the table last night. Yes, we all knew; the more you two drank, the more obvious you were. So now are you going to tell me you don't know why he would do all that for you?" Another snippet of memory plays in my head. Was it from last night or this morning? Michael's soft voice as he whispers into my hair as he softly kisses my temple.

"I'm done pretending. I'm not hiding how I feel about you anymore. You are mine, and I will do all I can to make you realise we belong together."

Michael

"Mum, where are you?" I call out as I close the front door behind me.

"Mikey, is that you?" I hear her calling from upstairs.

"No, it's a burglar. I just wanted to lead you into a false

sense of security by calling you Mum," I call back, rolling my eyes.

"Well, whilst you rob me, make me a cup of tea to make up for the inconvenience, will you?"

"Are you not ready to go yet? I only have a couple of hours spare." I pull my phone out of my pocket and check it for the tenth time since I left Daisy. I hate not knowing if she is awake yet or if she's okay. What if her wolf tries to shift again?

"I will be ready when I'm ready. Now put the kettle on, as I'm not leaving until I have a cup of tea."

I find myself growling as I walk into the kitchen and switch on the kettle.

I am just putting Mum's favourite mug on the table when I see her enter the kitchen. She walks over so I can plant a kiss on her cheek before heading to the sink to wash her hands. I look over at her and smile.

My mum hasn't changed since the day I was born. She had my sister and me young, so she is only now in her late fifties, although she doesn't look a day over forty-five. Her short brown hair is still cut into the same bob you see in every picture of her from the age of fifteen. I once asked her why she doesn't grow it out; she responded, "Why? The only person I ever wanted to impress was your father. Even though he has passed away, I like to think he looks down on me and falls in love with me again every day." I couldn't really argue with that, could I.

"Well, I know I'm asking a lot for you to take me to your auntie's today, but it's not like you had anything else on. So lose the face."

I turn and look at her as I lean against the door frame.

"I wasn't aware I had a face on," I snap. Mum just looks at me, raising her eyebrows.

"Want to tell me what's crawled up your backside and why you are wearing…" she sniffs the air quickly, "Carl's clothes?"

"Because I had to stay at theirs last night, and my clothes got damaged."

Mum just looks at me, and I can see the disappointment in her eyes; she thinks I was fighting in the bar.

"Look, I'm sorry I've had near to no sleep and a very long, eventful night. Which I realise I may need to tell you about."

"Why do I have a feeling I need to be sitting down for this." I watch as she pulls out her favourite chair and sits down. At only five foot one, she always looks so tiny, sat at the massive wooden table my dad built when we were kids. "Go on, what's happened?" she asks, placing her elbows on the table and leaning on her hands.

"Why do you look so worried?" I ask, unable to stop the smile that creeps on my face. Mum lifts one eyebrow at me again.

"Because I have dealt with you and your brother for twenty-eight years. I know when one of you turns up in another person's clothes, saying it was an eventful night, as well as you have something to tell me that I need to be prepared for the worst." I have to laugh as she is not wrong, especially when it comes to Jonathan.

"Well, for once, it's not all bad; it's complicated, and you need to remember that when I tell you. But it will hopefully all be good in the end."

"Okay, I am listening."

I take a deep breath.

"I had to stay at Carl and Richard's last night as a student, who is also a wolf, had her drink spiked with what we believe to be a date rape drug." I watch my mum's eyes widen.

"Did they get hurt? Did they lose control of their wolf? Did you get hurt, which is why your clothes got damaged?" I hold my hands up to stop her bombardment of questions.

"Mum, please, let me tell you everything first. Then you can ask questions, but please drink up as I need to get you to Auntie Sherri's so I can get back and check on them."

"Okay, you start talking. I'll start drinking." I shake my head as I sit down in my usual seat next to her.

"As I was saying, a student was drugged and reacted badly to them. We had already safely gotten her into the flat above the bar when she started to shift. However, her wolf didn't know what to do because of what she was given, and she couldn't complete the change. We contacted Edward, and he told me to shift so that my wolf could calm hers. I didn't wait to strip; I just shifted there and then. It worked, though, and her wolf settled back down. She slept all night in human form, curled up with my wolf." I can tell by Mum's face that she is putting it all together.

"Why was it you that had to shift and not one of the others?"

"Because it was only my wolf who would have calmed her."

"Because?" I can tell she knows, but she is waiting for me to say it, like last night with the guys.

"Because she's my mate."

Mum's hand flies up to her mouth.

"You've met her?" I can see the tears in her eyes, her throat bobbing as she tries to stop herself from crying.

"Yes, Mum, I have finally met her, and she is amazing and smart and has a comeback for everything anyone throws at her. She has no problem with putting me in my place." I can see Mum bursting at the seams with excitement.

"And she is okay after last night? She's recovering?" I pick up my phone and see a message from Carl.

Carl: Daisy is awake. She was very confused and agitated when she first came to, but Tony talked her down. They're still talking, but she is calmer and knows that you looked after her all night. Maybe it's worth giving her a little time and then calling her later. Will keep you updated. But she is in one piece and in complete control of her wolf. So relax, she will be okay with us.

I show Mum the message, rather than reading it out, before replying.

Michael: I should be there. I shouldn't have left her. Tell her to call me if she needs me. I will call her as soon as I get back from taking Mum. Thank you for watching over her for me. I know Tony will know what she needs right now. Just please make sure she knows I didn't want to leave her.

I should have been there when she woke up. I should have stayed.

"Why didn't you ask Jon to take me today? I wouldn't have minded."

I lean back into my chair and rub my eyes. I am so tired and wired at the same time.

"The bastard wouldn't answer his phone. He left us around three AM and went back to mine. He didn't pick up, and I didn't have time to wake him up to come and drive you." My mum leans over and cups my cheek. She is the only person I will ever be able to put over Daisy. Mum is

Jonathan' and my world; there is nothing we wouldn't do for her.

"Okay, so let's go and get in the car, and we can talk on the way."

I nod as we stand. I grab Mum's bag whilst she locks up. Once we are settled in the car and on the road, she starts with the questions.

"How long have you known? Why did you say it was complicated?"

"It's complicated, as she is one of my students and has had a rough time since she was bitten." I watch as Mum's face softens. She leans over and places her hand on top of mine, squeezing it to give me the encouragement I need.

"Tell me what you can." So, I do.

I tell Mum all about the first day I saw Daisy sitting on that bench and how I felt the second her scent hit my nose. I tell her all about how intelligent and funny Daisy is and how she's so unbelievably strong. I tell her how Daisy suffers from panic attacks with the sheer mention of the arsehole who changed her. I can't stop boasting about how amazing she was the other night, changing and running and just being herself.

The whole time, Mum doesn't say a word. I see her wiping away the occasional stray tear from her cheek or laughing when she hears how Daisy has no problem putting me in my place. Or anyone else who oversteps the mark.

"I know that I need to take things slow, and I have no idea when or even if she will be ready for a relationship. But I will always be there for her, and I swear I will find the person who bit her, and I'll make him pay so that she never has to be scared of anyone ever again." My mum reaches over and places her hand over mine.

"Mikey, I wish you had spoken to me about this sooner,

but I understand why you didn't. That poor girl really has had it tough, and I am so proud of you for the way you have handled everything."

I glance over at her, frowning.

"I haven't done anything."

"Yes, you have. You've given her space, even though I know it must have killed you. You have let her have a typical student life, as it sounds like she has been held back for so long. She has experienced things she wouldn't have. Even though you hid on the outskirts, you made sure she was safe the whole time. But most of all, you have not given up on her, and you are letting her find her own way to you. Because it sounds like she is doing just that. I honestly believe that very soon, you will both get the happiness you deserve. Just carry on being there for her and let her know she is safe with you. She will appreciate it and love you more for it." I look at Mum and know that she's speaking from the heart.

"Did you realise that the whole time you were talking about Daisy, you never once used the words beautiful, gorgeous or any other description of her looks?"

"She's the most beautiful woman I've ever seen, but what she is on the inside is so much more. She's perfect beyond words, but her looks are just a bonus."

"That right there is how you know she is the one."

I look over at her and smile.

"I've never doubted it; that girl ruined me the second I smelt her scent. I told her this morning that I'm not pretending anymore that she is mine, as much as I am hers."

"No one deserves this more than you and her, Mikey. You have spent your life putting everybody else first. It's time to take time for you and Daisy."

I pull up outside of my auntie's and get out to help Mum with her bag; she is already standing by the garden gate when I get there. She takes the bag out of my hand and pulls me into a tight hug.

"Be happy, Mikey. Let yourself be loved and allow yourself to feel it," she whispers into my ear before she steps away from me. She gently places a hand on my cheek.

"Thank you, Mama."

She pulls my face down to her so she can kiss me on the cheek.

"You may be twice the size of me, but you will always be my baby. Now go and see your girl. She needs you more than I do right now. I will let your auntie know why you couldn't stay. Get going before you get dragged into the dragon's den."

I laugh and kiss her on the cheek before heading towards the car.

"Love ya, Mama," I call back.

"Love you, Mikey. Drive safely and bring this wonderful girl to see me as soon as you can," she shouts, smirking from the gate.

"What happened to taking it slow?"

"I don't count; I'm your Mama, which makes me hers too," she calls as the front door opens, and I have to drive off before Auntie Sherri sees me.

Chapter Fifteen

DAISY

Since waking up in The Crows, I have been struggling to keep my anxiety at bay. Waking up in a strange room like that brought back so many memories for me. Ones I'm trying desperately to put behind me.

Even though Tony, Carl, and Richard all promised me I was safe and that no harm had come to me physically, I can't stop thinking, "What if?"

What if Michael hadn't found me when he had?

What if he hadn't been able to calm my wolf down?

It's all too much to process. So, I've come to my favourite place in an attempt to do something, anything, other than obsess about last night.

My step falters as I walk through the front door, and the smell of old books hits me. Is there any better place to come to unwind and to think than a library? I greet the librarian as I walk past the front desk, heading to my usual spot, right at the back of the building. There is the comfiest chair I've ever sat in. I love to come here to study. It's always so much quieter than the library at the university; it's more extensive and better stocked as well. Michael had suggested trying here for some research material a couple of months back. I've been a regular visitor since.

Once, I picked out a few reference books, I make myself comfortable in my chair. Tucking my legs up underneath me, I place my headphones into my ears and turn my study playlist on low on my old, trusted MP3 player. Balancing my folder on my bent knees, I put a couple of books I had picked up next to me. Wishing I had a coffee with me, I start working on my notes for the essay I'd planned on finishing today. But as hard as I try to get into the swing of it, I keep thinking about last night.

Every time I think about it, I feel myself starting to shake. I'm instantly back there, waking up tied to that stinking mattress in the room he held me.

I quickly shake my head in an attempt to push it all to the back of my mind. I don't want to remember it anymore. I don't want to remember the smells, the feel of the mattress against my skin, or how cold I was as I wasn't allowed a blanket.

"Stop, you are safe. You aren't there," my wolf whispers. I try, I really do. I attempt to distract myself by reading through my notes again. After five minutes, I realise I'm still trying to read through the first page. Nothing is going in; I just keep flashing back to that first night. I lean my head against the back of the chair, throw my arms over my eyes and moan out loud.

"Sounds like someone needs this."

My head shoots back up, pulling my headphones out as I move. Sending my folder crashing to the floor. Standing in front of me is Michael, holding out a cup from my favourite coffee shop. I look up at him, amazed.

"Is that for me?" I ask. Michael smiles, his signature

one-sided grin making my heart race. God, this man is something else. He reaches down, picks up my folder, and places it on the table.

"I hope so because I don't know anybody else who would want a full-fat caramel latte with two added shots of coffee plus extra caramel," he winks as he takes a step towards me so I can take the coffee from his hand. I can't believe he is actually here, holding my favourite coffee. He really is every woman's dream guy.

"Thank you." I take a sip, closing my eyes and savouring that first sip of milky heaven. "I need this right now. But how did you know my order?"

"You told me the other day that you had been with Beth and Tony for coffee in BEANS. You mentioned it's your favourite place as they have your favourite caramel syrup and let you have two shots of it. I also noticed you always have flavoured lattes in class, which always smell stronger than most people's. So, I put the two together. Seems I was right judging by your face right now," he laughs as he sits down in the chair to the side of mine. I just sit, shocked that he remembers all the little details.

"You went to a lot of trouble, thank you," I smile as his face softens.

"Maybe it was worth it just to see you smile. You looked stressed when I walked in. Is everything okay? How are you feeling after last night?" Just as I open my mouth to answer, a librarian approaches us.

"Excuse me, there is a no food or drinks policy here," she says sternly, pointing to a sign on the wall. As I am about to apologise and tell her we will take it outside, Michael turns and faces her. I see the moment she realises just how gorgeous he is; her jaw drops, and her eyes fill with lust.

"I am so sorry, it's completely my fault. I had no idea; I just wanted to surprise my friend as she'd had a rough time. If I promise we won't spill a drop and will finish them as quickly as possible, will you please let us off this once?"

Is he flirting with her? I watch as she becomes flustered and starts to flutter her eyelashes at him. Oh, dear goddess, he is!

"No, no, it's fine. I will … I'll just pretend I haven't seen anything." With that, she spins around and hurries back the way that she came. Michael turns back to me, smiling as I start giggling and shaking my head at him.

"Did you enjoy doing that to her?"

Michael frowns, looking confused.

"What do you mean?" Does he really not realise the effect he has on women?

"You know full well what you just did to that poor woman. I wouldn't be surprised if she comes back in a bit trying to give you her number," I reply, laughing. I watch as Michael looks in the direction the librarian went, then back at me.

"Do you really think she thought I was flirting with her?" He looks so shocked; I can't stop myself from laughing.

"Do you really not realise the effect you have on the female sex?"

"I have no idea why they act like that around me," he shrugs. I shake my head at him again. He looks up at me with that sexy, one-sided smirk on his face, as well as the sexiest eyes I have ever seen. "So, do I have that effect on you as well?" I quickly take a sip of my coffee and give him my best come-to-bed eyes.

"Wouldn't you like to know?" I wiggle my eyebrows at him. Michael leans forward, giving me a look that makes a knot form deep in my core, causing my thighs to clamp together tightly as an aching sensation spreads between my legs. I watch as Michael glances down at my legs as his smile widens.

"I think I already do." I find myself biting my bottom lip, wishing it was his. His eyes travel to my lips and become darker; there is something almost primal about them. We both stare at each other, locked in a moment. A moment which could see us both tearing each other's clothes off right here in the library or us leaving extremely frustrated. Michael seems to come to the same realisation and sits back in his chair. I watch as he lets out a deep breath and then winks at me. Extreme frustration it is, then.

"You did that to prove a point, didn't you?" I huff. Michael smirks as I slump back into my chair, folding my arms across my chest, pretending to sulk. Michael just keeps staring at me with that goddamn smirk on his face. I pick up my coffee and take a sip, trying to calm my racing heart. "I hope you are happy with yourself playing with people's emotions and hearts like that."

Michael's face alters slightly, but just as quickly, his smile returns.

"I don't play when it comes to the heart. Especially yours." The knot in my lower stomach tightens; this man is good. But, knowing I need to do something before I end up begging him to take me right here against the shelves, I change the topic. Reluctantly.

"How did you know I was here?"

Michael leans back into his chair, sipping his coffee.

"I messaged Tony as you weren't answering your phone."

I dig my phone out of my bag and see I have missed calls and a few text messages.

"Shit, sorry, I had it on silent. I have a habit of doing that. Everything okay?"

Michael nods.

"I just wanted to check how you are. Carl messaged me earlier and told me you freaked out when you woke up." Michael leans forward in his chair. "I'm so sorry I wasn't there. I hated leaving you. Mum had to be at Auntie Sherri's as she is having surgery in the morning. Jon wasn't answering his bloody phone, so I had to take her."

I place my face in my hands and moan with embarrassment. I had been so humiliated when I realised Carl and Richard had heard my mini freak out.

"I still can't believe everything that happened. The only thing I remembered when I first woke up was you saying you wouldn't leave."

"Tony said. I really didn't want to leave you, Daisy; I'm so sorry I had to. Why didn't you call me when he offered you his phone? I would have come to you or at least talked to you until you felt calmer."

I lower my hands from my face before leaning over and taking Michael's, which is resting on his leg.

"Because you were with your mum, I'm not selfish enough to demand you choose me over her," I reply, smiling at him, "I'm so glad you found me when you did last night." I watch Michael's eyes close, and he takes a deep breath while squeezing my hand. He moves off the chair and kneels in front of me, folding his arms over my knees and taking my hands in his.

"Not being able to find you was one of the scariest moments of my life. When I think of what could have happened-" I cut him off and place a finger over his lips. I quickly glance around to check we are alone before looking back at Michael.

"But I'm fine, and it's all thanks to you. I will never be able to thank you for what you did for me. Tony told me how you shifted to calm my ... to calm me."

Michael places a hand on my cheek. I feel my head leaning into his touch, his warmth.

"I don't want you to thank me. I have told you before and will tell you again: I will always comfort you, protect you and find you. Whatever you need of me, I'll do it. Nothing on this Earth can stop me from being there for you." I feel his thumb run over my cheek, and a calming sensation spreads slowly through me.

"Tony also told me what Kellan said about me leaving with another woman. But, darling, I can promise you there was nobody else. When I left you lying on that bed this morning, I told you something. I told you I'm done acting like this between us is just playful flirting. I refuse to continue hiding my feelings from you anymore."

I look straight into his eyes as I finally open myself up to him.

"I don't want to hide anymore, either. It feels like my heart is being ripped apart every time I'm with you, and I have to pretend that you are *just* my lecturer or *just* a friend. Because you are so much more than *just* anything."

"What am I?" he asks quietly. I lean forward until our foreheads are resting against each other. I place my hand over his on my cheek. Closing my eyes as I whisper.

"My mate."

There is only a moment's pause before Michael's lips crash into mine. I throw my arms around him, pulling him as close to me as I can in the position we're in. Michael's tongue runs across my lips, which I open greedily for him, hungry to feel his tongue against mine. Just as my hands find his hair, noise from within the library causes us to separate. We look at each other and start laughing.

"If we nearly got kicked out over coffee, we definitely will for making out for all to see," I laugh as I lean my head into his shoulder, my arms around his neck as he pulls me against him, chuckling.

We stay holding each other for a few precious moments, both breathing deeply as we relax, enjoying the closeness and the fact that it's now out there. We are true fated mates, and everything we have been fighting against since September is now out in the open between us.

"I've waited so long to hear you call me your mate. I was starting to wonder if the day would ever come." He pulls away from me, so we are face to face again, both grinning like a couple of teenagers. Michael leans in to kiss me again, but his phone rings, interrupting us.

"Shit. I'm so sorry," he curses as he pulls away, leaving me breathless, wanting to throw his phone out of the nearest window. "Alpha." I quickly busy myself, realising that it's obviously important, and I start gathering my stuff together. "Can't Marcus lead just this once … oh shit, okay, I'll sort it." Michael hangs up and looks at me.

"I'm so sorry, there has been a pack issue which I need to take care of." He jumps to his feet and grabs both of our now empty cups. He looks down at me, torn between staying and doing what his Alpha has asked of him. It's almost impossible to ignore an Alpha's order. But I think Michael is considering doing just that.

"It's okay, go. I will be waiting for your call when you have time. I understand."

He quickly places the cups back onto the table and grabs my hands to pull me to my feet straight into his arms. As he wraps his arms around my shoulders, I wrap mine around his waist, resting my head against his firm chest. It feels so good to be here, encased in his strong arms.

"I feel like all I'm doing today is leaving you. I'm so sorry." He leans down and kisses the top of the head. "Keep away from Kellan. Something tells me that he spiked your drink last night, and I think he may try something else. If you need me for anything, call me. I don't care what time of day or night it is."

Michael places a finger under my chin, lifting my head so that he can look me in the eyes. Slowly, he leans down and gently touches his lips to mine for the softest of kisses. A few seconds later, he pulls away from me and gently kisses me on the forehead.

"It may not be much of a kiss, but if I kiss you properly again, I really won't leave. However, I promise you the next one will leave you weak at the knees," he winks at me as he turns and walks away. He looks back one last time before rushing out of sight, his phone already by his ear.

"Marcus, get the call out. We meet in half an hour at HQ," is all I hear as he walks away, leaving me speechless, weak at the knees and touching my just kissed lips.

Damn, that man is smooth.

Chapter Sixteen

MICHAEL

"Stuart, find him. He's gotten past Will."

"On it, boss," Stuart's voice calls out through the earpiece. I look around, spotting Will and Jon. I know Marcus will also be close by. We've been hunting a rogue for the past twenty-four hours. Every time we get close to him, he gets away again; he knows this area too well. Or he has been on the run for so long that he knows all the tricks. He doesn't realise that the longer I run around after him, the longer I go without seeing or speaking to Daisy, which puts me in an even worse mood. I am well and truly pissed off, which does not bode well for him when I finally get my hands on him.

This rogue has been coming onto our pack land and has assaulted two separate women who had been running when he spotted them. That automatically gets our attention, as it's essential our pack feels safe on their own land. Also, no rogue should be able to get on to our territory and off again without somebody knowing about it.

These types of attacks are incredibly personal to our

team after what happened to my sister. They are too similar. I immediately checked his scent to see if it was the same wolf, but it wasn't.

This guy is a real piece of work. He's wanted for a string of sexual assaults on women, not just the two on our land. The last thing we need is a rogue in custody, especially as it's too close to home and a full moon in a couple of days. If he is caught before, then he could be forced to shift in the cell. I don't think I need to explain why that would be the worst thing that could happen. There would be no way of hiding what we are if there were witnesses as well as CCTV.

"Boss, I have him. He has run to the trees around the corner. He was taking off his top; I think he's going to shift."

"Fuck," I curse as we all head at speed to Stuart's location. I can hear sirens getting closer in the distance. "Double fuck."

As soon as we get to the trees, I hear moaning and cursing from within.

"Boss, what's the plan? He is getting fully undressed. Are we still going to bring him in?" I think for a second. This rogue is dangerous. He's a threat, not only to women but also to exposing our kind to the human world. We had hoped to capture him alive, but then he attempted to attack another woman tonight; he sealed his own fate. Luckily, we intervened, and the woman was unharmed, but she called the police, and now they are out in force searching for him.

I'm about to start throwing out commands when I hear a howl. Oh great. Just freaking great.

"I'm going in." I strip down completely; as Jon appears to my right, he grabs my clothes and equipment, shoving them into a bag.

"What are you planning, Mikey?" I look at him and see that he is down to his joggers.

"I'm going to chase him back towards pack territory. There, we capture him if we can. Otherwise, you know what I need to do." Jon nods. I can tell from his face he isn't happy about it; we never are, but sometimes we have no choice but to take out the rogues that are too much of a threat. I drop to my knee. Before I even touch the ground, paws are in front of me rather than hands within a second.

"Be careful, bro," Jon whispers to me as he turns around, jogging in the direction he came from.

I stretch my wolf's body quickly before heading off in the direction of the rogue's scent. I find it easy as my senses are the strongest in this form. I run, knowing that I must find him before he gets away again. I spot Marcus's wolf to my right and Will's to the left, both keeping their distance, waiting for my command. I communicate with them through our mind link, letting them know I see them and to be ready for anything.

I hear a whimper and quickly slow my pace; the others do the same. I can't feel Jon or Stuart, so I know they are staying on two legs so they can intervene with any humans that may get too close.

I crouch behind a bush, peering through it, and find the rogue lying down on the ground, recovering from his shift. He is obviously newly bitten; no blood wolf would need this much time to recover. I watch as he pants, not even attempting to get up. It's now or never if I want to get the element of surprise on him.

I jump out of my hiding space and land next to him; I can smell the fear pouring from him, but there is also an equal amount of arrogance. I shift back after checking the others are still close and hidden. I hate leaving myself vulnerable, but I need to communicate with him.

"Can you shift?" I ask; he shakes his head but gets to his feet and growls at me. He tries to intimidate me. "You are already in enough shit, so I would fucking behave if I was you. We know who you are, and we know what you've done. If you wish to live through this, you will shut up and do as you are told. Is that understood?" The wolf looks at me, and even though I watch as he bows his head in submission, I can't mistake the look in his eyes. *Fuck.*

As he springs towards me, I jump at him, taking him down and shifting simultaneously. We roll around in wolf form, snarling and teeth clashing for a few seconds until I get him pinned on his back, my jaw around his throat. I growl to let him know I am not backing down. But he keeps trying to fight me.

"Michael, the police are coming," I hear Marcus through the mind link. I tighten my grip on the rogue's neck, hoping he will stop, and he does. I look at him and see in his eyes that he will fight me as soon as my grip loosens again. I don't want to do this; I don't like this part of my role and will always give extra chances to avoid it. I put it to the test and loosen my grip on his throat, but the second I move just a tiny bit, he tries to get the jump on me.

This time, when my teeth find his neck, they don't stop until his blood hits the inside of my mouth, and his body goes limp.

Chapter Seventeen

MICHAEL

It's been four days since I left Daisy in the library. Four days since my lips last briefly brushed against hers. Four long days since I told her how I felt, and we decided to stop fighting the bond between us. It has been the longest four days of my life. Although we have texted and spoken on the phone at some point every day, it's not the same. I'm ready to spend some quality time with her, even if it is with my brother.

Tonight, it's a full moon, and Jon has invited himself along for a run with Daisy and me in the forest. I'd been looking forward to spending some time just the two of us. However, I also want Daisy to feel comfortable around other wolves whilst in wolf form. What better wolf to start with than my brother? He is great at putting people at ease, even if his sole purpose in life is to piss me off.

As soon as the small parking bay comes into view, I see Daisy's car and smile. Seems I'm not the only one eager tonight, as I'm fifteen minutes early.

I park next to Daisy and get out of the car. I turn and

lean against my roof, looking over at her. She is already standing by her driver's side door, looking straight at me with the most beautiful smile. Unfortunately, Jon blocks my view of her as he removes himself from my car. He throws me a cheeky wink before turning to face Daisy.

"There she is, my new baby sister," Jon claims excitedly, holding his arms out and pulling Daisy into a hug. She laughs as she hugs him back.

"Jonathan. So, it's not just alcohol that makes you annoying," Daisy chuckles as she looks over his shoulder at me, smiling.

"Jon has a knack for being the most annoying person on Earth multiple times a day. You get used to it," I point out as I walk around to join them. Daisy instantly moves away from Jon and straight into my arms. I love that when I hold her like this, her head rests perfectly under my chin. I lean down and plant a kiss on her head, inhaling her heavenly scent. Gods, I've missed it.

"Hey, I can guarantee you'll love me by the end of the night. You never know; you may have some competition on your hands, little bro." Jon pushes me; I shove him back, which earns me another push. I quickly retaliate by punching his arm. As he turns to punch me, both of us grinning broadly, Daisy jumps in between us, holding her hands up.

"Children. Pack it in. Gods, are you two always like this?" she demands, with her hands now firmly on her hips.

"Yep," Jon and I reply in unison. Daisy throws her hands up in despair.

"Remind me to send your mum lots of wine and a medal for dealing with you two." The whole time, her eyes are glistening playfully; she glances over at me and starts chuckling. I love the sound of her laugh; it never fails to make me smile.

"Oh, she does love her wine." Jon laughs.

As I'm watching Daisy, I catch a flash of pain in her eyes as her smile falters for the briefest moment. I know she is feeling the ache of the oncoming change. I signal Jon to get the bags from the trunk of my car. He nods before walking away, giving Daisy and me a little bit of privacy.

"Hey," I whisper, looking down at her as I pull her back into my arms. Daisy smiles and looks back up at me, placing a hand against my chest.

"Hey, yourself." Her arms slowly move up and wrap around my neck, pulling me towards her. I lean down to kiss her on the lips for the first time since the library. Instantly, her fingers are in my hair, her tongue against my lips. The kiss deepening quickly. I turn us so her back is to her car as I push her up against it, desperate to feel every inch of this extraordinary woman against me.

"Yeah, I know you haven't seen each other for a few days, but we are losing time here; we need to move." Jon's voice carries from the forest. I pull away from Daisy, groaning, as I know he's right. As Daisy pushes herself away from the car, she places a hand against my chest as if to steady herself.

"Well, you weren't wrong," she giggles, trying to catch her breath; I look at her and frown. Daisy rolls her eyes and, in a deep voice, to imitate me, "I promise you the next one will leave you weak at the knees." I hear Jon laugh from where he is standing as we walk over to him, hand in hand. He claps me on the back.

"Smooth, bro, real smooth."

I just shrug, smirking.

"Left you frustrated and wanting more, didn't it?" I raise my eyebrows at her, smiling, as Daisy smirks back at me.

"Who said I'm still frustrated from then?" she says, looking at me with a sexy glint in her eye.

"Oh really? So how did you ease said frustration?"

"Oh, handsome, wouldn't you like to know." I stop in my tracks, watching as she walks ahead with that swagger she had in the bar the other night. She glances over her shoulder and blows me a kiss before walking away again. The image of her lying naked in bed, touching herself, moaning as she finds her release fills my head.

"Man, you are one lucky bastard," Jon exclaims next to me, clapping me on the shoulder before he jogs off to catch up to her. Yeah, I really am.

As soon as Jon reaches Daisy, he drapes his arm over her shoulders.

"So, any chance you would consider giving the hotter brother a trial run and then deciding which one you want to be stuck with?" he says, smirking at her. I can't stop my wolf as he growls out loud; I give Jon a warning look, but he just laughs, holding his arms up as he removes himself from Daisy. "She knows I'm only joking; I like her, but she's all yours, Mikey." Jon glances at Daisy and wiggles his eyebrows quickly, "Unless he just isn't manly enough for you, then you know where to find me," he adds, winking. Daisy shakes her head from side to side slowly.

"I am more than happy with the brother I have, thanks." She wraps her arms around my waist as I reach her. I put an arm around her shoulder, tucking her into my side. "I do have a question for you, though, Jon?" Daisy adds, looking at my brother. "How do you not trip over that big head of yours?"

Jon just waves her comment off,

"Please, I'm like a finely oiled machine in human and wolf form; I never trip." Jon is vain at the best of times. When he is showing off to someone new, he's a nightmare. Daisy doesn't seem to be buying it, though.

"Is that so?" She looks up at me, smirking. I'm sure I see her mouth something, but I get distracted by the sound of Jon cursing to the side of us.

"What's up with you?" I glance over at my brother, who is looking around at the ground.

"Nothing." He replies, looking confused. I laugh out loud when he trips, only just avoiding falling over completely. He starts looking around on the floor again. He shakes his head before continuing; Daisy is chuckling against my side. When Jon trips over completely, Daisy laughs louder and harder than I've ever seen her laugh before. She's doubled over, clutching her stomach. I start laughing as Daisy wipes tears from her eyes.

"What the fuck is going on?" Jon shouts, looking around the ground. It takes Daisy nearly a full minute to stop laughing long enough to speak.

"Not such a well-oiled machine, after all, Jonathan. Here, this may help your old eyes see better." I expect her to hold out a torch of some sort, but instead, she opens her hand, and there, hovering above her palm, is a perfect sphere of light. Jon and I both jump back in shock.

"You're a witch?" I ask, amazed. She looks at me, shocked.

"What? Didn't you know?" For a second, she looks worried.

"No, that's amazing! I had no idea." Daisy relaxes as she starts smiling again. Suddenly, it dawned on me, "Hang on. There was meant to be a witch on the course with you who never showed. Their name was N. Evans, though." I watch as Daisy looks confused.

"Nigel Evans is my uncle. There must have been a mix-up on the council's side with the names." Well, that explains a few things.

"Did you have something to do with Jon tripping?" I ask, smirking. Daisy shrugs and smiles.

"Oh, it's on witchy," Jon curses as he playfully nudges her with his shoulder.

"Bring it, wolf boy," she retaliates, punching him on the arm. I step back, watching them as they start throwing insults and punches at each other.

"Gods, what have I done letting you two meet?" They both turn to face me at the same time.

"What?" they ask innocently in unison. I throw my hands up in the air as I walk off ahead. I can hear them laughing and play fighting behind me, which brings a smile to my face. I glance over my shoulder just in time to see Daisy push Jon away from her. She looks so happy and at ease. Bringing Jon tonight has turned out to be a great idea; I see a budding friendship forming here. I can see these two are going to be a nightmare together.

I lean against a tree with my arms crossed against my chest, watching the two of them play fight. Daisy turns towards me; she has the biggest smile on her face as she jogs over before jumping into my arms. I catch her laughing as we nearly fall; the only thing stopping us is the tree I'm leaning against. Daisy presses her lips to mine quickly before jumping back down. Grabbing my hand, she pulls me in the direction of the clearing.

With me on her right and Jon on her left, the three of us make our way to where we plan to shift. Playfully, she nudges me with her shoulder; I chuckle as I throw an arm over her shoulder, pulling her closer to me again. I can't remember the last time I felt so at ease and full of life as I am when Daisy is around. I don't feel like the stoic, disciplined, assertive, and sometimes downright dull leader I have become. When Daisy is near, I feel alive again. I feel like I have a reason to be happy once again and, more importantly, that I deserve to be.

I look down at Daisy talking and laughing with Jonathan and wonder what she would think about what I did the other day. Ever since I walked away from the mission, I've dreaded her finding out that I'd taken another male's life. Could I've let him go? Could I've captured him and made him pay for his crimes another way?

"*No, you gave him the chance to come quietly, and he decided to fight you,*" my wolf clarifies. I know he's right, but the thought of this woman being scared of me or, worse, disgusted with me makes me feel weaker than I have ever felt. I look down at her again, catching her looking up at me; I can see the concern in her eyes and realise I've been trapped in my own thoughts a little too long. I quickly plaster on a smile, lean down and kiss her gently.

"What's the matter?"

I look into those bright eyes and instantly relax.

"Nothing, baby, just relax." I lean down and kiss her again quickly. I can see she isn't buying it, but she lets it drop for now. I need to be honest with her; I'll tell her everything, but not tonight. Tonight, she doesn't need the added stress.

As we walk closer to the clearing, where Daisy and I had shifted the other night, I sense her becoming increasingly tense. I lean down and gently place my lips against her hair.

Daisy looks up at me and forces a smile; her heart's beating so hard I can hear it. I look over her head to get

Jon's attention. He quickly nods and sneaks off into the trees next to him. We had already agreed that he would find his own area to shift to ensure that Daisy didn't feel any extra pressure or stress, making the shift harder on her.

"Where's Jon gone?" Daisy asks, looking around.

"He's going to change in another part, then meet us here afterwards," I reply. "He's just giving you some privacy; he didn't think you would want some weird guy being too close when you are shifting."

Daisy looks up at me with one raised eyebrow.

"I manage okay with you, don't I?" she chuckles in my arms. I grab hold of her and throw her over my shoulder, causing her to squeal as I walk towards a break in the trees.

"Call me weird again, and you're going back into the pond." I pick up my pace, and Daisy starts yelling for me to put her down.

"If you throw me in that pond, I'm taking you with me, Adams," she screams. We are both still laughing uncontrollably when we get to the clearing.

We've made good time. There are still around ten minutes until we shift.

"Can we change early, or do we have to wait?" Daisy asks as she sits down on a fallen tree trunk. I turn to answer her, but the air gets knocked from my lungs. Her long dark blonde hair has fallen over one shoulder; her cheeks are slightly flushed from laughing, and those gorgeous green eyes shine brighter than usual with the pending shift and the full moon's light.

"Michael?" Her voice breaks my train of thought.

"Sorry, you are just so damn distracting." I watch as she blushes, which distracts me further.

"Focus, you idiot," my wolf growls.

"On a full moon, it's best just to let it happen, as

changing early can confuse your wolf. How are you feeling?" I ask as I watch her rubbing her arms. She shrugs and looks around, trying to avoid eye contact; her smile has vanished. "Be honest with me, darling, so I can help you."

"I'm anxious." She whispers, looking back at me. I walk over and sit next to her on the fallen tree. She is playing with her hands on her lap; I take one of them in mine. Daisy sighs as she relaxes into my side, leaning her head against my shoulder.

"What about?" I ask.

"The pain, I guess, as well as the fact that I've spent the last two years dreading every full moon." She looks up at me, her head still resting on my shoulder, her face softens slightly. "I really enjoyed myself the other night. It surprised me how much fun I had and how exhausted I was afterwards." I smile, remembering the feeling of her sleeping in my arms as I carried her back to the car. "But what if I just freeze like I've always done, this time? What if I spend the time on my own hiding?" I lift myself off the log and kneel before her, just like in the library. I take her hands in mine as I stare into her eyes, ensuring that I have her full attention.

"If you freeze and want to stay here, I'll be staying right here with you; you will never be alone again." She tries to protest, but I give her a look to stop her. "Darling, I promised you I would help you to learn how to enjoy your wolf. I only make promises I fully intend to keep, especially to you. I'm here to help you in any way I can. If that means just being by your side while you lay low, then that is where I'll be. I can run any time."

Daisy pulls her hands from mine and throws her arms around my neck. I smile as I hold her.

"Thank you," she whispers into my shoulder. I can feel

her breath on my neck, which sends heat rushing through my body.

"*Now isn't the time, Michael.*" I know he is right, but damn, it feels so good. A werewolf's sex drive is heightened during a full moon. Being so close to Daisy will be difficult tonight, but I'm determined I will not make *that* move, not yet.

"You never have to thank me for being here for you when you need me," I reply as Daisy pulls away, smiling again.

"I'm glad we aren't pretending anymore," she whispers softly.

"So am I, especially if it means I can do this." I kneel up higher and kiss her on the lips tenderly. Just as we start losing ourselves in the kiss, Daisy pulls away from me as she clenches her stomach, moaning. I can feel the change starting, but I hold it off. With years of experience, I know I can hold mine for about five minutes if I need to.

Daisy looks at me, the fear back in her eyes. I quickly help her remove her clothes, leaving on just an oversized t-shirt. I can see the sweat beginning to pour from her as she is obviously fighting the change. My body is hurting, but I know she will be feeling worse. I take her hand and pull her to me.

"Breathe, darling, let the change happen."

"It hurts," she gasps. I hold her gently, trying to reassure her.

"The more you fight it, the more it hurts, I promise, just breathe and relax into it. It will be over in seconds if you do."

"Why aren't you shifting?" she gasps in between cries. I rub her back and can feel the bones changing, taking on their new form.

"I will oncc I know you're okay," I reply through gritted

teeth, my own pain getting harder to ignore. But I can't allow myself to give in until Daisy is okay. I hold her as she releases a loud cry. "Breathe, baby. Just allow your wolf to do what it needs to. I'm right here; I'm not going anywhere. Just try and relax into it, please."

I hear Jon whimper behind me, who has completed his shift and can see what's happening.

I feel Daisy allowing her body to relax, the shift now speeding up. She is letting the wolf come to the surface. Her breathing is still rapid, but she's no longer crying out. I'm forced to let go of her in just a few seconds so she has the room to complete the shift. My heart is racing, and the pain becoming unbearable, but I won't give in.

I hear Jonathan snap behind me, telling me to let go, but I can't, not until I know Daisy is okay. My body is shaking violently. I don't remember ever fighting the change this long; I know I need to release it, but she's almost done. Jonathan is furious with me; I can see it in his eyes. I nod towards Daisy as I sway on my knees.

"Protect her," I gasp as I start to lose consciousness and fall to the forest floor. The last thing I remember is seeing a large pair of bright green wolf's eyes looking at me as I feel my body crash to the ground.

"I swear to the gods I'm going to kick his sorry ass when he wakes up the stupid, overprotective bastard!" Slowly, I start becoming aware of my surroundings. I can't get up yet; my body needs to recover from holding back for too long.

"Jon, give it a break, will you? Check he's okay," I hear Daisy say, and instantly relax, knowing that she's okay.

"He's fine. He will hurt for a few minutes but will be back to his

dickhead self in no time." I can tell Jon is a little further away than Daisy, who seems right beside me.

"*Dickhead seems a bit harsh,*" she sighs.

"*Is it?*"

"*Yes, I prefer arse.*" I can hear them both chuckling down the mind link.

"*I hate you both,*" I chime in. I instantly feel something rub against my neck and shoulders. I lean into Daisy, savouring the feel of her whilst I recover.

"*No, you don't,*" Daisy whispers, causing me to chuckle.

"*Okay, I don't hate you.*" I open my eyes and look at her. Everything about Daisy puts me at ease. "*You, okay?*" I ask as I slowly move so I lie on my stomach. It's easier to stretch this way.

"*I'm fine! Other than worried about you. What were you thinking?*"

I lift myself up on my front paws to help me stretch, but she knocks me back down to the ground.

"*Hey!*" I laugh, but with one look from Daisy, who is standing over me, I know to stay down.

"*Don't you 'hey' me, Adams. What did you think you were playing at? Why the hell did you hold off for so long?*"

I look up at her from the ground.

"*I'm sorry, I was worried about you. You were my priority.*" Daisy nudges me hard with her head whilst Jon is chuckling to himself in the back of my mind.

"*Shut up, Jonathan,*" Daisy snaps, looking behind her at him.

"*Shutting up,*" he answers as he lies down. I watch as Daisy turns and looks at me again.

"*I'm only going to say this once. You pull a stupid ass stunt like that again, even if you are worried about me, and I'll make sure you don't wake up until the next full moon. Is that clear?*"

Fuck, she's hot when she's mad but also absolutely terrifying. I'm sure if we were in human form, she would be kicking my ass right now.

"Yes, baby, abundantly clear. I'm sorry, it won't happen again."

She pushes her nose into the side of my face again before walking off. I finally get to start stretching out my wolf body, which is stiff from the shift. It doesn't take Jon long to come to my side; I can hear him still chuckling in the back of my mind.

"I never thought I would see the day the big bad Michael Adams was submissive to a rogue." I look up at him, raising my wolf eyebrows. Then, nodding my head towards where Daisy has gone to the stream for a drink.

"Would you want to piss her off further?"

Jon looks over at her and shakes his head.

"Nope, good luck with that one, bro. I have a feeling you are going to need it with her crazy ass."

"Hey!" Daisy and I both shout at the same time. I hear Jon curse as Daisy flies towards him. He dodges her and starts running towards the trees with her hot on his tail. Oh, Gods, give me the strength to deal with these two tonight, please.

Daisy

If you had told me that I would be sad to shift back after a full moon one day, I would have laughed in your face. However, tonight has been brilliant. I've had such a fantastic time with Michael and Jonathan. I didn't want it to end.

As soon as it's time to shift back, we head to the clearing, where Michael changes first before putting a blanket over me for privacy again. I quickly get dressed before rushing into his arms. He catches me with ease as I wrap my legs around his waist and arms around his neck so I can bury my face into his neck. I hear him chuckling as he does the same. Michael's arms are my new favourite place to be.

"You really are a natural," he whispers into my hair. I lift my head away so that we are face to face, just a few inches between us. Our eyes locked,

"You make it easy," I whisper back. Michael leans in to kiss me as I lean towards him.

"You both make me sick." Jon's voice rings out. I drop my head into Michael's shoulder and moan; I swear Michael growls as he answers.

"Impeccable timing as always, brother." Which makes me chuckle into his neck; I feel his body tense against me as he moans. I press my lips against his neck once, twice, three times before Michael moves his hands down to cup my backside, grinding himself against me.

"Jonny, kindly disappear for two minutes, please," I call out. To my surprise, he quietly walks away. I lift my head to look where he has disappeared and find Michael looking, too.

"How did you do that? You told him to do something, and he did it," Michael asks, looking amazed.

"Michael?" I say quietly, knowing we don't have much time.

"Yes, baby?" he replies just as quietly.

"Shut up and kiss me already." He doesn't need telling twice. He places a hand behind my head and pulls me in for a hot-blooded, passionate kiss. I entwine my fingers into his thick hair, causing him to moan as I tug it slightly. He pulls me harder against him as the kiss deepens; I tighten my legs around his waist, causing friction in the right place. Gods, I think I could fall apart entirely just by kissing his lips and the feel of his abdomen against my throbbing clit.

Michael turns us and pushes me against a nearby tree in seconds. The feeling of the sharp bark against my protected back, his hands kneading my ass cheeks, with pressure between my legs from his rock-hard cock pressing in just the right place through my leggings, has me squirming in seconds. Michael lets out a primal growl as he moves his lips from mine and almost holds me at arm's length.

"Do you have any idea what you do to me?"

I glance down between us and see his giant bulge. I look up at him, wiggling my eyebrows.

"I have a good idea." Michael looks at me and grins whilst rubbing himself against me, teasing me in just the right spot.

"Your two minutes are up," Jon calls as he walks out of the trees. Michael rolls his eyes before he places me back on my feet. Once again, I sway slightly as my legs have turned to jelly.

"You are going to be the death of me," I whisper, smiling as I turn to walk away from him, but Michael lets out a loud, deep moan as he tightens his hold on my waist, causing me to squeal as he spins me back into him, forcing me to lean back into his arms as his lips crash into mine. I lift my arms so they are back around his neck. Gods, I could kiss this man all day.

"As glad as I am to see you all happy and shit, little bro. I am not partial to playing the third wheel, so can we press pause, and you two lovebirds can continue this when you are, in fact, alone."

I feel Michael's lips leave mine. When I open my eyes, I am looking straight into his.

"I am seriously up for continuing this alone very soon,"

Michael whispers, as I feel my cheeks heating further as I blush.

"So am I," I reply, smiling. Michael gently kisses my lips before setting me back down so my feet are firmly on the ground. He keeps his hand on my lower back until he knows I am steady on them, and we start reluctantly, heading back to reality. After a few minutes, realising how tired I am, before I get to voice it, Michael scoops me up and holds me against his chest.

"I'm starting to think you like me being in your arms," I mumble as I snuggle into him. I feel his laugh vibrate through his chest like a lullaby.

"Maybe I do. Now sleep, baby; I've got you."

I nod as I start drifting off. I feel him kiss the top of my head, and a smile creeps onto my face.

"Michael?" I whisper sleepily.

"Yes, darling." I smile to myself slightly, as I always do when he calls me baby or darling.

"The librarian stopped me when I was leaving the other day and asked me if I would give you her number."

"What did you say?" Michael chuckles.

"I told her it would never work between the two of you, as I am a very jealous person, and I don't like people touching what's mine."

Michael stops in his tracks. He stares down at me in amazement, then slowly, a smile appears on his face.

"Is that so? Well, it's a good job I have no intentions of being touched by anyone but you. But remember, if I'm yours, that makes you mine." I feel a smile spread further on my face as I lean my head into his chest, closing my eyes, feeling more content than I have in a very long time.

"That's good. Because I like being yours."

Chapter Eighteen

DAISY

It's taken two full days, but I've finally woken up ache-free. The guys really ran me ragged Tuesday night during the full moon, and every muscle in my arms, shoulders, hips, and legs has ached since. Deciding to take advantage of the lack of pain, I head out for a short, slow run. I love my five-mile loop, which I run daily; I don't have to pay attention to where I am going as it's instinct now.

As I turn down a dirt track three miles in, I pick up on that scent that hits me every time I run down here. I know who it is, so I am considering calling them out. But, instead, I decide to play. I come to a stop before slowly pulling my running top off, so I'm left in just my running bra and trousers. I may not have the thinnest waist, but I am happy with my slightly rounded stomach. Who wants to be stick-thin anyway? I tuck part of the shirt into the side of my trousers, stretch a little then take off running again. I pick up on the scent a few times during my little strip show, which makes me smile.

I carry on running, wondering if they're still watching when out of nowhere, a man runs straight towards me. I've never seen another person down here before; my wolf instantly becomes alert, sensing danger. My back straightens so I'm at my full height; holding my head high, I keep going straight on. Today may not have been the best day to strip down to my bra. Fuck.

At first, the guy just looks at me and carries on running, but just as he gets past, he turns and starts running beside me.

"Hey," he smiles at me.

"Morning," I reply, looking ahead. Whilst searching for any signs, he's going to cause trouble. I can hear my wolf growling as she isn't happy.

"Mind if I run with you? A gorgeous girl like you shouldn't be alone out here at this time of the morning. You never know who's about."

I know he's not really asking for permission and will follow me, regardless of my answer.

"That's funny, considering you're the one following a *woman* who was happily minding her own business," I reply sharply, hoping to let him know that I'm not intimidated.

"Well, you can't blame a guy for trying, can you?" He reaches out, but before he can even touch me, I stop running and step away from him. I look over and see a glimpse of something in his eyes. My wolf's getting louder, and I notice the guy looking towards the trees as if hearing something. Maybe it's not *my* wolf, then. Which means my usual stalker hasn't left. Shit.

As if realising there is a chance we're not alone, the guy grabs my arm and tries to pull me towards him. I instantly pull out of his grip and turn to stare at him, refusing to be scared.

"I think you need to back off now," I warn through gritted teeth as I gather some power in my hand, ready to send him flying if I need to. But instead of being spooked, he makes a run for me and tries to take me down. Thanks to my wolf instincts and speed, I quickly jump out of his way, and he doesn't make contact. I use my magic to give him a push, knocking him to the ground. But he jumps up quickly.

"I don't feel like it. So stop trying to fight what you know is going to happen," the guy replies. As he steps towards me, I see a large brown wolf jump between us; it hunches down and growls. The guy stops dead in his tracks. The wolf stands tall on all fours, not taking his eyes off the threat as it positions itself in front of me so I can't move around him.

"What the hell is that?"

"What does it look like?" I ask smugly; the guy looks around as if checking to see if there are any more surprises about to jump out at him.

"It looks like a fucking wolf. That's what it looks like." I can see and smell that he is terrified to move. I smile as I cross my arms over my chest.

"We don't have wolves in the UK, must be a very big dog," I reply sarcastically.

"Call the bloody thing off, will you?"

The wolf growls as if daring him to do anything other than leave.

"It's not my dog; I think it's wild." I laugh out loud at the terrified expression on the man's face. Slowly, *the wild dog* backs up and sits right against my leg. He's so close if he leans against me anymore, he will knock me over. I instantly push my fingers into Michael's fur at his neck. His tail swipes the back of my legs; I look down and notice he won't take his eyes off the guy as he continues to bare his teeth, still seeing the threat he poses.

The guy turns and runs, muttering to himself as he gets as much space between him and us. Neither of us moves until he is out of sight. I pivot on the spot and point towards the trees.

"Right, you. Get back in there and shift, and then we can talk." I watch as Michael looks at me and then in the direction that guy just ran off in. I know he's worried about leaving me alone in case the guy returns. I walk over to the trees and lean against one of the trunks.

"I'll stay here, where you can be close. But I'm not waiting long, so hurry the hell up already." I arch my eyebrows, emphasising my stubbornness. Finally, Michael huffs and runs off into the trees.

In what feels like only a handful of seconds later, Michael walks out, pulling on a running top. I take a quick second to appreciate his toned muscular body whilst he is preoccupied. Then, quickly look away before he can catch me staring.

"Are you always this stubborn?" Michael asks as he walks closer to me. I stay leaning against the tree; arms crossed against my chest, one foot planted against the trunk behind me.

"Do you stalk all your students? Or only me?" I fire back in return. He stops in front of me, standing at full height with his shoulders pushed back.

"Only the ones which run at stupid o'clock in the morning in the dark and head straight towards danger. So yeah, only you." He takes hold of my arm and gently lifts it so he can check it over. I notice a few scratches, probably from when I'd pulled my arm out of the guy's grasp. I hear

Michael growl under his breath; he looks in the direction the guy had gone. He sniffs the air, trying to pick up his scent so he is easier to follow. Michael's wolf is fighting to take over and go after the person who threatened and hurt their mate.

"Hey, look at me. I'm okay. It's only a few scratches," I whisper as I place a hand on his chest; Michael doesn't move an inch.

"It could have been so much more than a few scratches," he replies through gritted teeth.

"But it wasn't, thanks to you. I'm fine, I promise." I watch as he closes his eyes and takes a deep breath. He gently places my arm back against my side before placing a hand over my own, which is still resting on his chest. We stay here for a minute while Michael calms down, and I just enjoy being close to him again.

Even though I know I could've protected myself, that had been a scary couple of minutes. It brought back memories I've been trying to forget. Having him close now helps my anxiety to calm down quicker than it has before. Michael is my anchor; he keeps me from drifting into the sea of panic.

Michael takes a step forward, keeping his hand over mine on his chest, and he places the other just to the side of my head on the trunk, sandwiching me between him and the tree. I can feel my head starting to race due to his proximity. I look into his eyes and notice they have darkened. The intensity with which he is looking at me is causing me to heat in places I haven't felt in a very long time.

"He is the second person in a week who feels it's acceptable to put you in danger. It makes me want to keep you with me at all times so I can ensure you are safe and unharmed," Michael growls into my ear.

"As nice as that sounds, I would end up losing my shit with you. I'm a big girl who can look after herself. One day, very soon, you and I will have to have a long chat about my past and why. If this is going to work between us, I need you to stop protecting me and stand beside me. You need to let me fight my own battles. I don't need a protector, Michael; I need a partner and an equal. I've been a victim, and I will never be one again."

Michael leans his head against mine, eyes closed as he nods.

"You are unbelievably strong; I know you can do anything you put your mind to. I'll always be by your side. Even though it goes against everything my wolf tries to do." He lifts his head from mine and looks down at me. I lift myself onto my tiptoes so I can plant a soft kiss on his lips. I wrap my arms around his neck, and he wraps an arm around my waist, closing the small gap between us.

"I've missed you," he whispers as he leans down and kisses me back gently. I chuckle. This man is forever turning me into a giggling schoolgirl.

"You only saw me yesterday," I tease, even though I've missed him too. I've started sneaking up to his office at least once a day just to get a minute or two with him. But we're forever getting interrupted by other students or members of staff.

"We managed to get a whole three minutes alone yesterday; it's not enough." I watch as Michael gets a glint in his eye. I instantly know he's up to something. He kisses me before pulling me away from the tree.

"I have a few things to do. You get back home and wait for my text," he winks as he turns his back on me. Then, as if forgetting something, he spins around and pulls out the t-shirt still tucked into my trousers.

"Pull a stunt like your little strip tease when you are alone again, and I won't be held accountable for my actions. No one gets to see this but me now," he growls as he slips the top over my head. I chuckle as I thread my arms through the sleeves.

"I knew you were watching me. I've always known you were here every morning. I just never said anything in case you stopped."

Michael wraps an arm around my waist again, pulling me flat against him again.

"We've wasted too much time being stubborn. I plan on making that time up to you every day for as long as you will have me." He pulls away, leaving me breathless like he always does when he's ridiculously smooth. Michael slaps my backside, making me squeal and winks at me. "Now get your sexy ass home and wait for my text." I watch, speechless, as he takes off, running back through the trees whilst shouting. "And keep your clothes on; I will be watching." I bet you will, Adams.

Michael

As soon as I know Daisy is back in her dorm safely, I pull out my phone to start putting my plans into action. But first of all, I have one important call to make.

Even though it's only six in the morning, he answers after three rings.

"Marcus, I'm sending you a street name and a description. I need you to access the CCTV around the area between five and six this morning. Some guy tried to grab Daisy whilst she was out running. When I scared him off, he mentioned it not being worth the money. It was planned by someone I want to know who." I hear Marcus agree it sounds dodgy as I hang up, trusting him to get answers.

Marcus will find out who the hell is trying to get their hands on my mate so I can make sure they never try anything like that again.

Chapter Nineteen

DAISY

"Hooky? This was your grand plan?" I call out as I close my car door before heading straight to Michael, who's leaning against the front of his car, holding his arms out proud as punch. I'd only been home for five minutes when I received an email from Michael explaining that class was cancelled for the day due to him being ill. Within a minute, my phone beeped, signalling a text.

Michael: You, unlike the rest of the class, don't have the day to yourself. I expect you and your fine ass to meet me at 9 AM in the usual spot. Don't bring anything; I have the whole day covered. Your ever-brilliant mate. 😊Xxx

"So, what is this illness that you've come down with?" I ask as I walk up to him. He slips his fingers into the belt loops of my jeans before tugging me in between his legs so I'm pressed against him. His lips find mine all too briefly.

"I'm sick from never getting more than a couple of minutes with you alone."

I raise my eyebrows as I put my arms around his neck.

"So, what is the cure for this sickness?" I ask as he wraps his arms around my waist, holding me tight.

"A full day just you and me. Lots of holding each other, talking, laughing, having a good time in general. As well as a little bit of this..." He leans down and kisses me. Now, this is how you skive a day off classes when you are dating the lecturer.

Michael grins as he stands and takes my hand before leading me into the forest; both grinning and excited to spend a full day just the two of us.

We spend nearly two hours walking around, talking about anything and everything, from favourite films, books, and bands. To whom would win in a fight: Superman or Ironman; Dumbledore or Gandalf. Michael informs me he's never watched or read the Harry Potter series. I calmly explain that I could not possibly be mated to someone so poorly educated on the subject of muggles, witches and wizards and that it needs to be rectified immediately. I don't think he's taking me seriously, but he will learn.

As always, the conversation flows flawlessly between us. The only time we are ever silent is when our mouths are busy doing something other than talking.

Around lunchtime, Michael leads us into the clearing where we usually shift. As much as I like it here at night, it looks completely different in the day. There are so many colourful wildflowers in all shapes, colours, and sizes. Michael tells me to wait where I am as he walks a little way away from me. He climbs a tree with ease and pulls out a bag.

"Well, look at you all organised," I call as he jumps down, landing perfectly. He reaches into the bag, pulls out a blanket, shakes it, and places it on the ground.

"Only the best for you, darling," he grins as he holds out his hand for me.

"Cheese ball," I whisper as I step onto the blanket. He laughs whilst sitting, pulling me down with him.

"I know; I don't know what's come over me. Just don't tell Jonny." He says as I sit between his legs, my back to his front. He wraps his arms around me as I lean into him. Whenever I'm in his arms, no matter how I'm standing or sitting, it always feels like I fit there perfectly. I hear him mutter something about waiting a moment as he reaches to the right of us, pulling something out of his bag; I watch as he pours something into a cup. I smell the coffee before it's even in my hands. The second it's in my grasp, I lift it to my nose so I can inhale the scent of caffeinated nectar.

"Man, that's good coffee." I sigh as I relax further into his arms, sipping my drink. I can feel Michael's chest vibrate as he chuckles.

"Is there anything as important to you as coffee?" he asks. I think about it for a moment.

"Pizza. Pizza is definitely up there with coffee."

"I'll remember that then. When you feel up to it, we'll make pizzas at mine and have a pizza and coffee date," Michael says. I turn my head so I can see him.

"Make? You mean you can actually cook?"

"I certainly can," he replies, looking very pleased with himself. I face forward again.

"I hit the jackpot," I exclaim, smiling. I feel Michael resting his cheek against mine before planting a kiss on it.

"No, I did," he whispers in my ear. I close my eyes and just enjoy being in his arms for a moment, listening to the sounds of the forest mixed with his heartbeat. Like mine, his runs a little faster than an average human; it's like music to my ears. I feel my whole body relax into him as we enjoy the moment of peace.

"I love it here," I whisper, looking around at all the plants and wildlife I can hear.

"I do, too. It's peaceful. At least it is when Jon isn't being a giant bulldozer."

I chuckle as he isn't wrong.

"Did he tell everyone about me giving you hell? He told me he couldn't wait to." I feel Michael laugh behind me.

"Oh yes, I'm surprised my phone didn't wake you up whilst driving you home. The whole team knew within minutes of him getting back to the car." I feel Michael stop laughing suddenly as I turn to look at him over my shoulder.

"Team?" I realise he looks paler than he did a few moments ago; he seems worried. "What's the matter?"

Michael takes a deep breath and moves so he sits to the side, facing me. I turn so I can look at him without twisting my neck.

———

Michael

"I need to talk to you about something. To be honest, it's one of the reasons I wanted us to come here today. I don't know how you are going to feel about it. But it is something that we need to discuss." I take a deep breath, trying to ignore the giant ball of tension that has formed in my stomach. I look at Daisy and can see the worry on her face.

"Okay?" she whispers nervously. I close my eyes, and I

attempt to hide how nervous I am. How scared I am that I'm about to lose this remarkable woman.

I'm not ashamed of what I do; I might not always like the decisions I'm forced to make, but I know I make the right ones. Wolves brought up in a pack know from day one about Pack Protectors; they understand what we do and the decisions that we have to sometimes make. But people like Daisy, who have no experience of packs, don't realise that we exist.

"Almost every pack has a team of Protectors. It's their job to protect the pack from all dangers. This can mean making sure no one gets too close to pack territory and ensuring the members of the pack and outsiders respect the Alpha, Beta, and Luna at all times. To ensure that no rogues cause any issues in our areas. They dedicate their time to protecting all wolves who need protection and enforcing pack and wolf laws. If a rogue or pack member starts drawing too much attention to us or our kind, we get called in to handle the situation." I glance up and see Daisy looking at me, a little pale, but she is still listening.

"That doesn't seem too bad. So, you are like the supernatural police or something? I take it you are part of your pack's team?" I rub the back of my neck, smiling nervously.

"Kinda, I'm not just a member of the team; I'm the leader. I'm the one who has to make all final decisions and tend to be the one who handles the most dangerous situations." Daisy looks a little taken aback. Gods, I wish I knew what was going through her head right now. Does she realise that I may have to make calls like I did on Monday?

"Maybe she doesn't like the idea of you being on the firing line?" my wolf suggests calmly, thinking he could be right.

"Is that why you ran off on Sunday? Were you called on a ... job?"

I nod.

"A mission, yes. We rarely get any notice. Sometimes, if it's just small and I'm busy with marking, or now you, I will ask my second to lead."

"I take it Jon is your second?"

I can't help but chuckle, which helps me relax a bit.

"No, Marcus Williams is my second; he is also our tech guy. There is nothing that the guy can't do with a laptop and internet connection. Jon is the one who gets the answers. Some might call him an interrogator, but to be honest, he has the ability to make people spill their guts without much violence needed most of the time." I'm shocked when a laugh burst from Daisy's lips. She slams her hand over her mouth for a second before removing it to speak.

"Sorry, probably shouldn't laugh, but I can see that. I would spill my deepest, darkest secrets to get that guy to shut up at times." I find myself chuckling again, relaxing a little further. "So, who else is on your team?" Daisy asks; she places her hands behind her before leaning back, her leg stretched out over mine. She isn't cowering from me yet, at least.

"There's Will Matthews; he is my organiser. I tell him what I need, and he helps me develop a solution to make it happen. He will find the best route, the best place for surveillance, where we can take someone when we capture them if we are too far from pack territory, all that kind of thing.

"Then there's Stuart Harvey. He is the newest on the team. He still feels like he needs to prove himself, but he is a good lad and works bloody hard. He is our hunter. In human or wolf form, no one I know has his sense of smell. Even Jon's isn't as strong, and Jon's is something else. As soon as Stuart knows a wolf's or person's scent, he never seems to forget it. He is like a walking index of scents." I watch Daisy take a sip of her probably now cold coffee.

"Can you tell me about the mission on Sunday?"

This is the moment I have been dreading. Now we are here, I'm not sure I want her to know this side of me.

"Trust her, like she is trusting you, to be honest." Okay, here it goes.

"A rogue was travelling around Wales, leaving a string of warrants for his arrest in his wake. Unfortunately, he came onto our territory and caused a couple of problems. It took us two full days to finally catch him and handle the situation." Daisy cocks her head to the side.

"You're being very vague. Is that because you *can't* tell me or because you think I will run?"

Man, she's good. She can read me like a book already.

"I can talk to *you* about it as you are my mate. Protectors are allowed to give details to mates as it's hard to hide things from them. But I couldn't give details to my mum or if you were just someone I was dating."

Daisy looks me in the eye as if waiting for me to tell her more details.

"He was wanted for a string of sexual assaults; he assaulted two of my pack sisters when they were running on our own pack land in two separate incidents. The police were getting closer and closer to catching him as he was getting sloppy. But we couldn't stop until we found him … and handled it." I watch Daisy's every move. Her eyes don't give anything away; she just looks at me, but I can't tell if she is actually seeing me or realising I am a monster.

"By 'handle it', you mean …"

I look down at the ground, terrified of how she will look at me, as I answer.

"I killed him."

I hear her take a deep breath before asking, "How?"

I don't want to answer.

"I ripped out his throat whilst in my wolf form."

There is silence. Even the forest seems to be on tenterhooks, waiting to see what her response will be. I hold my breath, scared that a single sound will be the one that breaks me, and I crumble as I wait.

"Okay."

It takes me a second to realise what she said; my head shoots up, and I look at her. She is still sitting in the same position, looking at me the same way she was a few short moments ago.

"What?" I force myself to ask. Daisy just looks at me as she finishes the last of her coffee and places the cup on the grass.

"You heard me; I said okay. Was there any way he was going to go with you quietly and make up for all the wrong he had done?" I shake my head, not knowing what to say. This was not the reaction I was expecting. I watch Daisy move towards me and kneel so our eyes are at the same level. She places a hand on my cheek like I have done to her so many times; she looks me in the eye as she speaks.

"What you did saved many more women from being abused, humiliated and scared. Men like that don't stop. Not until they are caught or killed. They don't ask for help; they just progress and become more dangerous until one day they kidnap a woman and hold her hostage in the attempt to force the mating bond and make her a birthing mule." Slowly, what she is saying starts to sink in. She isn't just speaking in general; there is a significant amount of truth in it.

"That's how you became a wolf?" I ask. Daisy nods. I

watch as she pulls the left side of her t-shirt collar to the side, along with her bra strap. This one is much thinner than the sports bras I have seen her in, and I realise what she's been hiding. On her collarbone, where I had planned on marking her, is somebody else's mark.

Chapter Twenty

DAISY

"He marked you?"

I feel the fear I've been trying so hard to ignore rush to the surface. I can't say or do anything except watch Michael's reaction. I wait to see the disgust and hate in his eyes. Nothing but rage radiates from him for a moment, causing the hairs on my arms to stand on end. But then his face softens. Slowly, he reaches over and brushes a finger over the teeth indents on my skin.

"It's not a real mark," he whispers, brushing his finger over the skin again. I shake my head.

"No, he kept trying to mark me, but because we weren't mates, it wouldn't take."

Only a true fated mate can leave a mark on their mate's skin. It's like a very pale tattoo with no bumps or grooves. No one knows how it works; it just happens when a mate bites their partner whilst they make love. This on my shoulder is pale but raised from the rest of my skin.

"So, he scarred you instead?"

I nod slowly. I watch his eyes as his mind starts putting it all together.

"I was his property; he had to make sure that everyone who met me would know I belonged to him. Once I was 'trained' enough to be allowed out of my prison cell, that is."

Michael looks at me with his eyes wide with realisation.

"None of it was consensual, was it?"

My whole body slumps as I look down at my knees and slowly shake my head.

I've been dreading this moment when Michael learns what really happened to me, how I became a wolf. Will it change the way he looks at me? Will he decide that it is all too much for him to handle and leave?

I feel Michael move in front of me, but I can't bring myself to look up at him. My whole body tightens again as the fear of him leaving takes over. I'm just about to tell him he is okay to go when he leans forward so his lips gently press over the scar.

"This changes nothing for me," Michael whispers. Every nerve in my body relaxes to the point I worry I may fall over. I look up to find his blue eyes watching me intently.

"Now, do you see why I won't condemn you for taking a life as evil as that rogue's? He wouldn't have stopped. What you did was so brave; you have saved so many other women from the pain and humiliation of being forced upon. They would never have gotten real justice through the courts because he couldn't be allowed to be captured. He would've known that. I am so proud of what you did, as I know it must have been the hardest decision to make, but it *was* the right one." I'm shocked as Michael leans forward and places his forehead on my shoulder; I tilt my head into his and run my fingers over the back of his neck and into his hair.

Neither of us says anything or moves for some time. I close my eyes and relax against him, rubbing his neck as he composes himself against my shoulder. I meant every word; I am so unbelievably proud of what he does.

"I was sure you would leave me," he whispers, breaking the peace around us. I chuckle, shaking my head against his.

"It will take more than that for me to run. Side by side, remember."

"Hand in hand," Michael whispers. I turn my head to kiss the top of his.

"Will you lie down with me?" he asks as he sits up. I smile, nodding. Michael lies on his back as I curl up against his side, resting my head and hand on his chest. One of his arms is around my shoulders as his hand plays with my hair.

"One day, when you are ready, will you tell me what happened to you?" I knew he would ask when he saw the bite. So, I have already prepared myself. I nod into his chest and start talking as he plays with my hair and holds my hand against his chest.

When I was nineteen, I rebelled a lot. I was hanging around with a different group of people that my auntie and uncle didn't approve of. I was drinking, smoking, and even having a joint or two every night. My auntie and uncle tried everything to stop me, but I just wouldn't listen; I was in self-destruct mode. I knew what I was doing, and no one was going to stop me.

One evening, we were all in a beer garden, and this guy approached us; he asked if we had a spare lighter and ended up chatting with us for a couple of hours. He seemed like a decent guy. I knew he was some kind of sup, but as I had never met a werewolf, I had no idea what he was. He told us his name was Jack; he piled on the charm, and we all fell for it. I remember thinking that he was a good-looking guy, although my instinct was that something about him wasn't right. But I put it down to having drank and smoked a little too much. So, when he offered to walk me home, I didn't think twice about letting him. I lived about five minutes away from the pub. What could happen in that amount of time—apparently, a lot.

I don't think we were even far from my friends when I felt something sharp dig into my back; I froze. I knew instantly what it was. I wanted to scream and fight, but all common sense disappeared. He leant over and whispered that if I did anything to get the others' attention, he would kill us all. I could never put the others in danger. He slipped something around my wrist, and I felt my magic instantly weaken. I was helpless as I had no idea how to defend myself without magic.

I followed him around the corner, so I was out of view of the pub and house. He pushed me into the back seat of a car, and before I even had a chance to turn around, he injected me with something. I remember trying so hard to fight the drugs but to no avail. I was under in less than a minute.

I woke up sometime later in a pitch-black room, tied to a single bed. My wrists were tied to the headboard. I tried to get loose, but nothing worked; the more I pulled on the rope, the tighter it seemed to get around my wrists. Then, when I tried to move my legs, I realised that my ankles were also tied up. I tried to think of any spell that would help me, only to realise I still couldn't feel my magic. It was like an empty hole where it usually was.

Feeling helpless, I came to terms with the fact that this was how I would die, there in that dark room. Mary and Nigel would never know what happened to me. They would never be able to find my body like we never found my dad's. The tears started falling down my cheek, and I didn't even bother to try and stop them. All I wanted at that moment was my mum and dad. They would have known what to do. They would've known the best way to get back home. I was so lost in my grief and fear that I never heard him unlock the door. It was not until it opened, and the light rushed in, blinding me temporarily I realised I was no longer alone.

"Look who's finally awake. Good morning, sweetheart." His voice went straight through me. I wanted to scream at him to let me go and to kill him with my bare hands, but I knew that there was something about him that made him stronger than me, and I knew there was little chance of escape. I had to play my cards right, and hopefully, he wouldn't kill me straight away.

I watched as Jack walked over to the bed and sat down on it next to me.

"Why am I here?" I asked. Jack looked at me, smiling.

"Because, sweetheart, I have some big plans for us. We're going to change so much together. But first, I am going to have to change you." Before I even realised what was happening, he shifted into a wolf and bit my ankle. Within seconds, the burning pain started, first in the ankle, then up to my leg. I tried not to cry out as I didn't want to give him the satisfaction, but then the pain increased further, and I knew there was no way this would get any better. I think it was around that point it all started to click into place, and I realised he had changed me into a werewolf.

It took three days for the change to finish. Jack, who I learnt was really called Jackson, popped in every couple of hours to check that I was still progressing and that my body wasn't rejecting it. He would tell me all the things he had planned for us, how I was going to be his mate, how I would give him lots of pups and that we would live together in that house. We were going to become the strongest pack around. But I didn't want any of that. I just wanted to go home and forget anything had ever happened; I just wanted to leave.

I couldn't tell you how many times I tried to kill myself during *that time; I remember trying to rip out my own wrists one of the times my teeth extended into fangs. Still, nothing worked; I would bleed for a moment, and then the wounds would heal; there was some kind of magic there to stop me, but I never found out what it was.*

The first day that I was pain-free was when he came in and forced himself on me. He didn't need me to be coherent or responsive for that. By this point, I had broken the bed during the transitions between human and wolf; all I had was a dirty mattress on the floor. I don't think I need to go into details about what he did to me, what he took from me.

After that point, there's not much to tell. Other than that, for five months, I was stuck in that room chained to the wall, abused in every way you can think of. He was desperate to mate with me and impregnate me, but nothing would work. What he didn't realise was that I had been on the injection for the last four years. I had received a dose only two days before he took me. There was no way I would get pregnant at that time. I was terrified of what would happen once the injection wore off, though.

I also discovered that he had placed an anklet on my right ankle. He had asked a sorcerer to make it so that I could not use my magic. He had been watching me for a while and had so many plans in place to make sure I had no choice but to stay with him. I gave up; I started agreeing to everything he asked of me. I started believing he would protect me if I behaved. But then, one day, he went too far, and I decided I needed to fight back. If I really wanted to get out of there alive, I had to do it my way, not his.

"How did you escape?" Michael asks as he kisses the top of my head.

"It was sheer luck that got me out of there."

It was a full moon night; I knew Jackson would leave me in the house while he went for a run. But, after the first time I turned, he had learned that I couldn't be tied up when I shifted. So, he would undo the chains and just lock the door instead.

That night, I listened until I heard him leave. I tried the door, and it opened. I waited until the change started.

I lift my head to look at Michael.

"I think that was the first and only time before that night with you that I changed quickly, as I was so desperate for it to happen."

Within a flash, I was a wolf, and I jumped out of a window that had been left open. I ran as fast as I could. I knew that he would chase me as soon as he realised I was gone. I ran and ran until I got a bearing of where I was.

I ran until I got all the way home.

I was terrified; I honestly thought my aunt and uncle would disown me for what I had become. Jackson had fed me so many lies I no longer knew what was real and what he had created to control me. But I needed to see them one last time before I disappeared for good. Even if they would never know it was me, they saw.

I finally got to the back garden, and even though it was midnight, my auntie was sitting there with her shawl around her shoulders. She was just staring up at the sky like she was waiting for someone. I could hear her talking, thanks to the wolf hearing.

"Please, Goddess, send our girl home. We need her here; we need her to know that she is loved, so loved, no matter what has happened. She is our world, and she doesn't even realise it. So please just bring her back to us, keep her safe. Please protect our girl."

I fell to the ground, the sight of her tearing me up. I wanted to run to her and tell her I was there, that although I was broken, I was alive in a way. I longed to see my uncle and feel their arms around me. But I just couldn't bring myself to take that first step. What if my being a wolf was too much? What if they wouldn't be able to look past the shame of having a werewolf for a niece? What if Jackson found me here? Before I could stop it, a whine left my throat as my heart broke. Mary spun around to the sound. I shuffled backwards on my belly, not wanting her to spot me, not wanting to scare her.

"*Daisy, is that you?*" *Mary called. The sound of my name on her lips caused me to cry, even in wolf form, and I heard my heartbreak. I needed to get out of there. But I just couldn't get my body to move. All I could see was this woman standing in the garden; she had lost weight and looked so tired in the moonlight. I wanted to go home. Again, I find myself whining with the pain that filled me.*

I'd lost my parents; now I had to lose my aunt and uncle, godparents, best friend, and coven. Why? Why had everyone I loved been taken from me? The anger started to build in my chest, and a howl tore through me. I wanted to shift back, but I didn't know how. I wanted to go home.

Whilst I'd been wallowing in my self-pity, Mary had walked towards me, following the sound of my whimpering. I only realised when I heard the back door slam open, and my uncle's scent filled my nose as he barrelled out of the house.

"Mary, where are you?" I watched as he spotted her and rushed to her side. "Was that a wolf I heard?" he asked as he reached her. He placed his hands on her shoulders, trying to steer her back to the house. But she shrugs him off. They were so close now I couldn't move; they might see me, and they would be terrified. I didn't want the look of fear to be in their eyes the last time I saw them. Because I had decided then, I was going to leave, not because I wanted to, but I had no choice if I was to protect them from him.

I watched, trying to be as still as possible; Mary held her hands up to stop Nigel and took another step towards me.

"We don't have wild wolves in the UK," Mary pointed out. "So, if it wasn't a normal wolf, what was it?" I watch as Nigel's back straightens even more; he pushed Mary behind him as he turned to the left. His face changed as his eyes widened with fright. I know what he fears; even if he doesn't know who it is, he just knows there is a threat.

It's me. I'm that threat.

I take the opportunity as their backs are turned to me, and I jump to my feet, turn, and run.

However, I didn't even get fifty feet when I heard my uncle's voice.

"I don't know who you are, but we don't want any trouble."

In that second, two things happened. First, the breeze changed directions; second, his scent hit me like a brick wall. He was there, Jackson was there, and so was my family.

I didn't stop to think. I turned on the spot and rushed back. He had destroyed my life, but he would never touch them.

I rushed to the garden, and that's when I saw it all unfolding. Jackson was in wolf form; he slowly advanced on my uncle, who had my auntie still pressed against his back. I knew he would rather die than have anything happen to her.

Jackson pulled his lips back in a snarl, and I saw my uncle gather a magic ball in his hand, ready to defend them both. As Jackson took another step towards them, I sprang out of my hiding spot and put myself between Jackson and my family. Behind me were the two people I love more than anything in the world. In front of me, the person who had beaten, violated, changed and controlled me for the last five months.

I knew I would die that night; he had starved me, and I was weak from the run there, but I didn't care; I was willing to die to make sure these two beautiful people survived.

"Daisy," I heard my auntie gasp behind me. I didn't allow myself to turn towards her; I couldn't risk taking my eyes off Jackson. I took a step backwards, knowing they would eventually have no choice but to step back as well. They did, but Jackson also advanced. He looked smug, as if it was going to be an easy win for him. But I was done being weak.

Jackson stopped advancing and growled at me. I could see from his face he was pissed and wanted me to behave myself. He really thought I was going to go quietly.

I leaned forward on my front paws and growled to tell him it wasn't happening. I could see he was getting wound up and starting to move to the right, obviously trying to get to my auntie and uncle. But I followed each step he took. I could feel my wolf getting more and more pissed off with his, and it was like I knew she would also protect my family. "Protect them, save them." *I heard her agreeing as I let her take over as Jackson launched at me.*

I don't remember much of what happened next. There were flashes of teeth, claws, pain, and splattered blood, but the whole time, I knew my wolf was standing on her own and doing what she needed to do. I trusted her. Every time Jackson started to get the upper hand, she was right there putting him back in his place. I didn't realise until Jackson fell that we were away from the house. Jackson was covered in blood. I didn't know if it was mine or his, but I didn't care; I knew it was not theirs.

Jackson shifted, right in front of me, back to human form. I didn't risk it because if I needed to fight again. I knew I was better in this form, as much as it pains me to say it. I noticed his leg and arm were in a bad way, and I felt so proud of my wolf; she had fought fantastically.

"Enough!" Jackson growled at me; I just growled back. He tried to hide that he was scared, but I could smell the fear radiating off him. "Change back right now!" he demanded; I just growled at him louder. "He is too injured; he cannot fight us," *my wolf informed me. I could see she was right. He was swaying slightly, looked pale, and was losing a lot of blood.*

"You are coming back with me, and we'll forget that this little incident ever happened. Do you understand me?" I didn't move, didn't growl, just stared at him. I was not scared for the first time since I was dragged into his world; he didn't intimidate me.

I had no idea what was going to happen or how this was going to end, but I knew I couldn't back down. I stepped towards him and growled; maybe if I showed him I wasn't scared of him anymore, he'd back off enough for my family and me to run. I took another step forward, and he instantly took one back. "See, he's scared; keep going, and he will have no choice but to run."

"Stop! Step down now! This is an order from your Alpha." Jackson roared at me, but nothing happened. "He's not our Alpha; he is no Alpha." I could feel that my wolf was right. Even though I knew a true Alpha could command their pack to do anything they wished, I felt nothing. He was not my Alpha; I have no Alpha. I growled again, taking another step forward. I saw it then on his face; he could see that he would not win whilst I had the upper hand; he would need to strike when I was vulnerable— it was time to end this.

I took another step forward, and this time, I followed it with another, and another, and another; Jackson had no choice but to keep going backwards. "Kill him." My wolf growled, and I agreed it needed to be done. I launched myself at him, taking him down. I stopped when my jaw was a couple of inches from his face. I wanted my eyes to be the last thing he ever saw; I wanted him to feel the fear I had felt for the previous five months.

"You don't have it in you; you'll never have the guts to kill me. You are nothing without me." He nodded his head in the direction of the house. "Those people will never accept you again. You are tainted to them. Why would they want a wolf as a niece? Why would they want to risk their lives? You could hurt them. You would be an embarrassment to their coven, to their friends." I faltered for a second. He must have seen it because he took full advantage of it.

I howled as pain radiated down my right-hand side, causing me to jump off him. I looked down and saw a branch in his hand, one end of it covered in blood, my blood. I took a step towards him, baring my teeth again, ignoring the pain radiating through me with every step. Jackson swung the stick at me as he jumped back.

"Enjoy your freedom whilst it lasts, sweetheart. I will come back for you and make you pay for your behaviour tonight. You have twelve hours to come back to me. Otherwise, I will come for you and kill all those who stand in my way; the choice is yours." With that, Jackson jumped up and ran away from me through the trees, away from the house.

I stood there watching where he left, waiting for him to come back. After a few minutes, I relaxed enough to start feeling the pain and collapsed into a heap on the ground. Unable to move or shift. I lay there trying to decide what to do next when I heard someone or something walking towards me. I moved back up onto my feet and turned to the sound, expecting it to be Jackson coming to finish off what he started earlier. But instead, I saw my uncle, who was holding what looked like a blanket in front of him.

"Daisy dear, is that you?" he asked quietly. The last thing I remember is whining as he placed the blanket over me and ran his fingers through my fur.

I am not sure whether he used his magic to put me to sleep or if I passed out, but I woke up three days later in a different room; Auntie Mary was there the second my eyes opened. They had asked a local Alpha for help. They had moved us to a safe house that same night.

Before I was taken, we had lived in Exeter; the safe house was down in Cornwall, and that was where we stayed until I knew I was ready to start living my life again.

I take a deep breath as I finish telling Michael about my past and how I came to be a wolf. Reliving it is always hard, but it feels like a weight has been lifted from my shoulders. Michael needed to know the truth. *I* needed him to know. Whatever happens between us now, I have been honest with him, and that's all I can do.

Michael lifts up slightly, looking down his chest at me. He places a hand on the back of my head and starts stroking my hair.

"You won't ever have to run from him again, that I promise you. if you ever get an idea of where he is, I want you to tell me. I can get in touch with other packs and get them to keep an eye out for him. You and your family are not alone in this; you have us now. Even if you don't join my pack, you will always have their support."

I know that he means every word; I believe he would protect me. If anybody has a chance of beating Jackson, it's Michael. But that doesn't mean I would ever let him put himself in harm's way. I would never forgive myself if anything happened to this man because of me.

Chapter Twenty-One

DAISY

The whole day yesterday was beyond perfect, excluding the jogger.

Michael and I had such a fantastic time in the forest. We talked, we laughed until we cried, and our stomachs ached. We got to be a typical couple, so lost in our own happy little bubble nothing else existed or mattered.

I can't wait to see him again in class. As much as it sucks that our relationship must remain secret until Michael can find somebody to replace him in his role here. It's still amazing that I get to look at him every single day and know that he is now mine.

I'm just putting the finishing touches to my makeup when Tony rushes in, closing the door behind him.

"Hey! Have you ever heard of knocking?"

Tony raises one eyebrow at me.

"Oh, please bitch, you ain't got nothing I haven't seen before." I shake my head as I go back to applying my mascara. "Right, wolf girl, spill it. I want details no matter how messy," he says, jumping on my bed and making himself comfortable. Unfortunately for him, I'm running late for coffee with Beth.

"Well, you should have woken up earlier then because I'm heading out. You will have to wait for your gossip," I answer, not taking my eyes off my reflection as I slowly put on some lip gloss, trying hard not to laugh.

"What? Are you for real? I want details, and I want them now!" he demands, sulking. I shake my head and smirk. "Bitch, come on. I need to know if Michael at least treated you like the queen you are. Plus, if he's a good kisser." He looks at me in the reflection of the mirror and winks. I place my hand on my chest, pretending to be outraged.

"Tony, I've no idea what you expect to hear. A lady does not kiss and tell."

"Daisy, we have been over this. Just because you call yourself a lady does not make you one. You, my dear friend, are a first-class kick-ass bitch, own that shit. Now spill witch."

I roll my eyes, laughing while shaking my head.

"Fine, yes, it was amazing; he treated me like his queen, and he is the most amazing kisser," I say through my smile. Tony has the biggest grin.

"Right, that will do me until later. I expect to see you in my office at three; by 'my office', I mean The Crows."

"Kellan isn't there tonight, is he?" I ask nervously; Tony shakes his head.

"He hasn't been back since that night. Carl has been trying to get in touch with him to collect his coat and wages, but he won't answer his phone."

"Okay, great, as I've no intentions of seeing him any time soon. Make sure you have a drink waiting for me. Gin and tonic, please." I wink as I get my stuff together. I sling my bag over my shoulder and pocket my phone before turning to my best friend and pointing towards the door. "Now get the hell off my bed and bugger off; you have class in an hour."

Tony jumps off the bed and plants a kiss on my cheek.

"You are lucky I love you. I'll be going straight to work after class to help with a big delivery, so I'll see you at three; I want all the details." I roll my eyes at him as he walks out of my door. Just as I leave my room, I feel my phone vibrate in my pocket.

Michael: Good morning, beautiful. Xxx

I start grinning like a teenage girl. Is there anything better than a good morning text? I quickly type out a reply before heading off to the cafeteria.

Daisy: Good morning, handsome. Xxx

I shove my phone back into my pocket before heading to meet Beth. I know she'll be cursing me for being late.

As I enter the cafeteria, I spot Beth in the usual spot holding up a coffee cup to show me she already has them. I head over and take the cup she holds out for me, taking a large sip as I sit down. I swear I feel the caffeine giving me energy, causing me to moan softly as I lean back into my chair, feeling very content. I open my eyes to see Beth shaking her head at me.

"What is it with you and coffee?" she asks as I shrug.

"I don't know what you mean. My love of coffee is perfectly normal. It's people who aren't obsessed with this brown nectar that I don't understand. I'm sure the dislike of coffee is a sign of insanity."

Beth looks lost for words, so she settles for calling me a crazy bitch. I shrug, smiling. I feel my phone vibrate again and quickly pull it out of my pocket.

Michael: Do you think you'll ever look at me the way you look at your first cup of coffee? Xxx

I quickly turn around, spotting Michael as he walks out of the door. As amazing as he is to look at from the front, it's a damn good view when he walks away from you as well.

Daisy: That depends. Can you make me feel as good as my first cup of coffee? Xxx

It doesn't take long for my phone to vibrate with a reply. My pulse rate shoots through the roof when I read it; my body reacts in a way it really shouldn't when there are this many people around.

Michael: Oh, baby, the difference between me and that coffee is you can only have one first cup a day, whereas I can make you feel like that multiple times. Xxx

"Who the hell are you texting? They have either really embarrassed you or sent you a dick pic," Beth exclaims, causing me to choke on my coffee. It takes me almost a full minute to stop coughing long enough to respond.

"What the hell, Beth! Next time you are going to say something like that, make sure I'm not drinking or eating," I laugh, using a napkin, Beth hands me to wipe down the front of my top.

"Well? Are you going to tell me which one it is?"

I shake my head at her, grinning.

"Nope, I think it's more fun letting your imagination run away with you," I reply as I stand up and head out of the canteen. I can hear her begging me to put her out of her misery, but I keep walking with a smile on my face.

As we walk to class, I quickly text Michael again.

Daisy: I'll have to change your name on my phone so no one can see who I am texting. I wonder what I should call you? xxx

It doesn't take long for him to reply.

Michael: You have so many creative names for me already; I'm sure you'll think of one. Could I suggest Mr Macho Man, My Brilliant Mate, Mr Perfect, or even a straightforward World's Sexiest Wolf? I'll let you decide. Xxx

I'm chuckling to myself, trying to decide on a response as we get to class. Beth is still nagging at me as we walk into the room. We are the first ones besides Michael, who I smile at sheepishly as I enter. I'm just sitting in my chair when Beth decides to change tactics.

"Michael, you will help me out here, won't you?"

I spin around and stare at her.

"What do you need help with?" Michael asks as he leans against the front of his desk, his legs stretched out in front of him.

"Nothing," I jump in. Michael looks at me and raises an eyebrow. Balls, I responded too quickly, and now he's intrigued.

"Daisy has been acting weird, looking all flustered and smirking like a madwoman at her phone, and I think it's only fair that she shares what's got her panties in such a hot mess."

I throw my hands up over my face and sink into my chair. Ground, swallow me up whole, please. I hear Michael laughing from the desk, making me even more embarrassed than I already was.

"That depends on what you mean by having her 'panties in a hot mess'."

"Shut up, shut up now!" I hiss through my teeth at her, too scared to look at him.

"Well, the last message had her going bright red and biting her lip like she was auditioning for a porno," Beth chuckles next to me.

"Dear gods, kill me now," I beg as I place my head on the table, putting my arms over it as if trying to block out these two discussing me. But, instead, I can hear them both laughing, knowing full well what they are doing.

"Well, that definitely sounds like it was an interesting message. Would you say Daisy looked as excited as she does when she has her first cup of coffee?" I hear Michael ask. My head shoots up off the table, and I stare at him wide-eyed. he is almost bursting at the seams and loving every moment of this, the bastard.

"More, way more," Beth answers, smiling.

"Now that is interesting," Michael answers. I raise my eyebrows at him, wondering how far he is going to take this. He looks at me and winks. "I'll have to say if it causes that much of an extreme reaction, then maybe you should give her this time to enjoy whatever has put that smile on her face. Given how close you two are, I'm sure you'll be the first to know when she is ready to tell." Michael looks at me, smiling. I can't decide whether to kill him or hug him right now. Is he giving me permission to tell her about us?

"See, shut up about it, please," I beg Beth. She just rolls her eyes at me and smiles.

"Fine, but I'd better be the first to know, and that means before Tony."

"I don't have a say, really, do I?" I laugh as people start piling into the class. I look over at Michael whilst Beth is distracted for a second. Michael grins at me, and I notice he has his phone in his hand; at the same time, mine vibrates.

Michael: If you react like that to a message, imagine how you'll be after the real thing. 😉 xxx

Oh, gods, this man is going to be my death.

Daisy: FYI, your name is now saved as DICK!! xxx

Michael actually laughs out loud from his desk, making everyone turn and face him.

"Sorry, somebody thinks they're a comedian," he says, holding his phone up.

"Well, they made you laugh," I reply, winking at him.

Yeah, maybe hiding our relationship will be harder than we originally thought.

Chapter Twenty-Two

MICHAEL

I knew it would be hard to be in the same room as Daisy and not act on my feelings after yesterday. But, after Beth and I had spent five minutes winding her up, it'd been near impossible not to walk up to her and kiss her. Knowing that I had that kind of effect on her was affecting me, too. Keeping this quiet between us may be more challenging than I anticipated. It was so hard not to watch her during class. I'm sure people are going to start noticing something soon.

Once class had finished, I returned straight to my office, hoping to catch up on some work after skiving all day yesterday. I'm just typing up a message to Daisy on my phone when my mum's name flashes up on my screen.

"Hi, Mum," I answer, leaving the phone away from my ear so I can complete the message. Thank you, wolf hearing.

"Hello Mikey, I waited for you to call last night, but you didn't. I take it you were busy with a certain lady?" I can hear the excitement in my mum's voice. I smile, knowing how happy this is making her.

"Sorry, Mum. I didn't get home until the early hours of this morning. But, yes, I was with Daisy. We had a fantastic time. It was all perfect."

"I'm so happy for you, Mikey." I'm about to ask how she is when somebody knocks on my office door.

"Hang on, Mum, don't go anywhere," I say before calling out, "Come in." As soon as the door opens, her scent fills the room.

"Hey, have you got a second?" Daisy asks, putting her head around the door, smiling. I smile back, so happy to see her again so soon.

"That depends. Is it just you?"

Daisy nods as she walks in, closing the door behind her.

"Yep," She answers, smirking.

"Then baby, I'll need far more than a second for what I want to do right now," I reply, leaning forward on the desk and giving her my best sexy eyes. I watch as she blushes, biting her bottom lip as she walks towards me.

"Michael Graham Adams, you *did not* just say something so vulgar!"

Daisy stops abruptly, mouth open wide. I look down slowly at the phone on my desk, sucking my lips in between my teeth.

"Shit, sorry, Mum. I forgot you were there." I look back up at a gobsmacked Daisy.

"I'm so sorry, Daisy; he's obviously been spending too much time with his brother and team. I expected better from him. I didn't bring him up to be that crude," Mum calls down the phone. Daisy smiles as she dumps her bag in front of my desk before walking around to my chair and leaning on the desk between my legs. I move the phone so it's between us.

"Don't worry, Mrs Adams, he isn't usually like that; he was a gentleman the majority of yesterday," she replies, winking at me.

"Good, I'm glad to hear it. I don't want any of that *Mrs Adams* business; it's Barbara, dear." Daisy smiles and agrees. "Now, as you are there, Daisy, you can answer a question for me, as Mikey ignores it every time. When are you coming to see me? I can't wait to meet you." I expect Daisy to feel a little overwhelmed, as I know meeting the parents is a big deal. I place a hand on her hip, giving her a reassuring squeeze. Daisy looks into my eyes with the sweetest smile.

"Whenever Michael wants to bring me, I'll be there." I look at her amazed; every time I'm sure things will be getting too much for her, she shows me she's stronger than I think.

"Can you do tonight?" Mum asks excitedly, and both she and Daisy start laughing. I'm just at a loss for words.

"I can't tonight; sorry, I have plans. However, I'm free any night next week if Michael is." She looks at me, raising her eyebrows as if asking me to pick a date.

"Uh, Monday?" I suggest as it's the first day that comes to my mind. Daisy nods as I hear Mum say she is free. "Great, so we will be with you Monday around four, Mum."

"I'll make dinner. Is there anything you don't eat, Daisy?"

Daisy shakes her head before answering. "Nope, if it's food, I'll eat it," she laughs. "That's easy then. I'll get on it. See you Monday, Daisy. I can't wait now. Oh, bye, Mikey," she calls as an afterthought. I roll my eyes, shaking my head at the phone.

"Yeah, I'm still here, Mum. I will call you later when I'm free," I reply before hanging up.

I look up at Daisy, who is grinning from ear to ear. I take in the view of her leaning against my desk, standing in between my legs; her cheeks are pink from blushing, and her eyes sparkling. I place a hand on each hip and tug her slightly, making her move even closer to me so I can kiss her silky lips.

"Hey," I whisper, smiling up at her.

"Hey, back," she replies before gently kissing me once more; she then stands back up and leans on the desk again. I refuse to take my hands off her. Instead, I start rubbing small circles with my thumbs. I watch as she takes in a deep breath as her scent changes, giving away her arousal. I love the effect my touch has on her.

"Does everyone call you Mikey?" Daisy asks, tilting her head to one side. I smile and shrug.

"Mum and Jon always do; the team and some of my oldest friends do, too, most of the time. More so when they are after something."

She places her hands on my shoulders, leaning into me slightly whilst giving me the sweetest look.

"Does that mean I can?"

I tug her hips so her body is pressed as tightly as possible against mine.

"Baby, you can call me anything you want." I grin up at her. "Although calling me a dick this morning was a little uncalled for."

Daisy rolls her eyes as she pushes against my shoulders so she is standing back up straight.

"Why was it? You were both picking on me. You're lucky I didn't call you worse."

"Okay, point taken. Maybe I got a little carried away

after hearing how you reacted to my text. Plus, you were so embarrassed it was super cute."

Daisy looks at me, shocked again and tries to walk away, but I just laugh and pull her onto my lap, not allowing her to move until she stops fighting me. I have to remember to keep the noise down as we know people are in the offices on either side of mine.

"Anyway, what have I done to deserve this unexpected visit?" I ask as I release her enough to sit comfortably on my knee. Daisy looks at me, and I can see she is nervous.

"I wanted to talk to you about Beth. I don't like hiding this from her. I know we need to keep it quiet, but it's Beth."

I smile knowingly.

"I knew you would want to tell her. I'm actually surprised you haven't already. Or that she didn't notice how we were together at the pub on Saturday. Everybody else seemed to realise that something was going on."

"Yeah, but it's Beth. She isn't the most observant person when she has had a drink. It has been hard keeping it from her, though. I can't usually hold my own piss when it comes to her and Tony. I tell them everything."

I start laughing, loving the mad little sayings that come out of this woman's mouth.

"As long as you are okay with me telling her, I'm going to take her with me to see Tony at work in a bit to tell her. Are you still going up to speak to the council tonight?" she asks. I nod in confirmation.

I informed her yesterday that I planned to go in front of the pack council tonight to inform them about the two of us. As she is a rogue, they will need to know a little about her. It's common practice to announce when we find our mate this way. Usually, the two of us would go in front of them together, but I want to use the fact that we can't be seen together as part of the argument for me leaving my post here.

"Are you sure you don't need me to come with you?" she asks nervously.

"No, darling, it'll be fine. I have to attend these meetings anyway with Marcus. I'll call you when I'm done. The meets usually finish around ten, so just let me know if you are asleep before then."

"I won't be. Tony doesn't finish until late, plus I was promised a lock-in, remember." I'm just about to remind her to be safe when a knock comes from the door. Daisy quickly rushes around to the front of the desk and sits down. Signalling for me to wipe my mouth at the same time. I do and see her lip gloss on my hand; I can't help but chuckle. That could've been interesting.

"Come in," I call out. A year three pokes their head in. "Sorry, Michael, are you busy?" Daisy stands up and picks up her bag. "It's okay. I've finished with him. Thanks for putting my mind at ease, Michael," Daisy says, winking at me while her back is turned to my other student.

"Any time, you have my details if you need anything." Daisy nods as she walks out of the door, waving behind her. I have to remind myself that another student is present; otherwise, I would chase after her just for one more kiss.

Chapter Twenty-Three

DAISY

"Hey Carl, is Tony here?"

Carl turns to face me from behind the bar.

"Hey, Dais. He's just sorting the delivery out for me; he shouldn't be too long. Want a drink whilst you wait?"

I pull myself up onto one of the bar stools.

"Yeah, the usual, please."

Carl gathers his shoulder-length blonde hair into a top bun whilst walking to the other side of the bar where the gin is kept. I use the time to check for the hundredth time since leaving Michael's office for a message. There's none. He said yesterday he rarely has his personal phone on him at work, but I miss him. Gods, I sound like a deranged stalker again.

Carl places a glass in front of me, dragging me away from my phone and my thoughts.

"Cheers, how much do I owe?" I ask, pulling out my bank card.

"That one is on the house." I look up at him, shocked.

Carl reaches over and takes my hand. "It's just a little something as your night out ended so badly on Saturday. How are you feeling after it all?"

"I'm okay; luckily, there's been no side effects. Thank you again for letting me crash here that night." Carl is about to say something when Beth walks in, stopping him.

"Best let go of her hand, Carl. She is a taken woman now," I hear Beth call out as she walks around to where I'm sitting. Carl looks at me, smiling, lifting one eyebrow.

"Well, it's about bloody time," he exclaims. I can't stop the smile that spreads across my face.

"Hang on, how does Carl know, and I don't?" Beth exclaims next to me.

"Because he gave the guy a talking to," Tony calls up from the cellar. Carl laughs as I look at him, shocked.

"It's true. Actually, I think we all told him, especially Tony, who declared, and I quote, 'I will not think twice about cremating you if you hurt her." I look at him and Tony, who is walking into view.

"How do I not know about this?" I ask, shocked.

"Does it matter? At least, it seems to have worked out for the best. It's an amazing feeling when you find your other half. I remember the first time I saw my Richard; I swear the moment will be imprinted on my heart forever," Carl explains as his whole face lights up.

"That's because you were drunk and threw up all over his brand-new boots. Richard told me you were lucky he knew you were his soul mate; otherwise, he would have killed you," Tony adds, walking up to us and leaning on the bar. I glance over at Carl as he throws back his head and roars laughing. I love Carl and Richard, they both look like a couple of Hell's Angels throwbacks, but they have the biggest hearts and will do anything for their friends and family. But goddess help anybody who hurts their mate.

"But we both still remember it, so like I said, imprinted." I'm impressed with the guys; neither has said 'mate' knowing there's a human around. I look at Beth, who is just staring at me wide-eyed.

"Hang on, are you telling me this guy isn't just a fling; he is the real deal?"

I nod, shrugging at her.

"I think he might be, yeah."

"Hang on, you really don't know who it is?" Carl asks Beth, then looks at Tony and me. All three of us shake our heads. Tony and I share a grin, which causes Beth to let out a deep sigh of frustration.

"Dude, I didn't even know there was a *who* until this morning. I only know it's some kind of secret," Beth replies.

"So you didn't notice anything suspicious at all Saturday night?" Carl asks, frowning at her. She frowns back at him, shaking her head. Carl turns around as he roars, laughing.

"Girl, you were more drunk than I thought. The whole bar knew who she was flirting with."

Beth opens her mouth to shout at me, but Tony intervenes.

"Hey, I need to know about yesterday before all the drinkers come in; it was their first real date. Why do you think I told her she had to come and see me whilst I was working? I need the low down like now!" Tony exclaims. Carl just looks at me, amazed, ignoring Tony.

"I want to know how you kept it from Beth. You two tell each other everything."

I just shrug.

"It's complicated, isn't it." I can see Carl weighing up all the information and nodding in agreement.

"Wait a minute. You told me you couldn't hang out yesterday after class was cancelled because you had plans. Did you make plans with this guy as soon as you got the message?" Beth asks. I consider telling her straight then, but teasing her is more fun, especially after this morning, so I smile. "Hang on, if he was here Saturday, that means I must have met him!"

I open my mouth to answer when we hear the front door of the bar open. We all immediately turn towards the noise.

"Well, if it isn't my new baby sister, Daisy!" Jon calls from across the room. Tony who has been trying desperately not to laugh at Beth, roars laughing as she stares open-mouthed between Jon and me.

"Baby sister?" She looks at Jon, obviously recognising him. "Hang on, you're Michael's brother. You were here Saturday."

Jon strolls up to us, all beaming. Beth looks from him to me, and I can see the moment it all clicks into place.

"Surprise!" I exclaim sheepishly as her mouth and eyes widen with shock.

"No. Freaking. Way. Michael is your mystery guy? No wonder you were so quick to make plans yesterday. You were both skiving together!" Beth just stares at me as she slaps my arm. "Bitch, what the hell?"

"Oh shit, have I just outed you to the wrong people?" Jon asks, looking around, obviously remembering that we are meant to be keeping things quiet.

"Thankfully, no, you gobshite. Do you have a brain-to-mouth filter, or do we just have to wait and see if what comes out of that gaping hole in your face is appropriate?"

The guy next to Jon howls, laughing, as Tony and Carl join in. I look over at him and realise he's another wolf.

"Wow, Mikey wasn't wrong when he said you are as fierce as you are beautiful," he says, grinning.

"Michael said I was fierce and beautiful?" I ask, swooning a little at the compliment. The guy steps forward, holding out his big hand; I lean forward to shake it.

"He sure did, as well as that you could kick all our arses if we pissed you off, so this is me being good. I'm Stuart, Stuart Harvey."

"Hey! Wait a minute!" Beth demands as she steps towards me. Everyone turns and looks at her.

"I get that you guys need to keep it secret, but how long has this been going on? When did you start dating? Was it after your birthday when he looked after you?" I can almost hear all the cogs turning in her head as she tries to get her head around it all. As much as I enjoy winding her up, I feel a little guilty for hiding it from her.

"It's only been since my birthday. Feelings for each other may have started a little earlier," I mumble. Tony looks at me, tipping his head to one side whilst raising his eyebrows. Beth just looks at me dumbfounded.

"How much earlier are we talking about here? A week? A month?"

I slowly shrug whilst holding my hands up, scared to tell her the truth as I feel like she will flip. Then, of course, the gobshite, a.k.a Jonathan, opens his mouth.

"Mikey saw her sitting on a bench on the grounds of the university. He said the second he saw her, he knew she was the one, but she ran off, and he didn't see her again until walking into his first class." Jon answers like it's old news. Beth stares at him in complete shock.

"Okay, so let me get this straight: Michael and you have fancied each other since the first day of classes, and you *never* acted on it. I can't believe this. You have listened to everyone saying how hot they thought he was all those times, and you never said a word. I thought you didn't even fancy him. When, in fact, you were falling for him, big style, and I had no idea! I can usually read you like a freaking book. So how the hell did it start?"

I quickly explained that we would occasionally flirt when we saw each other in the gym.

"But I figured it was just playful banter. Then things started to change after I came back from Christmas. Michael jumped in when someone tried to threaten me. He then helped me carry my stuff up to our dorm. There was a moment then when I thought he might actually feel the same way about me, but I panicked again and rushed into the dorm. Too embarrassed to find out if he did or not."

"It started earlier than that for Mikey," Jon says as he leans on the table where he is now sitting next to Tony. He turns and looks at Stuart, who is directly next to Beth. "Remember the Christmas night out when he sliced his hand up with that glass?"

Stuart frowns, nodding.

"The night he walked out and left us all in the club? I thought that was because of Michelle?" Jon shakes his head.

"No, he had seen Daisy and this dickhead Kellan together in town and gotten himself worked up after a few too many drinks."

I look at Jon, confused.

"But there was never anything between Kellan and me. If I was in town with Kellan, Tony would have been there as well."

"Mikey saw Kellan put his arm around you and kiss your head or something like that. He thought it meant you were together. He really struggled with the idea of you being with someone else," Jon explains. I'm about to say some choice words about Kellan when what Jon said hits me.

"Hang on, Michael sliced his hand on a glass?" I ask, feeling guilty. Jon and Stuart both nod at me.

"One minute, he was staring into space. The next, he had squeezed the glass so hard that it smashed." As if he had never told me about that yesterday. I'm about to ask for more information when Jon continues.

"Mikey nearly told you everything outside your dorm that day when you came back from Cornwall, but you ran off. Just as he decided he was going to knock on your door and make you listen, Kellan arrived. The little prick told him the two of you were together. Mikey left, thinking you had chosen Kellan. I know all this because I dragged it out of him the other night before our run."

"Oh, goddess," I gasp as I cover my face in my hands; I feel sick with guilt. Then, I feel someone squeeze my shoulder. I turn to see Tony looking at me.

"You didn't know how he felt about you like he didn't know how you felt about him. It's not your fault. Kellan seems to have been stirring the pot for a while with all his lies. He is to blame, not you."

"I must have led Kellan on somehow; otherwise, why would he say we were together when we weren't?"

"Who knows why Kellan does anything? You were always honest with him. If anything, it's my fault. I offered to let him stay in our dorm over Christmas. I never thought it would do so much damage."

"Well, none of it matters now. Mikey and you seem to be on the right track and are no longer hiding your feelings from one another. So, Kellan loses anyway, doesn't he," Jon says, winking at me.

"I still can't believe I missed all of this, as well as you guys flirting Saturday. Do I live in a separate bubble from you all, or what?" I look at Beth and laugh as I stand up and stand behind her, wrapping my arms around her shoulders.

"You are the least observant person I have ever met at times, but it's what makes you, you," I laugh, kissing her on the cheek; she swats at me as I walk back to my seat, laughing.

"Think this calls for a celebratory drink." Carl walks up to our side of the bar carrying a tray of drinks. Everyone agrees wholeheartedly, taking their drink of choice.

"Oh shit!"

I look at Beth, who is looking at me with her hand clamped over her mouth. "It was Michael texting you this morning, wasn't it?" I start laughing whilst nodding at her. "Oh god, no wonder you were begging me to shut up!" She throws her hands over her face.

"What?!" Tony and Jon both ask at the same time. Beth quickly fills them in on how I had been left flustered by a text because I wouldn't tell her who it was from, so she asked Michael to help her find out. Soon, everyone is laughing, demanding that they see the text he sent; as you can guess, I refused.

What was meant to be a quick chat and a few drinks turned into an entire evening of drinking and chatting shit. Beth had to leave after an hour as it was one of her dormmates' birthdays, but she promised to try and get back later.

As much as I love Beth, the conversation flows a little easier once she has left. We don't need to worry about saying too much in front of a non-sup. We all start chatting loudly. Tony sticks some music on, and Carl ends up just bringing over the bottle of bourbon for the guys as well as a jug of gin and tonic for me.

A couple of hours later, the party is in full swing. We are all quite tipsy, and Carl has told Tony he can just concentrate on our table. If we don't need anything, he can sit with us and drink. Tony is more than happy with that, especially as he has been working most of the day. Richard is out with his family for the evening and will be back around closing, so Carl is keeping busy. I've already started dancing to the odd song, as the dance floor has been calling me. Our own little party is in full swing.

"Mikey is going to kill me if you get drunk," Jon says, pointing at me from across the table. I just laugh and shrug. I know he is probably right, which just makes it even more fun.

"I'll tell him it's all my fault. Tony and I can't get too drunk anyway, as we have a full weekend of partying ahead of us. The last thing I need is to be dying from three days' worth of hangovers when I meet your mum on Monday. She'll be telling Michael to reject me." The nervous knot in my stomach tightens at the thought of it.

I still can't believe I agreed to meet his mum already. When I spoke to her on the phone, I was so relaxed, and she sounded so happy I got caught up in all the excitement. But now I've stopped and thought about it, I realise that I'm terrified she'll hate me. What if I'm not what she expected for her son? What if she thinks he can do better?

"Trust me when I say you have nothing to worry about when it comes to Mum. She's going to love you," Jon says, winking at me, "Just be yourself, and you two will be inseparable in no time."

Stuart nods in agreement; he's a little too drunk to put

words into sentences right now. I'm just about to respond when I hear someone say my name behind me.

My back instantly straightens at the exact moment Jon and Tony jumped to their feet, quickly followed by Stuart. I turn slowly, coming face to face with Kellan.

Chapter Twenty-Four

DAISY

"I think you need to leave."

I hadn't noticed Jon move until he's standing between Kellan and me. It looks like Jon is going to be as protective as his brother. That's just great. I stand up and put a hand on Jon's arm.

"It's fine."

He turns and looks at me, his eyebrows raised. I can feel the anger radiating off him.

"Like hell it is. He drugged you and let you wander off alone," he snaps, pointing at Kellan. Then, out of the corner of my eye, I see Stuart's back straighten; he takes a step towards us with one of the most threatening looks I have ever seen. His eyes trained on Kellan the whole time. Great, this is all I need: two overprotective wolves. I need to defuse this situation quickly.

"We don't know that do we? Plus, even if he did, he isn't going to cause any trouble now, are you?" I ask, looking at Kellan, who shakes his head. I glance over my shoulder to where Kellan is looking. Tony stands with his arms crossed over his chest, staring at him, his eyes darkening. Why have I got to be the sensible one here? I've had too much to drink for this. I quickly roll my eyes at Tony, which earns me a raised eyebrow in response. I turn back to Kellan as he starts to speak.

"No, I only came in to pick up my wages. When I saw you were here, I just wanted to talk, that's all." I take a step forward to talk to Kellan in private, but Jon places a hand on my arm to stop me.

"I don't like this, and a certain person won't like this either," he whispers in my ear. I lean back to look him in the eye as I whisper just as quietly.

"No, they wouldn't, but they have promised to let me fight my own battles. I expect you to let me do the same." Jon lifts his hand off my arm, frowning. It is written all over his face that he isn't happy about any of this, but I turn away from him and nod to the other side of the bar, signalling Kellan to follow me. I purposely stay within sight of the others as I know Jon would be straight on the phone to Michael if he thought I was doing something stupid.

"You are doing something stupid," my wolf groans. I quickly tell her to be quiet as I pay attention to my surroundings.

I stop with my back to the others; Kellan turns to face me. In all fairness, he looks like hell; he has lost weight, his face is covered in stubble, and his hair looks like it has lost all life. Once again, I find myself feeling sorry for him.

"How have you been, Kellan? You haven't been in classes all week." Kellan shakes his head as he takes a seat at a table. I sit down opposite him, keeping plenty of space between us.

"I figured it was best I stayed away. Tony and Michael both threatened to kill me if I went back, so I didn't." I knew they had warned him; we all took the fact that he had stayed away as an admission of guilt.

"Will you be coming back?" I ask; Kellan shakes his head. I inwardly relax as I really hadn't wanted him to. It's been nice not feeling his eyes boring into the back of my head through every single lesson.

"I can't be in that room and see you and him flirting together, rubbing it in my face that you chose him over me."

"Kellan, who are you on about?" I don't know why I'm denying it; I know, he knows. That's proven when he just looks at me as he leans back in his chair.

"Daisy, everyone in here on Saturday knew what was going on between you two. If you were trying to hide it, you did a really poor job." He looks down at the table again. His face drops, and I feel the guilt I feel every time I hurt him by not having any feelings for him.

"Kellan, before Saturday, nothing was going on between us other than flirting. The fact that he had to look after me because somebody spiked my drink with a drug is how we ended up acting on our feelings."

Kellan laughs out loud and starts rubbing his forehead.

"Only I could screw that up."

My wolf instantly stands to attention. Did he just say what I think he said? *"Yep."*

"It was you that drugged me, wasn't it?" I ask cautiously, knowing that this could escalate quickly if not handled properly. Kellan doesn't say anything; he just looks at the table, fidgeting with a beer mat. "Why Kellan? Why would you put me through that?"

Blood starts pounding in my ears. I can feel myself getting angrier and angrier. I can also hear the other voices getting louder. Carl is telling them all to let me handle it,

Tony is trying to get to me, and Jon and Stuart are debating whether they need to contact Michael. I spin around in my chair and stare at them as I snap.

"Stop it. This is between Kellan and me. Sit down and shut the fuck up."

They all instantly sit down quietly; I turn back to Kellan and stare at him.

"Answer me, Kellan. Why did you do it?" When he looks up at me, it isn't the Kellan I'm used to seeing. This, I realise, is the real Kellan. Not the version carefully put together for others to see. Everything about him screams danger, and I can't put my finger on it. For a brief second, I am scared of what he'll do.

"You weren't meant to wander off. You were meant to go where I told you to. If you had just done as you were told, just for once in your life, then you would've been okay. But no. You had to do things your way." I stare at him, lost for words.

"What would you've done if I'd done as I was told? What would've happened when the drugs kicked in and I was unconscious? Would you have forced yourself on me? What about when they had worn off? Would you've just drugged me again and again until I just did as I was told? Did you think I would have fallen madly in love with the person who drugged me and held me against my will?" My voice is getting louder and louder with each question. What the hell did I ever do to him for him to resort to drugging me? I feel physically sick.

"No harm would have come to you. You would have been safe. I'm not a pervert. I would never have taken advantage of you. I would have just made you see that you belong to me and not him." Oh, screw this being calm shit. My anger gets the better of me as I jump from my seat, slamming my hands onto the table as I lean against it.

"I don't belong to anyone, I don't belong to Michael, and I certainly don't belong to you; I belong to me and only me."

"YOU BELONG TO ME!" Kellan roars as he jumps to his feet; he sends the table and his chair flying. I fall backwards as I move out of the way so as not to get hit. Kellan grabs hold of my wrist and pulls me back onto my feet, my head spins. Kellan holds my wrist, so I am forced to stay near him.

"You have always belonged to me, not to *him*, not to anyone else, ME. The sooner you learn that, the sooner we can stop all this ridiculous drama and move on together!" I can hear the others shouting, but I just hold up my hand to stop them.

"I belong to nobody but myself," I reply through gritted teeth. I try to pull my arm out of his grip, but I can't. When did he get so strong? Or is it because I'm feeling weak? Why am I feeling weak? The room is spinning. Did I hit my head? I feel like I am using my powers, but I'm not, am I? Kellan just looks at me with those black eyes and laughs.

"If you say so, princess, but you'll see, you will be begging me to come back to you." With that, Kellan leans over and kisses me on the cheek. "I'll be waiting for you," and walks towards the back door, waving at the others as he walks through it and out into the street behind the bar.

The second the door closes, Jon is by my side, grabbing hold of my shoulders and checking me over.

"Jon, I'm fine."

His face is bright red, and his jaw is clenched so tight that I swear he's going to crack his teeth.

"You're not fine; you're shaking like a leaf and freezing

cold." He starts rubbing his hands up and down my arms as if to warm me up. "What happened to 'I can look after myself'? What were you playing at putting yourself in danger like that?"

I shrug him off as I wrap my arms around my body. He's right. I'm freezing, and I have no idea why.

"I am fine, aren't I? Not a scratch on me. Just leave it." I turn to walk away, but Tony is there in front of me, his expression matching Jon's, who remains by my side.

"What the fuck was that?" he growls. I just roll my eyes at him, not needing the lecture.

"You saw what that was. Enough already. I need a drink and my hoodie." I try to step around him, but he blocks me. I let out a sigh, might as well get the lecture out of the way.

"I'm referring to you blocking us; none of us could get to you; it was like there was an invisible barrier around the two of you. All we could see was you two stood so close that there was hardly a gap between you. We couldn't get to you or hear what was going on." Tony grabs hold of my shoulders and grips them hard. The anger in his face melts away, and I see he is terrified.

"Why the fuck did you do it? If he had pulled out a knife or hurt you, we couldn't have helped. I'm all for you being able to stand on your own two feet but block us like that again, and I will fucking kick your arse myself, do you understand? I couldn't get to you, Daisy!"

I just look at him wide-eyed.

"Tony, I didn't do anything. I certainly didn't use any magic." I can tell by the look on his face he doesn't believe me. Did I block them? Did I do it without even realising it? Hadn't I been wondering if I was using my magic whilst Kellan had hold of me? No, I know I didn't. But if I didn't, then who did? I start looking around the bar, which is surprisingly quiet for a Friday night. Every single person in there is supernatural. Thankfully, it's a members-only night.

"Could you have done it without realising? I have felt your magic before, and it felt like you," Carl asks as he reaches over and places a hand on Tony's arm, reminding him he's still gripping me. Tony seems to realise, and his arms drop quickly. Carl hands me my hoodie, and I thank him quickly as I pull it on. I lift my hands to my face and try to think, but I can't, my head hurts so much. I have lost control of my magic in the past; I've cast spells without realising it. But that was when I was coming into my powers. It's been years since I've lost all control like that. I don't even know if it's possible to do it now; I'm experienced. I'll have to ask my uncle.

"I don't know. I just know I need to sit down. I feel like crap." I take one step and hear Stuart call across the room.

"Jon, the boss is still on the phone." Oh shit. I turn to Jon, who walks to Stuart to take the phone.

"You called him?"

Jon turns around to face me, the phone in his hand, and he looks furious.

"What choice did I have? You were going to get yourself fucking killed," he shouts back before taking the phone off Stuart. I moan, rubbing the back of my neck. I swear every muscle is knotted about ten times.

"Boss?" Tony asks as I sigh, shaking my head, and walk over to the table, ready to face the music.

I can already hear Jon telling Michael that I am unharmed and giving him an update on Kellan. I could wait for him to finish, but I'm not feeling the most patient, so I walk up to him and snatch the phone away from his ear. He starts to protest, but I just hold up my middle finger as I walk away from them all. Even with the phone in my hand, I can hear Michael shouting at Jon, and he is furious.

"Stop shouting; I'm fine," I snap, heading towards a sofa at the back of the bar, where no one is sitting, for some privacy. Michael's volume changes instantly, but I can tell he is still pissed off.

"Are you sure? You don't sound it. Jon said Kellan threw a fucking table at you. I'm going to kill him, no arguments." I can hear the anger in his voice, and I find myself wishing he was here so I could put his mind at ease.

"Mikey, I'm fine, just tired. All I want to do now is go home and go to bed. Kellan has put a real damper on what was a great night." I can hear a car engine in the background. "Are you driving?"

"Yeah, I was trying to get in touch with you to let you know I'll be away for the weekend; I'm on guard duty. I'm driving the Alpha to that large multi-pack meeting in Birmingham. So, I have to cancel our plans for the pizza and coffee date, sorry."

Damn it, I've been looking forward to having a pizza lunch at Michael's tomorrow before going out with Tony in the evening. I feel my mood plummet further.

"How come you have to go? I thought Marcus was?"

I hear Michael sigh and know he's as gutted as I am.

"He's been called away to a family emergency. I hate leaving you when that prick is causing shit, darling. Are you going to be okay?"

"I'm fine, I promise. Kellan won't cause any more problems." I hope not, anyway. I hear Michael sigh again.

"Look, I know you are going to hate this idea, but-"

"Nope," I cut in before he can carry on.

"You don't even know what I am going to suggest." I hear Michael groan.

"Yes, I do, and it's not happening. Jon and Stuart are not staying at mine, and I am not staying at theirs. You promised to let me fight my own battles. I managed just fine on my own tonight." I hear Michael curse and know I was right.

"I get that, darling, I really do. But I promised you I would be beside you, and I can't do that when I'm not there. I'd feel better if you at least let one of them stay with you. Just in case." I know his heart is in the right place, and I know his wolf demands he protect his mate, making it even harder for him. But I don't want to explain to my other dorm mates who the guys are.

"I tell you what, how about a compromise?" I ask hopefully.

"I'm listening." I can hear the concern in Michael's voice and can't help but smile.

"The guys were already going to join Tony and me on a night out tomorrow as we're going to watch that band I was telling you about. I was going to ask you when you called to see if you wanted to come, but you are away now. I know Stuart lives near me, so why don't we stick together when out and about? But I go home with Tony only. Jon can stay at Stuart's, so they are close if we need them, but I still get my privacy and don't feel like I am being babysat."

"And what about Sunday?" Michael asks.

"Tony and I are going to come here for a roast with Carl and Richard, followed by a few drinks, so I'm sure you'll agree I am safe here with them. You will be back on Monday, right?"

"Yes, I will be back by midday."

I smile to myself, knowing that I could win this one.

"So, I will be a good girl and stay in my room under lock and key. I'll even throw in a few spells for good measures until you get back. I will get Tony to walk me to my car when I leave to meet you. How does all that sound? I'll never be on my own. And on the off-chance, Kellan makes a fresh appearance, I won't face him alone again." I can almost hear Michael thinking it all through.

"Michael, there's no denying she has covered all bases. I would take it and count your blessings; you aren't there to have your nuts handed to you," I hear someone say down the line and realise it must be the Alpha who can hear everything.

"Thank you," I say, unsure how to address him as I'm not one of his pack, plus I have never really dealt with an Alpha before.

"Yes, thank you, Alpha," Michael adds sarcastically; I can hear the Alpha chuckling, followed by Michael sighing, "Fine, I'll agree to all of that. On one condition." Oh fuck.

"Go on," I say, dubious of this condition.

"Every night before you go into your apartment, Tony and Jon walk through it and check it's safe. Stuart can stay with you outside. After they know you are safe, they can go to Stuart's, and you can do whatever you do when at home. Also, you text me every now and again, so I will know you are safe, and I will be able to rest easier."

"Fine deal. I will agree to that," I smile proudly after winning this one.

"Fuck, you're not going to make my life easy, are you?" Michael groans down the line. I can hear the Alpha laugh in the background, and I can't help but smile.

"Nope. Get used to it, handsome. I'm like a handful of glitter, great to look at and fun to have around, but once I get in your space, there's no getting rid of me, no matter how hard you try." I hear the two of them roar with laughter.

"Go and have a drink, and please try to stay away from any more trouble this weekend."

I smile to myself.

"Will do my best, and Michael?"

"Yes, darling?"

"Be careful. I'm starting to like having you around," I say as I stand up and start walking towards Jon.

"Good, because I like being around you. Now give the phone to Jon and be good. Bye, darling."

"Bye, handsome," I reply, smiling, handing the phone back to Jon.

Chapter Twenty-Five

DAISY

Oh crap. Why did I think this would be a good idea? I'm in Michael's car as he drives to his mum's house. HIS MUM'S! I'm meeting the parent, and I'm freaking the hell out! Plus, I'm a little hungover.

Bloody Jon and Stuart had us drinking in the bar until two am last night. Carl finally called it a night after Tony fell off the table he and some random girl were dancing on. It had been a great night, though. In fact, it had been a fantastic weekend, considering how it had started.

"Penny for your thoughts?" I hear Michael say to my right. I turn to look at him as he smiles and places a hand on my knee. "What's going on in that pretty little head of yours, darling?" I mutter that I'm fine, but I feel Michael squeezing my knee slightly.

"Oh please, you are going to chew through that bottom lip in a minute." I can't help but chuckle; Michael glances at me quickly and smiles. "Not too hungover, are you? You had a bit of a crazy weekend, from the sounds of it." I feel myself groaning at the thought of it. Gods, there was so much gin.

"I'm not hungover. Although I'm never drinking again."

Michael laughs at me. I can't blame him, famous last words and all that shit.

"So, what's going on?" Michael asks again; I take a deep breath.

"What if your mum doesn't like me? What if she thinks I'm all wrong for you and tells you to reject me?" I blurt out. Michael laughs; he is actually laughing at me whilst I'm sitting here panicking to the point of feeling sick.

"Darling, you were all up for this when you spoke to Mum on Friday. You really don't have anything to worry about. She is going to love you; actually, I think she already does," he chuckles.

"How do you know?"

Michael takes my hand and pulls it up to his mouth, where he gently kisses the back of it.

"Because you're the most caring, loving, smart, strong, and extremely gorgeous woman I know. I don't think people can meet you and not fall instantly in love with you."

I feel myself huff playfully.

"You have to say that you're my mate."

Michael turns and smiles at me.

"This is true; however, being your mate just proves that my mum will love you. Remember how easy it was with Jon the first night you met him? That was because he is my family. You and they will have an instant connection due to the mate bond. I'm sure it will be the same when I meet your auntie and uncle. I hope so anyway," he playfully winks at me, and I laugh and relax a little. I know my auntie and uncle will love Michael.

"Anyway", he continues, "Even if Mum did say she

thought I should reject you, I wouldn't. I'll only do it if you order me to. You are mine, and I'm not going anywhere." He kisses the back of my hand again, and I lean into his shoulder quickly.

"You always know what to say to put me at ease," I whisper. Michael kisses the top of my head gently before I move away so he can concentrate on driving.

"That is what I'm here for, darling," he replies, not taking his eyes off the road, but I can see the side of his lips curl up in a smile.

"Cheese ball," I mutter, smiling. Michael roars, laughing.

"Why can I see that nickname sticking?" he asks, raising one eyebrow at me; I just shrug.

"If the shoe fits," I wink at him before adding, "Not that it's a bad thing."

"That's okay then, as I don't plan on changing. I want to spoil you and give you everything you could ever ask for, whether it's with gifts or just being there for you when you need me." I find myself leaning into his shoulder again.

"Major bonus points, cheese ball," I mutter as Michael kisses the top of my head again. I can feel his smile in my hair. "That's what I was aiming for. Now sit up; we're nearly there."

Ah, crap.

Michael

I can't believe I am taking my mate to meet my mum. It's a wolf's rite of passage I never saw myself actually doing. Poor Daisy looks terrified, but I know she has nothing to worry about. There is no way these two ladies will not get along. In fact, after seeing how well she obviously got along with Jon and Stuart this weekend, I think it should be *me* worried about Daisy and Mum meeting. They are going to enjoy making my life hell together.

I pull the car up to Mum's house, my childhood home, and look at Daisy, who is staring at the house and taking in the beautiful garden my mum spends so much time tending to.

"It's beautiful." I hear her whisper; I can't stop the smile from appearing on my face. I jump out of the car and head over to Daisy's side. "Has your mum always lived here?" Daisy asks as I help her out of the vehicle.

"Yes, my dad built it before they were even mated. He said it was like he knew what his mate would want before he had even met them. Mum has always said it took her breath away the moment she first saw it, and it still does now." I look back at Daisy and see her still looking at the house.

"That is so romantic."

I nod and smile at her as she turns to look at me.

"They were perfectly matched." I feel my smile becoming broader. "My dad had a way with words and actions when it came to my mum; maybe that's where I get it from with you." Daisy laughs at me before reaching up and giving me a quick kiss on the cheek.

"It sounds like it, cheese ball." I'm about to respond when the front door opens, and Mum appears in the gap.

"Are you going to stand out there all afternoon?" she calls. Daisy giggles next to me. I take her hand and lead her to my mother. Daisy grips my hand between both of hers as she takes a deep breath. I pull my hand free and put my arm around her shoulders, tugging her slightly so she is pressed against me. I lean my head down to kiss her head.

"She will love you," I whisper into her hair. I can feel Daisy relax slightly against me, which makes me smile, loving that I make her relax in such a way.

"Mum, this is Daisy," I announce as we get to the front door. Daisy steps out of my arms and towards my mum, holding out her hand.

"Nice to finally meet you," Daisy says. Mum grabs her hand and pulls her into a hug. I hear Daisy giggle nervously as she hugs her back.

"Well, aren't you just the cutest thing? Mikey, you never told me how beautiful she is." Mum says as she holds Daisy at arm's length, looking her up and down with the biggest grin on her face.

"I'm pretty sure I did," I reply. My mum just looks at Daisy, smiling. Daisy blushes but smiles back. "Have you finished embarrassing her yet?" I ask, crossing my arms across my chest. Mum looks up at me with one raised eyebrow,

"It's not Daisy I'll be embarrassing today." I open my mouth to respond, but Daisy beats me to it, jumping up and down and clapping her hands in excitement.

"Please say there are baby pictures?"

I look at Daisy, shocked, my mouth hanging open. Mum grabs her hand, pulling her in through the door, both giggling.

"So many baby pictures," I hear her reply as they head out of view.

Oh shit,

"Mum, don't you dare!" I call as I follow them into the house, closing the front door behind me.

Chapter Twenty-Six

DAISY

I now see why Michael said I had nothing to worry about; his mum is amazing. I'm so in love with her. We haven't stopped talking since I walked through the door. Barbara has shown me so many pictures of Michael and his siblings as they were growing up. Michael had never looked prouder than when Barbara had told him that Michelle would have loved me as much as she and Jon do.

From the pictures and the stories Barbara has told me, I can see just how close Michelle and Michael were. In every photo from their birth until Michelle was taken from them, they were always together. Either holding hands or Michael had his arm over his sister's shoulders. It really is lovely to see.

We've been here for a couple of hours now. Michael's currently up on the shed roof, fixing a hole in the felt. Barbara has asked me to help her make a list of uses for her herbs. Although she has no magical blood other than the wolf gene, she likes to make her own natural remedies and balms.

I'm just writing down the properties of the common dandelion for her when I hear a car pull up outside the front of the house. I turn just in time to see a sweaty, shirtless Michael jump from the top of the shed, landing perfectly as he looks over at me and winks.

"I'm sorry, I missed that. Can you do it again, please?"

Michael walks over and kisses me.

"Perv."

"Only at you, handsome."

Michael grabs the back of my head as his lips are crushed against mine. He pulls away far too quickly for my liking, and I actually pout as he pulls his t-shirt back over his head, hiding the eye candy.

Spoilsport.

"In that case, you can perv all you want later. But first, why are the guys here?"

"I invited them," Barbara calls from the other side of the garden. I look at Michael, who's frowning.

"But I told you Daisy wasn't ready to meet them yet."

I can see the concern in his eyes as he places a hand on my shoulder.

"That was before she was forced to spend the weekend with Jonny and Stuart. I asked her yesterday on the phone, and she told me she was fine with it."

Michael looks at me, and I realise I forgot to tell him about the call. Actually, I forgot until now. Oops.

"Hang on, you spoke yesterday?" Michael looks down at me, frowning. I bite my bottom lip and quickly pull out the puppy dog eyes.

"Oops, I knew I forgot to tell you something."

Michael opens his mouth to say something but is interrupted.

"Don't blame, Daisy. Do you have any idea how much

gin that woman put away this weekend? I'm surprised she's even sober."

I turn to see Jon walking through the back door and into the garden, closely followed by Stuart and two other guys.

"I wouldn't have had to drink so much if I wasn't stuck with your company all weekend. You would cause the pope to need AA." The sound of laughter fills the air as we all gather together.

I turn to face Michael's team as they stand before me. Jon is standing at one end, Stuart at the other, and they are all built like they work out at least twice a day.

"Fuck me, are you wolves or bears?" I knew Michael was built well for a wolf, but these guys are just as big. They all laugh as I quickly turn to Barbara with my hand over my mouth. "Shit, sorry, didn't mean to swear … Twice."

But Barbara just laughs, shaking her head.

"Daisy, when you have had this lot around all their lives, you get used to the bad language." She turns and faces the guys with a straight face, "That doesn't mean they can let their potty mouths run wild, though." They all look straight at Barbara, shaking their heads

"Never, Mama B," they all say in unison. Barbara gives them a curt nod before quickly winking at me. I smile back before turning to Jon.

"How's the head today, Sis?" he asks as he walks up and hugs me.

"Mine's fine, how's yours? You been causing any more trouble since last night?"

Jon steps back, placing a hand on his chest as if shocked.

"I don't cause trouble."

"No, it just always finds you," Michael adds as he walks up to us and places an arm over my shoulders, pulling me close to him. He turns towards the other three guys, who are now facing Michael and smiling.

"Well, as these morons are here, I might as well introduce you. Daisy, these are my pack brothers and teammates." He points from left to right. "This is Marcus, Will, and you know Stuart." I step forward and say hi to each of them. Marcus and Will reach out, and we shake hands. But when I get to Stuart, he scoops me up in a massive bear hug; I squeal in shock and then laugh as Michael growls a warning next to us. I turn and frown at him as Stuart places me back down before holding his hands up in defence.

"Oh, pack it in, you idiot," I sigh "worse things than a hug." I turn and look at Stuart, grinning, "Good thing he didn't see us dancing on the tables last night."

Michael slowly lifts his eyebrows, looking at Stuart like he is seconds away from killing him. Stuart, very wisely, takes a few steps back.

"It wasn't that kind of dancing; I swear there was no contact. Jon, back me up here."

Jon and I just look at each other, grinning.

"Oh, there was definitely contact, from what I remember," Jon answers. Stuart looks even more shocked and terrified as Michael takes another step forward, forcing him to take one back.

"Will you two tell him the truth? I never touched Daisy."

"Oh, I never said you were touching me; you were too busy bumping and grinding with that guy. What was his name, Jonny?"

"Paul," Jon responds as he stands with his arms crossed, acting as if the whole thing is boring him. Michael looks from Stuart to Jon and then to me. I wink at Jon, who starts grinning like the cat that's got the cream. Stuart, on the other hand, looks like he is ready to pass out. Will, Marcus and Barbara are all shaking with laughter. I look at Michael and shrug innocently.

"You bastards," Stuart mumbles as he relaxes; now that he is no longer Michael's target. Jon and I high five without even looking at each other. I watch Michael cross his arms across his chest.

"Have you quite finished winding me up?" he asks, stepping towards me; I cross my arms over my chest and look straight back at him.

"That depends on you and if you have finished being a jealous arse? That look may intimidate other rogues, but it doesn't work on this one, so pack it in, Adams," I declare as I raise my eyebrows to show I'm not backing down. Michael looks down at his arms and quickly uncrosses them.

"Yeah, okay, point made. Sorry," Michael mutters, looking down at me, a slight grin tugging at his lips.

"See what I mean, guys? She has him well and truly under her thumb already," Jon laughs next to us. "As for the jealous thing, don't worry, Mikey, it's Stuart after all; no one would willingly pick him unless they were steaming drunk and blind," Jon says as he steps next to his brother. I look at him, tipping my head to the side.

"So, he still has more chance than you then?"

Jon looks at me, shocked, and I wink at him as I wrap my arms around Michael's waist from the side. Barbara walks up to Jon and gently taps his cheek,

"It's okay, Jonny; I still love you."

Jon looks at her, grinning, then turns to me, sticking his tongue out. He's been doing it all weekend after I did it to him. He's such a child, which is probably why we have such a laugh together.

"You have to; you're his mum," Michael laughs. Barbara looks at him straight-faced as she replies.

"I might have to love you both, but that doesn't mean I have to like you. I like Jonny more than you right now."

Michael stands with his mouth hanging open as Barbara pulls me away from him.

"But I brought Daisy to see you. That must count for something?" Michael calls as we walk away. Barbara doesn't reply; she just winks at me.

"Come on, I've a bottle of wine with our name on it. We're going to need it with this lot here."

I can already hear them bickering playfully among themselves.

"Is it just the one bottle? Because I'm not sure it's going to be enough."

Barbara looks at me and smiles.

"I always have more than one bottle just for times like this."

I hug her arm as I rest my head on her shoulder.

"I can see you becoming my favourite person," I say, smiling.

"I heard that!" Michael calls after us. I hold my hand up and flip him the bird without turning to face him.

"Don't listen then." I can hear the guys all start laughing out loud as Barbara laughs next to me.

"Oh, you are already my favourite person," she replies, patting my hand. I'm just about to reply when I hear Jon shout, "Incoming." I jump from Barbara, spinning around just in time to see Michael as he grabs me before throwing me over his shoulder. I squeal as he turns away from Barbara.

"Sorry, Mum, I need to borrow my mate for a moment," he says as he heads back towards everyone else.

"Save me a glass. I'll kick his ass and come straight back. It'll only take a minute." I call to Barbara as I push myself up straight using Michael's trousers as leverage; I can see her shaking her head, laughing at us.

Michael walks past his pack brothers and heads to the gate by the side of the house, kicking it closed behind him.

"Where are you taking me?" I ask, trying to sound bored, but I can't help smiling. Michael turns as he lowers me slightly; I wrap my legs around his waist as he pushes me against the house wall.

"I can't do this with that lot watching," he says as his lips crash into mine. I instantly melt into him as I shove my fingers into his hair. I feel him growl deep in his chest. His tongue traces my lips, begging for access, which I grant hungrily. His tongue finds mine instantly, causing the kiss to deepen further. I feel his hands move from my hips to my ass as he pulls me closer. "Fuck, I can feel the heat coming from you through our clothes."

I rub myself against him, finding myself moaning as I feel his rock hard member being restricted by his trousers. He curses again as he moves with me, causing the kiss to deepen even further.

Michael ends the kiss with a deep growl before placing his head on my shoulder, both of us trying to catch our breath as I sink into his shoulder and close my eyes. My heart is racing, in time to his, like they are beating as one.

"I don't suppose you know an invisibility spell, as I would love nothing more than to sneak you to my room right now," Michael says into my neck as I giggle.

"No, sorry, the closest thing to one wouldn't work as you have to stay very still." I push my hips into him, slowly teasing him. I watch as his eyes roll into the back of his head, groaning deeply.

"The last thing I want to do right now is stay still. I need to feel myself moving in and out of you at various different speeds." He starts rocking against me to prove a point, rubbing me in just the right area whilst kissing my neck. I lean back against the wall as I can feel myself heading towards climax. I place my hands on his shoulders and reluctantly push him away.

"You carry on like that, and I am going to be forced to sit around four male werewolves who will be able to smell the fact that I orgasmed in my jeans." I feel Michael's whole body stiffen as he glances at the garden gate.

"Fuck. I didn't think of that."

I can't help but giggle as he places me back onto my feet.

"What brought that on? I thought we were waiting?" I ask, lifting my head so I can see him better. Michael looks at me, smiling softly.

"Oh, we are waiting until you are ready to complete the bond and let me mark you. But seeing you so at ease with my family. Made me feel things I never anticipated." I lean into him to kiss him softly on the lips.

"Mikey! Mum says put Daisy down and let her drink this wine before Marcus drinks it all!" Jon calls from the garden. We both start laughing as Michael steps back from me. "Also, dinner is on the table!" Jon adds. I look towards the house and smile.

"Let's go before we get dragged in there." I look at Michael's trousers, noticing the bulge from his manhood standing to attention. "Umm, do you need a minute to right yourself?" I ask, winking at him, Michael growls.

"Keep looking at it like that, baby, and I'll need more than a minute."

I turn my back to him and place my hands on my hips.

"Better?"

"Not really, that's one fine ass," he purrs. I throw my hands up in the air and start walking back to the house.

"Catch up when you are in more control of your body," I call, opening the gate. I only take a few steps before Michael scoops me up from behind and carries me back to the kitchen, both of us giggling like school kids.

Chapter Twenty-Seven

DAISY

As we walk into the house, we find everybody already sitting around the table, the chatter filling the room.

Barbara is handing out plates as Jon and Stuart pass around a plate of jacket potatoes and bowls of salad. I look at the table and see a platter piled high with steaks. Considering we have only been gone about ten minutes, Barbara has managed to put together a feast. I know she said the cooking was done, but there is no way ALL of this was just waiting to be plated up.

"Barbara, I take it back. You *are* my favourite person," I say, smelling the amazing aromas coming from the food. Michael growls as he slaps my ass, making me squeal. "What? There's steak and wine!" I point out, holding my hand towards the table.

"Darling, if you want steak and wine, just say the word, and I'll cook it for you," he says as he pulls out a chair for me next to Will before taking the seat between me and his mum. "Hang on, what happened to *'I'm never drinking*

244

again?"' he asks, smirking as I pick up a glass of wine. I shrug my shoulders whilst taking a sip.

"That was hungover Daisy; she's gone now, so drinking is back to being an okay sport." Michael slowly shakes his head at me. "Anyway, don't offer me steak and wine when I'm still waiting for my coffee and pizza," I point out.

"Is that what they call sex now?" Marcus mocks from across the table; he winks at me and laughs as Michael growls at him. Barbara quickly slaps Marcus across the back of the head.

"Marcus, behave. Otherwise, I'll let Michael have your steak," she warns as she walks past him.

"Sorry, Mama B," he mutters, looking at her sheepishly.

"If the five minutes you were gone for is anything to go by, you could have pizza, coffee, steak and wine in one evening," Will says next to me. I turn and punch his arm, not holding back the wolf strength.

"Ouch, Mikey, sort your mate out, will you!" he groans, rubbing his arm. Michael just shakes his head.

"Nope, you piss her off at your own risk. But so that you know, she can be scarier than me when she wants to be."

I turn, looking at Will whilst grinning broadly, showing all my teeth. Michael puts his arm around the back of my chair and kisses my head whilst chuckling. I watch as Will swallows deeply, looking at me nervously.

"Didn't anyone tell you to never piss off a witch?" Jon calls from across the table. All the guys stop passing the food around and stare at me. I feel myself lean back into the chair, suddenly feeling under the spotlight.

"You're a witch as well?" Marcus asks, amazed. I feel Michael's hand rest on my shoulder as if to offer me support.

"Yeah, didn't you know?" I turn to Michael, who just shrugs casually.

"It just never came up."

I take a sip of my wine.

"Some warning would have been good before the weekend," Stuart groans from across the table; Michael frowns at him, then at me.

"I was being helpful," I protest. I can hear Jon trying not to laugh and purposely avoid looking at him, knowing I will crack up.

"Helpful? You froze my feet to the floor, and I had to listen to that girl crying about her failed relationships for nearly half an hour!" He exclaims as Jon, and I crack up at the same time. Everyone else frowns at us. "It wasn't funny. That girl really thought I wanted to stand there to listen to her relationship troubles. How was I meant to tell her I was only there because I physically couldn't move!"

Everyone burst out laughing as Barbara looks at me, shocked.

"Daisy, you didn't?"

"In my defence, she *really* needed someone to talk to, and Stuart just has one of those faces that puts people at ease. It worked anyway; she left with some guy at the end of the night." Stuart frowns at me.

"I didn't see her leave with anyone."

"You didn't? Oh, hang on, you were dancing with Paul at the time." Stuart flips his middle finger up at me whilst everyone else laughs.

"I'm not leaving you three unsupervised anymore."

"It's not us you need to worry about," Jon, Stuart and I all protest at the same time. Michael just rolls his eyes.

"Do I even want to ask what Tony did?"

The three of us all share a look and shake our heads,

muttering various versions of "nothing" whilst drinking our drinks. I can see Marcus and Will looking at us all, desperate to know who Tony is and what he did, but we're not saying anything, especially as it would mean admitting to Michael that Tony did not, in fact, come home with me last night. Instead, he was off having a threesome with a couple he met in the bar.

I feel Michael move next to me as he puts some salad on my plate. I turn to him and smile before mouthing a thank you. He smiles back at me before passing the salad bowl to Stuart and taking my hand in his. Michael gently kisses the back of it whilst smiling softly at me. I melt as I look deep into those blue eyes.

"You doing okay?" he asks quietly. I can't hide the smile on my face as I nod. "If it gets too much at any point, just say, and we will leave." I shake my head at him.

"I'm fine, I promise. I've never felt so relaxed and..." I can't seem to find the right word, but Michael smiles knowingly and answers, "Complete?" I nod back. He leans in and kisses me gently on the lips.

"Someone pass me a bucket," Stuart groans from across the table. Michael looks at him and frowns but Stuart just smirks as he takes a sip of his drink. Suddenly, his bottle tips up a little too far, and he splutters as the lager he is drinking pours all over his face and nose. Michael glances at me knowingly; I just wink as a way of confirmation. I look at Stuart, who is using a kitchen towel to try and dry himself off a little, whilst Marcus, who is sitting next to him, laughs loudly. I casually cut into my steak. Michael places his hand on my knee as he chuckles at his friend.

We spend the rest of the meal talking among ourselves. Barbara asks me what I like to do in my spare time and about my auntie, uncle, and our coven. It's so easy to talk to her; it's like I've known her my whole life. I know my aunt Mary, and she will get along like a house on fire when they meet.

I look around the table and watch the guys all laughing and joking with each other. The room is just filled with so much love. Here is an extended family that laughs and plays together. They are all so at ease with each other and welcoming to me. I don't feel out of place like I feared. Instead, I feel like I've come home, which is crazy as I've just met them all.

I feel Michael's arm go over the back of my chair as Jon says my name.

"Sorry, what did you say?" I ask him. Jon is leaning back into his chair and drinking beer out of the bottle.

"I asked when we are going for a run next."

"Want a rematch, do you? You know I'll just kick your ass again," I grin as I lean into Michael's side, smiling.

"Witchy, I could beat you any time; just name the time and place." He takes a sip of his drink, looking at me with those cocky eyes. Suddenly, he chokes on his beer as it tips back too far and covers his face. Michael roars, laughing next to me, as Jon splutters for a second before pointing at me. "I knew it was you!" he calls, jumping to his feet. I laugh, jumping up, ready to run if I need to. I glance over at Stuart, who is looking confused, but slowly, I see the realisation on his face.

"Oh, you sneaky witch!" he gasps. "You caused me to spill my drink, didn't you?!" I slowly move around my chair, still laughing, watching Jon and Stuart look at each other, both now standing; I know they are ready to pounce.

"Mikey, how attached are you to her?" Jon asks, not taking his eyes off me, grinning. I stare right back at him.

"Very, so be warned," I hear Michael say next to me.

I see Stuart move slowly to my right and hold a hand up to stop him, freezing him to the spot. He nearly falls over when he tries to move his feet.

"Oh, come on!" he exclaims as he tries to move again. With Stuart taken care of for a moment, I look at Jon and wiggle my eyebrows at him, daring him to make a move. Jon takes a step forward, then another and another. I consider freezing him, too, but where is the fun in that? I turn quickly and plant a kiss on Michael's cheek.

"I'll try not to hurt him too badly," I say, releasing Stuart as I run out the back door, narrowly getting past Jon as he makes a grab for me. I squeal with laughter whilst running for the path to the back of the garden, Jon quickly on my tail. I can hear laughter and yelps of pain behind me but daren't turn to look, knowing Jon is only a few steps behind me. I spot a large tree and jump as quickly as possible into it, climbing up a few branches.

Jon stands at the bottom and folds his arms.

"Daisy, I spent my childhood climbing these trees, so you can either come down or stay up there; either way, I'll get you." I hear Michael laughing in the back garden, telling Stuart he is levelling the playing field. The sound of Barbara laughing mixed with Marcus telling Michael to get off Stuart makes me laugh out loud. Jon looks around at the sound of his mum's laughter combined with Stuart's groaning.

Whilst Jon's distracted, I take my chance and jump from the tree, landing straight onto his back knocking him to the ground.

Jon yells in shock as he hits the dirt, getting a face full of old dead leaves and twigs. I quickly pin his arms against his back and sit on him. I can feel him trying to buck me off, but I hold on tight.

"Oh, you are in for it when I get you, witchy," he growls, thrashing under me. I hear the sound of laughter closing in. Jon and I both look up as everyone walks into our line of sight. Michael stands at the front, arms crossed against his chest, grinning from ear to ear at his brother and me.

"Beaten by someone nearly a foot shorter than you, bro. You're obviously losing your touch."

"It's not a fair fight; you'd kill me if I hurt her," Jon huffs at him, having given up fighting underneath me. Michael just shrugs his shoulders, smirking.

"I don't think Daisy would get hurt; she is too quick for you." I pull in some of the power from the earth below me, and suddenly, Jon starts wiggling, laughing, shouting, and cursing.

"What the hell is crawling all over me? Are we on an ant's nest?" I start laughing and make it stop. Jon seems to realise then that it was me. "Oh, Daisy, you are pushing your luck, hun." He says as I cause the sensation to start again and let it continue as he thrashes, moaning that it tickles.

"I'll make it stop when you admit you'll never be able to beat me," I demand. Jon shakes his head, laughing. Everyone else roars with laughter; Barbara is next to Michael, and tears are rolling down her face. I close my eyes and cause the sensation to travel over his legs and stomach.

"Okay, okay, you win, make it stop!" Jon calls, gasping for breath. I close my eyes and pull my magic back in. Jon stops wiggling and lies on the ground, gasping for breath; I lean down to plant a kiss on his cheek.

"Good boy," I jump up and rush over to Michael, holding my hand up for a high five, which he gives me, grinning, before pulling me into his front so I am facing Jon.

Michael's arms wrap around me from behind, holding me close.

"Where the hell did you go?" Jon demands as Stuart helps him up and nods towards Michael.

"Mikey blocked me and held me off. They tagged teamed us." Stuart explains. Jon looks at Michael and crosses his arms.

"Mikey, I don't like this one; send her back and get another one."

I just stick my tongue out at him as Michael pulls me tighter against him.

"Oh no, this one is staying right where she is," he says. I feel a hand on my arm and turn to see Barbara now standing next to me,

"Too right she's staying; she is going to help me to keep you all on the straight and narrow. Plus, I need another female around here again."

I smile at her as she smiles back at me. I can't wait to spend more time here, drinking wine or coffee with Barbara as we put the males in their place.

"Mikey, definitely keep her, purely for that fact she takes no shit," Will says next to us as he holds out his hand for a high five, which I give willingly.

"Plus, she could come in handy with that magic of hers," Marcus says next to Will. He winks at me before smiling up at Michael, who tightens his hold on me, smiling at his brother and Stuart.

"Hell, there's no way I would vote for her to leave. One, you would kill me and two, I'm already attached to the little witch. She's my new drinking partner," Stuart says, smiling at me. Jon and Michael look straight at each other.

"Five against one, Jonny. Looks like she's staying for as

long as she wants," he looks down at me, and I smile, unable to speak. I hear Jon sigh and look over at him.

"Well, I guess all there is left for me to say is welcome to the family, baby sister." Jon's face lights up as everyone starts cheering. Michael spins me around before lifting me so my feet leave the ground; I wrap my arms around his neck and bend my legs behind me as I kiss him. I've never felt so accepted and cared for outside of my family and coven. I now know what I want and can feel it's the right choice for me.

Chapter Twenty-Eight

MICHAEL

I can't remember the last time my childhood home was so full of fun and laughter, and I didn't feel out of place. It's been a long time since I participated in the antics when the lads are all around. But today, I was in the thick of it all. It's all thanks to the amazing woman I get to call my mate.

We all laughed until we cried. Jon and Daisy have been throwing insult after insult at each other all evening, which has been hilarious. It's incredible how quickly Daisy can go from a strong, independent woman to cowering behind me because she's pushed Jon too far. Not that I mind, as I think it'll be the only time she'll ever allow me to protect her. She loves standing on her own two feet, and I could not be prouder of her.

I've been so worried about Daisy meeting my team; I was scared it would be too much. But once again, I've underestimated how strong she truly is. Witnessing Daisy being accepted by those most important to me had made my heart swell with pride. I knew they would love her. But I never dreamt she would instantly love them all right back.

It's like Daisy is a piece in our family puzzle we had no idea was missing. My ex, Carly, had never fit in with my friends; I always felt I had to choose between her and them. But it isn't like that with Daisy; she just belongs with us.

We are all hanging out in the garden around the fire Jon and I had built earlier; Daisy is sitting across my lap, talking to Mum and Will. I'm chatting with Marcus about a new computer program he is putting together whilst playing with Daisy's hair absentmindedly. I glance down at her as I feel her head press against my chest; she looks exhausted. It's no wonder after the weekend she's had. I dip my head down and rest my lips against her hair.

"Tired, darling?" Daisy looks at me and smiles.

"If I said no, would you believe me?"

I shake my head, smiling at her.

"Not at all. But if you don't want to go home just yet, how about I take you to one of my favourite places? Just me and you."

Daisy nods, smiling sweetly at me.

"Sounds good to me, cheese ball."

We quickly say our goodbyes before leaving the garden as Mum walks us out. She hugs me tight as we get to the car, catching me off guard.

"You look better than you have in a long time, Mikey. That spark is finally back in your eyes." She turns to Daisy as she lets go of me and pulls her into her arms. "It's all thanks to you, sweet girl. Thank you for making my boy so happy." Daisy smiles, hugging Mum back.

"He makes me happier."

Mum steps back and places a loving hand on Daisy's cheek.

"You are part of this family now; whether you decide to join our pack or not, this is always going to be your home.

So don't rush into anything you are unsure of. Mikey has waited this long for you; make him wait a little longer," Mum winks at her as Daisy chuckles. I put an arm around Daisy, pulling her to me to kiss her head. I glance down in time to see Daisy attempting to hide a yawn.

"Come on, you, I promised you one more stop before getting you back. Let's go before you fall asleep on me."

Daisy hugs Mum one last time before getting into the car. I lean over to kiss Mum on the cheek, quietly thanking her for a wonderful evening.

"Take care of each other. Your dad and sister would love seeing you so happy."

I suck my lips into my mouth and nod, refusing to let my emotions show.

"Thanks, Mama. Love you," I say quietly, kissing her cheek one last time before getting into the car. We both wave as we pull away from the house; Mum stands where we left her, watching as we drive out of sight. I turn and glance at Daisy, who is looking right back at me.

"You survived then," I say, smiling at her.

"You're all mental, you know that, right?!"

I can't help but laugh. She isn't wrong,

"They're all bat crap crazy, always have been. You seemed to have made quite an impression on them all. They'll be talking about how you handled Stuart and Jon for quite some time."

I hear Daisy chuckle in her seat.

"Yeah, that was fun. I don't think I've ever felt so at ease with people I've just met before, other than Tony and Beth. I meant it when I said your mum is one of my favourite people; I love her."

"I said you would; there is no denying she loves you too. I wouldn't be surprised if she wants us to go over for dinner twice a week from now on." I glance over at Daisy, smiling. She's curled up in the seat, looking at me, with her head resting on her hands. She looks so content. But I can't shake the feeling things are moving too fast for her. I know the intensity of the mating bond has been a little overwhelming for her; I don't want things to move too fast and scare her off, and I don't want to lose her. Not now that I know how good things could be.

I pull over to the side of the road and turn off the engine. Looking over at Daisy, I wonder if she will be up for a short walk. But when I ask her, she rolls her eyes before exiting the car.

"Come on, cheese ball, you promised me some alone time," she calls over to me as I follow suit. I walk around to where Daisy's leaning against her now-closed door and reach down to take her hand.

"Come on then, but if you get too tired, you have to tell me, and I'll get you straight back." I feel Daisy lean into me as she promises.

I lead her through the thick trees; they've grown a lot thicker since I was last here; even with the wolf sight, it's difficult to see in the pitch black. But just as I am starting to think I've made a mistake bringing her here and that we may need to head back, the area brightens up as a sphere of light hovers a little way in front of us, lighting up the darkness. I turn to Daisy and smile.

"I think having a witch as a mate will come in handy."

Daisy winks at me, smiling. Within a few minutes, I realise we are here. I hold back a branch, letting Daisy walk a little way in front of me. She stops dead in her tracks and gasps as I walk out and step beside her.

"Mikey, this is beautiful," she whispers as she looks over at the view in front of her. We are high up on a ridge, looking down as the valley dips to the river running below. Each side is covered in trees of all types, nature at its purest.

"Look up," I whisper in her ear; slowly, I watch her face change as she takes in the night sky above her. Because there is no artificial light out here, and it's a clear night, there are thousands of stars as far as the eye can see. There are very few places where you will be able to see so much on a night like this.

I take Daisy's hand and pull her down to the ground with me so she is sitting between my legs, her back to me. I wrap my arms around her and hold her close. Even with the view before me, nothing compares to looking at her in the moonlight, the way it makes her skin glow, and her eyes glisten like emeralds. She turns her head, catching me admiring her. Her cheeks blush as she leans in that little bit before kissing me softly on the lips.

"However did you find this place? It's beautiful."

I tighten my hold on her as she faces forward again; I lean in, letting my cheek rest against hers.

"Michelle and I used to come here all the time. It was like our secret spot. Whenever things became too much for one of us, the other would find them here. It was the first place I looked when she went missing. I've not been back since." I feel Daisy lean further into me as she places her hands on mine.

"Why tonight?"

I tip my head so I can look at her again. I gently press my lips to her temple before leaning my cheek against hers once more.

"Because tonight was the first time since she died that I didn't feel like an intruder in my childhood home. Not only did I feel like I belonged, I felt like I was a part of it again.

"When I went upstairs, I went into Michelle's room; I

never go in there. But today, it felt right, like she was telling me everything would be okay and that it was time to be happy without the guilt that she wasn't here with me. I realised that it's okay to miss her, but it's not okay to stop living because she has."

I look down as I take Daisy's hand, entwining my fingers with hers; it always feels like they fit together perfectly, just like we do.

"Before you, darling, the only thing that mattered to me was keeping those I love safe, making sure they never got taken away from me the way Michelle did. But now, even though I would still fight till my last breath to protect them all, to protect you, I know that as long as I have you by my side, I can face anything that life throws at me. Even if you decide that you never want to complete the bond and want us to stay as we are, I am okay with that because I still get to be with you.

"I would give it all up for you, my pack, my team, all of it. If you ever wanted to move back to your auntie and uncle's, I would drop it all to be with you." Daisy spins around and throws her arms around my neck, launching us both backwards until I am lying on my back, my arms holding her against me. I can't stop the laugh that escapes my lips as she has such a tight hold of me; I wonder how I am still breathing.

"You know I would never ask you to do that, don't you? I would never ask you to leave any of it behind for me," she declares. "Today, spending that time with you and your family made me realise that I want it all: you, your family, and your pack. Of course, I want to complete the mating bond; I want to be with you, always."

I push myself up on my elbows so I can sit up with Daisy straddling my lap.

"Are you sure, darling?" I ask, my heart racing; Daisy just sits nodding at me; her face comes alive as she smiles.

"I'm yours, Mikey. I was yours from the moment I saw you. I've never wanted anything as much as I want this, as I want us." I grab her face and pull her towards me to kiss her; she giggles before kissing me back.

"Darling, you have just made me the happiest wolf on Earth. I don't even know what to say." I rest my head on hers as she chuckles in my arms.

"So, what do we do next?" she asks. I pull away and look at her, unable to do anything but smile.

"Well, to start with, I would like to speak to your auntie and uncle. It wouldn't feel right not to have their blessing. How about we take a trip down there this weekend?" I watch as Daisy's face lights up.

"Really?"

I nod, smiling. She throws her arms around my neck and pulls me into another death-grip hug. I know how much she has been missing them. This way, she can spend some time with them, and I can speak to her uncle about the bond. I know they'll know a little about it as they are supernaturals themselves, but I want them to understand what it will mean for us.

"Darling, just one thing I want you to consider for after we have been to see your auntie and uncle." Daisy looks up at me, confused and a little worried. "When I told the Alpha about us at the meeting, I also asked him to find a replacement for me at the uni. He said he would try his hardest. I explained to him that I plan on living with you. I want us to live together as soon as possible and start our mated life in *our* home." Daisy pulls away from me,

"Are you asking me to move in with you?"

"Of course I am. As far as I'm concerned, once we are

mated, that's it. There's nothing more important than you and me. Even though we won't be legally married, I'll see you as my mate, wife, and world. So why wouldn't I want to build a home with you? So yes, I'm asking you to move in with me." I watch as tears roll down Daisy's cheek, and she smiles and nods at me. "Is that a yes?" I ask. Daisy just nods again, then lets out the cutest little sob. I pull her into my arms, holding her tight; I can hear her sobbing while giggling.

"You have made me happier than I ever thought I could be," she sobs; I run my hand over her hair and kiss the top of her head.

"Darling, you deserve the world and more. You have no idea how happy you've made me, and I don't just mean tonight. I promise you I'll spend every day of our lives making you smile and laugh. The only tears you're to shed now are happy ones, is that understood?" I feel her laugh against my chest as she nods.

"How soon can I move in?"

"As soon as you want, just say the word," I reply. I watch as she pulls away from me and wipes her tear-soaked cheeks with her hands.

"Can we manage it before we are mated?" she asks; I nod at her, smiling.

"How about we spend this week moving your stuff in and making any changes to the house you want; we'll go down to your family on Friday and stay until Sunday. Then, when we get back, we'll complete the bond. I want the first time I make love to you when we mark each other to be in *our* bed in *our* home. It will be perfect, just as you deserve it to be." I place a hand on her cheek and look into her eyes, still filled with tears but sparkling with happiness. "I love you, Daisy Andrews. I have from the moment I saw you sat on that bloody bench." Daisy looks at me and giggles.

"I love you too, you big cheese ball." At that moment, my heart became full, so full I swear it would burst through my chest. I pull her into a kiss like no other.

"*Mine.*" My wolf growls inside of me. "*Ours*," I reply.

Chapter Twenty-Nine

DAISY

I finally get back to my dormitory building a little after one in the morning. As soon as I walk into the room, it hits me: in a little under a week, I'll be leaving this tiny bedroom for good. I'll be living with Michael, and we'll be starting our new lives together, side by side, how it's meant to be.

Looking around now, it's hard to believe how much has changed in the five months since I left my family down in Cornwall and moved to Wales. Although the only thing I had planned was to study and work hard for three years to get my degree in law, making friends and enjoying my new life was just going to be an added bonus.

As for finding love, well, that just wasn't on the agenda at all. I never thought I would ever let another male anywhere near me; I would never let a man have an ounce of control over me again. I had a plan for my life, and I was sticking to it.

Yet, here I am, in love with not only a man but a shifter who hasn't tried to control me in any way. He lets me make all my own decisions. He even left me to work out that we are mates on my own, knowing that I needed this control; I needed to know that this was not another part of my life that my wolf had taken over. This was something that I decided for myself. I decided when I would let Michael into my life. I decided when I would accept our bond and choose my happiness and future.

After telling Michael I wished to be bonded tonight, we talked for nearly two hours in that beautiful spot. Michael offered time and time again to move down to Cornwall to be near my auntie and uncle so I could be part of their coven again. He even said that we could become part of a pack down there if that was what I wanted. He loves me and respects my wishes so much that he's willing to walk away from everything he has ever known, from the people he loves, to ensure that I'm happy. I don't know what I've done to deserve him. But I could never let him do all of that.

Cornwall may be where my family is; it may be where we ran to ensure we were safe, but it no longer feels like home. Tonight, I realised that Wales feels like home because of the life I've created for myself here and because of Michael and his family. Tonight, when we were all sitting in the garden, the fire pit burning, beer bottles and wine glasses in our hands, I realised that I've never felt so at peace, not since losing my parents.

At one point, I'd been sat across Michael's lap, talking to Barbara and Will about some of the books we've read, whilst Michael spoke to Marcus. I realised this is where I want to be. Barbara was right when she said that they were my family, as it was exactly how it had felt. It was like finally coming home, which was why it was an easy decision to make when Michael asked me if I wanted us to stay up here or move down to Cornwall.

While I was recounting this evening, I realised that I had not paid any attention to my phone, which is flashing at me. I unlock the screen and see that I've had a message from Michael and Tony. I open the one from Tony first.

Tony: Alright, Wolf girl, hope you had a good night with matey boy and his mother. I want all the gossip tomorrow. I'm staying out tonight but expect me to be at your door by 9 AM. Phone if you need me for anything. Also, an envelope was in the post box for you, so I put it in the kitchen. See you tomorrow, Luvs ya. Xx

I had a feeling he'd be out tonight; he tends to stay out on Mondays to look after the bar for Carl and Richard so they can go and see Carl's parents. I walk out of my bedroom, opening Michael's message on the way to the kitchen.

Cheese ball: I'm home and lying in bed, and it feels too big for the first time ever. I can't wait until you are here with me every night. Good night, darling. Sweet dreams xxx

I can't wipe the smile off my face. I can't believe that very soon I'll be mated to this remarkable man, living with him, and never having to be without him again.

Daisy: I can't wait to fall asleep in your arms every night, wake up with you every morning and know that you are mine and I'm yours. Always. Good night, Cheese Ball. I love you. Xxx

Whilst I'm in the kitchen, I make myself some toast and a cup of tea. I watch my phone for a few minutes to check if he will message again, but he doesn't. I guess he has fallen asleep quickly. I grab my plate of toast and the envelope from the table before heading back to my room.

Whilst eating the toast, I plug my phone in to charge and then pick up the envelope again. My address isn't on it; it just has my name and apartment number. I figure it must be a letter from the university or some promotion for the student union. I tip it upside down, and four pictures fall out, as well as a piece of paper. I instantly panic when I notice that the pictures are of me. One from last night in the bar with Jon and Stuart, one of Tony, Beth and me in the café, one of me running, and the last one is of Michael and me kissing in the forest the other day.

My stomach ties into knots. I pick up the piece of paper with shaking hands. I manage to read the first line before I've to run to the bathroom to throw up the toast I've just eaten. No, no, no, not now. Not when everything is going so well. I throw up until my stomach is empty, my throat burning from the stomach acid. I sit there on the toilet floor, shaking too hard to get up. Trying desperately to stop the panic attack from taking hold.

After about ten minutes, I pick up the letter next to me and manage to read it. It's not long, but it's enough to realise all my dreams and plans I've made can never be. Not here, not now and not with Michael.

I've got to get away from here; I need to go and never come back. I need to be gone by morning. I rush into my room and throw everything into my bags; I can't leave anything as I'll not return. I can't risk it.

Less than two hours later, utterly broken-hearted, I'm driving away. I'm barely able to see the road due to the tears, but I can't stop; I have to make sure I'm far away by the time everyone starts waking up.

I open my window and feel like I'm going to be physically sick as I throw my phone out of it. I have to make sure there is no way to track me because Michael will find me. This is why I have to leave now; whilst everyone is safe and asleep in their beds, I have to make sure no one is around to stop me, so I leave to protect them and save them from what is waiting for them if I don't. I'm driving away from the university, my new friends, new family, but worse of all, away from Michael.

Chapter Thirty

MICHAEL

I roll over and look at the alarm clock; it's only 5 AM; why is it going off?

Crap, it isn't my alarm; it's my phone. I pick it up and look at the screen.

"This better be life or death, Jonny; I'm knackered," I mumble down the phone, rubbing my eyes.

"What the fuck did you do?" he roars at me. I feel my eyebrows pinch together.

"What the hell are you on about?" I haven't got the head for this on less than four hours of sleep.

"What the fuck did you do when you left here last night to scare her off!"

I sit up, trying to work out what he's shouting about. Gods, it hurts to move.

"Jonathan, are you pissed? Who's been scared off?"

"Daisy, you fucking idiot."

I just roll my eyes, rubbing the pain in my chest; I must have slept on a full stomach or something, as my chest and abdomen are really aching this morning.

"Daisy's fine, better than fine, actually. We're going to complete the bond, and she is moving in on Sunday. Why did you think she had been scared off?" I hear Jon cursing on the other end of the phone.

"She sent me a message at two this morning saying she was leaving. I was to make sure you didn't try to follow her." No, that can't be right. I want to believe this is some kind of a joke, but I know Jon wouldn't joke about something like this. I quickly look at my phone and see I also have a couple of text messages from Daisy.

"Hang on," is all I manage to say; my mouth goes dry. My hands shake as I open the message, the first saying goodnight and that she loves me. But when I read the second message, I can't breathe.

Daisy: This isn't going to work. I'm sorry; you deserve so much better than me. I've left. Please don't try to follow me. I'll be long gone by the time you get this message. I'm so sorry. As much as this kills me, it's for the best. Thank you for everything. I'll never forget you. Daisy xxx

I just stare at the message, the pain in my chest getting worse. I don't understand. What's happening? Why's she left? I look at the time of the second message, and it says three AM. Just two hours before, everything had been perfect. My brain is telling me something is very wrong here, but I can feel my whole body starting to shake; I'm losing control. I'm aware of Jon shouting down the phone at me. I've got to get out of here. I have to … What do I have to do?

I look at the clock again; it's been two hours since she messaged. She really will be long gone by now. I hang up on

Jon and call her number. It goes straight to voicemail. My heart stops when I hear the new message she's done.

"This is Daisy. I've destroyed this phone; I'm no longer reachable on it. If you are looking for me, please stop." I can hear the tears in her voice; I can hear the pain that echoes my own. "I'm so sorry." Then silence. Then, finally, I hear the beep signalling for me to leave a message.

"Where are you? Why have you left? Where are you!? I love you. Come home, please? Whatever has happened, we will sort it out. We don't have to move in together yet, we don't have to complete the bond, just please don't leave me," I beg down the line, knowing that she'll not hear it if she's really destroyed her phone.

The second I hang up, it starts ringing, and I pray it's Daisy, but Jon's name is flashing on the screen. I just hold my phone as I walk out of my room, feeling the pain in my chest getting stronger, the feeling of rocks filling my stomach.

"*We need her. We can't lose her,*" my wolf growls at me. I get to the bottom of the stairs and see the set of keys I had put on the side, ready to give to her today. I vomit, unable to stop it; everything comes up until it's just bile.

I can feel my wolf taking control, trying to force the change, forcing me to shut down. I walk to the back door and open it. I let my wolf take over as the shift happens. I do not care anymore; I just need the pain to stop and the confusion to halt, even if only for a few minutes. More importantly, I need Daisy.

Chapter Thirty-One

JON

What the fuck is going on?

The last thing I expected to wake up to this morning was a message from Daisy saying she was leaving. I was sure Michael must have done something on the way home last night to scare her off. But after speaking to him and hearing the shock and pain in his voice, it's evident that he was completely blindsided.

Since Mikey hung up on me, I've not been able to get a hold of him. Luckily, I'd already been heading to his when I'd phoned. If Daisy really has gone, he's going to need as much help and support as possible. I just pray this is all some big misunderstanding that they can sort out. I don't think I've ever seen Mikey as happy as he was last night. She worships the ground that man walks on, so why would she run?

I think back to last night when we had all been at Mum's, and everything had seemed perfect. Daisy had been so happy and confident there was no way that was an act. The way the two of them had looked at each other, I don't think I've ever seen two people more in love. None of this makes sense. What could have gone so wrong that she felt she had no choice but to leave?

I pull up outside Mikey's place, breathing a sigh of relief as his car is still there. At least he hasn't tried to follow her. I just hope his wolf hasn't taken over and attempted to track her on foot.

I jump out, rushing into the house. As soon as I open the front door, I'm hit with the unmistakable odour of vomit. I see it all over the bottom of the stairs. My heart drops.

Mikey is by far the strongest of us all. But judging by the state of this place, he has gone into complete shock. I call out to him but am met with silence. I feel a cold breeze comes through from the lounge. I walk in and find the patio doors wide open. Just outside are the signs that he has shifted whilst still in his nightclothes. The remains of which are lying in tatters all over the garden. Oh, shit, has he lost all control? Has his wolf taken over? I quickly strip off my own clothes and shift so I can find him. I run into the trees behind his house, listening for any signs of him, but I'm met with silence. I pick up his scent, but it's impossible to follow; it's everywhere. Finally, I hear a wolf whine in the distance; quickly, I take off following the sound.

"Mikey, can you hear me?" I call through the mind link as I run. He doesn't respond, but I hear the whimpering again; it's getting closer. *"Mikey, answer me for the love of Mother Earth."* I hear a growl ahead of me, and I stop short of crashing into my brother. He's lying on the ground, still in wolf form.

"Mikey, come home; let's see what we can do. Let's find her."

"I don't even know where to start, Jon." He stands, turning away from me. I jump in front of him.

"You must have an idea?" Michael just looks at me, and I can see the defeat in his eyes. I watch as he moans in pain, the pain of a bond being stretched too far. She must have really put some miles between them for him to feel this much pain. I worry for Daisy as she will have no idea what is going on. Does she understand that a bond can't be stretched without both parties knowing where the other is?

"Daisy doesn't want to be found. I promised her if she told me to leave her, I would. So I'm keeping my word." He turns from me again and takes a step forward before turning to look at me. *"I need to be left alone, Jon; I need to work this out."* With that, he takes off at a run. All I can do is watch my brother's heart break. This man has spent his life helping others, helping me. But now that he needs me, I have no idea what to do.

I watch him disappear into the trees before heading back to the house. I quickly shift back before dressing. I look around at Michael's shredded clothes and start picking them up. Underneath a piece of fabric, I find his phone. I open it to check if there is any indication of what has happened. I need to find a way to help him, to help her. I open his messages and see the last message she sent last night. Then, two hours later, the message saying goodbye. Something awful must have happened, as there is no way Daisy would purposely cause Michael this amount of pain. There is no doubt in my mind that she loves him with all of her heart.

I finish tidying up the garden before heading back into the house. I'm once again greeted by the smell of vomit. I can't let him find the place like this. I grab what I need to clean it up.

As I'm cleaning, I find a set of keys on the floor; picking them up, I spot the keyring on them. It's a heart with an engraving.

The keys to our future, as you already hold the key to my heart.
I love you. M xxx

Oh, shit. In the rush to get here, I forgot that he had told me they were moving in together; they had planned on completing the bond. The more my head clears, the more I think something terrible must have happened. But what if I'm wrong? I'm scared to mention it to Michael if I am; I don't know what to do for the best. I pull open the drawer of the dresser, carefully hiding the keys in there out of sight.

I'm just finishing cleaning up when I hear the back door opening; Michael strolls through, completely naked.

"How are you feeling?" I ask. He stops on the bottom step and doesn't even bother to turn around when he replies.

"Like my heart is being ripped out of my chest and stretched a hundred miles and more. I feel like I've lost the most important person in my life again! I feel like every time I get the slightest bit of happiness in my life; it gets snatched away from me. I feel like just giving up."

I take a step towards him.

"Mikey, you are the strongest guy I know. You need to stop with the self wallowing and think about this logically." Before I get the chance to finish, he launches at me, pinning me against the wall. I don't fight him; I know he needs a release.

"Don't tell me how I should be acting right now. You all think I'm this emotionless arsehole who takes everything in stride. To you and the pack, I'm 'The Protector', the leader of the enforcers, a force not to be reckoned with. You all think that nothing scares me, that I can handle everything that is thrown at me. I fight for every wolf and human that cannot fight for themselves. Christ Jonathan, I've *killed* to protect them. It's a reputation I've had to build to ensure I'm feared by those we hunt. It was a reputation I was happy to uphold if it meant my family and pack were protected.

"But then, she walked into my life, and everything changed. Now, I would crawl on my hands and knees over hot coals and broken glass in front of everyone just to beg her for one more day. One more fucking day where nothing else matters; it's just her and me. I would throw away every ounce of respect and fear I've spent the last sixteen years building for her because that single rogue has walked into my life and brought the big unstoppable protector to his knees. And without her, I don't think I'll ever be able to rise again." Finally, he releases me and walks up the stairs, slamming his bedroom door behind him.

I hear the shower being turned on in his room. Knowing he will be in there for a while, I make a fresh pot of coffee before heading into the lounge. I read through the message Daisy had sent me last night over and over again, just praying something would make sense.

Daisy: Jon, I have to leave. I need you to promise me you will take care of Mikey and watch his back. I'm sorry for the pain this will cause him. Don't let him try to follow me. It's for the best. I'm so sorry. Daisy. xx

There is nothing to indicate why she feels running is her only option. Why would she say she'd move in only to leave two hours later? Had something happened when she got home? Had something happened with Kellan? Was she scared? Had she become overwhelmed by it all? No one would have blamed her if she had. She has been through so much, but we would have helped her; Michael would have never held it against her if she needed to slow things down.

I'm in my own head when I hear a phone ringing from Michael's briefcase; I quickly grab it in the hope that it will be Daisy. I see Tony's name on the screen of his work mobile. Dickhead. Why hadn't I thought to call him? Surely, he'll know what the hell is going on,

"Hey Tony, it's Jon."

"Where is he?" Tony roars down the line; shit.

"He's in the shower. What the hell's happened, Tony? Why has she run?"

"That's what I want to ask your prick of a brother. What the fuck did he do?"

I sigh; judging by Tony's reaction, he is as much in the dark as the rest of us.

"Nothing. Michael didn't do anything."

"Bullshit, you would back him up; he is your brother. If he didn't do anything, then why the fuck has my best friend left without even saying goodbye? Just a note saying she won't be back and for me to hand her keys into the office for her."

"Tony, I can promise you Michael hasn't done anything. He only found out she had left an hour ago himself. At one o'clock, she was messaging him, telling him how much she loved him. Two hours later, she told him not to follow her and that it was for the best. Complete radio silence in between." I can almost hear Tony's attitude start shifting as he curses down the line.

"So, he really didn't do anything?"

"No." I hear Tony sigh as he calms down a little. "I'm at a complete loss here, Tony. I'm trying to be the strong one, but it's not a role I'm familiar with. Any ideas what could have happened on your end?" I can hear Tony sighing and doors opening and closing. Tony tells me he is going to check out her room and will call back.

I hang up the phone and head back into the kitchen for another cup of coffee. It's going to be a long day at this rate, and I think I'll need a few more cups to get through it until I can hit the beers.

I'm just about to make Michael a cup when his phone rings again. Tony's name flashes back up on the screen.

"Did you find anything?" I'm sure Tony sounds like he is outside now.

"Yes. I need to see you both. How quickly can you get to the bar?" I tell Tony we will meet him there in half an hour, then head up the stairs to Michael's room. I stand outside his door for a moment to prepare myself for what I may walk into.

I find Michael sitting on the bed with nothing but a towel wrapped around his waist, flipping through his personal phone. He must have grabbed it on the way through before. He doesn't even look up as I walk in. I can see pictures of him and Daisy on his screen.

Time to be the big brother he deserves.

"I need you to get dressed and come with me."

He looks up at me, and my breath catches in my throat. Before me is my powerful brother, who was right when he said the whole pack sees him as unbeatable. But now he is completely broken, his eyes red from crying, his knuckles look like he has gone ten rounds with a tree, and his eyes have lost all colour and are just black where his wolf is so close to the front.

"Where to? Cause I'm really not in the mood for your cryptic trips." I can hear the pain in him as he speaks. I want to walk over to him and hold him, tell him everything will be okay, but I can't promise that. Not yet.

"Tony called. He might have answers; we're going to meet him at The Crows." I see the red flash through Michael's eyes and realise he is fighting to keep control of his emotions.

"What's the point if she doesn't want to be found." I spin around and face him, my hands balled into fists, ready to lay down some home truths.

"If you are going to sit there and play dumb, then fine, the rest of us will find her without you. You might have decided that this is what she wants and might be happy to sit there sulking like a child. But the rest of us aren't. I don't know why it's so hard for you to believe that Daisy wants and loves you as much as you do her. Because she does, I've seen it firsthand this weekend while hanging out with her. Her face lights up the whole damn place whenever your name's mentioned. Whenever you texted her, I swear she looked like she was going to explode with excitement.

"For fuck's sake, Michael, just last night, we were all in awe of the love between the two of you. Even Mum and Dad never looked at each other the way you two do. So, if you want to sit there and believe that she has run away, then fine. But remember, this is a woman who has been on the run for nearly three years from her past. She has admitted she would rather give up her own life than allow him to hurt anyone else.

"So no, I don't think she has just left. Not for one minute. I think she needs help, and the rest of us will look for her until we ensure she is safe. *If* then, and only then, does she say she left willingly, *then* we will walk away, but before that, we will do what we do best, and we will track her down and protect her." I kneel in front of Mikey as I watch it all sink in.

"Now, are you going to do what *you* do best and lead us

and take control, or are you going to sit here and let the best thing that has ever happened to you disappear?" I hold my right hand out, offering it to him. Michael looks at it, then at me, and takes the hand offered to him. We both pull each other up until we are standing tall, and I pull my little brother into a hug.

"Thank you, Jonny," he mutters into my ear.

"Thank me when we find her. Now get dressed; we leave in five."

Chapter Thirty-Two

MICHAEL

"I thought you two hadn't started the bonding process yet?" Jon asks. I look over at him, frowning. He nods to my hand, which is rubbing my aching chest. I hadn't even realised I was doing it.

"We haven't," I force myself to put my hands on my lap. "I thought you only felt like this once both were marked."

"I thought so, too. Is there any way you could have accidentally started the process? I mean, I know you two haven't … you know … done the deed yet. But-"

"I'm not talking to you about our sex life. But no, there is no way anything has been started." I turn to look out the car window, thinking about all the times I've just felt something was happening to Daisy, that she was hurt or in trouble, even before we were in a relationship.

The night of her birthday, I had felt an aching in my chest and stomach for about half an hour before Beth told me Daisy was missing. Could we really be connected without the bond being completed? How's that even possible? Is there a different type of bond between witches and their version of mates? We've never really discussed her witch side; we have been so focused on her accepting her wolf that it hasn't come up yet.

"I hate to put this out there, but do you think something's wrong with Daisy, and that's why you're feeling like this? Do you think the pain is because she is hurt?" as he says it, I feel the pain in my chest tightening again.

"Gods, I hope not. If her pain is linked to me, I can't even let myself think about what she's going through right now. It fucking hurts Jonny."

I look at the clock on the dashboard of Jon's car. It's just past seven in the morning. It's been almost three hours since Jon woke me up, and I discovered Daisy was gone. How could I have been so stupid to have wasted so much time? I could kick my own arse for not seeing what was right in front of me. How could I believe that Daisy would cause us this much pain on purpose? How had I let my self-doubt take over so completely? Daisy is my mate; she's repeatedly told me how much I mean to her, yet the moment I read her message, I believed she'd walked away, that she'd washed her hands off me, of us and the plans we had made mere hours beforehand.

"We messed up; we need to put this right and find her," my wolf whispers, and I know he's right.

I don't bother looking up as the car rolls to a stop outside of the bar. As I open the car door and climb out, I almost bump into Jon, who is standing by my door, waiting for me. Jon places a hand on my shoulder and looks at me with a seriousness I rarely see from my joker of a brother.

"I need you to promise me something, Mikey. I need you to promise me you won't do anything rash. I know logic will go out the window if it turns out she is in danger, but I need you to remember what happens if we rush in.

You are our leader, and I'll not make you step back from that role yet, but if I think you are making decisions based on emotions rather than logic, I'll force you to hand over the reins to Marcus. I'll die before I let anything happen to that woman. But I need you to promise me you will let me take on some of the burden. I'll not let you or Daisy down. Let me be the brother you have always been to me."

I just stand looking at my brother. No words will ever express how much I need him right now. So, instead of responding verbally, I do something I've done only a handful of times in our adult lives. I pull my brother into a hug as I feel a few loose tears escape. This time, I don't try to hide them from the one person who has been with me through everything. With those heartfelt words, he breaks the barrier I've been working to keep up since leaving the house.

I feel him place a hand on the back of my head as he holds me, reassuring me that we will find her and that we will make sure she's safe. He'll face whatever happens with me. I let the weakness wash through me for just a few heartbeats before forcing myself to take a deep breath and rebuild the wall I build around myself when we are on a mission. I can't be weak right now; I need to gather all my strength and put on my leader's head. Daisy needs a man who will do everything in his power to find her. To get her back and protect her.

I pull back from Jonathan and wipe my face. I take another deep breath as he places a hand on my shoulder, supporting me.

"You've got this. If anyone can find Daisy and make sure she's safe, it's you. Now take a second, get that leader composure you're so famous for in place, and get in there and take control of the situation." I straighten up and take one last deep breath as I pull back my shoulders.

"Let's do this." I turn around and walk into the bar with my brother beside me, ready to face whatever we need to, to find my mate.

Tony is behind the bar by the coffee machine when we walk in. He looks up at me, and I'm not really surprised that he is a little taken aback.

"Gods, you look like shit Michael."

I can't help but bark out a laugh.

"Yeah, well, waking up to find you have lost the love of your life can do that to a man. The constant pain in my chest where our bond is being stretched isn't helping either," I answer as I walk up to him. He holds out his hand, and I grasp it. "Jon says you have some information; what've you got?" I watch as Tony pulls a piece of paper from his jeans pocket and places it on the bar.

"I found this in a bin bag in her room. She started writing it to me but changed her mind." I pick up the folded piece of scrunched-up paper, and I can immediately smell her scent coming from it. It's so faint, but it's enough to turn my legs to jelly. Jon grabs my arm, holding me up whilst I grab hold of the bar for support.

"I'm okay," I whisper; I hold the paper up to Tony. "Can I?" he nods, so I unfold the paper with my shaking hands.

Tony,

Fuck, I don't want to write this or know what to even say. Jackson found me; the letter was from him; he threatened every person I love here. I can't sit by and let him ruin all your lives. He sent evidence that he knows you all and my routines, including a picture of me returning home tonight. Which he left on my car whilst I was packing my room.

He knows about Beth, you, Jonathan, Stuart, and, of course, Michael. He has promised Michael will be the first one he kills; what am I meant to do, Tony? I can't let you all suffer or be hurt because he wants me. I have to go to lead him away. Why can't he just move on? What is it about me that he wants so bad? I know Michael and the guys would help me, but if any of them got hurt because of me, I would never ever forgive myself. When you see Michael, please let him know this has killed me. I love him so much that I feel like I'm leaving behind my whole being. Tony, it hurts so bad.

Throughout the letter, the ink is blotched in areas where apparent tears have fallen. Daisy didn't or couldn't finish the letter as she scribbled through it and then scrunched it up. *"How has he found her? How does he know about us?"* I can feel my wolf's confusion; it just doesn't make sense. There is no way he could have gotten close to her without me knowing. I look over to Jon, who is now reading the letter. I can see the pain on his face, as well as the confusion mirroring my own.

"Was there anything left in the room?" I ask Tony. He starts listing a few bits, and I tell him to wait. I realise I'm going to need the whole team on this. So, I ask him to make me coffee while I make a few calls. He agrees instantly, obviously needing to do something to keep his mind from worrying about his friend. I pull out my phone and get up the number of the one guy who will have my back as much as my brother.

"Marc, I need your help for a personal emergency; it's not pack related. Can you get the team together and get to The Crows as soon as possible? I'll explain when you all get here, and you can decide if you want to help or not."

"On it, Mikey. We'll all be there within the hour and will help in anything you need, you know that," Marcus replies before the line goes dead. I don't know why I even questioned whether he would help me. Marcus and I have been friends as long as Jonny and I. We are more like brothers.

"I've already spoken to Stuart; he'll be here in half an hour. He's at Will's, so he's bringing him too." I thank Jon. I know before anything else can happen, there is one more call I must make. The one person who will drop everything to help us. I take a deep breath and dial the number I know off by heart, desperately hoping this call will not break me wide open. It only rings twice before the voice I need to hear as much as I need to hear Daisy's answers.

"Hey, Mama."

Chapter Thirty-Three

MICHAEL

We've been at the bar for four hours, and things are in full flow. I've sent Tony and Stuart to go through everything left in Daisy's room. Stuart is trained to spot things that Tony won't think are relevant. I've also asked Tony to keep an eye on Beth. I need to make sure she is safe; Daisy would never forgive me if anything happened to her friends. Carl and Richard have closed the bar for the day so we can use it as a base. We are closer to Daisy's apartment here, and if, by some miracle, she returns, we can get there quickly.

Something about this whole situation feels off; I don't understand how Jackson could've found her. Daisy told me they had picked this area on purpose as the family has no connection here. She hadn't told anyone she was going to university. It's not information he could've gotten from anybody other than her auntie and uncle. I'm sure they wouldn't have told him, no matter what he did to them. So how did he find her all the way up here?

I've tried to contact some of the packs around Exeter, where Daisy lived when the arsehole turned her. But so far,

I've not found the pack that helped her. The Alpha is going to keep trying others to see what he can come up with. He has cancelled all his plans for the day to help from his office. I think my mum threatening to come over and 'put him in his place' may have had something to do with him dropping everything. Even the Alpha knows not to mess with Barbara Adams when one of her own is in trouble or danger.

I'm currently looking online at the information Daisy had given the university about her past. She's already told me it's all bullshit, that she made it up, but there must be some element of truth in there somewhere, even if it was just enough to help me find out where her family lives now in Cornwall.

If I'd had my way, I'd already be on my way down there to search for her, but Mum made me promise I wouldn't go until we knew what area she was in or if she was down there at all. Jon remembers her mentioning a coven in Ireland to which hers is linked. What if she has gone there and I go down to Cornwall? As much as I hate to admit it, they're right. I need to be here; at least it's near enough the middle of the two.

I'm in the middle of reading her application essay when a plate of sandwiches appears in front of me.

"Thanks, Mum, but I'm not hungry," I say without looking up.

"I don't remember asking if you were." I know that's her way of telling me to eat.

"I'll eat them in a minute when I've finished this, I promise." I look up at my mum, and for a blink of a second, I see her features soften the same way they did when she arrived earlier.

Carl had picked her up on the way back from his parents, who live on the street down from hers. Mum had taken one look at me and started crying. Now she's in full Mum mode, supplying us all with food and coffee and ensuring we look after ourselves. I watch my mum open her mouth to argue when someone walks through the back door.

"Boss, you need to see this." I hear Stuart call. I jump up, rushing to the back of the bar where Stuart is standing where Marcus has been working.

"What you got?" I ask. I notice Jon and Marcus are looking at something on the table. I walk over; the first thing I see is a picture of Daisy running. I would spot that form anywhere; I've watched her run nearly every morning since October. I pick up the photograph and notice it was taken recently. I know that she changed her trainers three weeks ago and the shoes she has in the picture are her new ones. I'm looking at the picture when I hear Stuart clear his throat.

"That wasn't the only one."

I look back at the table and see another picture of Daisy with Beth and Tony having coffee.

"Son of a bitch was right here!" I hear Jon curse. I look up to see him holding another picture and turning it to Stuart, who nods. Jon passes it to me, and if there wasn't so much pain and anxiety in my heart, I know I would have laughed out loud. In the photo, Daisy and Stuart are dancing on the table right here in the bar. She looks so happy; Stuart is laughing, and Jon is standing by the table, ready to catch her if she falls. Just like the protective brother, he was with Michelle.

"Mikey, if I had known." I turn to Jon, shaking my head at him.

"How would you have known? We only know his name, and we're not even sure it's his real one; he could've made it up." I look at the picture again and feel a slight smile appear on my face despite it all. "She looks so happy."

Jon takes the picture from me and smiles at it himself.

"She was. She didn't have a care in the world," Jon starts chuckling, "Plus, she had drunk a whole lot of gin."

"There were two others, one of her getting home last night, going by the way she is dressed, and this one."

I hold my hand for the picture, but Stuart looks at me. "You might want to prepare yourself for it." I take a deep breath and nod. Stuart hands it over, looking at Marcus nervously, who nods, reassuring him.

When I look at the picture, I swear my heart jumps into my throat in an attempt to escape. Jon steadies me for what feels like the tenth time today.

There in the picture is Daisy and me on our first actual date. It is a side portrait; we're standing in the clearing around sunset. My arms are wrapped around her waist, hers around my neck as she looks up at me. Even though I can see I'm smiling, her smile is lighting up the whole picture. We are staring into each other's eyes and oblivious to anyone or anything around us. I feel the photo slip from my fingers as I sit down in a chair Jon pushes underneath me.

"How did he get so close without me knowing we were being watched?" I ask out loud.

"Mikey, you were distracted by your mate. Why would you have been paying attention to danger?" I point to the picture of Daisy running.

"I was looking out for danger then, though, and I never realised there was another wolf around."

The guys look at me, confused.

"He's stalked Daisy since realising she was running in

the early hour of the morning back in October," Jon explains to them,

"I had to make sure she was safe. Considering she was attacked on one occasion and obviously being watched on at least one other, I was right in watching over her. But that takes us back to the question. How did a wolf manage to hide from not only her but me? I was always on high alert when she ran. There is no way he would have got past me."

"The biggest question is, how did *he* keep getting so close to Daisy without her picking up *his* scent?" We all turn and look at Marcus. "This guy held Daisy captive for five months, assaulted, raped and abused her, as well as changed her into a wolf. Are you telling me she wouldn't have picked up his scent at some point whilst he's been watching her? His scent will be embedded in her brain; there is no way she would be able to miss it."

"So, what are you saying?" I hear Mum ask behind me.

"I'm asking if there is any chance someone else knows about Daisy's past and is trying to scare her. I know I only met her yesterday, but she really doesn't seem like the type to have the guy who nearly killed her stalk her and not know about it."

"She never noticed Michael stalking her," Will chimes in.

"Yes, she did. She had known the whole time but never called me out on it sooner as she said she was worried I would stop. She liked knowing I was close by." I rub the bridge of my nose and sigh.

"So, if Marcus is right and it isn't Jackson who has taken these pictures, who sent them and made her think he had found her?" Mum asks as she sits down next to me, picking up the picture of Daisy and me. I look at Jon and can see he is coming to the same conclusion as me.

"Do you think Kellan knows anything? Even if just enough to make her think it was Jackson?" Jon nods. I shrug as I turn to Stuart. Time for him to do what he does best.

"You have met Kellan, haven't you?" Stuart's lips turn up like a bitter taste has entered his mouth; I know how he feels.

"Carl, any chance you know where he now lives?"

"As a matter of fact, I do. I gave him a lift to an apartment once; he said it was a friend's place, and he crashed in a lot. Do you think he is behind all of this?"

I shrug as I really have no idea. But for now, he is the most logical answer. I point to the picture of Daisy dancing on the table.

"That picture was taken here. I would guess it was taken through that window." I point to one of the windows at the front of the building. "It was late, obviously, as it's dark."

"Daisy didn't start dancing on the tables until about eleven. There was hardly anyone here then," Stuart chimes in. I just nod as I thought it had been around then by the messages I received from her that night.

"It would have been easy for him to take a picture and not be seen," I point to the one of Daisy and her friends in the café. "That could have been taken at any time. They are always drinking coffee in there; it's Daisy's favourite café." I look at the one of her running, "I hate to admit he would have got past me as I wouldn't have seen him as a threat back then. But this one…" I point to the one in front of my mum, the one of Daisy and me. "This one doesn't make sense at all. How would he have known we were going there? The whole thing was discussed via text message. He must have followed her, but we would've noticed if another car had pulled up; we certainly would've heard if anybody was following us. We were in a clearing, which is hard to find if you don't know about it. Also, he would have had to be close as the clearing isn't big. We would have picked up on his scent at some point."

That is when it hits me. I look up at Carl in shock.

"What does Kellan's scent smell like to you?" Carl looks at me, confused. I watch as he tries to think about it; his eyes widen and confirm my suspicions. Then, finally, he looks at Richard, who is mirroring his look.

"I don't know; it's like he doesn't have one." Richard nods to confirm he is thinking the same thing.

"Of course, he has a scent. Everyone does," Stuart pipes in. I turn to him, raising my eyebrows.

"What is it then?" I watch as he comes to the same realisation.

"Fuck, how is that even possible?" I shake my head; if Stuart doesn't know it, it doesn't exist; we need to confirm this. I turn to Stuart and Carl, pointing to them both.

"Carl, you take Stuart to Kellan's place and wait for him whilst he takes a look around." I turn my focus onto Stuart, "You are the best at tracking and sneaking into places. Do what you can, even if it's just a look through his bedroom window, see if you notice anything, and see if you can pick up an item with his scent. First, we need to confirm whether he has one or not." Both nod and rush towards the door.

I turn to Richard, "Can you call Tony and confirm how much Kellan knows about Daisy's past? I know at one point Daisy and Kellan were close friends, so she could've confided in him. Tony will know for sure." Richard nods, giving my shoulder a reassuring squeeze before walking around to the other side of the bar.

I reach across the table and pull the picture of the two of us towards me. I trace Daisy's smile with my fingertip. Now I see how she looks at me in this picture, I can't believe that I thought she had left because she didn't want to be with me.

"I told you; I've never seen someone look at anybody the way Daisy looks at you. At least it looks like she is safe," Jon says next to me, holding the picture of the three of them Sunday night. I nod. It's reassuring to know that it's unlikely the bastard *has* found her.

"But Daisy doesn't know that, and she is still missing. I've no idea how to find her to tell her." I take the picture from Jon and look at her, laughing. "If they find Kellan, do me a favour and keep him the hell away from me. I swear I'll kill the prick for what he has done to *my* girl. She must be terrified, Jonny. I can't believe he has done this to her, to us." I arrange the pictures so they are all in front of me. "There are so many other ways he could've made our lives difficult, to have tried to separate us; he doesn't know what our bond actually is. He just thinks we're dating. He could have taken evidence to the university and outed our relationship in public. Why attack her the one way that would cause her this amount of pain and distress? She never did anything to deserve this."

"He's done it to separate the two of you. By threatening to kill you if she stays, he's ensuring Daisy leaves you completely, and there's nothing you can do about it," Mum says next to me as I feel her rubbing my shoulder.

"I just wish I knew where she was so I could show her that everything is okay, that she's safe, and she can come home."

"I might be able to help with that." I turn to Marcus, who's speed typing on his laptop. "I've received a message from the Alpha; he has located two other packs in the Exeter area. They are both only small, ten to fifteen members, but there's a chance one of them will be the one that helped relocate her and her family."

"Send me the details; I'll contact them myself," I say as Marcus sends everything to me. I head back to my laptop and quickly send an email to the first whilst leaving a voicemail with the second. Explaining to both the situation and hoping they'll be able to help me. I'm not expecting them to just hand over the details if they are the ones that helped her, but I'm hoping they can at least hear me out. All we can do now is wait and hope we catch a break soon.

Chapter Thirty-Four

MICHAEL

"Bro, you need to try and get some sleep; it's past midnight. There is nothing more we can do today. So go to bed, rest, and we'll tackle more in the morning."

"How am I meant to rest when Daisy still believes that he has found her? She must be terrified. I need to find her and tell her she's safe."

Jon walks over to the steps I'm sitting on in my back garden and sits beside me. It's so quiet now it's just the two of us. Marcus took Mum home hours ago, and Will and Stuart left not long after, both taking turns to watch Kellan's place tonight, hoping he will return.

We left The Crows just before five so that Carl and Richard could make some money today, as they had closed the kitchen during lunch. I left a very generous tip in their till when they weren't looking, hoping to make up for some of the money they lost by not opening today.

I honestly don't feel worthy of my friends and family today. They all heard what happened with Daisy and came running. I don't know if that speaks more about my relationship with them or their love for Daisy. You can't meet her without instantly falling in love with her. I guess she is too easy to love, which is how this whole thing came about.

When Stuart got to what we thought was Kellan's friend's place, he found out he lives alone. There's no sign that anyone else has ever lived there. Marcus did a bit of digging and found that the house was bought outright by auction in September by Mr Kalvin. C. Jacks. We can't find any other information about the owner. Marcus is going to keep working on it and will let me know if anything comes up.

The fact that Kellan has a house in town has raised even more questions. Has he actually been living on campus like he claimed? When I spoke to Tony, he told me he had never been to Kellan's dorm. Kellan always made excuses so that they had to hang out at Tony and Daisy's. Tony just figured it was because he didn't get along with his dormmates or wanted a chance to see Daisy. Now, we think he never even lived on campus. When I checked the student records, I noticed that his address section was empty.

But why lie about where you live? There are so many unanswered questions about the kid that I would really like to have answers to. One of the more important questions is how he does not have a scent. Stuart confirmed that the only odours coming from his property are typical household smells, such as deodorants, cleaning products, food, etc. But he has no personal scent. I asked Mum about it; she is as stumped as we are. We all agreed that we think he was more than just human, but we have no idea what he is or if he is *aware* of what he is. The only thing we are one hundred percent certain of is that he is obsessed with Daisy on a dangerous level.

What Stuart found in his house was both sickening and

terrifying. I have never understood how someone can lose control, 'see red', and kill somebody. But after seeing the pictures, Stuart took on his phone of the inside of Kellan's house, the only thing I could think about was finding and killing him. It had taken all six men to restrain me. Just thinking of the shrine he had created for Daisy makes my blood boil and bile fill my mouth.

"Any signs of Kellan yet?" I ask Jon as I take a sip of the beer he has brought me. He shakes his head.

"Will has taken over from Stuart on watch. He is parked down the road from his place. Apparently, he had to force Stuart to leave as he wants to be the one to destroy him when he resurfaces." I've noticed that Stuart is very protective over Daisy already. I have started to wonder if he has developed some romantic feelings towards her, not that I think he will ever act on them if he has, but I don't know how I feel about it. It's something I'll have to deal with at another time. For now, I just need to make finding her my priority.

"He'll have to get in line. I'm going to relish in killing Kellan after everything he's done." Just the thought of that room, filled with photos of Daisy, as well as some of her own personal items scattered around the place, makes me sick. He has stalked her for months; there were even pictures of her sleeping in her bed. But the most unsettling thing for me was seeing the clothing items.

There were two t-shirts, both of which hung on a wall, with photos of her sleeping in them. Another item was a towel; Stuart said it smelt strongly of her and the shampoo she uses. The icing on the cake, the picture and item that made me punch my own brother in the face when he restrained me, was a picture of Daisy in the shower. In the photo, you could see someone holding up a pink lace bra and matching thong. Stuart had found the set under the pillow of the bed with two other sets. All three smelt of Daisy, but he had also obviously used them for his own personal release.

I turn my head to the side as I vomit the tiny amount of food I've been able to eat. The thought of someone pleasuring themselves with an item of her clothing whilst they thought of her and inhaled her scent, violating the trust Daisy has put in them in that way, keeps making me physically sick. That kid is a whole new level of sick and twisted; he needs to be stopped. I'll happily be the one to do it and end his obsession with *my* mate.

"What was that?"

I turn my head to my brother and raise my eyebrows.

"Every time I think about that arsehole's room, I puke." I rub my face, feeling absolutely drained and wired at the same time.

"Other than that, how are you feeling?"

I turn my attention back to Jon and frown.

"Daisy is still missing; I've no way of finding her. Every time I think I'm getting somewhere with the packs in Exeter, it turns into another dead end. How do you think I'm feeling, Jonathan?"

"I meant with the physical pain." Jon looks at me, waiting for my answer, as I take a deep drink from my bottle.

"It's not getting any better; in fact, I think it's getting worse, and I don't know what the hell it means. I asked the Alpha and Mum about it, and all they could think was that it had something to do with her witch side. But something is telling me it's more like it's an advanced version of the mating bond or something. Of course, Marcus finds it fascinating and is researching it."

I hear Jon chuckle as he stands up and places a hand on my shoulder.

"I'm going to try and get some rest. Please do the same. I've got a good feeling about tomorrow. I don't know why, but I do."

"I hope you are right, bro, as I don't know how much longer I can hold it together." I feel Jon's hand squeeze my shoulder.

"You are doing amazing, Mikey. I've never been prouder of you. The way you are handling all of this and doing all you can to get her home is amazing. This is why I know it will turn out all right in the end. You are too dedicated to finding her and keeping her safe. Have faith in your love, your bond, and you will get her back."

I stand up and hug my brother. In the twenty-eight years we had terrorised our mum, he has never been such a pillar of strength. I have always been the strong one of us, but today, he has stepped up and been more than I could ever ask for in a big brother.

"I love you, Jonny; I'm glad Mama kept you."

Jon chuckles as he remembers how Michelle and I used to say we loved him when we were younger; he squeezes me tighter.

"I'm glad she kept me, too. I love you right back, little brother."

We pull apart, both trying to hide the fact we are wiping away tears. "Right, I'm going to bed. Please try to get some rest and eat something. Mum will kill me if she comes round tomorrow, and that stew is still in the pan."

I force a smile and nod.

"I'll go back in soon, I promise, and I'll try to eat something."

Jon wishes me goodnight again before heading in. I sit back down, pulling my phone towards me.

As I hear my brother making his way through the house, I open up my pictures and look through some of the ones of Daisy and me.

I've never been one for taking pictures. But since being with her, I want to document everything, every smile, every laugh; I never want to risk forgetting a single moment I've had with her. I smile to myself as I can almost hear Daisy mocking me. *"Cheese ball."* I'll find you, darling, and I'll bring you home. I'll never let you feel scared again. I pick myself up and take myself off to bed. Jon is right; I'm no use to Daisy if I'm exhausted.

I wake up to the sound of my phone ringing. I scramble across the bed and grab it quickly.

"Daisy?"

"Oh no, sorry," a female voice stutters on the other end as my heart sinks. "I'm sorry to ring at this time, but I have some information that might help you find your mate."

I jump to the edge of the bed, looking at the clock to see it's four AM.

"Who is this?"

"I don't think you'll remember me; my name is Julia; you helped me once about three years ago."

I quickly try to rack my brains for any recollection of the name.

"You were chased from your last pack by a man obsessed with you and trying to kill your mate."

"Yeah, that's me; you helped us find a new pack and taught us how to defend ourselves if Zac ever turned up again. That's why I want to help you; you have no idea how much you helped us."

"How can you help me, Julia? How do you even know about it?" I ask as she takes a deep breath.

"My Alpha has taken over from the one who hid your mate when she was bitten. He knows the safe house which they placed them in. I overheard them talking about her to the Beta. I went through his files as I work in his office and wrote down the address. When I heard your name and learned what was happening, I had to do something. I still have your number from when you were helping us. I tried to explain to the Alpha that you are a good man and that there is no way you could plan on hurting this girl. But he wouldn't listen. I can't sit by and not help you when you and the guys did so much for us." I hold my breath as I can't believe my luck. But I also know the risk this places Julia and her mate in.

"As much as I want you to give me that address, fuck, I want nothing more than for you to give it to me. You do understand what it means to go against the Alpha's wishes. You could be banished from the pack. Are you sure you and your mate will be able to live with that?" I hear Julia take a deep breath.

"My mate is onboard; neither of us can sit by and let you and yours suffer because our Alpha is unwilling to listen. We have tried so many times today to get him to understand you mean this girl no harm, but it's falling on deaf ears." My heart is racing. Please, Gods, let this be legit.

"Okay, Julia, give me the address, and I will make sure you and your mate are safe. I already have a plan in mind."

Less than ten minutes later, I'm barging into Jon's room, fully dressed.

"Wake up! I need you to do something for me." I turn on the light; my brother is lying on top of the bed, completely naked, spread eagle on his front.

"What the fuck! Ever heard of knocking?" he curses as he tries to work out what is going on.

"When do you ever knock for me? Plus, it's my house. Now get up! It's important."

Jon jumps from the bed and starts pulling on his sweatpants.

"Have you found her?"

I throw a top at him and place a piece of paper on his bedside cabinet.

"I've got her family's address; I'm leaving now. I've messaged Marcus and asked him and Will to continue watching for Kellan, although I think he may already be long gone."

"So, we are going to get Daisy?"

"No, I am. You are going with Stuart to pick up my source. Her name is Julia, and her mate is with her. We helped them a few years ago. She is in the pack that hid Daisy. She has got the address for me without the Alpha knowing, so you guys need to get them out of there." I rush out the door, my phone, wallet, and keys already in hand as I head for the car.

"Wow, hang on, you're not going on your own. What if it's a trap? What did I say about doing something rash, Mikey?" Jon calls out behind me as he follows me out the front of the house. I open my car door and jump in.

"It's not a trap. I know Daisy's there; I can just feel it. Since I've gotten her address, the pain in my chest has become a dull ache. She's there. I just know it. I've already put Marcus in charge. I'm going to get my mate, and you can't stop me." With that, I slam the door closed and pull away from the house, leaving Jon at my doorway, looking completely bewildered.

Chapter Thirty-Five

DAISY

Whoever says that they feel numb after having their heart broken is lying. Cause this pain is unbearable. It's been relentless since I left.

As soon as I left my dorm, I headed straight to our old home in Exeter; he told me to go there, so I did. I hoped he would follow me as I needed to know he was away from everyone. I had only been in my old home for ten minutes when another note had been posted through the letter box.

I'm glad to see that you are finally doing as you are told. Wait here, and I will be back for you shortly. J

I didn't wait; I shifted and ran to a nearby garage in the early morning where we'd hidden my mum's old car a couple of years ago, just in case I ever had to come back here.

Once at the garage, I shifted back and dressed in my mum's clothes, which we had stashed in the car. I am thankful that we took the time to sit and make a plan for every situation. Using every spell I could think of, I checked for anyone being close or watching. Then, when I was sure I was alone, I pulled my hair up, chucked on my dad's old baseball cap and drove the longest way possible home to my auntie and uncle.

I know Jackson will find me eventually. If he is still looking for me after three years, he will surely do whatever he can to find me. Should I have let Michael and the guys take care of him? I know they would have if I asked them to. I know I wouldn't have even had to ask Michael. But, there again, that was before I went into a blind panic and ran away with no explanation. What if I've broken his heart to the point he will never forgive me?

Oh Goddess, what have I done?

I pull the duvet further around me as I start to shiver, not from the cold but from the physical and emotional pain growing within me. I feel like I am drowning, and there is nothing to help me to the surface. The pain of missing Michael and needing him has consumed me until I can think or feel nothing else.

I have lost all track of time and have no idea when I arrived. Was it yesterday? Have I gotten out of bed or eaten since? No, I know I haven't, as the mere thought of food makes me nauseous. Auntie Mary has been trying so hard to get me to eat and drink, but I just can't bring myself even to try. The only thing I want is to call Michael to hear his voice and know that he's okay. Why did I think throwing my phone and laptop away was a good idea? I don't have any contact details for him or anyone else now. I need to know that he's safe, that they all are.

A car pulls onto the drive, and my heart stops. I listen to the sound of someone running to the front door. It opens after the first knock.

"Where is she?" I hear that familiar voice, unable to miss the panic in his tone. Gods, I've missed that voice so much.

"She's in her room; I don't know what to do." I hear my auntie say, followed by the sound of footsteps running up the stairs; my door flies open as Uncle Nigel rushes in.

"Oh, Daisy, my sweet girl. I'm so sorry I wasn't here. I came back as quickly as I could." He sits on the side of my bed, stroking my hair like he has done so many times since I was little. But now it just makes me think of Michael. I throw myself into his arms as my heart breaks all over again. There, in the safety of his arms, I let it all out. All the pain and tears that have been building in my chest. My uncle holds and comforts me, whispering that everything will be okay. Telling me that he will help me with whatever I need. If only he knew.

I stay there in that safe place for what feels like hours, crying as he offers me words of comfort. As the tears recede, he lowers me gently back onto the bed, tucking the duvet around me and staying close the whole time.

"Daisy, please talk to me, tell me what's happened. Has someone hurt you? You sounded so happy when you called the other day." I can feel the panic building again within me. All I can hear is my own heartbeat in my ears, drowning out all other sounds.

"He found me. Jackson found me and threatened everyone there that I love and care for. I had to leave to protect them." I look up and see my uncle frowning at me.

"What made you think he'd found you? You were so well hidden." So, I tell him about the note and the pictures. I avoid mentioning the one of Michael and me as it's too painful. The thought of Jackson being close that day and ruining that moment is too much right now.

"I panicked, and now I'm so confused. I left to protect people, to protect those I love there. But what if I didn't have to leave them? They could have dealt with Jackson. But now, I don't think I can ever return, as I would have hurt them so much by running away without explanation. I feel so stupid."

"It wasn't stupid; you panicked and did what you thought was right. Yes, you could've probably handled the situation a little better, but nothing is really ruined. Let's see how we can fix it." That is my uncle all over. Always there to help me work everything out and to make sense of things. He has been my rock for so long; I don't know what I would do without him.

When my father was presumed dead shortly after my mum died, I thought I would have to go into care. I was terrified, but my auntie and uncle took me in. They've been my parents ever since, and I love them both to bits. But I've always been closer to my uncle. I was always a daddy's girl, so they say I transferred that love over to him. I don't think he has minded as he always says I'm the daughter they could never have.

"Daisy, I just don't understand how he could have found you there unless someone told him. This is why only the three of us know where you have gone. Alex, Sara, and Clare don't even know. As for not being able to go back, I don't understand. Why couldn't you just return if we can prove it's safe? Just say that it was a family emergency. I'm sure you still have your place on the course." With the thought of the course comes the thought of Michael, and the tears start again.

"Daisy, what are you not telling me."

"I met someone there, but when I panicked and ran, I didn't even say goodbye I just left a shitty text as I couldn't tell him the truth. He would have gone looking for Jackson, and I couldn't risk him getting hurt because of me."

"You mean a boyfriend?" my uncle asks. I shake my head.

"He's more than that." I take a deep breath, "He's my mate." The uncontrollable tears start again, and my uncle pulls me back into his arms, holding me tightly against his chest. I can't breathe, just the mention of Michael, and I feel myself falling even further apart. I'm hyperventilating and feel like I'll be sick, but there is nothing left in me.

"Oh, Daisy, why didn't you tell us you had met your mate? I'm sure he will understand and help you through all of this. That's what mates are for."

I can't control the sounds that escape me as my heart breaks even more. I know he's right, but I don't know how to face Michael now, not after what I've done.

"I miss him so much it hurts," I sob loudly. "I never thought the distance would hurt this much, but it does. I didn't even give him a reason why I left. He will be hurting, and it's all my fault. He must hate me," I choke out as another sob tears through my chest.

"I could never hate you, darling."

Chapter Thirty-Six

MICHAEL

For a second, Daisy just looks up at me with those big green eyes, and everything else stops existing.

I found her.

She is actually here in front of me.

Before I can even open my mouth to speak, Daisy launches herself towards me. Her legs get tangled in her duvet, and I only just manage to catch her by sliding on my knees before she lands on the floor of her room. She throws her arms around my neck as a sob, which tears my whole being in two, leaves her.

"You found me," she gasps. I place my hands on either side of her face and lean back so I'm looking into her tear-filled eyes.

"When are you going to learn? I will *always* find you, darling." I kiss the top of her head before wrapping my arms around her, burying my nose into her hair, inhaling her sweet scent. I notice that the constant ache in my chest has finally gone, and now my girl is back in my arms where she belongs.

Daisy pulls away from me, a look of sheer panic now etched on her face.

"But if you are here, who is watching everyone there? Jackson will -" I place a finger on her lips to stop her, shushing her gently.

"It wasn't Jackson, darling. He still has no idea where you are. You are safe, I promise."

"But he left me a note in Exeter. I went there first to trick him-" I cut her off again by shaking my head.

"Darling, I promise you, it's not Jackson; we found the camera which took the photos in someone else's room. So it couldn't have been him. We will work everything out, but the important thing right now is that you are safe." I feel a hand touch my shoulder and look up and see Daisy's auntie and uncle standing over us. I'd forgotten they were here in the room with us.

"We'll leave you in peace. Call if you need anything," her uncle says as he places a hand on his wife's lower back and guides her out as she cries silently.

"Thank you, both of you," I whisper as they leave. Her uncle gives me a curt nod as he closes the door.

As soon as the door is closed, I pull Daisy tightly against my chest. Her hold around my neck doesn't alter as she continues to cry. The relief of finding her and having her here in my arms, safe and well, is enough to open the gates within me. I allow the tears to fall into her hair, breathing in her scent repeatedly. After thirty-four hours without her, worrying that I would never see her again, I'll never get enough of her.

We stay holding each other, not noticing the hardness of the floor or the draft coming through the open window; nothing matters but us being together.

After some time, I slowly lift Daisy so that I can move

her onto the bed. I sit on the edge and place her onto my lap, her legs to one side so I can hold her against my chest. I take this chance to really look at her.

My poor girl looks so ill. I know I'm not faring much better, but to see Daisy's eyes so dull and lifeless seems wrong. I know I need to make her feel better, to put some colour in her cheeks and the sparkle back in her eyes. But first, I need to just hold her and try to wrap my head around the last half an hour, and how I finally have her back in my arms where she belongs.

When I had first arrived, I'd rushed to the front door. The second her Auntie Mary had answered, I knew I had the right house. There is no mistaking that they're family. Not only do they have the same colour eyes, but they also have the same sharp chin. Daisy's scent had hit me as soon as the door was opened, causing my knees to buckle; I held on to the wall for support.

"Are you okay? Can I help you?" I looked at her auntie and could feel the tears welling up in my eyes.

"Is Daisy here? If she is, you need to tell her she is safe. She thinks Jackson has found her, but he hasn't. Please just let her know she is safe."

Her auntie just stared at me, shocked. I must have looked and sounded like a madman; I felt like one anyway, but I didn't care. All that mattered was that she knew she was safe.

"Who are you to, Daisy?" she asked quietly. I looked up at her as I rubbed a hand against my aching chest.

"I'm Michael Adams, ma'am. Daisy's mate." Before I could add any more, I could hear Daisy sobbing from within the house. My whole body stiffened. The pain intensified with the sound of her crying as my wolf cried for his mate. I wanted to push past her auntie and run to her, but I couldn't. There was still that tiny part of me, wondering if she had left me.

"You better come in," I heard her auntie say as she took my arm to support me.

"Thank you so much," I answered, walking into their home. As I stepped over the threshold, I felt a tingle of magic race over my body. I spin around and look at her auntie as she closes the door.

"It's a protection spell. If your true intentions are to harm anyone in this household, you would not have been able to enter."

I have to admit I was impressed. I wanted to know more, but it could wait.

"Is she okay? Is she hurt?"

Her auntie just shook her head at me, looking at the stairs ahead of us.

"Not physically, no, but she's a mess. All she's done since she got home is cry and cry. She hasn't eaten or drank a single thing in over twenty-four hours. I don't know what's happened. All she has done is cry out for Michael. For you."

The tightness in my stomach instantly relaxed when I knew she hadn't run from me.

"Has Jackson truly not found her? Is she really still safe?"

I nodded again,

"She's safe; I can promise you she'll always be safe from him. I will never let any harm come to her." I ran my fingers through my hair as I tried to calm my racing heart. "Please, can I see her? I need to see that she's okay. I know I'm asking a lot, ma'am, but I love that amazing woman with all my heart, body, and soul. It's been killing me not knowing where she was."

Mary opened her mouth to answer when we heard a heart breaking sob coming from upstairs. I couldn't wait any longer for permission; I took the stairs three at a time, stopping dead in the doorway of a bedroom as I saw Daisy crying in her uncle's arms. Her auntie gasped behind me as she took in the sight of her niece sobbing uncontrollably. I felt her hand on my arm as she whispered,

"Help her."

I was just about to step into the room when Daisy muttered those words.

"He must hate me."

My soul broke in that moment. I knew in my heart she was talking about me. I couldn't stop myself from replying.

"I could never hate you, darling."

I glance down at Daisy; her hair hasn't been brushed for days, and her eyes are black and swollen from crying. I can't leave her like this. She is still the most beautiful person in the world, but I know Daisy, and I know as she starts to feel better, she will want to feel clean. She is my mate, and I'm here to care for her in any way she needs.

"Hold on to me, darling," I whisper as I move Daisy's arms back around my neck and place an arm under her knees. I slowly stand up once I know she is secure in my arms. "Where's the bathroom?" I ask; she points to a door at the far wall of the room. I start walking towards it.

"What are you doing?" she croaks softly. Her throat is not surprisingly raw from crying.

"I'm going to take care of you if you'll let me. Do you trust me?" I feel her arms tighten slightly.

"With every inch of my being."

I chuckle as I kiss the top of her head.

"Now, who's being a cheese ball?" I watch in amazement as the side of her mouth lifts into the slightest of smiles.

"I learnt from the best."

I glance down at her, curled up in my arms, the slightest hint of her cheeky personality there on her tear-soaked face. At that moment, I know she's going to be okay, eventually.

"You'll never get up to my standards. Now, let's get you into a deep bubble bath so I can wait on you like the queen you are. Play your cards right. I might even wash your hair for you, as I know how much you love me playing with it."

"Is this your way of saying I smell?" she asks, smiling a little bit more. I shake my head slowly.

"This is my way of giving you what I can. So, stop asking questions and just relax and let me worry about everything else whilst taking care of you.

An hour and a half later, Daisy is as fresh as a ... well, a daisy; after a deep bubble bath. She got out of the tub and into some fresh pyjamas with some clean bedding on her bed. I've even managed to get her to eat a little lunch. We are now curled up in her bed, and although it's only four in the afternoon, Daisy is fast asleep in my arms.

It'd taken all of three minutes for her to fall into a deep sleep once we had gotten comfortable. She hasn't moved an inch in the last two hours. I haven't been able to take my eyes off her; I can't believe I finally have her back. I'm scared to close my eyes in case I wake up, back in my bed, alone, still searching for her. I'm finally unable to stay awake any longer when I hear a faint tapping at the door.

"Come in," I whisper as loudly as I dare in fear of waking Daisy, but she doesn't so much as flinch. Her uncle walks in and leans against the door frame.

"How is she?" I can hear the concern in his voice. When I look up at him, I can see he looks as worried as her auntie did when she opened the door to me earlier.

"Sleeping peacefully at last," I whisper as I move to sit up. Daisy's uncle holds his hand out, signalling for me to stop.

"Stay where you are, Son. Apparently, she hasn't slept since she got here. The rest will do her good." He walks over to the bed and runs a hand over her head, soothing her now-dry hair. "This poor girl has been through so much in her life; the thought that she has finally found someone who will look after her the way you have this afternoon is a dream come true for us." He steps away from the bed again to lean back against the wall. "How did you find out where she was?"

"It wasn't easy. I spent all day yesterday trying to track down the pack that had helped you. No one was forthcoming for obvious reasons. But then someone I once helped overheard their Alpha talking about Daisy and me, and they got me the address." I look down at Daisy and tuck a loose strand of hair behind her ear. "They will be in big trouble when their Alpha finds out. I've already sent my brother to collect them and keep them safe." I look back up at her uncle. "Please don't be angry with them. She only told me because she knew me personally, and I saved her and her mate's life a few years back." I look back down at Daisy, taking in every figure on her face. "I would have found her eventually, even if I had to knock on every door in Cornwall. I wouldn't have rested until I found her again. Even if just to tell her she was safe." I look up at her uncle and make eye contact.

"I know you didn't know about us, sir. This wasn't how we planned for you to find out. We were planning on coming down this weekend to speak to you. I wanted to ask for your blessing so that we can complete the mating bond. It didn't seem right to do that over the phone." I watch as a smile plays on her uncle's face.

"I appreciate that, thank you. Daisy may not be my daughter by birth, but I love her as if she was. What do you plan on doing now you're here?"

I shrug slightly before responding.

"I didn't think that far ahead. It was four this morning when I received the phone call with your address. I didn't even grab a change of clothes to bring with me. I'll find a hotel once Daisy has woken up, and I know she's settled and calmed down. I'll stay there until she knows what she wants to do. If she wants me to stick around, I will. If she wants me to leave her, as hard as it will be, I'll do it for her." I quickly look down and check she's still asleep. She mumbles a little, and I can't help but smile, wondering if she can hear our conversation at all.

"I'm also hoping to meet with a pack down here. I know some of the Enforcers. I'm hoping to give them some information about who she is running from so that if they hear about him being near here, they can take care of it, so you and Mrs Evans are safe."

Her uncle raises his eyebrows at me.

"You can do that?" He looks at me, obviously impressed, as I nod. "Then, when we can speak alone, I'll tell you all I know about him. I've done my own research into the prick; excuse my French."

I can't help but chuckle.

"I've called him much worse," I say with a smile; Daisy's uncle smiles back at me.

"I bet you have. I'll share what I've got on him. Also please don't think we will allow you to stay in a hotel. You are obviously good for our girl and love her to have done all you have to find her. I would never turn away someone willing to do all that. Mary and I will pop out and get you a few bits just to see you through until you can go out and get yourself what you need. I don't think I've anything that will fit you; otherwise, I would lend you some of my stuff. But I am sure Daisy will enjoy dragging you to the shops."

I point to the chest of drawers by the bed, where I had placed my car key and now dead phone.

"My wallet is in the car. Please take my credit card; I'll let you know the PIN. Also, I would be extremely grateful for some shower gel; I don't actually remember the last time I had a proper wash."

Daisy's uncle chuckles, waving his hand.

"We will get you what you need; you can pay us back by continuing to look after Daisy the way you have been."

I glance down at her peaceful face resting against my arm, which died hours ago, but I can't bring myself to move her.

"That I can do."

I watch as her uncle pushes himself away from the wall.

"I'll send Mary up to make a list, and with some food, I bet you haven't eaten in a while. Please make yourself at home whilst we are out. What is ours is yours." He turns to leave the room and stops. He just turns his head to look back at us. "You are obviously a good man, Michael. I know she is safe with you." He then starts walking out of the room again.

"Thank you, Mr Evans," I whisper as loudly as I dare.

"It's Nigel, Son. Mr Evans was my grandfather and a miserable bastard," I hear him chuckle as I find myself smiling.

"Thank you, Nigel," I reply as he closes the door behind him.

Chapter Thirty-Seven

DAISY

I wake up to the feeling of someone breathing lightly against the back of my neck. There's also an arm draped across my stomach and legs tangled up in mine. I take a deep breath and breathe in Michael's scent, which instantly calms my racing heart.

I glance at the clock and see that it's gone midday. I've no idea what time I fell asleep yesterday; I remember waking up a few times in a panic, thinking I had dreamt Michael finding me. But each time, he'd just tightened his hold on me, whispering that he was there and wasn't going anywhere without me.

I listen to his gentle breathing and know he is still fast asleep; I gently unfold myself from his hold and slip out of bed.

"Darling?" he mutters, opening one eye.

"I'm okay. Go back to sleep, handsome," I whisper as I kiss the top of his head. He nods slightly before falling instantly back into a deep sleep, showing just how exhausted he still is.

I grab my old dressing gown from behind the door and slip it on as I sneak out of the room, not wanting to wake him again. I head downstairs to the kitchen, following the smell of that brown nectar I crave so badly.

"Hey, you're awake," Auntie Mary says as I walk into the kitchen. She looks behind me, "Is Michael still asleep?"

I nod before planting a kiss on her cheek on my way to the coffee machine. I hear Uncle Nigel chuckle from the kitchen table.

"Mary, you should know better than to speak to her before she has had her morning coffee." I walk over and plant a kiss on his mop of brown hair. How it's still so thick, I will never know when the rest of our family were all bald as melons.

"Correct," I mumble as I take the seat next to him.

They leave me in silence as I take the first two sips of coffee, waiting for the caffeine to hit my system. I look at the front of the paper, which my uncle is reading, and gasp.

"Is it Thursday? Have I really been here two days?" They both look at me and nod. I can see the pain I caused them written all over their faces. I can feel my eyes filling up again. "I'm so sorry."

Auntie Mary rushes over and wraps me in one of her hugs as a sob escapes my lips. I lean my head against her shoulder as my uncle takes my hand.

"Don't you dare apologise; you needed to feel safe, so you came home. There's nothing wrong with that. We were just so confused and worried. I couldn't get you to eat or drink; I swear you didn't sleep. I'll never know how you didn't pass out with exhaustion." Mary pulls away from me slightly and takes my face in her hands. "Please just remember that you can't run from a mate. I think it nearly killed you both from the way that poor man looked when he knocked on the door. I thought he was going to keel over with exhaustion," Mary explained. I feel myself nodding.

"So, you met my mate," I say, smiling sheepishly, trying to lighten the mood. Mary pulls away from me and slaps my arm.

"Ouch, what was that for?" I ask, rubbing my now bruised arm.

"That's for not telling us you had found your mate."

I look at Nigel, and he just shrugs.

"I was going to call before coming down tomorrow to surprise you."

"Oh, we were surprised, alright," Nigel laughs next to me. I look between the two of them, biting my bottom lip.

"So, what do you think?"

Uncle Nigel looks at me as Auntie Mary walks away towards the oven.

"He's a big lad and will certainly be able to look after you. Some might find him attractive." My uncle answers whilst reading his paper. I look at Mary, who is walking back towards me, fanning herself as if to back up my uncle's claim.

"Mary dear, I can see your reflection in the window," he adds, rolling his eyes at me playfully. I can't help but giggle.

"You're still my number one guy," Mary says, planting a kiss on his head before turning to me.

"That man loves you so much. When he knocked on the door, I honestly thought he was going to fall through it. Every time he heard you cry his whole body went rigid. Even though it must have been killing him to stay away from you, all he was worried about was you and that you knew you were safe. I think he thought you had left him. When I told him you had been calling out for him, he begged me to let him take care of you. Before I could answer, though, we heard what could only be described as your heart breaking; he stopped being polite then and raced up those stairs. Nothing was going to stop him from getting to you; he had to ensure you were okay." I could feel my heart tightening just thinking about how he cared for me. "The moment you saw him, the disbelief on your face, quickly followed by relief, was unmissable. When he caught you and told you he would always find you, I swear even old grumpy Nigel cried." Mary places a hand on her heart and pouts.

"I don't think he left your side for more than a couple of minutes at a time. Then, when I went in to ask him how you were doing, you were gripping his top like you never wanted to be without him again. The way he watched you sleep was like he was sure you were going to disappear if he took his eyes off you," Nigel explains. I look down at my hands and start fiddling with a loose strand on my dressing gown.

"I don't deserve him," I whisper. I watch as my uncle places a hand over mine, squeezing it slightly.

"You deserve this love and happiness more than any of us. He will protect you and love you for the rest of your days. You just have to learn to let him." I look up and smile, knowing he's right.

I hear the timer going off on the oven, and I sniff the air. I look over at my auntie, smiling.

"Croissants?" she confirms with a grin. I notice the tray on the side. She piles a load of the fresh-out-of-the-oven pieces of heaven onto a plate and puts it on the tray, followed by two cups of coffee before handing it to me.

"Go and take this up to the poor man. He only had a few sandwiches last night, and from the way he scoffed them down, I don't think he had eaten for a while." I jump to my feet and kiss them both on the cheek before taking the tray up to my room, where Michael is still fast asleep in my bed.

I gently place the tray on top of my chest of drawers and shrug off my dressing gown before crawling back into the bed. Michael instantly opens his arms for me, pulling me in tight. I snuggle into his chest, inhaling his scent again.

"Good morning, beautiful," he whispers into my hair as I plant a kiss on his chest.

"Good morning, handsome." I can feel Michael breathing in deep and realise he is sniffing to work out what he smells.

"Coffee and croissants?" he asks. I move back a little so I can see his face.

"Yep, fresh out of the oven too."

I hear him moan in appreciation.

"Your Auntie Mary has just become one of my favourite people," he murmurs before his mouth breaks into a big grin.

"Hey!" I protest. He pulls me in close and holds me tight so I can't escape or hit him. His laughter fills the room.

"Tell you what? I'll keep you supplied with coffee, pizza, wine, and steak, and you can keep me supplied with coffee and croissants, and then we can stick to being each other's favourite people." I pull away to look at him again.

"You are already my favourite person," I reply, gently kissing his lips.

"That's good because you are most definitely mine."

I look deep into his blue eyes as I whisper, "I'm sorry." Michael pulls me in close once more and holds me tight whilst resting his head on the top of mine.

"I'm only going to say this once, baby, so make sure you

are listening. Don't you ever apologise to me. You did what you thought was right at the time; you were in a panic, so you ran to the one place you felt the safest. How could I ever possibly be cross or upset by that?" He kisses my head again before continuing. "Next time, just tell me, and I'll drop everything and bring you home. I'll stay with you and hold you until you feel safe again. I know you can look after yourself, but let me help you and look after you when you are struggling. Use me and do whatever you need to feel safe. Just don't push me away again, please."

"I love you," I whisper against his chest.

"That's good because I love you too." He whispers back. "Your auntie and uncle kindly went shopping and picked me up a few bits. They have said I can stay here as long as you need me to."

I pull away from him and look into his eyes.

"I never want to be away from you again; it hurt too much."

Michael places a hand on my cheek before kissing me softly.

"Then we'll never be apart again. When you left, you took a part of me with you. I hated not knowing where you were." I open my mouth to speak, but he places a finger over my lips, stopping me. "I understand now, darling. Just do me one favour; never hide anything from me again. How can I help you and protect you when you don't tell me what is going on?" I look up at him and realise he's right. "Darling, you are my mate. I've known my whole life that you were out there somewhere, waiting for me. Please talk to me; let me help you; let me take some of the burdens. We're a team; it's you and me against the world. It may not always be 50/50; sometimes, it may be 20/80, and that's okay, as that's what a relationship is when a couple works as a team.

One holds the other up when they can't do it themselves. So let me hold you up and let me be strong for the both of us when you need me." I meet his eyes again and see nothing but pure love shining from them.

"I love you, Daisy Angela Andrews. I've loved you from the moment I saw you." I feel my breath catch in my throat, but I can't help but smile.

"I love you too, you big cheese ball."

Michael chuckles. It's like music to my ears. He leans over me until I'm lying on my back, and he is on top of me.

"But whose cheese ball am I?" he says as his lips softly touch mine.

"All mine, and I wouldn't change you for the world."

He gently kisses me, then pulls back a little.

"Good because I wouldn't change you either … well, maybe one thing." I look at him, shocked, but he just smirks. "Your last name, but we'll get round to that one day." His lips crash into mine before any more can be said.

A short while later, we are sitting in bed and eating our breakfast. Michael has plugged his phone in to charge with one of my old chargers. Apparently, it had died before he got here yesterday. He had just turned it on when the screen lit up and started flashing to signal a call. I watch as his eyes widen.

"Shit, I knew I forgot to do something." He answers the phone, biting his bottom lip looking worried. "Hey, Mama."

Oh shit.

"Don't you 'hey Mama' me. I've been out of my mind with worry. I've left message after message on your voice-mail and sent so many bloody text messages that my fingers hurt. The last any of us heard, you were heading down to find Daisy at four in the morning. We didn't know if you had found her or not. Or if you had even made it down, nothing!" As soon as I hear Barbara's voice, my stomach drops like a lead balloon. Oh, gods, she will hate me for putting her son through hell the last few days.

"I know I'm sorry, Mum, really I am, but Daisy was my priority, and I had to make sure she was okay." I can barely hear her, and her voice changes as she asks how I am. "It's taken a bit of time, but she's getting there." I put my face in my hands. I hear Michael mumble something and then tap me on the shoulder. I look up and see that he is holding his phone out to me.

"She wants to speak to you." I shake my head whilst on the verge of crying. Michael looks at me gently as he covers the voice piece of the phone with his hand. "Darling, it's okay. Mum has been so worried about you; she just wants to hear your voice and know that you are alright." He nods at me reassuringly, holding out the phone again. I take a deep breath before taking it from him.

"Hey, Barbara," I hear her gasp down the line.

"Oh, Daisy, my darling girl, are you okay? I've been so worried; we all have. Please know we are all here for you and will do anything you need. Just please speak to us when you need to." I can't bring myself to speak a single word; my throat has closed tight, and all I manage is a sob as tears start running down my face. Michael lifts me so I'm sat on his lap, pulling me into his chest as he holds me, offering the support I need.

"I'm sorry." That is all I manage to squeak out. Michael takes the phone off me as I'm shaking and holds it so we can both hear.

"Do not apologise. Never apologise for feeling scared.

Remember, you aren't on your own, and even if something worries you and you can't speak to Mikey, you can always come here or call me at any time. We are family now, and we are all there for each other."

"Thank you," I whisper.

"Thank you, Mum, we both really appreciate that," Michael says as he kisses the top of my head. "Daisy is still a little raw, so we're going to go. We'll call you later." We can hear someone shouting in the background. The noise gets louder before they take the phone from Barbara.

"Hey, little witch, before you go, do me a favour and punch Mikey for me?"

"Why?" We both ask together.

"For not letting me know you had got down there, okay, you dickhead. Marcus and I were planning on coming down to find you if you didn't get in touch soon. I'm going to kick your arse when you get back, and then Marcus is going to kill you. Daisy, I'm going to kick yours too for not coming to me. You know I'm always here for you, you moron." I can hear the humour in his voice. Michael doesn't seem to, though, as he growls at him.

"It's okay; we both know I can take him down," I say, winking at him. Michael laughs as Jon protests in the background.

"Everything go okay yesterday with Julia, Jon?" Michael asks next to me. I look at him, frowning. Michael mouths he will tell me later.

"Yeah, they are fine. They are settled into the safe house they were in before. But they don't want to go back. Apparently, they don't like how the new Alpha does certain things. So, Desmond is going to sort something for them and wants to wait until you come back before dealing with the things

Julia has told him." Michael thanks Jon and asks him to tell Marcus to email him an update on everything.

"Right, I'm hanging up now. I want to make sure Daisy eats her breakfast. We'll call you later," Michael calls out. Barbara and Jon both shout out a goodbye; Barbara shouts that she loves us as she hangs up. I can't help smiling to myself.

I had been sure they were going to go mad at me, but instead, they had shown me so much love and support. They still welcome me into their family, even after everything I put Michael through.

"Come on, you, let's have this food, and then you can show me where the nearest shops are. I have a feeling we both may need a few bits." He kisses the top of my head again as he passes me my coffee.

Chapter Thirty-Eight

MICHAEL

After we finish our breakfast, well lunch, in bed, Daisy heads off for a shower, and I take it as a chance to head off and speak to Nigel about all he has learnt about the bastard that turned her. I ask Daisy where I can find him, telling her that I plan on speaking to him about the mating bond. She tells me he will be in his office and where to find it; wishing me luck, she skips off into the shower, and I head off to speak to her uncle.

I find his office easily and knock on the door.

"Come in, Michael."

I walk into the room, smiling.

"I take it no one else knocks before entering?"

Nigel sighs as he shakes his head.

"If they started now, I think I would panic more than appreciate it." He pulls a flash drive out of the computer and hands it to me. "This is everything I have on the prick."

"That's great, thank you. I will forward it to our tech

guy, and he can do some deeper digging. No offense." I add quickly but Nigel just waves my comment off.

"None taken. I take it you have a database or something for things like this?"

"We do; it was actually built by my pack brother Marcus, who will put this into it and see what comes up." Nigel looks impressed. I put the flash drive into my pocket and lean back into the chair I am sitting on. "What can you tell me quickly about him?"

Nigel sits back in his own chair and rubs the bridge of his nose, taking a deep breath. I know it must be hard for him; from what Daisy has told me, he kept her captive for so long that Nigel and Mary were starting to give up hope of her ever returning to them.

"His name is Morgan Jackson, but he hates his first name, so he just goes by Jackson. I cannot find any history of him being part of a pack. He did approach one around Exeter about six years ago looking for sanctuary, saying he was running from someone hunting him. But they kicked him out after a week for trying to sleep with the Luna."

I find myself growling at the complete disrespect.

"I take it he didn't just walk out of there."

Nigel shakes his head.

"No, from what I can gather, he was beaten up pretty bad. A shame they didn't just kill the bastard." I can't help but nod in agreement as he continues. "From what Daisy has told me about him, he planned on forming his own pack. Saying no other pack deserved to have him in it and that he would build one so big and powerful that he would be able to destroy anyone that got in their way."

"How this guy hasn't made it onto our radars before now, I'll never know. Sounds like he has been causing a lot of trouble."

"I am surprised he's managed to stay off all our radars personally. I wish I could tell you what he looks like, but I have never laid eyes on him in human form. I think Daisy wants to believe she could defeat him. But you have seen for yourself he still truly terrifies her. It's not surprising, considering the state she was in when she escaped. There was nothing left of her; he had broken her in ways I didn't think was humanly possible. I have included a copy of the police report in the file, as well as pictures. I can't look at them again. We tried to keep the police out of it once we realised what he was and that he had turned Daisy. They think Daisy was a runaway who got into the wrong crowd and came home when things got rough. I hate that he will never face a jury for what he did to her, but I know sometimes the human courts are a waste of time for us supernaturals. The Supernatural Council has promised if he is ever found, he will pay for what he's done."

"Well, you have us now; we will get the son of a bitch. Trust me when I say he won't get within five feet of her ever again." I pick up a pen and a notepad next to it and write down Marcus's email address and my home and mobile number.

"If anything else does ever come to light, send it to this address or contact me directly. I will give Marcus a heads-up and tell him to hide it from the others for now. I think I will get my brother Jon and Marcus to go and spend a few days in Exeter to see if they can find anything out about him. See if they can find out where he has set up camp. I would like to keep Daisy here for a little longer, as I am worried the guy who pretended to be Jackson is still unaccounted for. However, it sounds like he followed her to Exeter somehow. The guys can check into that, too." I repositioned myself in the chair, knowing I also needed to discuss other things with him.

"I really do appreciate you letting me stay last night to be with Daisy. I don't think I could have left her in the state she was in. I was wondering if you would mind me staying as long as Daisy does."

"Like I said yesterday, you can stay as long as you like. If your brother and pack brother need somewhere to stay when in Exeter, we still own our old house. They are free to use it. Just let me know, and I will get it up to scratch for them." I thank him, but he just waves it off.

"You are good for my girl, and I really appreciate that you are willing to fight for her. You looked after her in a way I don't think anyone else could have last night. The way you both look at each other, I have never seen anything so pure and intense. I won't pretend that I know what it's like between a wolf and their mate. But I know what it's like to find your soul mate. The thought of ever being separated from Mary if she was in danger was enough for me to become the strongest sorcerer I could be. I would fight until my last breath for that woman. From what you have shown me, I believe you would do the same for our Daisy." I feel honoured that this man who loves his niece so much is willing to let me take over, look after her, and protect her.

"I really would do *anything* to protect her. I love her. I would love her just as much without the mate bond. She gets me in ways no one else ever has. I couldn't breathe when she left. I'm ashamed to admit I lost all hope for a while.

"When we had first discussed the bond, I had promised Daisy I would not push her into accepting me, that if she wanted to reject me, she could. I wouldn't stop her from being happy, even if it killed me. When she left, I thought she had decided she didn't want me, so I let her go. All I could see was the pain and sorrow of losing her. It wasn't until my brother Jonathan pointed out that for Daisy to run like she did something, or someone had scared her. Somebody had made her think that the only way to protect those she loves and herself would be for her to hide. As soon as he got that into my thick skull, I set about finding her.

"I am not giving up on us ever again. She can push and scream as much as she wants, but I know this is what she really wants. That's why I would like your permission for Daisy and I to move in together and complete the mating bond."

Nigel looks at me with a straight face, not blinking or showing any sign of emotion. I freeze with panic and start to worry he's going to say no. I watch on tenterhooks as he looks over to his right, where there's a picture of a very young Daisy with her parents.

"When Angela died, and then David was presumed dead, I didn't have to think twice about taking Daisy in. There was no way she was going to end up a child of the system. Mary and I may never have been blessed with a child of our own, but we were blessed with a beautiful, intelligent niece who is as much a daughter to us as our own child would have been. I have watched that girl's life fall apart four times in her life, the first two being when she lost her parents. The third, I honestly thought it had killed her; I thought he had killed her." I watch as Nigel rubs the bridge of his nose again. "Yesterday, when I came home and found her in that state, her life having obviously fallen apart for the fourth time, I thought there was no chance she was going to recover this time. I thought this was going to be the one that was too much. Then you walked through that door, and she threw herself into your arms. I heard you telling her you would always find her, and I knew she would be okay. You held her, washed and cared for her, got her to eat, I even heard her laugh again, and then you got her to sleep and rest. When she came downstairs for her coffee this morning, she looked so much better. Almost as if nothing had happened." Nigel leans on his desk, his eyes piercing my own. "You did that. You picked her up quicker than any of us ever could. Which is why I don't have to think twice about giving you both my blessing and wishing you all the love and happiness in the world."

I feel a lump form in my throat; I quickly clear my throat before attempting to speak.

"Thank you, Nigel; I won't let you down."

"I really don't think you will, Son."

I stand up to shake his hand, feeling honoured that he trusts me with one of the most important people in his life. Just as I sit back down, the office door flies open, and Daisy bounces in with a giant smile on her face and a skip in her step.

"There are my two favourite guys."

Nigel just looks up at her over the rim of his glasses.

"I suggest getting a lock on your office door, Michael. Daisy has a habit of just strolling in, uninvited."

I laugh as she sticks her tongue out at him and sits on my lap. I place a hand on her back and look up at her face. She looks so much better; her eyes are back to their usual sparkling green, her cheeks are flushed, and she is smiling from ear to ear.

"Feeling better after your shower, darling?"

She looks at me and nods.

"Much better, thank you. Do I smell better?"

"Yes!" Nigel and I both say together before laughing. Daisy just rolls her eyes at us, calling us both mean.

"So, what have you two got planned for today?" Nigel asks. I look at Daisy, who just shrugs.

"Didn't you say you needed to go shopping?" she asks me.

"Yes, I do. Unfortunately, I only have the clothes I am sitting in and the few bits your Auntie Mary kindly picked up for me last night. I guess if we are staying for a while, I better stock up on a few supplies."

"What about work?" Daisy asks, and I just rub her back.

"I am taking a leave of absence to concentrate on a family matter; I will work from my laptop a couple of hours a day to keep up with the marking. But other than that, I am finished for the school year."

"If you ever need somewhere to work in private, let me know, and I will clear out of here for you," Nigel says. I thank him and let him know I'll probably take him up on that offer.

"Well, if that's all sorted, let's go shopping; I need quite a bit as well," Daisy says, jumping to her feet and pulling on my hands until I stand up, too. I look at Nigel and frown.

"Is it a good idea to take her shopping?" I ask. Nigel shakes his head, laughing out loud.

"Nope. Not at all. Good luck, Son." He is still laughing as Daisy pulls me out of the door.

Chapter Thirty-Nine

DAISY

Getting to spend the day just the two of us, no sneaking, or hiding, has been amazing. Being able to walk around in the open, holding hands, kissing and being an average couple has been something we haven't been able to experience before. I can't wait until we can do this all the time. I know it may be a while until Michael has a replacement for work, but I'm okay with that, especially as I get to be with him every night from now on in our own home.

Michael wants to stay down here another week. He says it's because he feels we need a break from everything and everyone. But I know it's really because the guys still haven't been able to track down Kellan.

It would be an understatement to say I was shocked when Michael told me all about Kellan and what they found in his place. I had forced him to show me the pictures Stuart had taken from inside Kellan's house. I still feel physically sick at the thought of it all. There were so many photographs. Michael had asked about the ones when I was sleeping, and I have no idea how he got them. When he was staying on our sofa, I always locked my bedroom door. So, he shouldn't have been able to get in without me knowing. Michael had some other questions, but I asked him to leave them while we are here. I want to spend this time with him and not worry about Kellan. Michael agreed to leave it for now, but I have a feeling when Kellan resurfaces, so will the questions.

After I take Michael into St Austell to get a few bits, we head over to Charlestown to have a lovely lunch and ice cream whilst sitting on the outer harbour wall. We talk about anything and everything. I tell him all about my parents and growing up around Exeter. He tells me about his parents and all the trouble the three Adams siblings would get up to with the guys and a few of Michelle's female friends, Natalie, Jayne, and Carly. Michael tells me about his relationship with Carly and how he is now glad she wasn't his mate, as he loves the way the guys and I get along so well.

I don't remember the last time I laughed as much as I did, hearing about when they had a house party whilst Barbara and George, their father, were away for the weekend. Apparently, to this day, Barbara takes all their keys off them before she spends a single night away. My sides were still hurting from laughing when we got back to the house around five.

As soon as we get out of the car, the smell of BBQ hit our noses. We both smile because it's food, and we are always hungry. I grab Michael's hand and drag him around to the back garden. Uncle Nigel is standing over the grill, and a tall man with a shaved head and bushy beard is next to him.

"Yay, you are finally here!"

I spin around to see my best friend Clare rushing towards me, holding out her arms.

"What are you doing here?" I drop Michael's hand before racing to meet her halfway. We engulf each other in a hug, jumping up and down and squealing. I turn and realise who is standing next to my uncle.

"What the hell have you done? Your head's upside down!" I exclaim, still shocked by the sight of Alex, Clare's father, who just laughs. "What are you doing here? No one told me you were coming. Aren't you meant to be visiting the Coven in Ireland?"

"We had a call to say you had turned up hysterical and that you looked like hell, refusing to eat or drink, wouldn't sleep. Mary sounded so worried we jumped on the next available flight back. We expected to find you a mess, but you certainly seem fine to me," Alex explains, pulling me into a hug and kissing my head. When he steps away, he turns to Michael, who has walked over to where we have gathered.

"I hear it's all down to you," Alex states, looking straight at Michael, who holds up his hands defensively.

"The fact that she is now better; yes, I had nothing to do with the other part, that I can promise you." I watch as Alex stares at Michael for a second before a wide grin spreads across his face. Michael instantly relaxes and smiles back. Alex holds out his hand, which he takes and shakes it.

"I'm glad to hear it. I'm Alex, Daisy's father's best friend and, more importantly, her Godfather."

"I'm Michael, the uhm, boyfriend."

Alex smiles at him.

"It's a little more than that, I believe." Michael's eyes widen just a little, and Alex laughs.

"Don't worry; we know who you really are to her. The whole coven knows."

"What do you mean the whole coven knows?" I demand, placing my hands on my hips and looking at Uncle Nigel as he walks up to Michael and hands him a beer.

"Well, as you are still a member of the coven, we had to inform them that you had found your mate and would be moving to Wales," Nigel informs us as he turns to face me. I look at Clare and frown.

"I'm still a member of the coven?"

Clare rolls her eyes at me, shaking her head.

"Of course you are. We always thought you would come back eventually, but now you have met Michael, we are finally getting rid of you for good." She laughs as I push her away whilst everyone laughs at us.

"Bitch." I mutter as I walk back to Michael. He puts his arm around my shoulder as I wrap my arms around his waist. I face my best friend and stick my tongue out at her; she does it back, scrunching up her nose.

"Twenty-three years of age, and they are still as childish as ever." I hear a familiar voice sigh from behind Clare. I jump out of Michael's arms and rush to Sara, Clare's mum, and my Godmother. She quickly places the salad bowl she is carrying on the table before pulling me into her arms.

"Oh, Daisy, I have missed you so much. Next time, don't stay away so long," she says into my shoulder. She plants a kiss on my cheek and lifts her head, "Oh dear goddess, you weren't wrong, Mary." I look at her, frowning, and realise she is looking at Michael, who is currently talking to my uncle and Alex. My auntie is now standing next to Sara. Both look at Michael with a glint in their eyes. "Goddess, the things I could do with that man if I were twenty years younger." Sara sighs. Michael chokes on his beer as I burst out laughing, watching Sara go bright red. Mary and Clare quickly turn their backs to Michael, who's still coughing, trying to hide their laughter. Sara, however, looks horrified.

"Shit, I forgot about the hearing thing," she mutters, which just causes the three of us ladies to lose it completely. Nigel and Alex both look at us all with a look of confusion on their faces. Michael is trying so hard to disguise his laughter with coughing, but he has the biggest smile on his face.

"Oh, I have missed you and your big mouth," I say, pulling Sara into another hug as I finally stop laughing and can breathe again. Sara just looks at me and starts giggling. As I step out of Sara's arms, I feel Michael behind me.

"I thought I should come over and introduce myself properly. I'm Michael, ma'am," he says in his smoothest voice, holding his hand out to Sara, who just stands there, jaw hanging open, one hand on her chest and the other slowly reaching to take Michael's. She then lets out a girlie giggle as she whispers, "Ma'am."

I turn to Michael and slap his chest playfully whilst shaking my head.

"What have I told you about doing that to people of the female sex? You are playing with their poor, defenceless hearts."

Michael lets go of Sara's hand so he can wrap an arm around my waist, pulling me tightly against him. I have no choice but to lean back to look at him; my breath catches as our eyes meet. He smiles that lopsided grin that makes everything else melt away.

"And what did I tell you? I don't play when it comes to the heart, especially yours."

I feel the smile spread across my face, and all I can do is

stand there with a hand on his chest, staring into his deep blue eyes, which are making me weak at the knees.

"Oh, fuck, he's broken them all!" Alex's voice breaks through the silence. Michael chuckles as he releases me slightly. I turn, clearing my throat to see Sara, Mary and Clare all staring at us open-mouthed.

"Remember how we used to share everything," Clare mutters. I shake my head at her, grinning.

"Not this time. This is all mine and not for sharing," I grin, reaching up and kissing Michael on the cheek.

"Damn straight, I'm yours, baby," Michael replies, and I hear the ladies sigh beside us, and I can't help smirking.

"Smooth Adams, real smooth."

Michael winks at me as he turns away from us. I hear Sara mumble something about needing something from the kitchen, grabbing Mary's arm as she heads into the house. Clare and I each pour ourselves a glass of wine before taking a seat on one of the benches under the trees. I look over at Michael, who has gone back to talking with Nigel and Alex; he seems so at ease with them. He looks over at me, startled for a second, before smiling his crooked smile.

"Damn benches," he mumbles, low enough I know the others won't hear it. This time, it's my turn to wink at him as he turns his attention back to the men.

"You are one hell of a lucky bitch, Dais," Clare sighs next to me. I don't take my eyes off Michael as I nod.

"I really am Clare Bear. You have no idea."

Chapter Forty

DAISY

Six hours and a lot of food, wine and, of course, gin later, we're all standing on the driveway saying goodbye to Sara, Alex, and Clare. Michael has just excused himself to answer his phone, so I take the time to have a couple of minutes with my Godfather.

"You look so happy, Dais."

I turn and smile at him.

"I really am," I reply, looking behind me where Michael is still on the phone, looking tense.

"You are sooo lucky. Don't suppose he has a hot brother, does he?" Clare asks, nudging me with her shoulder, causing me to turn my back on Michael and face her.

"Actually, he does. Come and stay with us; you never know, I might introduce you," I say, smiling, looking for a reason for her to come and stay with us. We used to do everything together before I was bitten, I want to make up for the time we have lost and get my sister back.

"Your father would have my balls hanging from a tree if I allowed my brother anywhere near you. But I have a pack brother, Will, who I think you would get along with," Michael adds as he walks up behind us before wrapping his arms around my waist so that I lean back into him, placing my hands on top of his. I look at Clare, and I can see her and Will hitting it off. They are both loyal types who love nothing more than ripping into those they love, but goddess help anyone who tries to insult them for real.

"Good call!" I turn and look at him. I can see a flicker of worry in his eyes, which he tries to hide behind his smile.

"Who was on the phone?" I ask. Michael just kisses the top of my head.

"Just the Alpha, nothing to worry about. He was just checking in."

I don't believe him but decide to leave it until there are fewer people around.

"Right, ladies, time to get going," Alex says as a taxi pulls up. I hug both Sara and Clare whilst Alex walks over to Michael.

"Nice to meet you, and I mean that. Look after our Goddaughter; she means the world to us. I don't give a shit that you are the big bad wolf up there; I will hunt you down if you hurt her." I walk up to Alex and nudge him playfully.

"Behave, you goon." He just laughs and puts an arm around me, pulling me into him. I look at Michael, who just looks me straight in the eye as he replies.

"You may need to get in line. Daisy's best friend is a fire demon and has promised to cremate me alive if I hurt her. As for my family and pack brothers, they've already informed me they prefer her to me."

"That's because I'm amazing, and they are scared of me," I reply, winking. Alex kisses the top of my head, which makes me hug him a little tighter.

"That's my girl, take no shit."

Stepping back from him, I place my hands together before bowing to him playfully.

"You trained me well, sensei."

"Apparently, in the art of sarcasm as well," Alex replies, smirking as he slowly shakes his head. My eyes fly open, and I start hopping from foot to foot.

"That's why you have shaved your head and grown the beard, isn't it? You're going to dye it grey and become a martial arts master!"

Alex rolls his eyes as he turns and walks away, smirking.

"Goodbye, Daisy."

I jump in front of him, stopping him from leaving.

"Oh, you could be a bald Gandalf or Dumbledore. Please open a school for witches and sorcerers. Michael could teach magical law, and I could be the fitness teacher."

Alex grips my shoulders and turns so I am no longer in his way. He pushes me backwards until I am flush against Michael's front, who I can hear laughing as he wraps his arms around me. Alex lets go and glances at Michael, shaking his head in dismay.

"I guess what I should have said is good luck. You're going to need it."

"Wouldn't have it any other way," he replies. Kissing the top of my head before placing a hand over my mouth as I open it to add more to my beautiful plans.

Spoilsports, the pair of them.

As soon as the others leave, Nigel and Mary call it a night and head off to bed. Michael and I cuddle up by the fire pit we had lit a couple of hours ago. I am sitting in between Michael's legs as he holds me from behind.

"Thank you," Michael whispers into my hair. I turn my upper body and frown at him. His eyes are so soft as they look deep into mine, the light from the fire reflecting off them.

"What for?"

Michael leans down and gently touches my lips with his own.

"For letting me be part of your family. For just being you. For agreeing to be mine. For existing. The list could go on, darling," he replies, planting the softest of kisses after each declaration.

"I love you." It may sound cheesy right now, but I do. I love him with every part of me and will never tire of telling him.

"Good, because I love you too and plan to show you just how much every day for the rest of our lives."

"Cheese ball."

Michael laughs and pulls me closer.

"And always will be," he declares.

"Was it really the Alpha on the phone before?"

Michael lets out a sigh as he nods.

"Yeah, there has been a bit of trouble up that way. So he has put me on standby. I have asked Marcus to handle it for now, but with Kellan still at large, the team is stretched. There is a chance we may need to head back in a day or two. Sorry."

"That's okay, I understand."

"I'm sorry, darling. I can leave you here if you want, and you can come back when you are ready."

I turn around and kneel to face him. I place a hand on his cheek, as I can see that he's worried I will stay and we will be apart again. He's also afraid that I will resent him if I go home with him early when I really can't wait to leave.

"What day is it?" I ask. Michael looks at me and frowns.

"Thursday, why?"

344

"What are we meant to be doing this weekend?" I watch as Michael's lips curl up slightly as he realises.

"I wasn't sure if you would still want to after everything."

"Mikey, if these last few days have taught me anything, it's that I don't work without you. I stop existing without you. I don't want to wait anymore; I want to be with you in every way." I take a deep breath before continuing.

"I haven't told you before, but before he took me and did what he did, I had never had sex. He took my virginity." A look of shock very quickly turns to rage in Michael's eyes, and if he hadn't wanted to kill Jackson before, I can see he would now. I run my thumb over his cheek in the hope of calming him a little before continuing.

"Ever since I escaped, I have told myself that it didn't count. That the male I choose to sleep with would be my first. I want you to be my first Michael. I want you to be my first and my last." I watch as Michael's whole face softens before he lifts me, and I'm now straddling his lap.

"I want to be your first and last everything. You are my whole world, and nothing matters more to me than you and what you want. You just say the word and let me know when you are ready." Michael presses his lips to mine gently as I thread my fingers into his hair.

"I would say right now if it wasn't for the fact that my auntie and uncle are only in that room," I say, pointing to the upstairs window. Michael chuckles and leans in to kiss me again.

"So, what are you thinking? Do you have a plan in mind for how you want everything to proceed from here?" Michael asks, as always, ensuring that I feel in control of everything and it moves at my pace.

"I think tomorrow, we should leave here and go to your

house so I can move in. It's not like I have much stuff now, anyway. We make sure Jon and Stuart know to stay away and complete the bond."

"Tomorrow? Are you sure that is what you want?" Michael asks nervously.

"Tomorrow, Saturday, Sunday, Monday, whenever you want, but I just know that it needs to be soon, as I *really* don't know how much longer I can go without begging you to touch me."

Michael grabs me around the waist and lays me on the ground, leaning over the top of me, as his lips crash into mine.

"All you had to do was say the word, baby, and my hands would have been wherever you wanted them to be. Not touching you has been the challenge of a lifetime," he says, his lips still against mine. I feel his hand on my hip, slowly moving up my side until it's just touching the side of my breast. My breath catches as my body reacts to the feel of his hand so close. I kiss him and try to move so his hand is on me, but he moves it away again.

"Eager, baby?" he whispers as his hand skims back down my side, coming to a stop on my hip briefly before carrying on down my thigh. Michael starts kissing my neck softly, his touch leaves a layer of goosebumps in its wake.

"Every second I'm near you, I want to strip you so there is nothing in the way as I devour every inch of your body. I want to run my fingers over every part of you, feeling your soft, silky skin. I want to feel you squirm, just like this, as your body begs for release."

Every part of my body is aching and contracting in places I really wish those fingers were right now. His touch slides to the inside of my thigh, and I can't stop the moan that escapes my lips. I hear Michael's breath catch in his chest.

"Fuck, baby, I am seriously considering putting you in the car and finding the nearest hotel right now," he breaths against my neck.

"You started this. What are you going to do about it?" I whisper as I bite down on his ear lobe. I feel him moan, his whole body tensing as he grabs me right where I want him to.

"What do you want me to do about it? Tell me, and I will make your wish come true."

I feel every muscle from the waist down tense as I long for his touch.

"Touch me, Michael. I want to feel your hands cupping me, your fingers rubbing me, inside and out, until I scream your name."

"Fuck, you're so hot," he gasps as he massages me through my jeans. I wither under his touch as I reach down and place my hand on his growing bulge. We both gasp at the same time. Then, without even saying a word, we both start undoing each other's trousers. Just enough so we can touch one another without the constrictions of the material. Michael kneels up and grabs a blanket before throwing it over us. I feel his hand reach down and push under my underwear.

"Baby, you are so wet and ready for me." He gently slips a finger between my folds and pulls it upwards, skimming over my hole until it reaches that extra sensitive bundle of nerves.

There, he circles his finger over it, once, twice, three times, and I am already panting with a building orgasm. "So easy, so ready for me; tell me what you need."

"You," is all I get out in between gasps. I hear Michael's deep laugh against my ear.

"Not yet; this will have to do." He slowly slides a finger into me, hooking it at the right spot, quickly slamming his mouth over mine as I orgasm around his finger. My sex repeatedly contracts as his finger moves in and out of me, riding out the waves of pleasure that wash through me. I feel his thumb move over my clit as he starts rubbing it again, his finger still inside me; I can feel my body tensing again as another orgasm grows.

"Tomorrow night, it won't be my thumb here. Instead, it will be my tongue, my lips, eating this beautiful hot pussy until you scream my name over and over again."

"Michael," I gasp as another wave crashes through me. Again, he kisses me to block out the sounds I have no control over being released.

Slowly, his hand stops, and he removes it from my trousers. I watch as he lifts his hand to his mouth and sucks on a very wet-looking finger.

"Fuck, you taste as good as you smell when you are aroused," he says as he leans over me, placing soft kisses along my neck, running his nose along my collarbone. I reach down with my hand to give him the release he has given me, but he grabs it and pulls it up to his mouth before kissing my palm, smirking at me.

"Oh no, tonight is all about you. I don't plan on finding my release until I am deep inside you, with my teeth sinking into your skin as I mark you to make you officially mine."

"No fair," I reply as I snuggle into him, my eyelids becoming heavy as the exhaustion of my extraordinary climaxes, as well as the wine and gin, take effect.

"I think I'm very fair," I hear him say softly as he kisses

the top of my head, and my eyes lose their battle to stay open.

Chapter Forty-One

DAISY

When I open my eyes again, I'm in my bed, and I have no idea how I got here. Michael must have carried me up from the garden last night. I stretch my legs and realise that they aren't entwined in his for the first time in two days. I lift my arm behind me and notice he isn't there. The bed is empty, and the sheets are cold. He must have been up for a while. I sit up and call his name; even if he were downstairs, he would hear me with his wolf hearing. But when he doesn't respond, I quickly turn around in a panic. It's then I notice a piece of paper on his pillow.

Morning beautiful. Sorry, I've had to pop out early.
I'm hoping I won't be long and will be back before you wake up.
I'll bring breakfast.
Love you always xxxxxxxxx

I glance over at the clock and realise it's nine AM. I sit on the edge of the bed and notice for the first time that I'm still in my clothes from last night. Ever the gentleman,

Mikey obviously didn't want to get me changed without my permission. I look over at my bedside cabinet and see my new phone is there on charge. Last I remember, it was in my pocket. The man really does think of everything. I grab it and open up my messages.

Daisy: Morning, Handsome. I don't like waking up without you anymore. Hurry back, I miss you. Plus, I am famished 😌 Love you xxxxxxxxxx

I put my phone back on the side before heading for the shower, hoping to smell a little better than I do right now by the time he returns.

"Morning, Daisy dear," I hear Mary call as I walk into the kitchen half an hour later. I manage to mumble a quick response as I point to the coffee machine and head straight for it. I hear Uncle Nigel chuckle something about how's the head. I grunt another less polite response and take my coffee over to the table.

"Where's Michael? I noticed his car's gone."

"Not sure; he left a note about having to pop out and wouldn't be long. I hope he isn't, as he promised to bring home breakfast," I reply as I sip my coffee. As if on cue, I hear his car pull onto the drive. I jump up and rush to the front door excitedly, needing to see him.

"I never thought I would see the day you left more than half a cup of coffee!" Uncle Nigel shouts behind me. I don't bother replying; I just throw open the door and rush out to Michael jumping into his arms as he gets out of the car. He laughs as he catches me stumbling back against the car.

"Is it me you are glad to see or the food?" he chuckles as he holds me tight.

"That depends. What food have you brought me?"

"Fruit salad, muesli and natural yoghurt." I look at him, screwing up my face. That is not what I wanted to hear. But judging by the look on his face that's not what he's really picked up. "Alright, it may be a breakfast meal from that fast food place you love so much."

I squeal as I hug him tightly again.

"So, it's the food then?" he chuckles.

"Well, you brought me said food, so I have to be happy to see you more, as otherwise, there would be no food." My eyebrows bunch together as I try to determine if that makes sense.

"I am sure there is logic in there somewhere, darling, but I will wait until you have another coffee before I ask you to explain it to me," Michael smirks as he moves to place me back on the ground, but then realises I have nothing on my feet. He mumbles something about me being impatient before swinging me around, so I'm now on his back. He reaches down to get the bags out of the car and locks it before carrying everything in. I'm giggling like a little girl, which causes Michael to shake his head whilst grinning.

"I can walk, you know," I point out.

"You have nothing on your feet, and I am not going to be responsible for you slicing them open on the stones."

"Overprotective much?" I mutter as Michael laughs.

"Get used to it, darling. Now, hold on." I tighten my legs and arms around him, trying to take as much of my own weight as possible, leaning my head on his shoulder as he carries me back into the house.

As we walk into the hallway, my auntie and uncle are walking towards the lounge. Mary sees us and rolls her eyes.

"Michael dear, if you keep spoiling her, she will become a nightmare."

Michael laughs as I stick my tongue out at her over his shoulder.

"But she is worth spoiling," he replies. I turn my head and plant a kiss on his cheek before sliding down his back, so I'm standing. He holds up the bags of food and asks if anyone would like any before I eat it all. I'm secretly glad when they reply that they have already eaten and would not dare take food from me.

I head into the kitchen and put the coffee pot on. I am busy measuring the coffee when I feel two arms around my waist and Michael's lips against my neck. I instantly melt into him.

"I missed you. Where did you go?" Michael kisses my neck again before pulling away slightly so I can turn and face him.

"I was invited to a training session with the local pack enforcers; they sent me a message around midnight asking me to be there for six AM. I think they hoped I wouldn't get the message so that I wouldn't turn up. Which is why I made a point of being there early and already warming up when they arrived."

"How did they know how to contact you?"

"My Alpha got in contact with theirs yesterday. Because we will be down here quite often, I asked him to contact them, so they didn't think I was up to anything." I pour us both a coffee as he sets the food out on the table. Once we are both sat down, he continues to tell me about the pack.

"Their Alpha suggested I go to the training session and see if there is anything they could improve on. It turns out my reputation has spread further than I thought."

I lean over and plant a kiss on his lips.

"That's because you're amazing."

Michael rolls his eyes whilst shaking his head.

"You're just biased," he says as he leans over to kiss me again. "But I like it."

I wink at him as I take a sip of my coffee.

"So, was there anything they could improve on? Are their guys as fit as you lot?"

"Goddess, no! Considering they are wolves, they are weak. The problem is they don't realise how weak they are. They would never survive a full session with my guys. Apparently, the Alpha knew this, which is why he has asked if he can consult with me and get his guys up to scratch."

"Let me guess, you said yes, as long as they keep you in the loop about any rogues causing trouble, especially ones with names beginning with J." I watch Michael's face change at the sheer mention of him. I know how he feels about Jackson and that he's determined to get rid of him once and for all for me.

"Maybe that was my hidden agenda. Plus, their land isn't far from here, and yet they didn't know you were here. That just shows how much work they need to do as a pack. The leader of the Enforcers seems confident, but something tells me he has become lazy and just content with how things are. The problem is he is making life difficult for the rest of us." Michael takes a sip of his coffee, "Plus, having them on our side will keep your family safe from the arse-hole. If he did ever turn up here, they would be close to hand if we were back home. Which is why I want to keep the Alpha and leader sweet."

"Which means you can't tell the guy he is lazy as you need him looking out for my family, which makes me love you even more, by the way, but also because he is an Alpha."

Michael huffs before responding, which tells me he is using that title loosely.

"Correct, although if I'm careful about how I word it, he will hopefully see it as constructive criticism rather than me straight out saying, 'You are crap at being an Alpha.'"

"Have you ever thought of being an Alpha?" I ask. I watch as Michael's face freezes, food halfway to his mouth. I realise I have either struck a chord or there is something he hasn't told me. I kind of already know that Michael could one day be an Alpha; he has the Alpha gene. You can feel it radiating from him, especially when he gets cross or feels people are not listening to him. Once I realised what it was, I realised it explained how he would get during class.

"That is maybe something I should have already talked to you about. Like a month ago." He says as he puts down his breakfast muffin. I take a bite of mine and wink at him.

"What, that you could one day be an Alpha? I already figured that out." Michael looks at me and frowns. I just shrug, "Jonny let it slip that night; we all went running. Something about you 'not being Alpha yet.' I don't think you realised I heard, so I didn't say anything."

"Do you want to talk about it? Because if I become Alpha, that would make you the Luna. That's a lot of responsibility, and a lot of females don't want that." I can see he is worried; the panic I will leave is there in his eyes. I put down my food and reach over to take his hand.

"What are the chances of you actually becoming Alpha? Honestly."

"It's pretty much guaranteed. Desmond has already named me to replace him, as Alaric, his Beta, has no interest in taking on the responsibility. So when Desmond steps down or dies, I will take over, which is why I lead the guys. Marcus is my second, as he will take over leading when I step up as Alpha. Jon will become my Beta." I watch as Michael looks down at his food, his shoulders hunched over.

"Does it bother you?" I ask. Michael looks up at me, confused.

"What, becoming Alpha? It didn't. I always knew it would happen since I was sixteen, and Desmond picked up on my Alpha gene."

"You said it didn't. Does it now?"

"It does if it means I lose you! I will step away from the whole pack if you ask me to. You are more important to me."

"Do you honestly think I'd ask you to do that?"

"No. But I think you would keep quiet and be miserable if it meant I would be who I'm expected to be. That is what I don't want. I want you to tell me what *you* want, to tell me if you want all of this or not. Like I said, it's a massive responsibility for both of us. I would never put that pressure on you if you didn't want to do it."

"When you become Alpha, I will be honoured to be your Luna. I will do whatever you and the pack need me to do. Not because I *have* to but because I *want* to. We are a team, and we do things, hand in hand, side by side, always. Remember, 50/50 or 20/80, whatever the other needs, we will have each other's backs." Michael pulls my hand up to his lips and kisses it gently.

"What did I do to deserve you?"

I look at him and smirk.

"Something outstanding… or something terrible. Depends on the mood I'm in." I blow him a kiss and go back to my food whilst he just roars, laughing and muttering to himself about having his hands full. He's learning slowly.

Once we've finished our food, I take the empty plates over to the sink. Again, I feel Michael's arms go around me from behind. He holds me while I wash all the dishes in the sink.

"I didn't get to ask how you are feeling today," Michael asks. I can tell the sound of his voice and how his hands are wandering that he is referring to our alone time outside last night. I turn around and put my arms around his neck, trying to avoid getting the soap and water from my hands on him.

"I'm wondering if I say I am frustrated, we will have a repeat of last night?" Michael's lips gently brush against my own.

"Baby, as soon as I get you home, I will ensure you are never frustrated again. If that means I have to keep you in bed for the rest of our lives, then so be it." Heat floods through my body again and pools between my legs. Michael smirks, knowing what he's doing to me.

"You still want to leave today, or do you want to stay a little longer?" he asks. He looks into my eyes, and I can see that he is genuinely asking and would stay if I asked him to. But I am ready to leave; I am ready to complete the bond and become mated to this remarkable man.

"Take me home," I whisper as his lips collide with mine.

Chapter Forty-Two

MICHAEL

I glance over at Daisy sleeping in the passenger seat and still can't believe she is actually there, that I found her.

When I was woken up by Jonny on Tuesday and read that message from her, I honestly thought that was it; I'd lost her for good. But here we are on our way home, *our* home, together.

I hear Daisy murmur; I quickly glance over again, but she is still sound asleep. A strand of hair has fallen across her face, so I gently brush it away; she opens her eyes and looks at me, smiling.

"Have I been asleep long?"

"Only a couple of hours."

"A couple of hours? Where the hell are we?" she anxiously starts looking around out the window. I can't resist laughing at her.

"Relax, it's not far now. We should be home in about fifteen minutes."

Suddenly, my stomach drops. Daisy realises and places a hand on my knee.

"What's the matter?"

"I just realised you haven't even seen the house before. You have no idea where it is or what the area is like."

"So?"

"So? So, this isn't how I expected you to move in with me. I expected you to at least see where we would be living *before* we were living there."

Daisy laughs next to me, causing me to frown. I don't know what she's laughing at, I'm freaking the hell out! I wanted everything to be perfect for her. Right now, I don't even know if she will like the area, let alone the house itself, or that we are so far out of town and away from the university.

"Mikey, I'm sure I will love it. Unless you and Jon have used it as a bachelor pad and had different women in there every weekend, because then I may refuse to sleep on the bed until you get a new one." I take her hand from my knee and lift it to my lips so I can place a kiss on her knuckles as she grins at me. I know I can always depend on this woman to calm me down and make jokes about any situation.

"Just so you know, I have never taken any woman to bed in that house. I haven't been with anybody since Carly. Jon's bed, on the other hand, may need burning."

Daisy laughs again.

"There we go then, nothing to worry about."

"Darling, I want you to promise me that if you want to change anything about the house, you tell me, okay? We will turn it into our home. If it isn't what you want, then say, and we will look for a new one."

"Mikey, it's not the house that makes it home; it's who is inside it. We could live in a run-down old shed. As long as I'm with you every night when I fall asleep and every morning when I wake up, I will be the happiest female on earth."

I look at her again quickly and smile.

"Now, who's being a cheese ball."

"You must be rubbing off on me, handsome." I look back at her, smiling.

"Tomorrow, we will do some shopping and get a few bits for the house so you can start making it your home, too."

"How can we do that when we can't be seen out together yet?"

"It will have to be done online because, baby, you will be lucky if I even let you out of our bed until at least Sunday morning. I will only let you out then because Mum is demanding I take you to see her. Plus, I think she just wants to celebrate with us and the lads that we'll have completed the bond."

"Your mum wants to celebrate you getting your leg over? Gods, it really has been a while." I turn and look at her, shocked, but she has the biggest grin on her face; she then starts laughing.

"Really, baby? Carry on like that, and I don't think I will be able to do anything tonight other than hide in a hole and pretend you haven't implied my mother is excited by our sex life." I pretend to shudder, causing her to laugh harder.

"Yeah, okay, that was a little sick even for me!"

"A little? That was wrong in so many ways."

Daisy is clutching her stomach from laughing so hard; tears are running down her face. We are still laughing as I pull the car onto the driveway.

Chapter Forty-Three

DAISY

I am mid-laughing fit when I realise we have come to a stop outside of a cottage. My laughter stops immediately as I take it all in.

In front of me is the most beautiful property I've ever seen. The front garden is full of flowers and a white picket fence around it. Yes, that's right, a white picket fence that fits in perfectly. I slowly open my door and step out, unable to take my eyes off the property in front of me. I can feel Michael watching my every move, but I just can't seem to work out the words to describe what I'm seeing.

"Say something, darling, please," I hear him say.

"Is this your place?" I gasp.

"No, it's ours. As long as you want it." I run around the car and launch myself into his arms, squealing excitedly.

"Remember what you told me about your dad knowing what his mate would want before he even met her?" I hear Michael nervously answer, "Yeah," into my ear. "Well, this is what my dream house has always looked like. It's perfect."

I step back from his arms and watch Michael's whole body seem to relax, and he smiles brightly.

"Well, I hope you are ready to see the inside. You might change your mind then." I look at him and roll my eyes. Even though he's smiling, I can still see the worry still evident in his eyes. I wrap my arm around his and smile up at him.

"Lead the way, handsome."

Michael laughs as we head down the path to the front door. He opens the door, and as I'm about to step through, he grabs me, scoops me up into his arms and carries me over the threshold. I can't help laughing as I look up and see Michael's whole face lit up by his smile.

"I'm sure you are only meant to do that when you get married."

Michael shrugs.

"I will do it whenever I feel like doing it, and right now, I want you in my arms." He leans in and kisses me. I feel him move as he kicks the door closed behind him, his lips not leaving mine. Slowly, he pulls away, grinning, and doesn't break eye contact.

"Welcome home, darling." Gods, this man melts my heart.

I'm about to reply when I see him looking in front of us, his grin replaced by a frown. I turn to see what he's looking at. A vase full of flowers and a bottle of champagne are on display in the kitchen.

"They weren't there when I left."

I wiggle slightly; he seems to remember he's still holding me and places me on my feet. I will take the opportunity to get a good look at where we are.

We are standing in an entrance hall. The walls are all white and fresh, the wooden flooring is gleaming, and there is an oak sideboard to the left of me against a wall. On it is a small bowl, which I see Michael has already thrown his keys into. Next to that is a picture of Michael and me, which looks like it was taken in Barbara's garden. I don't remember it being taken, but there again, by the looks of it, we only had eyes for each other at that moment. We are both looking into each other's eyes, grinning. We look so happy and in love.

"That's new too. I think someone has been in and added a few personal touches for us," he says, looking around.

"Have they cleaned too, or was it always this spotless?"

Michael smiles, shrugging.

"I am house trained, I would have you know," he winks before looking around. "I think everywhere is white as it was easier. But feel free to add some colour to the place. To be honest, I was hardly ever here." Michael wraps an arm around my waist and pulls me close whilst grinning down at me. "But that's going to change now I have a reason to be." He presses a short, hard kiss to my lips before he takes my hand and pulls me to the right. "Come on, let me give you the guided tour, and then we will get our things in."

Michael shows me the rest of the ground floor, including a large dining room, an even larger lounge, and a kitchen. We find a card with the flowers and champagne, proving they're from Barbara and the guys.

Mikey and Daisy
Wishing you both all the happiness in the world as you start your lives together. Lots of love, Mama xxx
P.S. We have added a few things we think you may need, little bro. Have fun. Jonny and the team.

Michael curses and runs up the stairs, taking them three at a time and demanding that I stay down there to let him check. Of course, that means I follow and head straight into the bedroom with him, curious about what they've done.

We stop short when we see another bottle of champagne in an ice bucket; there is still loads of ice in it, so they've only just left. There are petals on the bed and leading to the bathroom. We follow them and see a basket full of candles, bubble baths, his and her towels and a box of matches. I cannot help but smile; they have thought of everything.

"This will have all been Mum. She's a sucker for anything romantic. It's what the guys have done that worries me," Michael says as he walks back into the bedroom and heads straight around to the far side of the bed and opens the bedside cabinet drawer, "Fucking children," he curses, I rush round to see, but he slams the drawer closed before I get there.

"Oh, come on, let me see," I beg.

"Nothing to see there. It's empty," he says as he moves his arm to block me. Only by some miracle does he fail, and I get the drawer open. Michael's arms are around my waist instantly as he tries to stop me, but it's too late. I've seen everything, and I laugh loudly.

"I know you said it had been a while, but has it been that long?" I hear Michael mumble a few choice words about his pack brothers as I pull out the three boxes of condoms and *The Beginner's Guide To Pleasing Your Partner.* I can't resist opening the book to wind him up.

"Chapter one, knowing what goes where." I don't get any further as he snatches it out of my hand and flings it across the room. He playfully pushes me onto the bed so that I land on my back as he leans over me.

"I don't need some book to tell me how to please you. I think I did just fine on my own last night." Instantly, my sex clenches, and my breath catches in my chest. He kisses me once on the lips, then looks down at me, grinning. Slowly, he lowers his head and runs his nose from my shoulder to my neck before kissing me gently there. My heart starts racing, heat pools between my legs as I gasp from the sensation that flows through my whole body.

"Do you have any idea how you smell when you get aroused? It's a subtle change, but fuck, I could smell it all day." As he kisses my neck again, I breathe in his scent and notice a slight change in his, too. It's a small one, but it makes me want him even more than I did five seconds ago. Michael lifts his head and starts kissing me. I feel his tongue rub against my lips slowly, asking for permission to enter, and I allow him greedily. The kiss deepens as I can feel myself melting into him.

"Baby, you have no idea how much I want you. But tell me to stop, and I will," Michael moans. I grab him around the neck and roll so I am on top, my legs on either side of him, his legs hanging off the bed. I sit up and place my hands on his chest. He puts his hands on my hips. Looking up at me, I can hear both our hearts racing in total sync.

I lean in and brush my lips against his. As I whisper, "Don't stop." I sit up again and grab the bottom of my top; with one tug, I pull it off over my head, leaving me in nothing but my jeans and bra.

"Fuck," Michael growls as he reaches up, grabs the back of my neck and pulls me down to him, our lips meeting in the middle of the space between us. I feel him reach around and undo my bra with ease. Pulling away from him again, I slowly peel it off. Michael is now leaning on his elbows behind him. I grab the bottom of his shirt and tug it, needing to see and touch him. He holds himself up and allows me to take the lead. When his shirt is off, I throw it onto the floor with my clothes and look down at his chiselled body. Michelangelo's statue of David has nothing on this man; his body is a work of art.

I gently run a finger over each of the ridges of his six-pack. I can feel his body tensing under my touch. His breathing becomes more profound as he fights control.

"Fuck this," Michael growls as he wraps an arm around me and stands up, lifting me with ease. He moves to the end of the bed and throws me back onto it. I can't help but laugh as I bounce on the mattress a few times from the force. Michael crawls onto the bed until he is over me again. He kisses me on the lips before moving down my neck to my breasts. Slowly, he runs his tongue over one of my nipples before gently catching it between his teeth. Instantly, my back arches as I feel myself growl.

"Fuck."

Michael chuckles as he moves over to the other breast; his hand moves up my outer thigh and across until it's over the waistline of my jeans, his finger running just between the fabric and my skin. As he bites down on my nipple again, I feel him undo my button. Followed quickly by my zip. He leans up and pulls my trousers down and off, leaving only my lace thong.

I watch as his eyes roam all over my body, taking in every inch of me. I quickly place a hand over my left hip, where there's a large scar left from my time in the hellhole. Michael notices and moves my hand away; slowly, he lowers himself to place a gentle kiss on the pale skin.

"Don't hide anything from me; I love every part of you, scars and all," he whispers as he kisses it again. I reach down to run my fingers through his hair, the same time as he slides one finger underneath my underwear. As soon as he touches me, my back arches, and I tighten my hold on his hair.

"Are you ready for me again, baby? It's so easy to make you wet." He runs his nose over my underwear until he is directly above my sex; I hear him inhale as he nudges that bundle of nerves that is waiting for him. I feel his fingers sliding between my folds as he starts circling my clit with his fingers, just as he did last night. My breath is ragged, and I find myself begging him not to stop. But he does, but only long enough to remove my underwear altogether.

Before I can even moan, he starts to flick my clit with his tongue. It doesn't take long before I'm shaking on the edge of ecstasy. Michael continues to kiss, lick and nibble me until I climax, my whole body shaking as I scream his name. Unlike last night, he doesn't try to silence me. He lets me scream and moan as he sucks on my swollen clit, making my climax last longer until it finally starts to subside, only for him to start rubbing me with his fingers. This time, though, he slowly moves his finger down until it is just over my hole. He slowly inserts one finger and starts sliding it in and out of me.

"Shit, I need you." I gasp; I need to feel him in me.

"Patience, baby, you are so fucking tight I need to make sure I won't hurt you." As he slowly inserts a second finger, I start to lose it again. Another orgasm begins to build, and I realise I am grabbing hold of the covers, trying to find anything I can use to ground myself.

"I'm going to cum again," I moan loudly.

"Cum for me, baby." As if he gives me permission, the floodgates open, and I scream his name again and again as I climax a second time. This time, he doesn't try to prolong it; he stands up and pulls his own trousers and boxers down.

I look at him and realise what he meant by making sure he wouldn't hurt me. The man is huge! I can't help but gulp at the sheer length and girth of it. He sees my face and smiles.

"I will take it slow, baby. Just promise me you will tell me if you become uncomfortable." I nod as he lowers himself over me again. "Are you sure you are ready for this? Just say the word, and I'll stop." I wrap my arms around his neck and pull him to me.

"Make love to me, Mikey. Make me yours." He growls as he brings his lips to mine. As I kiss him, I taste myself on him. I feel his hand go back between my legs as he inserts two fingers into me again, stretching me. I start to relax again with the feel of him in me, his lips and tongue kissing and licking my lips, my neck, nibbling my ear lobes. I am so lost in it all I don't even notice that he pulls his fingers out and slowly slides the tip of his penis into me, I thought I would panic, but instead, I relax further. I wrap my fingers into his hair again and pull him down to me, kissing him deeply. Slowly and carefully, he eases himself into me. When he is about halfway, I feel myself hiss with pleasure. He almost jumps off me, but I hold him tight.

"Don't you dare stop; fuck, you feel so good." He nods and keeps kissing me, slowly allowing himself to ease out a little and then back in a little bit further than last time. It may not be quick, but he is finally all the way in, and I let out a deep growl as he fills me, stretching me so I am the perfect fit for him. It's like we were made for each other. Slowly, he starts moving again. In and out, I can tell he is holding back, but any pain has eased, and I need him more than I realised.

"Are you okay?" he asks gently. I grab hold of him and roll, with him still inside me, and I'm on top.

"Better than okay," I reply as I start lifting myself up

and down on his solid member. His hands instantly grab my hips, and I place my hands on his broad chest to steady myself as I take control, feeling him touching every spot in me. I open my eyes and see Michael staring at me, looking deep into me. I bite my bottom lip and swear I hear him curse again. He pulls me down as he flips us again, so he is back on top.

"Fuck, baby, you are killing me here. I can't hold out much longer. Can I mark you?"

"Please," I beg. I feel Michael picking up speed; we move together, getting faster and harder.

"Let go for me, baby, cum with me, mark me." And just like that, my climax hits again at the exact moment I feel Michael's hit. We both bite each other on the shoulder at the same time. Straight away, I feel it, like a piece of string comes from him and me, meeting in the middle, and two pieces become one. It's like every part of our body and mind become synchronised, and everything he feels, I feel, too. I scream out with pleasure as Michael does. It is such an intense feeling for us both that we climax again instantly.

Everything feels perfect as we finally come down from the most intense high, sweating, gasping for breath and a tangled mess of limbs. Everything is as it should be. There is just us in this world. No one else matters, just him and me, together for the rest of our lives.

Chapter Forty-Four

MICHAEL

I thought my feelings for Daisy couldn't get any stronger than when we were down in Cornwall. But now the bond is nearly complete, and I've marked her. I know those few days down there had just been the foundation of what I feel now. From the moment our teeth sunk into each other, and we climaxed hand in hand, me filling her, I knew there was no doubt she was mine as much as I was hers.

We haven't left the house since. All of Daisy's new clothes are still in the car; I keep telling her I will get them, but as soon as I start putting my clothes on, they end up back on the floor, and me deep inside her.

We're currently curled up in front of the fire I had lit in the lounge. Lying on a rug, a throw from the sofa thrown over us, and our clothes discarded somewhere close by. Not that we have much need for clothes.

"Is it normal to feel this overwhelmingly needy after being marked?" I hear Daisy ask as she runs her fingers over my chest. I'm lying on my back with one arm under my head. The other is under her. I'm playing with her hair, as it always makes her relax.

"I'd heard it can be like this for the first week or so, but I never realised how intense it was." I look down at Daisy and see her smiling. "What are you grinning at?"

She rolls so she is lying further onto her stomach, allowing her to look me in the eye. I can see she is looking rather happy with herself.

"I just remembered the first day of classes. The girls and I were trying to work out if you were single, married or gay."

"Gay?!" I yell, sitting up, causing Daisy to start laughing.

"I said I didn't think you were."

"You didn't *think* I was?! Baby, if you need reassurance that I'm not gay, I think you need to only think back over the last twenty-eight hours." Daisy just laughs harder.

"Well, I wasn't sleeping with you then, was I?"

"Oh, so now you are only sleeping with me? Be careful; I might start taking offence." I'm laying the sarcasm on thick, and Daisy is now hysterical. "I don't know how to take it that you were thinking about the time you thought I might be gay after we have made love; Gods only knows how many times."

"Oh, stop it!" Daisy screeches, wiping the tears from her face. She's gone bright red and is gasping for breath. I lay back down, placing both arms under my head.

"Oh, it's fine, you carry on laughing at me. I'll just lie here and wait for you to finish so you can tell me more about the time you thought I was gay!" I've managed to keep a straight face so far, but watching her laugh so hard she starts hiccupping has me laughing right along with her. Eventually, the laughter subsides enough for us to speak.

"I love you," Daisy sighs, smiling from ear to ear, her face bright pink and eyes red from crying from laughter.

"Even though you thought I was gay?" I reply, rolling my eyes. Daisy laughs again.

"That wasn't where I was going with that conversation. You just blew it right out of proportion." I shake my head, causing her to laugh again. "What I was saying, before you went on your little rant, was that morning Sam, Rosie, Beth, and myself were all wishing we could do rather naughty and unspeakable things with you. Now here I am, lying completely naked in your arms, having done lots of naughty things. If you had told me five months ago, I would be here; I would have laughed in your face and said it would never happen."

"And yet here you are, lying naked in my arms, telling me you thought I was gay," I reply, shaking my head playfully. Daisy slaps my chest, making me cry out whilst laughing.

"You aren't going to stop about that, are you?" I shake my head at her again, grinning. I roll, so I am now over her. I nudge her legs with mine; she opens them willingly to make room for me to lie between them. I place my arms on either side of her head. As she wraps her arms around my chest, attempting to pull me down for a kiss, I stop just as my lips touch hers.

"I'm wondering if I should show you just how much I want you and nobody else," I whisper as I kiss her gently. I feel her moan against my lips, and my manhood instantly jumps to attention. Every sound this woman makes drives me wild.

"How do you plan on doing that?" she whispers back.

"By making you scream my name over and over again until you beg me to stop." I kiss her on the lips one more time before moving down to her neck, my hand moving to her breast as I feel her gasping underneath me. The house phone rings, causing Daisy and I to both groan in unison.

"Ignore it," I say as I carry on kissing and touching her. Then, just as I have her attention again, my brother's voice fills the house.

"Mikey, put Daisy down and answer your fucking phone. Alpha's been trying to get in touch with you all day."

"Fuck!" I mutter as I jump up, rushing to the phone in the hallway.

"Jon, what's happened?" I demand as I answer it, but he's already hung up. I stride back into the lounge as Daisy holds my mobile out for me. I check the screen to see ten missed calls and two text messages. Five are from the Alpha, one from Mum, two from Jon and one each from Marcus and Will.

"Fuck, something's going down." I turn to see Daisy throwing my t-shirt at me, the one she's been wearing all day. I grab my sweatpants and have both on before the Alpha answers.

"I hope I'm not interrupting anything," he teases down the line.

"Completely cockblocking me here, Desmond. What's happened?" I ask as I hear him laughing.

"Sorry, I won't keep you. It's nothing major. I just wanted to ask if you'd be able to come to your mum's a little earlier tomorrow, say midday?" I look at Daisy, who is frowning at me, obviously as confused as I am.

"Can't see why not. What's going on?"

"I was talking to your mum earlier; she confirmed you and Daisy had marked each other. Congratulations, by the way."

"Thank you," I reply as I sit next to Daisy, who is sitting on the floor still, holding the blanket in front of her breasts. I playfully try to pull it away, but she slaps my hand away, smiling.

"As you know, to complete the bond, you'll have to have me bless it, as well as allow Daisy to become part of the pack. I usually do this in front of everyone, but as Mama B said, Daisy can be a little nervous around other wolves, which is completely understandable. So, I thought I could perform the blessing and welcome Daisy into the pack at Mama B's before the rest of the pack descends on you guys for the BBQ. That way, Daisy will feel a little less pushed into the limelight." I look over at Daisy, who's smiling and nodding. I know this is something she's been nervous about.

"We would really appreciate that. Thank you so much, Alpha."

"Mikey, it's the least I can do after all you have done for this pack. We want Daisy to feel welcome and want her to know we are her family as much as we are yours." I glance over to Daisy, who has tears in her eyes but is still smiling.

"I think you may have made Daisy extremely happy." She nods and mouths *thank you*. I thank the Alpha again and tell him we will see him tomorrow.

"Oh, before you go, Mikey, do me a favour. Don't let Jonny know I will be there early. I need to get him back for something." Before I can ask any further questions, I can hear the Alpha laughing as he hangs up. I look at Daisy, who jumps into my arms. I chuckle, holding her tight.

"I take it you've been even more worried than you let on?" I feel Daisy nod into my shoulder. I kiss her head before pulling away from her slightly. I place a hand on her cheek and wipe away a stray tear with my thumb.

"Why didn't you tell me how you really felt? We don't

have to do this tomorrow if you don't want or we can do something different. Just tell me what you need. And again, stop keeping things from me, please!"

"I want to be with you. I will do whatever it takes to make sure we are together." I look at her and take in every feature of her beautiful face. Memorising every millimetre of it.

"I am so lucky to be able to call you mine." I whisper, kissing her gently, "I love you, darling." I hold her against me as I lower her to the floor so we can carry on from where we were so rudely interrupted.

Chapter Forty-Five

MICHAEL

I look down at Daisy as she sleeps soundly in my arms, resting her head against my chest, and I thank the Gods and Goddesses for bringing this amazing woman into my life.

Our first full day in our home has been magical and perfect in every way. I wish we could stay in our little bubble forever, just the two of us. There are too many things in the outside world that could take Daisy away from me. I feel the old panic building in my chest. The panic of not being able to protect those I love.

I close my eyes and count to ten whilst breathing slowly. I let my mind wander and am greeted with the images of Daisy lying naked underneath me as she screams my name. Her face flushed, hair fanned out around her, and lips swollen from me kissing them for hours on end.

Opening my eyes, I look down at her again and consider waking her just so I can see that look on her face again as I make mad, passionate love to her. I only consider it for a moment, though, as she is sound asleep and exhausted from all the lovemaking. We have been at it like a couple of horny teenagers, and it's been beyond amazing.

Out of the corner of my eye, I see my phone flashing, signalling a call coming through. I reach over and pick it up. Marcus's name is on the screen. I know I need to answer it; I need to check in and get an update on what's been going on while I've been with Daisy. I let the call go to voice mail and then send him a message one-handed.

Michael: Give me five, and I'll call you back.

I slowly pull my arm from underneath Daisy and lower her head to the pillow as I slide off the bed. She mumbles in her sleep as I place a kiss on the top of her head. I hate leaving her, even for a second. After those couple of days when I thought I had lost her, I hate every minute she isn't in my arms.

Slowly, so as not to wake her, I reach down and pick up my sweatpants from the bedroom floor before sneaking out of the room. I quietly close the door behind me before quickly pulling on my sweats on the landing and walking downstairs, heading straight for the kitchen. Opening the fridge, I pull out a bottle of beer and open it while calling Marcus's number. He answers on the second ring.

"Please tell me you weren't texting whilst fucking."

I choke on the beer whilst trying to cough as quietly as possible, hoping I won't wake Daisy.

"What the hell, Marc? Give me some credit, for fuck's sake."

Marcus roars laughing on the other end of the call.

"Just checking, didn't want to be interrupting anything. Heard Desmond did enough of that earlier."

I shake my head as I take another sip of my beer.

"So, other than being a prick, what's up? Anything to update me on?"

Marcus stops laughing instantly, and I know it's not good news.

"Yeah, there are a couple of things I think you should know about. Where is Daisy now? As I am not sure how much you will want her to know just yet." I sit down on one of the bar stools in the kitchen and rub the bridge of my nose.

"She's upstairs sleeping. I don't know how long for, though, so if I go off-script."

"She's up, got ya." I knew he would understand. I'm dreading what he is going to say.

"Go on, then spill it." I hear Marcus take a deep breath as I hold mine.

"Okay, so the first is that I organised another look around Kellan's place. As he hasn't been back, so I asked Stu to get me any laptop or electronic device he found, bank statements, all that kind of crap to try and find out more about him."

"What did you find?"

"A lot. It took a little bit of hacking, but I found his bank records. There was a name on there to which he transferred a substantial amount of money a week ago; we are talking three thousand pounds."

"How the fuck does a student have so much money?"

"Ohh, Kellan's bank account is huge; that wouldn't have even made a dent in it." I let out a whistle. Marcus continues with what he found.

"Anyway, I ran the name through social media, and two people came up as possibilities. One of the guys looked so familiar, but I couldn't remember where from. But then it clicked: the CCTV footage you asked me to dig up." I sit up straight as what he's saying clicks into place.

"The jogger?" I ask in disbelief.

"The very same. It was Kellan who paid for him to grab Daisy."

"The fucking bastard!" I have to clench my jaw to stop myself from shouting or punching something; I can't believe the extent to which this kid was willing to go to have Daisy to himself. "I want the jogger found, and I want five minutes with the fucker. I will get what he was meant to do with her out of him."

"Already done. I sent Jon and Will to his house. He lives alone; he's a normal human with a gambling problem. We thought Jon may need to use his expertise to get the guy to talk, but apparently, he took one look at the two of them and sang like a canary."

"What did he say?" I ask through gritted teeth.

"He said that some guy walked up to him at the bookies and offered to pay him six grand to grab a girl and scare her a bit to try and put her off running alone. He said he got half for agreeing to it and was meant to get the other half once he was done, but the other guy never paid up the second half."

"Kellan probably saw the way it all went down and realised his plan hadn't worked." I can hear Marcus agreeing down the line. I take a sip of my drink and quickly listen out for any noises from upstairs. Nothing. Thankfully, it seems Daisy is still asleep.

"So, there is no news on Kellan then? Do we think he has just left?" I know there is no way he would have gone through all this effort just to give up.

"I wish I could say yes, I really do, but this leads us to something else you need to know about. I have been looking into this, Kalvin. C. Jacks owns the house Kellan lives in. It turns out he owns a few more, but two stand out more than the others. You will never guess where they are." I feel the bottle I'm holding slip through my fingers, thankfully it lands standing up on the breakfast bar.

"You have got to be fucking kidding me, Marcus. You had better not tell me there is one in Exeter and one in St Austell."

"That's what I'm telling you."

"What the actual fuck?! There is no way that is a coincidence." That's when it hits me.

"What did you say the owner's name was again?"

"Kalvin. C. Jacks. I know what you are thinking, Mikey. It is too similar to Jackson. But surely Daisy would recognise him if he has been following her for the last three years?" I need to think about this. I don't want to take this to Daisy until we are sure, as there are too many possibilities. Plus, we have our blessing tomorrow, as well as a BBQ at Mum's. I don't want anything to dampen that. Daisy deserves it to be perfect in every way. I'm determined to make sure it is.

"Not if he's paying people to be his eyes." I rub my face in frustration. "Okay, I need time to process this. I'm going to sleep on it, and we'll discuss it tomorrow before the ceremony. I'll send Mum a message to ask her to distract Daisy for half an hour, and we'll have a team meeting. I will also need to speak to the Alpha, as I think this will require extra hands. The guys over at the Silver Sun Pack owe me after borrowing Will and Jon for a month. I'll see if I can put them on standby. I'll also need to contact the St Austell pack and ask them to constantly watch Mary and Nigel. If he owns property in their area, we don't know who is there, so they'll need to do some digging. Send me the addresses, and I'll forward them to the relevant people. I don't want to take liberties, but I want Daisy protected at all times."

"Mikey, that's not taking liberties. That's you protecting your mate. You would do it for any of us in a heartbeat. We're all more than happy to protect Daisy; she's our family now. Family comes before all else; you know this." I thanked him and let him know what time we would be at Mum's. We agree the entire team and Desmond need to be present for the meeting, and Tony, Richard, and Carl will need to be aware of what Marcus has found. Tony is already demanding that he help in any way he can; he wants to be kept in the loop about it all. I have agreed as it's for the best. There will be times that I can't be with Daisy, but Tony can.

Marcus promises to get the word out; he'll make sure everyone is there for the morning, and I'm to leave everything else to him. We both agree Daisy doesn't need to know anything yet, not until we know for sure what we are dealing with. I wish my pack brother a good night and thank him again for all his dedication. He has been everything I would expect in a second and more whilst I have been distracted with Daisy.

I sit in silence for a while, trying to process everything. Could Jackson have really known where Daisy was this whole time? If he did, then why didn't he act? Surely, if she's important enough to follow around and keep tabs on, why not grab her and be done with it? Nothing about any of this is making sense. I can't help wondering what his overall goal is and how it involves Daisy.

I down the rest of my beer and place the now empty bottle on the side next to the two empty champagne bottles. I pick up one of the bottles and smile. Picturing Daisy's face as she sipped the champagne from her flute whilst wearing nothing, but a thin white sheet wrapped around her. I place the bottle back on the side, grab a glass of water and leave the kitchen, turning all the lights off as I go.

Once upstairs, I quietly sneak back into the room and look at the bed. Daisy hasn't moved; she looks just as peaceful and perfect as she did when I left. I slowly make my way around to my side of the bed, pull off my sweatpants, and slide back under the sheets, gently moving her so she is back in my arms and resting on my chest once more. Just when I thought I had managed to get away with it, she smiles.

"Where did you go?"

I pull her to me and place a kiss on her head.

"I needed some water. Go back to sleep, baby," I whisper.

"And a beer?" she chuckles as she gets comfortable against my chest again. I smile into her hair.

"Busted," I whisper back.

"I love you, cheese ball," she murmurs as she drifts back off to sleep in my arms.

"Not as much as I love you, darling." I watch her sleeping peacefully for a few minutes, silently making a promise to her.

"I swear that no matter what has been going on and what we'll face in the future, you will never have to feel scared or worried again. I swear on my life that no one will ever hurt you again, darling." I close my eyes and listen to her soft breathing as I drift off to sleep.

Chapter Forty-Six

I'm so much calmer than I thought I would be today. The thought that by lunchtime, Michael and I will be bonded entirely, brings me so much joy that I honestly think I could cry.

"What's going on in that sexy little head of yours?" Michael asks next to me as he drives us to his mum's. I turn and look at him, and my stomach tenses when I take in his gorgeous face and smell his scent, which I'm sure has gotten stronger in the last couple of days. He is currently wearing a casual shirt with the sleeves rolled up and a pair of jeans that show off his amazing thighs as he drives.

"Baby, you keep looking at me like that, and I will be forced to pull over and ravish you in the back seat," Michael warns. I wiggle my eyebrows playfully, causing him to laugh. "We are running late because of your little distraction in the shower."

"Excuse me? All I was doing was *trying* to get clean. It's not my fault you took it as an invitation to join me and make me dirty again."

383

"You certainly weren't complaining. In fact, I distinctly remember you telling me, 'Don't stop!' I was just doing as I was told," he winks at me smirking. I roll my eyes, shaking my head at him whilst muttering that it still wasn't my fault. "Okay, I will take some of the blame. Now, will you tell me what you were thinking?" he asks again.

"I was just thinking how happy I am," I reply with a smile. Michael reaches over and takes my hand; he lifts it to his lips and plants a kiss on the back of it.

"I'm glad to hear it. I was worried you might be having second thoughts." I smile at him and shake my head.

"Nope, my feet are nice and toasty. Any second thoughts from you?"

Michael glances at me with a deep frown on his face.

"Baby, how could I possibly have second thoughts about being mated to you? You have made me happier than I ever thought possible. You are my world." He always makes me feel so loved.

"Cheese ball," I mutter playfully. Michael laughs.

"But I will always be your cheese ball, darling."

"Good," I say as I take my hand back while he takes the turn to his mum's house.

We're not even fully parked before Barbara comes rushing out of the house, grinning from ear to ear. She stands on the pavement, hopping from foot to foot, waiting for us to vacate the car. I don't even have time to close my door before she pulls me into her arms.

"Oh, my darling girl, I have missed you so much. Don't you ever feel that you can't come to me if you are scared again! Do you hear me?"

I can feel tears filling my eyes, but I quickly blink them away.

"I'm so sorry, Barbara."

She pulls away and holds me at arm's length so she can look me in the eyes as she responds.

"Don't apologise for going home when you were scared. You did what made you feel the safest, and no one will ever hold that against you."

"That's what I keep telling her," Michael says next to me as he leans over and kisses his mum on the cheek before placing his arm around my waist so I can lean into him.

"I'm not used to having people ..." I start when a sob closes my throat. Barbara steps forward and places a hand on my cheek.

"People other than your family? I get that; this is a big change for you. But you're our family now, and we look after our own." She looks from me to Michael and back to me. "Now, shall we go inside? People are waiting to see you, and the Alpha will be here in half an hour. By the way, Jonny doesn't know he is coming early." She places a kiss on my cheek and takes my hand, giving it a quick squeeze. I ask her why the secrecy, and she just shrugs.

"Goddess only knows with those two." I hear Michael agree and that it's better not to ask. "Mikey did warn you about your scent; now you are newly mated, didn't he?" I look at her and frown. I hear Michael curse behind me as Barbara turns around to face him. "You forgot, didn't you?" he nods; I notice that he is looking a little more on edge and watching the house with his eyes narrowed as if looking for a threat. I look at Barbara, who shakes her head and mutters, "Should have moved the valuables," under her breath. I stop and look at them both.

"Would somebody care to explain what's going on?" Michael lets out a grunt and places an arm around my shoulder, bringing me closer to him.

"When a wolf is newly mated, their scent changes to

ensure they keep their mate interested. Many, many, moons ago, it would have ensured the female was impregnated quickly, the male having another claim on her. But now, instead of going into heat all the time, thanks to modern-day contraception, it's just a pain, to be honest. In the first week, it's at its strongest. The problem is that it will also attract other males, not just Mikey."

I open my eyes wide and try to take in what she is saying.

"So other males will try to what? Jump me?"

Michael growls next to me.

"I would like to see them fucking try."

Barbara just rolls her eyes at him.

"As humans, we are a little more aware of our behaviours, so no one should approach you or try anything. The fact that you are Michael's mate will help, as every male in the pack has far too much respect for him."

"In other words, they are terrified of me and know I would fucking kill anyone who so much as looked at you the wrong way."

"Yes, that helps, potty mouth," Barbara says sarcastically as she rolls her eyes again. "The point is the guys inside may act a little differently when they first see you. It isn't intentional, and I *hope* they have enough sense not to push it with Mikey, as they are fully aware he will fight them and walk away a lot better off than they will," she winks at me. I know she is trying to lighten the mood. I thank her for warning me, and we head inside the house.

I don't even make it all the way into the lounge before I'm pulled off my feet and find myself in a crushing bear hug.

"Mikey, I have her; she isn't running away again, don't worry." I want to punch Jonathan, but I can't move my arms as they are pinned to my side by his. "Shit, you smell amazing," he mutters as he nestles his nose into my neck. I freeze.

"Jonathan!" Barbara snaps as Michael walks through the door; I can instantly see he has made himself as big as possible and looks like he could tear Jon from limb to limb, brother or not.

"Get the fuck away from her right now!" he growls. Jonathan drops me before stepping back with his hands up in defence. I step away from him and closer to Michael, wanting as much distance between us as possible.

"Sorry, Mikey. I was just joking around and got caught off guard." As Michael closes the last of the distance between us, I hear the kitchen door open, followed by the sound of three voices laughing. The next few seconds happen in slow motion.

As I watch Marcus, Will and Stuart all walk into the lounge laughing; in unison, they all stop and turn to look at me. Their eyes all turn black; for a split second, it's like nothing could stand between them and me. Then, as a unit, they all take a step forward. I feel a hand grab me and spin me around as a solid wall appears in front of me, blocking me from view. A deep, loud growl fills the room, and I am pinned to Michael's back.

"Step the fuck back!" he roars. The Alpha gene kicks in as magic fills the air, and I find myself stepping back as well. When an Alpha gives an order, it is nearly impossible to ignore it. The body does as it's told whether we want it to or not. I watch as Jon and Barbara also step back, not in fear but because of the order. I take a deep breath and step around so I'm now in front of Michael. I place one hand on his chest like I did the morning with the jogger and one on his cheek.

"Mikey, I'm okay; they'd never touch me," I whisper. Slowly, Michael looks at me, and I can see it in his eyes in that second that he would fight anyone to protect me, even his own pack brothers. I hold his stare and ensure my eyes are as soft as possible. "I am fine," I whisper again as I lean up and gently kiss his lips. I feel his arm go around me as he pulls me closer, his lips crashing into mine as he kisses me back. I let him hold me whilst kissing me passionately for a few more seconds before I push away from him. He leans his head down and rests his forehead against mine.

"I'm sorry," I hear him mumble. His body finally relaxes. I gently lift my head and let my lips brush his again.

"Overprotective much?" I whisper, and I feel Michael chuckle, the last of the tension leaving him, as he replies.

"Get used to it." I turn around and push my back against his front. He wraps his arms around me and holds me to him.

"We are so sorry, Mikey and Daisy. The scent just ... wow." Marcus mutters. I can see all three are near enough up against the wall, all looking extremely sorry for themselves. I realise then it is because they are bowing to an Alpha and asking for forgiveness. Michael sees it, too.

"It's fine, no harm done. Let's just forget it." Instantly, all three relax, look up, and smile shyly at us. I let out a breath I had held until now.

"Now that drama is over, Mikey and Daisy, you should come with us," Barbara says, coming into view smiling. I look around and see all the lads are grinning suspiciously at us.

"Why are they all smiling like that? Should I be scared?" I feel Michael's arms tighten around me as he lowers his mouth to my ear.

"I don't know; it's a little unnerving. Maybe we should just go with them; if they attack, we'll make a run for it," he whispers. I giggle as Barbara grabs my hand and pulls me away from him.

"Children, the pair of you." She tugs me towards the kitchen, and I quickly grab Michael's hand, pulling him with us. He tries to turn away from me, but I tighten my grip.

"Oh no, Adams, if I am being dragged to my doom, you're coming too. Side by side, remember."

I hear Michael curse under his breath,

"I knew that would come back to bite me on the arse one day."

Barbara chuckles but keeps guiding me through the kitchen to the back door. As we step into the garden, I stop in my tracks, my hand shoots to my mouth, and I hear Michael's deep intake of breath behind me as he bumps into me.

The back garden has been transformed into a beautiful party area. There are ribbons of all colours hanging from the trees and fairy lights hanging all over the garden. There are tables and chairs scattered over the lawn and patio, with a makeshift dance floor in the middle. I turn to the left and see a bar and BBQ set up. The place looks perfect for a huge family party.

"The guys helped me put it together yesterday afternoon and this morning. It's all for your mating celebrations. I know you wanted to keep the numbers low, but unfortunately, word got out about you two, and everyone wants to come and celebrate you both," Barbara explains next to us.

"Mama..." Michael starts, but I realise he is stuck for words like me. I feel his arms wrap around my waist again, and he pulls me back so I'm leaning against him.

"Barbara, I don't know what to say." I feel a single tear escape my eye, "It's beautiful." I step out of Michael's arms and straight into Barbara's. "Thank you," I whisper as a small sob leaves my throat; I hear Barbara chuckle as she holds me tight.

"That's the second time you have brought my mate to tears in the space of ten minutes. If this carries on, I will stop her from coming around," I hear Michael joke next to me.

"I would like to see you try to keep my new daughter away from me. She is my favourite person and deserves all of this, especially as she will have to put up with you for the rest of her life."

I giggle as I look at Michael, who is standing with his mouth hanging open; he pretends to think about it and shrugs. He leans over and kisses his mum on the cheek.

"Thank you, Mama." He turns to the guys as I do, and we both thank them too. I notice all four guys are keeping their distance from me in fear of upsetting Michael.

"Is anybody there?" I hear being called from the front garden. I watch Jon's jaw drop, and his eyes open wide.

"Shit, is that the Alpha? Hide me quick." I look at Michael, who is just shaking his head at his brother.

"What the hell have you done now?" Michael asks. Jon looks up at him, straight-faced.

"Nothing, it's just a misunderstanding."

"Debatable," Michael laughs as he stands in front of his brother with his arms crossed.

"Hey! I take that personally. I'm a freaking saint. It's not my fault if people walk around corners unexpectedly and get a face full of water." Every single one of us stops talking at the same time. Of all the people for Jon to soak, the Alpha was not a good choice. Marcus looks at Jon.

"You thought it was Stuart, didn't you?"

Jon bursts out laughing as Stuart punches him, complaining.

"I so did! I swear the water turned into steam as soon as it hit him. I just turned and ran. I could hear him yelling at me a mile away. I haven't shifted since because he will know and shout at me down the mind link as soon as I do. Man, he was maaaddd. But it was worth it. It was freaking hilarious."

Jon laughs so hard that he is doubled over.

"I suggest you head through the side gate; he has just coming through the front door," Michael says, moving out of the way.

"Cheers, bro, do your thing and let me know when it is safe to come back," Jon says, patting his brother's chest.

"I can't get you out of the shit every time Jonny," Michael calls after him.

"Sure you can. You've had plenty of practice." Jon calls as he throws us all a quick salute before rushing through the gate. The second he is out of sight, we all hear the sound of water splashing and Jon shouting. I run to the gate, not bothering to see if others are following. I throw it open to see Jon standing there dripping wet, with a man the size of Michael standing with an empty bucket. Jon looks speechless, while the guy is roaring with laughter and holding the wall for support.

"Next time you want to soak someone, make sure you can hide from them because payback is a bitch, Jonny." Everybody, myself included, is howling with laughter. That is possibly the funniest thing I have seen for a long while.

As the guy with the bucket straightens up, I notice everyone bow; I instantly follow suit, knowing this must be the Alpha.

Chapter Forty-Seven

MICHAEL

After Jon wanders off with his tail between his legs, I walk Daisy over to my Alpha and good friend.

"Alpha, I would like to introduce my mate. Daisy, this is our Alpha, Desmond Gibbs." I watch as Daisy bows her head to show respect. I know she has been so worried about coming face-to-face with the Alpha. She has quizzed me over every situation she could think of and how she should behave. I tried to tell her she had nothing to worry about, but then I remembered the only Alpha she had ever met was the arsehole who changed her. He filled her head with so many lies about what Alphas expect of their pack that it's no wonder she was terrified to meet Desmond.

"It's a pleasure to meet you, sir," she says as she lifts her head and looks Desmond in the eye. I would think she was at ease; her face is giving nothing away; the fact that I'm about to lose all my fingers on my left hand from her death grip is another story.

"Trust me when I say the pleasure is all mine. I've been waiting a long time to see someone put this one in his place, and from what I have seen and heard of you, I think you may have already succeeded."

Daisy smiles at him and nods playfully before looking at me.

"He wasn't that hard to train, really." I listen to them as they get to know each other, noticing that the feeling is coming back into my hand slowly as Daisy relaxes more and more. After a few minutes, Mum calls Daisy away. I kiss her quickly and watch as she heads into the house.

"She's good for you, Mikey. The same way as I think you're good for her," I hear Desmond say behind me. I don't turn to his voice as I watch Daisy until she is out of my line of sight.

"I spoke to her about being an Alpha. I offered to step down."

"And let me guess, she told you she would be honoured to be by your side, as Luna."

I turn and face him.

"How did you know?"

Desmond smiles at me as he places a hand on my shoulder.

"Because it takes a special mate to be a Luna, I can see it in her already. She will be loved and respected by all who meet her; she'll be strong, firm and supportive whenever you need her to be as well. There is a special type of magic between you two. I'm just not sure what it is yet, but I can feel it." With that, he turns away and heads to talk to Marcus, leaving me to work out what he means, as he always does.

Fifteen minutes later, we are all gathered around the kitchen table. Mum and Daisy are both upstairs. The Luna has joined them and will help keep Daisy distracted whilst we discuss everything,

"Mikey, we don't have to do this today. It's your blessing, for crying out loud," Jon protests next to me, his clothes still wet as he hasn't had a chance to change them yet.

"I want this sorted so that I can relax and enjoy our day." I look around at everyone gathered and can't miss the way my heart swells with gratitude once more. I take a deep breath and address everyone.

"Okay, as I know Marcus has filled you all in, I won't go over old details. But, we have no idea how close an eye Jackson has on Daisy or what role Kellan is playing in this and any others who have been working for Jackson. So, I want to ensure that Daisy is never left alone. I want one of us with her at all times." I turn and face Tony.

"I will be with her when she is in uni. Every class, trip to the café, canteen, gods, I'll even go to the toilet with her if I have to. She will not be out of my sight," he promises. I nod at him, knowing Tony will do everything in his power to protect his best friend.

"Michael, I have requested that the council find someone asap to replace you on the staff there, but there is only so much I can do," Desmond says beside me. I turn to him and nod. "What I did do, though, was apply for the psychology lecturer role on your behalf. I know it is your favoured subject. At least this way, you can stay there and protect her if you need to, but you won't need to hide your relationship."

I look at him, shocked. I hadn't expected my Alpha to do so much for me, for us.

"Thank you, Alpha." I look around at the rest of my

pack brothers. "From now on, when Daisy and I run, someone else will be with us. I want a second pair of eyes, as Kellan got close to us too many times for my liking. I need to know that if I miss something, someone else will pick it up."

"You know Daisy is going to fight you on this the whole way, don't you? You can't hide this from her forever. When she finds out she is being watched this closely, she will hit the roof," Jon says from across the table.

"What am I meant to do, Jonny? We have no idea who we are actually going up against here. We have no idea what Jackson knows. Once he knows that she is now mated, he may up his game to get her back. Kellan must be working for him. But we have no idea how or why or for how long. Plus, we have no idea what Kellan is! He has some sort of power; we just don't know what."

"Have you thought about what you're going to do when you get called on a mission, Michael? What about when we all go to Exeter? We *all* need to go; we need the full team to deal with the pack there and the search for Kellan and Jackson."

"Daisy will stay with us."

I turn and look at Carl and Richard. Carl is leaning on the table; his mate reaches over and takes his hand. "I might not be part of the team anymore, but I'm still trained to protect. We will protect her just as well as any of you." He turns and looks at Richard, who nods.

"There's no reason why she can't come to us. Even if she joins us downstairs in the bar, do you think a single person in that place would let someone harm one hair on her head? Shit, they would tear the place down to protect her." I know they are right. I have seen the way the regulars are with Daisy. The fact that they are all shifters and part of this pack helps put me at ease.

"It's settled then. We will work everything out as it happens. But no matter what, Daisy is protected at all times." They all nod in agreement. "Right enough for today. The plans will all be put into place tomorrow, but for now, I want to have my bond blessed and enjoy our day with my mate with no thought of the two pricks determined to harm her."

Daisy

I sit in Barbara's room and play with the hem of my dress. The guilt of what I put everyone through is playing on my mind. I can't believe I acted so irresponsibly. I know everyone has told me to stop worrying about it all, but as much as I try, I can't.

Ten minutes ago, when Barabara had stolen me away from Michael and the Alpha, I had been feeling positive about everything, but then I saw the one person I hadn't been able to face standing in front of me. My feet had stopped in their tracks at the sight of my best friend.

"Bitch, you better get over here so I can kick your ass for leaving me here with all these wolves!" Tony had snapped, and at first, I couldn't stop the smile that spread across my face as I rushed into his arms; we held each other tightly.

"I've missed you so much," I'd sobbed into his shoulder as he laughed at me.

"Please, you have FaceTimed me twice a day since Thursday." I felt Tony plant a kiss on my temple as he whispered, "Although I've missed you too." I quickly kissed him on the cheek as I pulled away from him. I turned and saw Barbara grinning at me; I felt my cheeks start to flush. Crap, what must she have thought of me hugging another male when I'm newly mated to her son? To my surprise, Tony had faced her and smiled.

"Hey Mama B! Carl and Richard are taking everything through to the garden; I'm on salad duty. Where can I set up?" Barbara walked over to Tony and pulled him into a hug.

"The kitchen's through there. I may have left a small tub of those homemade cookies you have been bugging me for on the side, just for you." I watched as Tony's face lit up; he bent down and kissed her on the cheek.

"Mama B, you are spoiling me. Do you fancy adopting another misfit?" Barbara laughed as she pushed Tony towards the kitchen, telling him to pack it in and get to work. She grabbed my hand again and dragged me towards the stairs.

"Okay, so I know I was gone a few days, but how and when did you meet Tony?" I chuckled as I followed her.

"It was that day when we had no idea where you were; the whole team gathered at The Crows to help out. Tony insisted on helping me in the kitchen with the food and drinks as everyone else worked and ran around. He's a good lad, and he thinks the world of you." She turned and smiled at me as she led me into her room and signalled for me to sit on the bed. "Stay there. I will be right back," she whispered before leaving the room.

Since she left, my mood has plummeted drastically, and I'm fighting back the tears as, once again, I can focus on nothing but the pain I caused.

"Oh my goodness, Daisy, whatever is the matter?" Barbara's voice startles me. I look up and plan on telling her everything is fine, but instead, I feel myself wanting to be honest with her.

"I caused everyone so much trouble, didn't I?" I whisper, looking at Barbara as she guides me to stand and moves me to sit in front of her vanity mirror. My chest starts to contract; as my throat tightens, I feel my eyes welling up.

"Daisy dear, it's no trouble when it's family. We were all there willingly, wanting to help find you and keep you safe. So, you really have nothing to get upset about," She smiles at me through her reflection. "Plus, the last thing you want is to be all puffy-eyed when Michael next sees you; he might follow through on his threat and stop you from coming to see me."

I chuckle as I jump up and pull Barbara into a tight hug. This woman means so much to me and has put me at ease with a simple smile.

"You know he couldn't keep me away from my favourite person," I whisper, enjoying her motherly hug.

Barbara pulls away and places a hand on my cheek.

"No more tears, and no more feeling guilty for what happened. It's in the past, and that is where it's going to stay." She encourages me to sit back down and face the mirror. "You are probably wondering why I dragged you away." I watch as she walks over to the chest of drawers and picks up a box.

"It's tradition for wolves to pass down a family heirloom when their children get mated. Jon is downstairs, giving Michael their father's watch. As I know your parents are deceased and your auntie and uncle are witches, I wanted to give you something I wore when mine and George's bond was blessed." She opens the box and reveals a beautiful hair comb. I look at it and feel my breath catch in my throat once more. Along the top of the comb are small white and pink flowers with tiny diamonds as centres. They look just like daisies.

"I would have given this to Michelle when she was mated. But I know she'd agree that you should have it now." I look up at Barbara, who is smiling with tears in her eyes. I can feel mine welling up again. "It's as if they were made for you."

"Barbara, it's beautiful. Are you sure you want to give it to me?" she nods, smiling at me.

"It would make me extremely happy and proud if you would allow me to style your hair. It's a traditional style females have worn for hundreds of years in our pack. Will you allow me to do it?" Barbara asks,

"Please," I reply, once again trying not to cry.

Gently, she gathers my hair and starts brushing it with her brush.

"What can you tell me about the Moon Goddess?"

"The Greeks named her Selene, the Romans Luna," I answer, frowning as I watch her in the mirror.

"I knew you would know. Do you know that it is she who chooses who will be our fated mate? She looks for people who are best suited for each other, who will love each other unconditionally and protect each other from all dangers. She understands that there are times when one mate will need to rely heavily on the other. So, she picks people who will support their other half when they need it and love them unconditionally. As you have probably seen and felt, the bond also makes us very protective of our mates." I feel her braiding my hair as she speaks. All I can do is watch her work in the mirror.

"I have watched my son bloom into a better, happier male since you came into his life. He has changed so much for the better. That is all thanks to you, darling girl. You've brought him back from the edge, the one he has been balancing on since Michelle was killed. His eyes are filled with love and joy again, and he is fighting to live and have the future he finally feels he deserves. You deserve it, too. You both do. I know with all my heart you will continue to love and support each other and grow together. I couldn't be happier for you both."

"Thank you, Barbara. Or can I call you Mama B now, too?" I watch in the mirror as Barbara places a hand on my shoulder and leans close to me. She whispers before planting a soft kiss on my cheek.

"To you, I'm just Mama."

Chapter Forty-Eight

MICHAEL

Half an hour later, I'm in the kitchen helping Tony. He seems in a much better mood than he's been in all week, now he has spent a few minutes with Daisy. I know how much he missed her when she was away. We are just putting the finishing touches to a bowl of salad when I hear my name.

"Mikey, the Alpha says it's time," Jon says as he sticks his head in the back door, now in dry clothes. I look down at my father's watch, sat on my wrist, and it is indeed one o'clock. I wish Dad could have been here today, but I now feel like he is part of this moment since Jon gave me the watch.

To wolves, the mating blessing is more important than a human wedding. Many mated couples only get married because of the legal side or to please their human friends and family. To us wolves, once our bond is complete, it is final; we are with our mates for life.

I take a deep breath and walk out into the garden to wait for Daisy.

Taking my place facing the Alpha a few steps back, I stand with my brother Jon, Tony, Marcus on the left, Stuart, Will, Carl, Richard, and the Beta Alaric on the right. Desmond has already explained to me what will happen. I'm to stay back until after he has welcomed Daisy into the pack, and then I will step forward when called for the blessing.

I sense her before her scent flows over me with the breeze. I turn to see Daisy smiling as Mum and the pack Luna walk with her out of the house into the garden. I look at my mate and swear she is glowing. Her floral summer dress moves slightly in the spring breeze, her hair is now up, and I can see my mum's comb, the one she wore to her blessing, placed on the side of her head. I know Mum always intended Michelle to wear her comb. Seeing it in Daisy's hair now makes it feel like Michelle is here with us. It feels like my watch gets heavier on my wrist, the reminder that both my Dad and twin are here with us, even if not in person.

As soon as Daisy's eyes meet mine, her face breaks into a broad grin as she winks before sticking her tongue out play-fully; I can't help but laugh. My eyes refuse to look anywhere but at her. Every step she takes to the front fills my heart with more love and pride than I could ever possibly imagine.

"*Our world,*" my wolf sighs inside me.

"Our everything," I reply.

As Daisy stands before our Alpha, my mum stands next to me. She takes my hand and squeezes it, making me look down at her.

"The Goddess chose well for you," She whispers quietly. I look at her and see that she has tears in her eyes.

"Thank you," I whisper, giving her a smile. I turn to the front again as the Alpha clears his throat.

"Afternoon all, so this is all a little different for us, but I couldn't be happier than I am now as I welcome Daisy into our pack and bless her and Michael's bond." Desmond turns to Daisy and smiles, "The gate is just over there; if you want to run for it, we should be able to hold him off long enough for you to escape." He winks at her, and she glances at the gate, then throws her hands up in the air dramatically.

"Damn it! I knew I should have brought my running shoes!" Daisy looks over at me and shrugs. "Guess I'm staying, sorry." I just shake my head at her whilst rolling my eyes. Everyone laughs around us, and I feel Mum squeeze my hand. I look down and see she is also shaking her head whilst muttering to herself.

"Goddess, give me strength to deal with another smart mouth."

Desmond looks at me, grinning from ear to ear.

"I like her."

"Everybody does," I reply, smirking. Everyone is nodding around me, including the Luna, who winks at Daisy. I should have known they would quickly become friends.

"Well, as Daisy is staying, let's get the show on the road." He turns to Daisy and places both hands on her shoulders. "Daisy Angela Andrews, as Alpha of the Blood Moon Pack, I ask you; do you promise to stand beside your pack brothers and sisters, to love, honour and protect those in need of it?"

"I do."

"Do you swear in front of all these present to honour our pack and wolf laws?"

"I do."

"Then, as the Alpha of the Blood Moon Pack, let me be the first to welcome you to our land, to our pack and most importantly to our family." As he says the last word, a strong breeze flows over us all. We all feel it as Daisy's own connection strengthens, the magic in the air binding her to us all as a pack sister. As the breeze dies down, my family and I start cheering and clapping for our newest member. I look at Daisy, who is grinning whilst taking it all in around her. The Alpha leans down and whispers something in her ear; she looks confused for a second and then nods slowly. He winks at her before looking at me.

"Michael, would you like to come forward?"

I don't need to be asked twice. I walk straight up to Daisy and place my arm around her waist, kissing her gently on the lips.

"You look beautiful," I whisper.

She looks at me and smiles.

"Mama can work wonders with a hairbrush."

I look at her and smile.

"I wasn't just referring to your hair, darling."

Daisy blushes and looks away.

"Michael, do you think you will be able to let go of Daisy for a couple of minutes or not?"

I look at Desmond and shake my head. He laughs as she shrugs out of my arm, muttering about me being a cheese ball. "You may be the leader of the team, but you certainly won't be wearing the trousers in this relationship," Desmond says with raised eyebrows.

"He knows his place," Daisy says as she taps my cheek playfully.

"Yep, doing as I'm told and keeping you supplied with coffee and food," I reply. Daisy nods once.

"See, you're learning." Everyone is laughing around us, and we both turn to the Alpha, who is watching, grinning at us.

"Well, there is no denying the Goddess could not have picked a better mate for either of you. So, all that is left for me to do is bless this bond. Michael Graham Adams and Daisy Angela Andrews, the Goddess Luna, has chosen you to be bound together, to love, protect, and support each other in all that you do. Do you agree with her choice of mate for you, Michael?" I look down at Daisy and smile

"I certainly do."

Daisy keeps looking me straight in the eye as the Alpha continues.

"Do you, Daisy, agree with her choice of mate for you?"

"I really do," she replies. I can see tears forming in her eyes as I blink back my own.

"Then all that is left for me to say is, as Alpha of the Blood Moon Pack, I bless this union and wish you both all the love and happiness in the world. May you both spend many moons as one."

Everyone around us starts cheering and clapping; I don't look around as I only have eyes for my mate. I sweep her up in my arms and kiss her passionately, hearing her giggle for a second before she throws her arms around my neck as she kisses me back. The breeze picks up around us again, and I can feel magic in the air, but I don't care. All I care about is the woman in my arms.

"Best day ever," Daisy says, but then I pull away from her, wondering how she had spoken so clearly while kissing me. Strange.

"What's strange?" Daisy asks, frowning at me. I look at her, shocked.

"I didn't say anything."

She just looks at me and smiles like I'm winding her up.

"You did; I heard you."

She couldn't have heard … could she?

"Can you hear me now?" I watch as Daisy's eyes widen; she nods slowly.

"Yes," I hear in return. I turn to the Alpha, who is frowning at us but then starts to grin.

"Ahh, I told you there was something magical about the two of you. Can you hear each other's thoughts?" Daisy and I both look at him and nod. "I wondered if that would happen. It seems Michael is not the only one with the Alpha gene. Daisy, after I welcomed you into the pack, I asked if you were ever considered to lead your coven, and you nodded?"

I look at Daisy, who nods again.

"I was going to take over from my uncle, but then I was bitten, so I stepped down."

Alpha nods and looks at us both.

"Daisy has much more power than she realises. She could lead any coven. Did you notice how the breeze picked up during the welcoming and the blessing? Both times when Daisy was probably at her happiest. I could feel the magic in the air. I believe it was all the Gods and Goddesses blessing this union as well as the Goddess Luna."

I look back at Daisy, who grabs my hand. I put my arm around her shoulders and kiss the top of her head, letting her know I am here with her.

"I'm not certain yet, and I'd like to look more into this, but I believe when Daisy was turned, the part of her ready to lead the coven changed, so she also can lead a pack. I thought I could sense the Alpha gene when I met you earlier, and now you are part of my pack; it's unmissable.

Together, you have become one unbeatable Alpha, Michael, with the muscles, Daisy with the magic, and enough brains between you both to overcome any obstacle. As two Alphas mated together, the connection between you can branch out, so you can hear each other not only in wolf form but now in human form, too."

"So, no thought will ever be our own?" I ask; Desmond shakes his head.

"No, you will be able to block it out. Even now, I bet both of you have a million things running around in your mind, and the other cannot hear them. You will need to project your thoughts for the other to hear. That first initial time was the Goddess's way of letting you know what gift she has given you."

I realise then that he's right. I can't hear Daisy's mind, but I can see she is thinking all of this through. I squeeze her shoulder, and she leans into me.

"This could be quite fun," I hear her say in my mind. I can't help but chuckle.

"I think it will be."

Chapter Forty-Nine

MICHAEL

The party is in full swing; nearly the whole pack has turned out to meet the woman who finally melted *The Protector's* heart.

I'm talking to an old friend when I feel someone tap me on the shoulder. I turn around and am surprised to see Carly standing behind me. Usually, it's tough when she and her mate are at pack meets; it's one of the reasons I've avoided them. But now, when I see her, I don't get the usual feeling of regret; I just see somebody I used to love a long time ago.

"Hi Mikey, I wasn't sure if I should come, but I wanted to say how happy I am for you." I lean over and kiss her on the cheek, smiling.

"Thank you, Carly; it's good to see you. I'm glad you came." Looking at this beautiful woman I have pined after all my life, it feels strange now, as I feel absolutely nothing romantically towards her.

"It's good to see you smiling again, Mikey," Carly replies. I look from her to Daisy and smile as she laughs and hits Will playfully on the arm, everyone laughing with her.

"Everything feels better now I have Daisy. It's as if she has erased the pain I was in," I reply as I look back at Carly, who's smiling at me, "I get it now."

Carly nods knowingly.

"It makes what we had feel like a brief fling in comparison, doesn't it?"

I nod in agreement.

"I'm glad you finally found her, Mikey. If anyone deserves happiness, it's you."

I look back at Daisy, who looks over at me and winks playfully before looking back at everyone she is talking to.

"She deserves it more. She has had it tougher than me, but I'm going to make sure she never has to suffer again."

Carly steps forward and gives me a one-arm hug.

"If anyone will protect her, it's you."

I am just about to reply when I hear Daisy scream. I spin around, expecting something terrible to have happened to her. But instead, I see Will slinging her over his shoulder and heading back towards me. Both of them are laughing so hard I'm worried he'll drop her.

"Here, Mikey, take this pain in the ass back; she is picking on me *again*." I take her off his shoulder and place her feet back on the ground.

"I wasn't picking on you. I just pointed out that between you, Stuart and Jonny, it's amazing that any female comes to these meets if all you three do is hit on them."

I laugh as Will throws his arms up in the air.

"Leave her at home next time." He says as he turns away from us,

"You would miss me if he did," she calls after him. Will gives her the one-finger salute without turning around.

Daisy calls him a child and turns to face us, laughing. "Oh, sorry, did we interrupt something?" Daisy says, smiling at Carly, who just smiles back at her.

"Not at all; I was just telling Mikey how great it is to see him so happy. Looks like you are keeping him and the guys on their toes." Daisy smiles and nods at her. She holds out her hand to Carly.

"I'm Daisy."

Carly takes her hand and shakes it, smiling.

"Carly."

I watch Daisy's eyes widen, and she smiles brighter.

"Oh, you're Carly. It's lovely to meet you finally. I've heard so much about you."

Carly looks a little surprised.

"There was me worried you would be a little put out by me talking to Mikey. I hope it was all good things."

Daisy waves off her comment.

"Of course, I wouldn't be put out. Your history means the world to Michael. We both have pasts, so no need to hide them."

Carly just shakes her head in amazement. I smile at her as I place an arm around Daisy's shoulders and pull her towards me, kissing her head.

"I like that way of looking at it. Anyway, I had better get going. It was lovely to see you again, Mikey, and to meet you, Daisy; I hope to see you both again soon."

"Take care, Carly," I say as she walks away, and Daisy waves at her. I turn to Daisy and look at her.

"You really okay? Sorry, I didn't know she would be here tonight."

Daisy just frowns at me.

"Why would I be bothered about her being here? Like I said, we both have pasts; she is part of yours, and I accept that. I'm sure if I had exes, you would be just as under-standing." I raise one eyebrow at her as she laughs. "Or not. It's a good job I have a very boring dating history then." I lean down and pull her into a passionate kiss.

"I don't deserve you," I whisper as I pull away. Daisy just giggles and pats my chest.

"I know, I'm a freaking catch. Now, come over here and help me wind Will up. It's so fun."

I laugh as she pulls me back towards my pack brothers.

It's coming up to midnight, and I'm ready to go home with my mate and lose myself in her over and over again until we pass out from exhaustion. But first, I have to drag her away from the dance floor. That in itself will be a mission and a half, as nothing comes between Daisy and her dancing.

I decided that the best course of action would probably be the less subtle one. So I walk onto the makeshift dance floor and sling her over my shoulder as she squeals in shock.

"Mikey, what you doing?"

I walk away from the rest of my pack sisters, including Luna Jayne, and Carly, as they all whine about me being no fun and taking their new best friend away.

"Go and find your own mates for the night; I'm taking mine home to bed." I can hear everyone wolf-whistling and cheering behind us as Daisy just laughs. "Sorry to steal you away from your new friends, but if I don't get inside you soon, I can't promise I won't bend you over one of these tables here in front of everyone and fuck you into next week."

"That's okay. I was getting warmed up for the main

performance anyway." I reposition her so she is now in my arms, and I can look into her green eyes. I frown at her, hoping she will elaborate.

"Do you know how many times I've looked at you sitting back in your chair behind your desk, wondering what it would be like to give you a lap dance until you beg me to ride your cock? A lot. Well, I noticed there is an office upstairs this morning, so I was thinking..." She starts wiggling her eyebrows at me as I pick up the pace and head straight for the car, with her giggling in my arms. I spot Mum, and we both shout a quick thank you. She just stands there laughing and shaking her head at us.

As we get to the car, I realise I'm not prepared to wait until I get her home. So I keep on going, knowing that there is a secluded area not far from here where no one will be able to hear us. Daisy instantly picks up on what I have planned and starts giggling whilst running her fingers through the hair at the top of my neck. Fuck, it's hard to concentrate when she does that, and she knows it.

As soon as we are in the woods, I find the strongest tree and hold Daisy against it as I slam my lips into hers. The kiss deepens instantly as our tongues become entwined, our hands groping at what they can reach. Daisy's legs are wrapped around my waist as I grind up against her.

"Loosen your legs," I gasp down the link, not wanting my lips to leave hers. As soon as they are loose enough for me to move, I hold Daisy's hips in place and drop to my knees and position her legs so they are now resting on my shoulders. I remove one hand from her hips and use it to rip away her thong, which I ball up into my hand and bring to my nose. I inhale her sweet, aroused scent before throwing them over my shoulder.

"Fuck, you smell so good. I need to taste you," I growl,

taking in the sight of plump, slick lips. I feel Daisy thread her fingers through my hair as I run my nose up before devouring her and her sweet juices. Within seconds she is panting and close to the edge. I continue to lick her playfully whilst pushing a finger, then two inside of her.

"Fuck, don't stop, babe, please." I love hearing her beg,

"Beg me again, but this way." I instantly notice that the woods go silent as I hear Daisy through our unique mind link.

"Babe, I'm going to cum; please don't stop." Fuck, that's hotter than hearing her out loud. I up the pace, and it takes only a handful of seconds before her orgasm fills my head, and all I can hear is her screaming my name whilst the outside world stays quiet.

As soon as she comes down, I lower her feet to the ground as I stand up, pulling her towards me.

"Do you want more here or at home?" I look down at her, expecting her to be completely spent, having climaxed so hard, but she looks up and bites her bottom lip whilst nodding.

"I need you now. Fuck me, Michael, hard." I look at her, amazed, then feel a grin spread across my face.

"Turn around and hold on to the tree." I watch as she instantly does as she's told. I undo my tight, uncomfortable trousers and release my rock-hard dick from its restraints. I run my hand down her back as I take in the view of her bent over, holding on to the tree for support. I lift up her dress and reveal her plump bare ass, which I knead with my hands. I lean against her, following the line of her bent body. As I do, I allow the tip of my dick to poke her sweet, puckered hole. I hear her gasp slightly as I lower my lips to her ear.

"One day, I'm going to claim this ass." Daisy moans and I can smell the arousal coming from her. "Oh, baby, you are always up for a bit of fun, aren't you?" I give her ass a quick slap and watch her gasp out loud as her eyes roll back. "You're going to love the feel of me riding your ass, but not today. Now I need to be in your sweet, wet pussy." I stand back up behind her and insert two fingers into her, ensuring she is ready for me.

"You asked for it hard, baby, but if it's too much, just say," I say as Daisy gasps and sends her own message.

"Fuck me, Michael. Please!" I pull my fingers out of her as I grab hold of her hips before slamming into her hard. She screams out, and I stop instantly.

"Are you okay?" I start panicking that I've hurt her.

"Fuck, don't stop."

I grin to myself as I start fucking her, as she holds on to the tree for support. I know I'm not going to be able to last long; I can already feel her tightening around me as she heads towards her own climax. Everything feels even better than usual after watching her all day, wanting to sink into her, reclaiming her over and over again. If this is how good it feels when she is on birth control and in heat, I can't wait until we are able to start trying for a pup. The sheer thought of it has me rushing towards my own release.

"Cum with me, baby."

As she climaxes, she screams in my head; she is my undoing. I slam into her pumping my own thick juices into her as her pussy milks me for every drop with her own orgasm.

I wrap my arm around her waist, taking the weight from her shaking legs and lowering us onto the woodland ground, where we curl up together. Daisy's wrapped in my arms as we both catch our breath and come down from the incredible high.

"I have something for you," I whisper in her ear; I feel

her moan slightly as she reaches up and pats me gently on the cheek, her eyes closed as if nearly asleep.

"Already? Can we wait until we get home before going again?"

I chuckle into her hair as I pull away from her and reach into my pocket, pulling out a small jewellery box. I watch as Daisy's eyes widen.

"It's not what you think it is; it's not a ring; you will get one in the future, but not yet. This is just a little mating gift."

She sits up and looks at me, panicked.

"From you? But I didn't know we were meant to do gifts; I didn't get you anything!"

I kiss her gently to stop her from talking.

"Baby, you didn't have to; agreeing to be mated to me was the best gift you could ever give me." I hold the box out to her again, and she takes it as she smiles at me, muttering "Cheese ball" under her breath. I watch as she opens the lid and pulls out the necklace. She holds it up and stares at it open-mouthed.

"Is that two wolves on a heart?" she asks. I nod whilst turning it around to show her the back, where there is an engraving.

Hand in hand,
side by side,
Always xxx

"Do you like it?"

"Like it? I love it! I'm never going to take it off. Wherever did you find it?" she smiles as she looks at it in the palm of her hand. I take it from her, undo the clasp, and place the necklace around her neck as she pulls her hair to the side so I can fasten it.

"I designed it. Jonny told me that during that first run with the three of us, there was a moment when he turned around and saw the full moon shining behind us. We were just looking at each other; he said that we wouldn't have noticed if the world had exploded around us. We only had eyes for each other." Daisy lets go of her hair and turns to face me, one hand on top of the charm.

"I remember that moment. It was when I realised that you had fixed me and made me whole. You made me love the part of me I hated the most." I shake my head at my brave mate.

"Darling, you fixed yourself. I just held your hand whilst you did it. As for making you love your wolf, you did that all on your own; I just showed you that you could." Daisy doesn't let me say anything else. She jumps on me, wrapping her arms around my neck and thrusting her fingers into my hair as she kisses me. I pull her to me and kiss her as I lay back down on the ground. Our lips and hands wandering until we start to make love under the night sky once more.

Chapter Fifty

DAISY

"Tell me again what the Alpha said."

Michael rolls his eyes as he continues to drive before answering.

"Just that he needed to discuss something with us both and if we could be there for one o'clock."

"And he didn't give you any indication what it was about?"

Michael quickly glances at me and smiles.

"If he had, darling, I would tell you. I know as much as you do. Why are you so worried?"

"I don't like not knowing what this is about. What if I did something wrong the other night? What if I upset someone? What if he regrets me becoming a member of the pack and wants to banish me?"

Michael's hand moves over to mine, and I'm rubbing them together nervously. He takes one and pulls it up to his mouth to kiss my knuckles, instantly calming me a little.

"Darling, if it was any of those things, he would've told

me or given me some indication of what the issue had been. You forget I've worked for him for eight years; I have trained under him for twelve. I know when he wants to talk about something serious or when it's just an 'I know, so you need to know' kind of thing. So please stop fretting and relax."

I know Michael's right. If anyone knows the Alpha, it's him. I sit back in my seat and try not to worry, but I can't help it. Everything has been so perfect the last week. Knowing my luck, something is on the edge, waiting to pull the rug from under my feet and put me back in the black hole I'm constantly being thrown into.

It's been the same since my mum died; it was like it was the start of the never-ending drama that became my life. That was until I met the wonderful man beside me. Michael has become my light, starting as a tiny spot in the far distance, a beacon guiding me back to safety, back to where the sun shines and the darkness fades away. He doesn't even realise it; I was so lost, but then I found him, and through the love he has shown me, I've found myself.

"Darling? Did you hear me?"

"What? No, sorry. What did you say?"

Michael looks at me and frowns.

"I asked if you wanted to pop to Mum's after we have spoken to Desmond?"

"Do you think she will mind?" I ask, which earns me a side glance and a raised eyebrow.

"If I turned up without you, then yes, but if we both go, I think it may make her day." Michael smiles at me, and I can't help but smile back.

"Well, she does like me the most."

Michael laughs, giving my hand a squeeze.

"She loves you more than anybody else on this Earth, darling."

I smile, knowing it's possibly true.

I realise we are pulling up outside the Alpha's house. As soon as the engine is off, Michael turns to me.

"I have no idea what this is about, but whatever it is, we will face it together, okay? Side by side, hand in hand." I look at him and nod, smiling whilst playing with my necklace. "Come on then, let's get this over and done with."

We both get out of our seats and meet in front of the car. Michael takes my hand and gives it a reassuring squeeze before we head to the front door.

Before we get a chance to knock, the door opens, and Jayne stands before us, smiling.

"Afternoon, you two. Early as always, Mikey." Jayne steps forward and pulls me into a hug. I smile as I hug her back. The two of us spent lots of time talking and dancing the day and evening of our blessing. The Luna and I quickly became good friends.

"You are glowing today, Luna," I say as she lets me go.

"If you had seen me an hour ago with my head down the toilet, you would take that back," she laughs, rubbing her slightly swollen belly. Michael bends down and plants a kiss on her cheek.

"She's right, though; pregnancy suits you. Michelle would have been so happy for you," he adds. I watch as Jayne playfully taps his cheeks,

"And for you, Mikey." I watch as she runs a hand over her bump again and smiles at me. "It will be you two next."

"No!" "Maybe?" Michael and I both spin around to face each other.

"No?" Michael asks with one raised brow.

"Maybe?" I reply, mimicking him. Jayne's laughing next to us, knowing full well what she has started.

"No, as in never?" Michael asks, frowning, but I can see the playfulness in his eyes.

"No, as in *not yet*," I reply, looking at him sternly.

"Glad to see you are keeping him in line, Daisy," a voice says from behind me. Michael and I turn around and instantly bow our heads.

"Alpha," we say in unison. Desmond just waves for us to follow him.

"I'll bring the coffee," Jayne calls as we follow him into his office.

"No, you won't; I've already done it. Now, sit down and relax. Get Josh to do a bit to help you," he calls back as he closes the door, smiling to himself.

"You know she won't listen," Michael laughs.

"Oh, I know, but at least I can try."

I watch as he walks around his desk and holds his hands out for us to take the seats in front of it. The Alpha sits down and leans his elbows on the desk in front of him.

"So, I guess you are wondering why I asked you to come in today." We both nod before he continues. "As it is something that will affect both of you, I wanted to see you both at the same time."

"What is this about Desmond?" Michael asks; he reaches over and takes my hand, probably realising that my heart is pounding. If I can hear the blood pumping in my ears, I'm sure he can.

"I'll get straight to the point. The university has declined your request to change courses. Instead, they have asked that you stay on in the Law Department for at least another six months as they need to find a replacement before they can transfer you."

I watch as Michael sits up, his back poker straight.

"What?" he asks.

"You heard what I said."

"I know, but I wanted to make sure I had heard right. How the fuck am I meant to stay on there when I am mated to one of my students?"

"I know it's not ideal, but I need you to stay on a little longer, which means you will need to hide your relationship for the time being." The Alpha looks between the two of us, and I don't miss the fact he looks more apologetic to me than Michael. None of this is ideal; it was never going to be. But I had always prepared myself for this. But Michael was so sure he was going to be transferred, and everything was going to work out.

I look over at Michael, who looks like he is on the verge of losing it.

"Okay," I respond. Michael turns his full attention to me, staring at me wide-eyed.

"Okay?"

"Yes, Michael, *okay*. What other choice do we have?" I point out.

"We have plenty of choices. First being me telling them to go fuck themselves and walking out."

I shake my head while giving his hand a reassuring squeeze.

"That would leave the students at a serious disadvantage, and you know it."

"I don't give a shit," he declares.

"You do, and you know that too. Especially as one of those students is me."

"How are we meant to hide from them that we are living together? Do we really want to keep hiding in the shadows? Because I sure as hell don't. I want to scream from the rooftops that you are mine."

"I get that, but it's only for six months. Tony is looking for housemates. I can have a room there." The pain in Michael's eyes stabs me like a knife in the heart. I open my mouth to explain, but he cuts me off.

"You want to move out?"

"NO! That's not what I'm saying. Will you just shut up and listen to me for one second?" Michael looks at me and nods reluctantly.

"As far as the university will be concerned, I will live with Tony and Beth. But we can still live together most of the time, but when I need to study, I will stay at their place. That way, no one can say you have helped me or that I have had an unfair advantage when you do leave."

"It makes sense, Michael," Desmond says from his seat; I turn and nod at him. Michael, however, growls. Desmond just raises his eyebrows at him in silent warning.

"He knows it does; he just doesn't like it. There is one other option," I say, looking at Desmond, too worried about Michael's reaction to look at him. I can feel his body tense and know he knows what I'm referring to. He drops my hand and jumps to his feet.

"No! Not happening! I'll give them six months; I'll even agree to the shared residence at a push, but I will not agree to that!"

Desmond looks at me with that one raised eyebrow.

"He means he won't allow me to give up my studies."

"Damn right, I won't! You had your life planned out when you moved up here. I will not make you alter your future for my sake. I'll not take another choice away from you."

"That path was changed the day I met you, you arse," I

laugh. "What is the point in me getting a piece of paper that says I understand a subject when I'll never use it again?" Michael kneels in front of me and places a hand on my cheek.

"You can use it; you can do whatever you want with it. I will never stop you."

"I know you won't, but one day, we are going to rule this pack; there is no other job I want. I want to be here by your side, not doing my own thing."

"But it's your dream."

"Was. It *was* my dream. That's the thing with dreams; they can change. The day we stopped pretending is the day my dreams took a whole new form."

"You can be so stubborn," Michael says as he leans his forehead against mine. I cannot help but giggle.

"It's why you love me."

"One of the many reasons," he mumbles before lightly pressing his lips to mine. I turn and look at our Alpha, who is watching us, smirking.

"Tell the uni they have six months. Any longer than that, and I leave." Alpha gives me a smile and one stiff nod.

"You okay with that, Michael?" the Alpha asks, looking at Michael.

"No, but I am not fighting her over this. She will end up winning anyway," he replies, sulking as he gets back into his chair. Desmond laughs at him.

"Spoken like a true mate. We males are better off just doing as we are told, Mikey. On another note, I need to speak to Michael about the trip next week. Would you mind checking on Jayne for me, please, Daisy? I know she will be trying to do something she shouldn't." I nod as I stand and bow slightly to the Alpha. "Thank you." He says. Michael stands and kisses me quickly on the lips.

"We won't be long, and then we will head to Mum's." I smile at him and wink before heading out of the office in search of the Luna.

My heart starts racing, and I quickly step away from the office so Michael can't hear it. I had known the university wouldn't allow him to leave so soon; the students love him, and there is a rumour that Martin wants to retire. We can do this for six months. I bloody hope so, anyway.

Epilogue

"Alpha."

I look up from my laptop at my Beta with my eyebrows raised.

"Do we not knock anymore, Simon?" I watch as he bows to me, keeping his head down.

"Sorry, Alpha, but you would want to know this instantly."

I wave my hand at him to go ahead as he looks up. Already bored of this conversation.

"Go ahead. But keep it quick. I have things I need to do."

"There has just been activity at the Luna's house."

I almost get whiplash from looking up at him so fast.

"She's there?" I feel my hope slip away as he shakes his head.

"No sir, she was, but we think she may have left again. Her car and belongings are all there, so she'll have to return."

I jump up from my seat behind my desk and grab my coat from the back of it.

"I want someone watching the place at all times. I want to know the second somebody goes anywhere near the place."

"Already done. Tobin has been watching it all morning. But that's not all, sir." I turn, giving him my full attention. "He noticed someone had broken into the premises, and when approached, they tried to run. So, he brought them in."

"Who is it?" My Beta looks at me and smiles.

"The traitor."

I look at him, shocked. What the hell is he doing here? He must know that by showing his face around here again, I would have him killed. I feel my hands ball into fists by my side as my anger soars.

"Take me to him now."

I follow my Beta through the pack house and down to the basement I had added when I purchased the large building.

This is where I keep wolves who piss me off. There is also a room ready for her, for when I manage to get her back with me, where she belongs.

She should be here with me now, standing behind me as I lead this pack. But instead, she escaped three years ago, thanks to the prick that is now, finally, in the holding cell. I'll never know how they've both avoided me this long, but I'm sure he has had something to do with it.

The bBta knocks on the cell door, which opens from the inside, and I walk in first.

"Everyone, get out now," I growl out, not taking my eyes off the arsehole sitting in a chair in the middle of the room, his hands cuffed behind the back of the chair. He's facing away from the door. I don't have to look around to see that everyone has left; even the Beta knows better than to stay when I'm in this kind of mood.

"You finally got your pack then?"

Gods, the sound of his voice still grates me; it's taking every ounce of strength not to rip his throat out. Instead, I walk around until I'm standing directly in front of him.

"Hello, brother," he smirks up at me. Before he even has a chance to prepare, I punch him straight in that smug face. I'm sure if the chair wasn't screwed to the ground, it would have tipped, judging by the way his head whips to the side. He turns his head back to look at me, moving his jaw from side to side, then licking his now split lip. "I guess I deserve that."

"You deserve a lot fucking more than that. If you want to live to see the end of the day, I suggest you start talking quickly."

The bastard actually looks at me and smirks.

"What would you like to know?"

I lean on the arms of his chair so our faces are mere inches apart.

"How about starting with explaining to me how it's possible that she comes back, and you reappear in her fucking home the same day?"

The smirk never leaves his face as he looks straight at me.

"Because I never lost her. I always knew where she was. I've been by her side since the day she beat your ass and got away." He leans forward, shortening the distance between us further. I step back and punch him again. I watch as he spits blood from his mouth onto the floor before looking up at me, the smirk still on his stupid face.

"I see your temper hasn't got any better, Morgan."

I punch him again whilst growling.

"You know that is no longer my name."

"Of course, I forgot. It's just Jackson now, isn't it?"

"And what, pray tell, is the name you are going under these days, Kalvin?"

"Well, that would be telling, wouldn't it?"

I walk over to the far wall and grab the chair that is resting against it. Slowly, I drag it to the middle of the room. I place it in front of my little brother and sit down. We stare at each other in silence for a moment, the tension between us building.

I take in the change of his appearance; he has gained muscle mass in the three years since I last saw him. He no longer looks like the stick-thin nerd that was so easy to manipulate. It seems he has also grown a backbone in his time away. Good, it will make kicking the shit out of him more fun. But first, I need quick answers from him.

"Where is she?"

"Not here."

I close my eyes and take a deep breath.

"Where have you been all this time?"

The smug prick actually crosses one leg over the other and has the nerve to look bored.

"I have been with *my* girl for three years, keeping her away from you and anyone else who thought they would get a look." I jump to my feet so quickly that the chair tips over behind me.

"Enough, she is *my* girl, *my* Luna. So enough of these games, brother. Tell me where she is."

"I will never tell you where she is. I'm not one of your minions you think you can boss around. I'm not scared of you anymore, *Morgan*." I stand back and look at him. I see it now; he is still obsessed with her. The only thing that is going to break him is her.

"If you don't tell me where she is, I'll have to have her tracked. She will obviously be back because her car and things are at the house. Plus, her scent is fresh there now. So I will just get my tracker on the case." I see a flicker of concern on his face.

"What makes you think he will find her? You haven't been able to find her yet."

I righten my chair and sit back down on it. I cross an ankle over a knee. I lean back into the chair and cross my arms over my chest.

"This time, we have her car and belongings. I bet if we went through everything there, we would find something to give us a clue about where she has been hiding. I have some of the smartest wolves around in my pack, and I know with the right information, they could have her here in a week, two tops." I uncross my legs and lean on my thighs with my elbows.

"Things have changed here as much as they have changed for you. Why do you think I've let her have these last few years away? It's given me time to get things into place ready for her return." I pull out my phone and dial my Beta's number as I stand up and start wandering around the room like I am bored.

"Simon send Bastian." I hang up and watch my darling little brother. He tries to hide that he's getting anxious, but I can see the sweat on his upper lip and smell the fear seeping from his pores. "Don't think the little magic tricks that you learnt from Mother will save you both now. Mother didn't survive me; what makes you think you will?"

"I don't give a shit whether you kill me or not, but you

will not harm Daisy, not again. If I can't protect her, her coven and pack will." I spin around and stare at him.

"Pack? This is her pack!"

He grins at me smugly, shaking his head.

"Oh no, Morgan, Daisy has a pack now, a big one. Oh, and did I forget to mention the mate?"

I feel my eyes widen.

"Lies! I'm her mate!"

But the bastard just shakes his head at me again.

"Nope, she has a big fucker of a mate, and even though I have led her away from him, he will find her. Especially now, I'm not there to keep her moving. He will find her, and then he will kill you because he knows all about you and what you did to her. I wouldn't be surprised if he turned up looking for you soon anyway."

"What's his name?"

"Michael Adams, I'm sure you have heard of him." Now it's my turn to sweat; if it's the one I think it is, then every wolf knows of him.

"The Blood Moon Pack Adams?" The smug prick grins at me again.

"The very same." Fuck, this complicates things. Or does it? I turn around and grin at my little brother. He might have grown a bit of a backbone and added a bit of muscle to his physique, but he hasn't gained any brain cells.

"Well, at least I know where to start looking now. Thank you, little brother, you have just made my life a lot easier." I watch the colour drain from his face as he realises his mistake.

"I swear to every God and Goddess, if you so much as touch her again, you prick, I'm going to rip you to fucking pieces and feed you to your fucking pack in a stew." Just as I turn to respond, there is a knock at the door. I open it to find Bastian there holding out a phone.

Bastian is just short of seven feet tall and built like the fucking Hulk. There is yet to be anyone who has been able to defeat him. He is not only great in a fight; he has the nose of a tracker. I open the door for him and take the phone.

"Beta has already unlocked it; he said you will want to see what is on there as well as this." He passes me a driving license; I look at the name and picture, and a smile spreads across my face.

I open the phone and am instantly greeted with pictures of *my* Daisy. She smiles in some and sleeps in others. There are even a couple of her in the shower.

"Oh, little brother, it seems you are still using those powers of yours to be a sneaky bastard. I hope you have enough photos to see you through, as unless you play ball and help us get her back, you will never be within sight of her again."

"I will never help you, never." I turn to Bastian and give him the nod.

"Do what you must to break him, but don't kill him. He has certain powers I will need if we are to get the Luna back." Bastian nods and heads towards my brother.

"I'll not help you again, Morgan; you might as well kill me now." I walk up to him and look him straight in the eye again.

"You will help me; you will help me keep her this time, too. Otherwise, I will make sure that Bastian here has fun with Daisy before we do. If she fights me, I will make sure the whole pack gets a go, and they will not be gentle. They will destroy her until all she is good for is breeding." I watch as my brother starts fighting against his restraints. Screaming all kinds of filthy language at me and threatening to end me. I just laugh as I walk to the door. I open it but turn back to look at the back of my brother one last time before I leave.

"I will be back later to see if you've changed your mind, and I strongly suggest you do, as I am sure you don't want anything to harm your precious Daisy." I glance down at the driver's license again and see his new name. "Would you, Kellan?"

vinci-books.com/BloodMoon-HerProtector

He's feared by many—but for her, he'd burn the world.

Daisy finally has the life she dreamed of—friends, a loyal pack, and the mate who makes her feel whole. But when danger stalks their doorstep, Michael will risk everything to protect her. Because this time, The Protector has everything to lose.

Turn the page for a free preview…

Her Protector: Prologue

What the fuck was I thinking?

Why did I think trying to scare Daisy by pretending to be Jackson would be a good idea? Never in a million years did I expect her to head back to Exeter. I was sure she'd run back to her family in Cornwall.

I should have known the whole plan would go wrong. Everything I've ever done to protect that girl has gone to pot. At least, it seems that she's gotten away, for now. He might be a moron, but Michael should have found her by now and will keep her reasonably safe. At least she's not here with me, tied to a chair in the middle of a room, beaten and starved.

I have no idea how long I've been here. There are no clocks or windows to see whether it's day or night. I'm sure I'd be dead by now if I were human. My brother has made it abundantly clear that I'll stay here until I agree to work for him. He doesn't realise I've been conjuring some plans of my own. He's mistaken if he thinks I'll let him hurt her again.

"Have you come to your senses yet?" I turn slowly to my brother's monotonous voice as he strolls into the room.

"I give up. You win." I whisper as I force a cough from my dry throat. Time to play the role of the pathetic, weak brother, who has barely a brain cell in his thick skull. It's an act I've played for many years, hoping to hide the truth from him. "I'll do whatever you want. Just untie me from this fucking chair, and please, give me something to eat and drink." I whine. My brother turns to face me with that evil look he gets in his eyes when he thinks he has broken somebody. I've always hated that look. He would get it after each beating he issued to Daisy when he held her captive. I was too scared and weak then to help her, but I now know how to beat him at his games. I've become stronger for this moment.

"Have you finally come to your senses, little brother? I have to give it to you; you took longer to break than I thought you would." Jackson squats in front of me so he can look me in the eye. "But why should I believe you've finally seen sense? How do I know you won't just disappear as soon as I release you?"

"Tell me what you want me to do, and I'll do it. I don't have the energy to fight you anymore; you win. Like you always do." I answer, trying to appear as submissive as possible.

"Of course, I always win. Because I never give up on what I want."

"Answer me one thing. Why her? Why has it got to be Daisy?" I ask. Jackson looks at me and frowns.

"Why does it matter?"

"Of course, it matters. Why go through all this trouble for one girl?"

"Because I know how powerful she can be. With her by

my side, I would never lose. My pack would be unbeatable. Her magic would make her the most powerful Luna in this sad, pathetic world. Together, we could achieve amazing things," Jackson states, grinning. "I don't care what anyone says; she is my second chance mate. I can feel it every time she is in my precious. Maybe if I get her first mate out of the picture, the bond will finally click into place."

"How do you plan on getting her to leave the mate?" I ask, digging for information.

"That won't be hard. The mate bond isn't as strong as they make out it is. If it were, I wouldn't have been able to kill mine so easily," Jackson shrugs. Maybe he's right, and the bond isn't that strong.

"Seems ironic that it had to be Adams your Luna would be mated to," I point out. I watch that evil grin spread over his face again.

"The fates have had their fun with this one, that's for sure," Jackson chuckles before turning to face me. "You never told me, little brother. Why do *you* want the girl so bad? Since I picked her up, you've made it your mission to stay close to her. You hid her from me and followed her around like the lost sheep you are."

I look up at my brother and sigh whilst letting my head drop.

"Mother once told me I would meet someone I would love, but another would want her. She said I would have to fight for her, that love wouldn't be enough to keep her." I take a deep breath before looking up at my brother. "I guess she was right because even when I was right there in front of Daisy, giving her everything she wanted, she didn't even look at me that way. I was always in the 'friend zone', as they call it these days. Even the fucking fire demon got closer to her than I did. You win. I give up."

Jackson walks over to me and places his hand on my bruised shoulder.

"Welcome to the world of females, little brother. Even those fated to love you don't. Look at my first mate; she was beautiful and strong but already belonged to another. She had the nerve to reject me for someone else," Jackson growls.

"So you made sure that if you couldn't have her, then neither could he," I whisper, knowing this story like the back of my hand. I've listened to it so many times in the last few years. Jackson winks at me as he smirks, once again proud of himself for taking a life. I've never understood why he feels the need to be so brutal and evil. We really couldn't be more different, even though the same family brought us up.

I feel him untying my hands at the back of the chair. I know there are cameras in here, so I have to appear as the obedient little brother he loves to push around. Even though the thought of turning around and breaking his jaw is really appealing right now.

"So how do I know you won't try and double-cross me? What can you give me to ensure that you stay on my side and don't run off with Daisy once I have her?" Jackson asks.

"I'll perform a blood oath to stay by your side and do as you ask until you get Daisy back. I'll stay until you have her safely in your den and hidden from Adams," I answer as I run my now released, aching hands through my dark brown hair, which has been irritating my eyes for ages.

"I'll agree to that," Jackson says as he pulls an army knife out of his pocket and flips it open. He cuts his palm and then holds the knife out for me to do the same. This is old magic neither of us has done in many years, but it's all I can think to ensure Daisy and I survive my brother again.

"Last chance to back out, Brother. Will you help me get

Daisy back, no matter how difficult it is?" I look at the knife in his hand and nod as I take it to slice open my own. I hold my bleeding hand out to him, and he takes it in his as we shake to seal the deal whilst I feel the magic forming the bond with our blood.

"I swear it."

Her Protector: Chapter One

MICHAEL

"Hey Mikey, you getting close?" Carl calls through the cars hands-free. I hear music in the background and know he'll be sitting in his usual place by the bar in The Crows, which he owns with his fated mate Richard.

"Yeah, I'll be five minutes tops. Does Daisy know I'm on my way yet?"

"Nope, she's still oblivious. I'm warning you, though; she's been on the gin again tonight," Carl laughs.

"I never dreamt she'd stay away from it." I roll my eyes, knowing how much that girl loves her gin.

"That's okay then; knock on the door when you get here, and I'll let you in. We've been keeping it locked and 'members-only'." What he means is pack wolves only, with the exemption of one fire demon they employ to work the bar, who also happens to be Daisy's best friend, Tony Simons.

"Thanks, Carl, I owe you. See you in a few," I reply, smiling as I end the call.

It's been the longest three days away from Daisy, my

mate. I hate it when we're apart. I feel like I'm missing part of my soul. I wouldn't have left her if it wasn't essential.

Almost two weeks ago, Daisy had fled back to her old home in Exeter in the middle of the night. She feared somebody from her past had tracked her down and threatened her new life here in North Wales. She had no plans to return when she ran, so she'd taken all her belongings. Once in Exeter, she'd ditched everything, including her car and travelled to a safe house where her family live, down in Cornwall. That was where I tracked her down and made her realise that Jackson, the guy she was running from, had not found her, that it was someone pretending to be him.

That someone had been Kellan Cole. A guy from Daisy's university class, which I teach. It seems Kellan intended to scare her away from me so he'd have her to himself. We can only guess that was his overall plan, as he's been missing since. He has to resurface at some point, and I'll happily kill him when he does.

I'm on my way back from Exeter, where I went with my team of werewolf enforcers to collect Daisy's things. We looked around for signs of Jackson, the male who kidnapped, tortured, raped, and turned Daisy into a werewolf without her consent. We think he initially paid Kellan to keep an eye on her for him.

Whilst in Exeter, my Alpha visited a few shifter packs to update them on the situation and ask them to report any sightings of either Jackson or Kellan to the Supernatural Council or us directly, hoping we eventually can free Daisy from her painful past. But so far, there has been nothing.

I pull up outside the bar and push all thoughts of Exeter out of my mind. Inside is the most beautiful woman ever to walk this earth, and she's all mine. All I can think about is getting her home and burying myself deep inside her, making up for the time apart. I jump out of the car, head straight to the front door, and quickly knock. Carl opens it, grinning.

"Hey Mikey, how you doing?"

I squeeze his shoulder as I walk past him into the bar. "I'll be better in about ten seconds," I reply as I look straight to the one place I know my mate will be.

There she is on the dancefloor, her hips swaying in time to the music, her long dark blonde hair cascading down her back, stopping halfway between her shoulders and her perfect grabbable ass.

"I swear you get more beautiful every day." I send down our unique mind link, which allows the two of us to communicate telepathically. She spins around and stares at me. The world stops for a second, and all I can see and hear is her.

Daisy screams and launches herself towards me. I take three long strides, meeting her halfway before she jumps into my arms and wraps her legs around my waist as I hold her tightly against me.

I hear her sob as she buries her head between my neck and shoulder. I lean into her so I can inhale her sweet floral scent.

"I've missed you so much, darling," I whisper down the bond.

"Not as much as I've missed you, handsome," she sends back.

I chuckle as I lean back to see Daisy's face properly. Before getting a good look at her, she threads her fingers into my hair and crushes her lips into mine. I don't care who's around and watching; I kiss her like I've been starved of her because I have. The last three days have been torture without her.

"For fuck's sake, bitch. Let the man breathe," I hear Tony groan as he walks past us. Daisy pulls away and winks at me before jumping down from my arms.

"You're just jealous as you aren't getting any," she replies. She turns in my arms to face her friend with her back against my chest, and I hold her close.

"Please, I can get what I want when I want, and you know it." He looks at the two of us, smirking. "But I'm always open to making this a threesome; you know you would love it," he winks at me before wiggling his eyebrows at Daisy.

Daisy walks out of my arms and towards Tony, patting him on the chest as she passes.

"Sweetie, you couldn't handle us," she looks over her shoulder at me and winks. "Plus, I don't share."

"I'm never sharing you, baby," I reply as I rush up to her and grab her around the waist, pulling her back into my arms so I can kiss her again.

"Uhh, get a room," Tony groans as he walks past us. I look into Daisy's eyes, and I reply, smiling.

"I plan on it. Go get your stuff and get in the car so I can get you home and be inside you within the next half hour," I whisper, nibbling on her earlobe. She rushes out of my arms, squealing as I slap her ass. I watch her run up the stairs and into the apartment she's been staying in. As soon as she's out of sight, I lean against the bar where Tony and Carl are sitting on stools and take the bourbon drink Richard hands me.

"You look like you need that," he says as I take a sip.

"You have no idea," I reply, holding the glass up as thanks.

"How did it go?" Tony asks. I put my glass on the bar and check Daisy's still upstairs.

"Someone has been through all her stuff in the car. They've also broken into the house. I called her uncle Nigel, and we decided to board the house up for now. The guys and I did it today; it's why we stayed the extra day," I explain quietly.

"Any sign of the arseholes?" Tony asks. I shake my head and take another sip of my drink.

"No, but there were signs of a fight, but only one scent, so we think one of them was Kellan since it seems he can hide his scent. It could have been him and Jackson, but as none of us knows Jackson's scent, it's hard to say for sure."

"Do you think Kellan's gone for good?" Richard asks. I down the rest of my drink and shrug.

"Who knows? He could be anywhere, but so could Jackson. We all felt like we were being watched the whole time we were there. I was glad to get away, if I'm honest. It was exhausting being on edge all the time. Alpha seems to have made some progress with the packs around there. It turns out they've all been working against each other rather than together, and that's why so much has been missed. There's still a lot of work to do with them, but the Alpha has it under control." I take a deep breath and look at Carl, "He asked me to ask you something, and I'm not sure how you will take it."

He holds up his hand to stop me. "Don't bother; the answer's yes." He says as he looks at his partner. Richard reaches over and takes Carl's hand, giving it a reassuring squeeze.

"Are you sure? I know you wanted away from that life," I ask, checking.

"I left the team as I wanted to protect Richard after that mission followed us home. But I know you're stretched, and I'm here to help. Even if it's to watch Daisy for you. I'm at your disposal."

"Thank you, Carl. You have no idea how grateful I am."

He looks at me and nods once.

"I promised to protect the pack like the rest of you. I stand by that promise." Just as I'm about to respond, a bang comes from upstairs, and we all turn to see Daisy rushing down the steps with her bag in hand. I smile when I see the grin on her face.

I hold one arm out for her as she rushes straight to my side, dropping the bag by our feet.

"You ready to go, darling?" I whisper as I kiss the top of her head.

"Yep, take me home, handsome," she replies as she walks out of my arms and hugs Richard and Carl simultaneously. "Thank you for keeping me sane whilst he was away."

They both chuckle, "Thank you for not drinking us out of house and home," Richard smiles, winking at her as she pulls away.

"Do I even want to know how much that bar tab will cost me?" I ask as I shake Richard's hand, and he shakes his head.

"I'll send you the bill. Just make sure you're sitting down when you open it," he jokes.

"Hey! I'm not that bad!" Daisy protests next to me; I put my arm over her shoulder and laugh.

"Oh, darling, you are so much worse. Now get in the car; I want to get you home to bed."

Her Protector: Chapter Two

DAISY

It's been the longest two nights and three days whilst Michael's been away. I'm so glad he's finally here.

I glance at him as he drives home, one hand on the steering wheel, the other holding mine.

"Is that it now? Or will you have to go back to Exeter?" I ask as I watch Michael's expression change.

"I can't promise anything, darling, as the Alpha may need to sort out the other packs further. He wants Marcus and me to go with him as security." He lifts my hand and kisses the back of it. "I hate it when I have to leave you, especially with everything going on."

I squeeze his hand, hoping to give him some reassurance.

"I know you do, Mikey, but it'll be over soon enough. With Kellan not making himself known, I think we're over the worst of it," I say optimistically.

"Darling, I wish it was that simple. But I want to know where he's hiding as I'm worried about his overall plan."

I bite my bottom lip, realising there's no way Michael will agree to my next request.

"So not being babysat whenever you have to work or go on a mission isn't an option anytime soon?" I ask carefully.

Michael glances at me, and I can see the pain in his eyes before he turns back to the road.

"Darling, I know you hate it, but I don't know what else to do here."

"You promised to let me fight my own battles, Mikey. You promised to stand beside me, not in front of me, protecting me." I can feel the tension in the air as this is something that has been building for the last week or so.

Since we came back from Cornwall, Michael's ensured I'm never alone. I get that he panicked, especially as he admitted he's worried Jackson saw me when I was in Exeter. But I'm not scared of him, not like I was. When I ran two weeks ago, I didn't care if Jackson had found me or not; I was more worried about what he would do to everyone here. I wanted to lead him away from them. But since seeing how well Michael and the guys can look after themselves, I'm no longer worried.

I turn and look at Michael and see from his pained expression that he's fighting with his wolf.

The problem with wolves is that we mate for life. When we find our fated mate, nothing or no one else matters. For a male, it's down to the primal need to protect what's theirs. It's more complicated for Michael as he's also an Alpha fighting the urge to protect his mate and his pack, even if he isn't the pack's Alpha yet.

I know how hard it is for him, as I've felt it myself the last few days. Knowing that Michael may be facing unknown dangers and I wasn't there to have his back was hard. All I want to do is protect him, our family, and our friends. So I get why he is being overprotective; I do. But that doesn't mean I have to like it.

I've been so lost in my thoughts that I don't realise we're home until the car stops. I look across to Michael and smile, hoping to lighten the mood.

"Home, sweet home."

Michael turns to me and smiles, nodding, before climbing out. As I climb out, I spot my car parked on the driveway.

"You brought her back!" I yell excitedly.

"I told you I would. Marcus drove her; I figured you wouldn't want to risk her in Jonny's hands," Michael calls from the trunk of his car as he grabs our bags.

I laugh as I make my way to my car. I peer inside and realise there seems to be more space in the back than when I left it in Exeter. I turn to Michael, frowning.

"Has someone moved some of my stuff? It's not all here." I can see the change in Michael's face as he sighs deeply.

"Come inside, darling. I'll explain everything over a glass of wine. I think you'll need it."

I follow Michael into the house and watch as he places our bags at the bottom of the stairs before heading into the kitchen. When I join him, he's in the fridge, pulling out a beer and a bottle of wine. I watch as Michael pours me a glass of wine before opening his bottle. Now he's finally home, and in proper lighting, I can see how exhausted and worried he is.

I walk up to him and wrap my arms around his waist. He lets out another deep sigh, tightens his arms around me, and buries his nose into my hair.

"What's the matter?" I ask. I feel his lips rest on the top of my head.

"I'm sorry, darling. I've not been honest with you; I'd planned to tell you everything tomorrow. I promise. I just wanted you to have one last night of peace," Michael says into my hair.

"Mikey, please, stop trying to protect me." As he takes a deep breath, I feel him kiss the top of my head one more time.

"We think Jackson has always known where you were and that Kellan has been working for him."

It takes a second for his words to sink in. I let my arms drop from around him and step away. Michael goes to step toward me, but I hold up my hands.

"What?" I ask, unable to grasp a word he just said. Michael closes his eyes before answering.

"Kellan's house in town was owned by someone who owns property in Exeter and St Austell. He's also been receiving substantial payments from the same name." I clutch my stomach as a knot forms, and my chest tightens.

"When did you find this out?" I ask as Michael looks down at his hands resting on the breakfast bar in the middle of our kitchen.

"The night before our blessing," he replies quietly.

"A week? You've known for seven days and didn't think to tell me? Were you going to tell me tomorrow? Or are you just saying that now I'm asking questions?" I demand as I take a step back from him, my voice rising with my temper.

"I was going to tell you, I promise, but things kept coming up, and I didn't want to scare you without some sort of confirmation we were right."

I turn as I throw my hands up in the air and storm out of the kitchen. I can hear Michael cursing as he starts to follow me. I spin around and hold my hands up in front of me again.

"Give me space, Michael." I don't wait around to see if he does. Instead, I walk up the stairs and into our room, closing the door behind me.

I look around, instantly regretting my decision to hide in here. There's still very little of mine in this house, as I've only been living here for ten days, and my belongings were in Exeter. I remember the stuff in the car and feel my temper rise further.

I storm downstairs and find Michael in the lounge with his head in his hands and a bourbon on the coffee table.

"Why is some of my stuff missing? You never got to that bit."

Michael looks up at me, and I know I'm not going to like what he has to say,

"When we got to your old house, we found somebody had been inside and in the car; they had gone through all your stuff. We weren't sure anything was missing, but now you've confirmed it," he explains.

"Do you think it was Kellan or Jackson?" I ask.

"We don't know Jackson's scent, and as you know, Kellan doesn't seem to have one," Michael says, shrugging. Well, there's one way to find out.

I walk out of the lounge and head to the bowl by the door, where we always put our keys. My car key has been placed in there, probably by Marcus. I take it and storm towards the car. I know Michael's behind me, but I don't acknowledge him. My need for some truths overpowering the need to look at him.

As soon as I reach the car I realise this may be a bad idea. I have no idea how Jackson's scent is going to affect me. I haven't smelt it since the night I escaped him three years ago. I grip the back door handle and press the unlock button. I take a deep breath to settle my nerves and open the door. Marcus's scent is the first thing I pick up, quickly followed by Will's. Their scents are focused around the front seats, so I'm guessing they travelled back together. Without turning to Michael, I start asking questions.

"Other than Will and Marcus, who's been in this car."

"Stuart and me," he answers.

I sniff and pick up on Michael and Stuart's scents. I let out a sigh of relief when I don't smell Jackson.

"There are two scents I don't know, both wolves. Are you sure none are from the Exeter packs?" I hear Michael mumble that he's sure. I look through what I can see from where I'm standing.

"If they've gone through all this, they will have my dorm address and course details," I point out as I stand up straight and close the door before relocking it.

Fuck. I can't believe I was so stupid to leave all this stuff in Exeter. When I ditched it, I believed Jackson had already found me, So there was no point hiding everything.

"I figured they'd been looking for something like that, so I was loud when discussing your new living arrangement. I know we were being watched, so the word should have gotten back that you no longer live in the dorm. Your friends and Tony will be safe." Michael explains. I nod and head back to the house.

I walk into the kitchen and grab my glass of wine. I'm going to need the bottle to deal with this shit. I have my back to the kitchen door, but I can feel Michael watching my every move.

"Darling, talk to me, please. Everything I've done was to protect you. Do you think I wanted to hide this all from you? The last week has been a complete whirlwind of emotions, with the blessing and the intense mating bond. Plus, I've had to return to work, and you've been trying to keep up with all the assignments that you have due. I kept going to tell you, but you would be exhausted, and I told myself I'd tell you later, but later never came."

"How many people know?" I ask. I hear him taking a deep breath before answering.

"The team, Alpha and ... Tony."

I spin around and look at Michael.

"Everyone knew except me. You told all of them before your own mate!"

"Marcus and the team knew because he worked it out when we were in Cornwall. He didn't tell me until the night before the blessing."

"And Tony?" I demand. I'm going to kill Demon Boy for hiding this from me.

"He demanded to be included in anything that involves you or Kellan."

I can feel my anger getting the better of me and know I need to put some distance between Michael and me, especially as he looks like he's waiting for me to explode.

"Oh, he should be prepared. I'm going to kick his ass; I don't care if he's fucking sorry," my wolf growls, and I agree. I want to scream at him, but I know it'll solve nothing.

I turn around and grab a bottle of gin, a bottle of mixer from the fridge, and a glass from the cupboard.

"I'm going upstairs. Don't follow me; I can't even look at you right now." I storm past Michael, heading straight to our bedroom. As soon as I'm in there, I walk into the bathroom and start running the bath. The only thing that might calm me down right now is a few drinks in a deep bubble bath.

Grab your copy...
vinci-books.com/BloodMoon-HerProtector

About the Author

D.E. Bartley lives in Wales, UK, with her husband, three feral boys, four cats, and a budgie.

To say her home is a madhouse would be an understatement, but she wouldn't have it any other way.

When she isn't running around after her tribe or driving her husband up the wall, she can be found reading and hoarding books like a dragon.

Nothing is as important to her as time with her family, and she loves her trips home to Cornwall with them more than anything in the world. What could possibly compare to sitting on a Cornish beach, with a glass of Cornish gin in one hand and an authentic Cornish pasty in the other, while the monsters, I mean children, play and bodyboard in the sea?

Absolutely nothing.

Acknowledgments

Where do I even start? There are just far too many of you amazing people to name individually. But I will try and get through as many of you as possible without writing another book.

Of course, none of this would have been possible without the love and support from my husband Nick and our three boys. They are my biggest support group, and there is no way I could have survived editing *Rogue* without their endless hugs and love. However, although they have all been supportive, my eldest deserves an extra mention as he's been telling me for years to do something with this story. I hope he knows how unbelievably proud I am of him; and how he always makes me want to better myself for him and his brothers.

Outside of our family home, the support I have received from friends and family, especially my parents, has been amazing. As much as I can't wait to hear what you think of the book, I also don't want to know what you think of specific chapters (maybe skip chapters 43 and 48, seriously, miss them).

There is no way I couldn't acknowledge my crazy work colleagues. I never dreamt I would have so many people shouting at me to "get the bloody book finished, woman!" on a daily basis. Seriously, to everyone in the care home I work in, you are all amazing. Not just for the work you all do in our day/night roles, but for the friendship and support you have given me whilst I wrote this book and juggled our crazy pandemic work schedule, family life and health issues. Thank you all, from the bottom of my heart. I love all you crazy ass bitches, and yes, that includes the significant pain in my arse, real-life Tony, George!

I wanted to acknowledge everyone who has helped me write this book, including all my amazing Facebook/Bookstagram/Booktok friends. You have all showered me with love and support, even if it's just a like or a comment on a post. Especially the friends I've made on the amazing group *Geek Girl Review Café*, you guys rock on all levels, thank you.

However, there has to be a special shout out to a friend and fellow author, Alexandra. A. Black, you were the first person EVER to read Daisy and Michaels shifter story. You were the one to tell me to get it out there and that people would want to read my rambling. Without you, there is no way this book would have been published. So, thank you for the love, support, patience and encouragement. I hope one day we can meet in person and share that bottle of wine, or three. I still think Italy next year should be a possibility.

If I have missed anyone out, please don't think I didn't think of you because I did. I just had to keep this within a certain number of pages, and I could have gone on and on naming all the fantastic people in my life.

The biggest thanks to everyone who's taken the time to read this book and buy a version of it. I hope you've enjoyed it and will continue to read the antics of The Blood Moon Pack and friends, as I promise they all have their own stories to tell and have a habit of finding themselves in deep trouble, some more than others.

Thank you all again from the bottom of my heart. xx